WHEN IS A PET NOT A PET?

When it is gifted with the powers of enchantment, with the ability to help its chosen witch, warlock, wizard, sorcerer, or enchantress to work magic, from the everyday variety to the truly spectacular. Now thirteen masters of the art of enchantment offer you some of the most original stories about some of the most unique familiars:

"And So, Ad Infinitum"—She knew the Summerland was a dangerous place for the living, but she would be careful not to leave her spell's protection. But if she made even one mistake, would her familiar's power be enough to keep her safe?

"Dog Spelled Backward"—When the ancient Pomeranian died, Sasha's mistress was bereft, filled with grief and unnecessary guilt—feelings that drew the Shadow-creatures. Only if Sasha and her fellow dogs, living and dead, could find a way to break the spell of sadness could they keep their human from falling prey to these soul-devouring creatures. . . .

"Business As Usual"—If anyone had told her that the way to succeed in business was to have a rat as her mentor, she would have thought the person was crazy. But that was before Tiff. . . .

FAMILIARS

FAMILIARS

edited by Denise Little

DAW BOOKS, INC.

DONALD A. WOLLHEIM, FOUNDER

375 Hudson Street, New York, NY 10014

ELIZABETH R. WOLLHEIM

SHEILA E. GILBERT

PUBLISHERS

www.dawbooks.com

First Printing, July 2002
1   2   3   4   5   6   7   8   9

DAW TRADEMARK REGISTERED
U.S. PAT. OFF. AND FOREIGN COUNTRIES
—MARCA REGISTRADA.
HECHO EN U.S.A.
PRINTED IN THE U.S.A.

ACKNOWLEDGMENTS

Introduction © 2002 by Denise Little.

"Searching for the Familiar" by Kristine Kathryn Rusch. Copyright © 2002 by Kristine Kathryn Rusch.

"And So, Ad Infinitum" by Jody Lynn Nye. Copyright © 2002 by Jody Lynn Nye.

"First Familiars" by Laura Resnick. Copyright © 2002 by Laura Resnick.

"Dog Spelled Backward" by P.N. Elrod. Copyright © 2002 by P.N. Elrod.

"This Dog Watched" by Von Jocks. Copyright © 2002 by Yvonne Jocks.

"On the Scent of the Witch" by Jean Rabe. Copyright © 2002 by Jean Rabe.

"The Familiar" by Andre Norton. Copyright © 2002 by Andre Norton.

"Alliance" by Bill McCay. Copyright © 2002 by Bill McCay.

"Catseye" by Laura Anne Gilman. Copyright © 2002 by Laura Anne Gilman.

"Business as Usual" by Diane A.S. Stuckart. Copyright © 2002 by Diane A.S. Stuckart.

"Modoc Rising" by Gary A. Braunbeck. Copyright © 2002 by Gary A. Braunbeck.

"Goodness Had Nothing to Do with It" by Susan Sizemore. Copyright © 2002 by Susan Sizemore.

"Swordplay" by Josepha Sherman. Copyright © 2002 by Josepha Sherman.

"Thieves in the Night" by John Helfers. Copyright © 2002 by John Helfers.

"Legacy" by Michelle West. Copyright © 2002 by Michelle West.

CONTENTS

INTRODUCTION

by Denise Little

HUMAN beings are determined to believe that we're not alone. Whether we're searching for aliens in the sky or looking at the cat on our lap, we're absolutely sure that there are other intelligences out there, sharing our world with us and interfering where necessary. Perhaps because of our long association with the animals of our planet, both wild and domestic, the most common manifestation of that need is the tale of the animal familiar. Almost every civilization has had some form of it as part of its folklore. From the carved totem poles of the Inuit to the spirit guides of Native American tribes, from witches' mascots in the European tradition to the household spirits of the Far East, from the cherished well-worn animal toys of small children to glittering gemstone-encrusted bits of personal adornment, tales and legends and comforting mythology of familiars crop up everywhere and flavor our world.

Right back to the days of cave paintings, it's clear that mankind has believed that animal spirits have had an important part in our lives here on Earth. What if folklore is right, and spirits do haunt us in the form of our animal friends or totem belongings? Are these familiars reincarnated human spirits returning to help us through hard times, or something else? Maybe even something alien? If they're reincarnated humans, who would choose to come back, why, and as what? How would they share their knowledge with us? (Think what Winston Churchill would have to say as Bill Clinton's cat, for example.)

If familiars are forces from outside our daily existence, what kind of forces are they—alien infiltrators, divine avatars of all sorts, revenant spirits from a distant time or place? And what happens the first time a familiar reveals its larger-than-life side? How do people react when they realize something isn't exactly normal? And are there furry paw prints on major junctures of our history, as many tales from many cultures indicate? However the stories got started, they make for interesting reading—and lead us to imagine stories of our own. So here, collected for your enjoyment, are a charming assortment of new and original tales of familiars, written by some of today's finest authors. Enjoy!

SEARCHING FOR THE FAMILIAR

by Kristine Kathryn Rusch

Kristine Kathryn Rusch is an award-winning fiction writer. Her novella, *The Gallery of His Dreams*, won the *Locus* Award for best short fiction. Her body of fiction work won her the John W. Campbell Award, given in 1991 in Europe. She has been nominated for several dozen fiction awards, and her short work has been reprinted in six *Year's Best* collections. She has published twenty novels under her own name. She has sold forty-one novels total, including pseudonymous books. Her books have been published in seven languages, and have spent several weeks on the *USA Today* Bestseller list and *The Wall Street Journal* Bestseller list. She has written a number of *Star Trek*™ novels with her husband, Dean Wesley Smith, including a book in last summer's crossover series called *New Earth*. She is the former editor of the prestigious *The Magazine of Fantasy and Science Fiction*, wining a Hugo for her work there. Before that, she and Dean Wesley Smith started and ran Pulphouse Publishing, a science fiction and mystery press in Eugene. She lives and works on the Oregon coast.

RUBY was gone.
      Winston leaned against the front counter of his magic shop, rattling the empty glass potion bottles. Behind him, the beaded curtains clinked, still moving from the violence of his panicked run through them.

He had searched every inch of the shop, called her name, looked beneath shelves and inside boxes. He picked up his coat, peered behind cabinets, and tossed aside piles of books.

Ruby, his familiar, was missing.

His hands shook, not sure what to do next. Ruby was a petite black cat, barely nineteen months old—a child really, a teenager, who thought she knew the world and didn't.

Had she slipped outside? It was March, cold, damp, drizzly March. Ruby loved her comfort. She hated getting her paws wet. She often asked him to carry her from the store to the car.

She would never go outside in this kind of weather, at least not voluntarily.

And that's what scared him.

He took a deep breath. He had to calm down. He had to go about this logically. Ruby was a familiar, and she had a distinct personality, but she was a cat. Perhaps something intrigued her enough to overcome her aversion to cold air and water-covered sidewalks. Maybe she had gone outside and he hadn't noticed.

But how? He'd been working in the back all morning, doing potions. He'd worked steadily and quietly, no radio, no stereo, nothing to accompany his work except his own breathing. He hadn't heard the bell over the door jingle. He hadn't felt the wall shake as it often did when the door closed.

Ruby had come in with him that morning, like she always did. She watched him mix for a while, and then she went through the beaded curtains to flop on the counter.

He hadn't seen her since.

"Ruby," he said, "if you've somehow made yourself invisible, please make yourself visible again."

He knew that wasn't possible, but she was a familiar, and she was young. Maybe she'd learned new tricks and hadn't told him about them.

"Or speak to me. Please." His mouth was dry. "This isn't funny and I'm really scared."

There. He'd said it. He was scared. For Ruby, yes, because even though she was smart and funny and strong, she was still a six-pound cat who had not spent much time outdoors. But he was also scared for himself.

Wizards needed their familiars to keep their spells pure. When he was a young wizard, fresh out of training, he'd thought he didn't need a familiar. He'd thought himself too good, too talented. Then he'd mixed an aphrodisiac for a young woman in San Francisco. She'd nearly died. Fortunately, her boyfriend hadn't tried it and managed to rush her to the emergency room.

She lived, but the cops were after Winston, thinking him a drug dealer. He'd left San Francisco so fast that his head still spun thinking about it. He didn't stop running until he found Seavy Village and its Gothic landscape.

At the cliffside house he rented and eventually bought, he found his first familiar, Buster. And when Buster died almost two years ago, Ruby showed up.

Winston hadn't been alone since.

He had to think. He bowed his head and rubbed his nose with his thumb and forefinger. He was so terrible in emergencies—the kind of man who usually froze, thought too much, and acted way too late. He was behaving that way now.

Panicking would do him—would do Ruby—no good.

He needed to search for her and he had to have some questions answered. He also had to stay here, in case she turned up somehow. She'd expect him to be here.

She would also expect him to find her.

He raised his head. He couldn't do this alone.

Winston slipped behind the counter and picked up the

phone. Only one other person in Seavy Village knew that Ruby was a familiar. One other person had ever heard Ruby talk, and that was a policeman. Officer Scott Park had been introduced to Ruby—the real Ruby—in the middle of a murder investigation the year before. Ruby convinced Park that magic existed and that Winston wasn't guilty of the crime, and she did it with her usual grace and finesse.

Winston's heart twisted. He clung to the phone as if it were a lifeline, dialing Park's number direct. The line rang, and for a moment, Winston was afraid Park wasn't there.

That would be odd, because Seavy Village was a small town with almost no crime. Everyone got traffic duty, of course, but Park usually avoided it. He handled the real crimes—the thefts, the rapes, the once-every-ten-years murder—and he usually solved them.

Then he picked up. "Park."

"Scott." Winston's voice didn't sound like his own. It sounded strangled and small, as diminished as he would be if Ruby didn't come back. "It's Winston."

"Winston? What's wrong?"

"Ruby's missing."

"What?"

He had Park's attention now. He could tell by the sharpness in Park's tone—all business.

"She was in the store, then she wasn't. No one came in, and I didn't open the door. I don't know what to do, Scott. I know I have to look for her, but I also have to check on some magic things about familiars—"

"Can she just—?" Park lowered his voice, as if he were afraid someone would overhear him. "Can she just come and go on her own?"

"No," Winston said. "She's a cat. In most things, she's just a little house cat."

His eyes burned. She was all he had. Surely Park would understand that.

"Would she come to me?" Park asked.

"Of course," Winston said.

"I'll be right there," Park said, and hung up.

Winston let out a small sigh. He wasn't going to be alone with this dilemma after all. He had help.

He'd never really asked for help before.

He went around the counter, and pulled open the shop's front door. The bell jangled, just like it was supposed to. Still, he slipped outside, pulling the door closed behind him.

A rainstorm had blown in from the ocean. The rain slanted sideways in the wind, cold and harsh. Ruby wouldn't be here, not voluntarily. He called her name, crouched and looked up the sidewalk, under awnings, at the concrete entrances of nearby stores. But he didn't see a slight black cat huddling against the wood doors, trying to keep dry.

Then he made himself look in the street. His shop was off Highway 101 on a side street that rarely got traffic. Still, tourists drove by very fast, forgetting that speed limits applied even when someone was on vacation.

No black cat lay injured on the road. No black cat lay against the sewer grate. No black cat had died in front of his store that morning.

Winston went back inside the store. He was soaked through, and he'd only been in the rain a few minutes. He shook himself off, then went into the back and grabbed a towel, wiping his face and hands.

Ruby's food dish sat in the bathroom, the Fancy Feast Turkey and Giblets mush still sitting in the bowl. She usually ate her morning treat right away, even though she complained that it wasn't people food. She had taken a bite that morning, and told him she would come back later for the rest—after it had a moment to settle.

She hadn't been back.

The bell above the door jingled. He tossed the towel on the sink and went out front.

Scott Park stood in the center of the store, looking official. He was a freckle-faced redhead who looked younger than he was. For once, his Seavy Village Police Uniform was pressed. He must have just got it from the dry cleaner.

"Winston," he said. "Has she shown up?"

Winston shook his head. The panic that had threatened to overwhelm him since he knew she was gone surfaced again. He pushed it down.

"What do you think happened?"

"I don't know." But Winston told him the entire series of events, from the lack of a jingle at the door to the uneaten cat food. "Scott, she's ten percent familiar and ninety percent cat. I'm really worried about her."

"Hmm," Park said.

He went back to the door, examined it, then let himself out. He stood in the rain for a moment, looking up and down the street, then he pulled the door open. As he did, he reached for the bell, but he wasn't quick enough. It jingled.

"Well," he said, "that blows that theory."

Winston understood immediately. Park thought someone might have snuck in, made sure the bell didn't ring, and then left with Ruby.

Park was peering up at the bell. "No one tampered with this, right?"

Winston shrugged.

"You heard all the customers come in and out the last few days?"

"There haven't been any customers the last few days," Winston said. His business was mainly mail order. He kept the storefront so that he had a place to go every day. "And no one could have come in the back without me seeing him."

Park nodded. "All right, then. Do you have a picture of Ruby?"

Winston had to think. He hadn't done any of the normal cat owner things. She didn't wear a collar ("C'mon, big boy," she'd said when he had tried to put it on her. "What do you think I am, stupid? I'd find a way to call you if I got lost.") and she didn't have a little chip in her shoulder. She was fixed, even though she'd been mad at him for a month over that. ("I'm a big girl," she'd said as he drove her to the vet. "I know better than to let every Tom, Dick, and Harry—"

and then she'd chuckled at her own puns "—have his way with me. A littler of kittens is something I don't want.")

"Winston?"

"Sorry," he said. "I was thinking."

Park raised his eyebrows, as if he expected some sort of answer from Winston.

"You know, Ruby told me once she'd call me if she got lost."

"Does she know how to dial?"

Winston nodded. "I made her memorize the numbers. She can push the buttons with her paw. We tested it."

Park looked stunned for a moment, then he shook his head. "Let's call her fifty percent familiar and fifty percent cat, shall we? I'm not used to a feline phoning home."

"She hasn't done that yet."

"But she might. Have you checked the house?"

"She knows where I am. She has this number, too."

Park was still shaking his head. "So do you have that photo?"

"Let me see." Winston went through the beaded curtains. He pulled open a drawer and found old Polaroids he'd taken of his house for insurance purposes.

The cat in most of them was Buster. He'd been a marvelous cat, so very different from Ruby. Ruby was flash and sarcasm, mixed with some incredible gentleness. Buster had been stronger, quieter, and tougher. Exactly what Winston had needed in the old days.

It took some digging before he found a photograph of Ruby. She was sitting near the fireplace—her favorite perch in the house—and she had her "where's the tuna?" expression on her face. Her golden eyes looked at him through the photo, so alive, so vibrant.

"Ruby," he whispered and resisted the urge to clutch the photo to his chest. Instead, he took it to Park.

Park glanced at it. "Doesn't really do her justice."

"Nothing does," Winston said.

"Okay. I'm taking this around. I'll even make a sign for

you, and we'll post it. I hope someone just picked her up and brought her inside a store, but I'll check. I have a few ideas. What will you be doing?"

Winston bit his lower lip. He always felt uncomfortable talking about magic to anyone, even someone who knew it existed, like Park.

"I'm going to call an old friend."

"Here in town?"

"No, no." Winston wasn't explaining this well. "I want to know how much time I have. I might try a locate spell, but I don't dare try without knowing whether or not my familiar must be here."

"Locate?"

"It's a little sophisticated for me, but it should be able to give me Ruby's location."

Park nodded. "I was wondering why you weren't casting some kind of spell. I guess I know now, huh?"

That and the fact that Winston's magic was very small. He was stretching things when he said that a locate spell was very sophisticated for him. It was a degree of difficulty above most spells he tried. He used to think his magic would grow, but over time he learned that what he had was all he'd ever have. Enough to make one-time potions and do a few tiny spells. But never anything else.

"Please find her, Scott," Winston said.

"I'll do what I can," Park said, and left, Ruby's photograph in his pocket.

Winston watched him through the shopfront windows. Park was calling Ruby's name as he walked down the street. He looked concerned, as if he had forgotten to tell Winston something.

Winston didn't want to know. He was extra vigilant most of the time. He knew that black cats were often targets of teenagers, particularly at Halloween. But this was March. Surely no one would take her for violent purposes. Not out of a store on a weekday morning.

He picked up the phone a second time, and dialed slowly,

heart pounding. He hadn't spoken to his mentor in six years. Gerry Bellier was a bona fide wizard of the first order. He could cast a spell that could destroy a city, if he chose to do so, or he could make the wind blow in the opposite direction. He was so powerful that he forgot that others rarely had that kind of ability.

Bellier had hated having Winston as an apprentice. He'd thought Winston's small talent not worth his time at all. But he was a conscientious teacher, answering questions, helping where needed.

And he was a good man. Fortunately. With all that power, he could have harmed anything and anyone who crossed his path. But, so far as Winston knew, Bellier had never used his power to hurt a living creature.

Someone picked up the phone on the other end. "Gerald Bellier."

The voice made Winston stand straighter. Just the sound of it reminded him what a failure he was at everything he tried. "Gerry," he said. "It's Winston. I'm sorry to bother you, but I have an important question."

Bellier sighed. "Can it wait? I have a lecture in fifteen minutes, and I'm revising my notes."

"I'm sorry, no," Winston said. "My familiar has disappeared."

"Hold on," Bellier said. "I'm switching phones."

He hung up, but the connection remained. After a moment, he picked up. In the background, Winston could hear piano music—a CD of some sort. Obviously Bellier had moved into his office.

"What kind of familiar is it?" Bellier asked without preamble.

"She's a cat," Winston said. "Ruby."

"How long has she been gone?"

"That's what I wanted to ask you about. How long are my powers—such as they are—still fresh? I want to try a locate."

"Technical questions in a minute, Winston," Bellier said. "Answer me first. How long has she been gone?"

"I don't know exactly. I opened the store at ten o'clock. It's—" he looked at the clock he kept beside the cash register, "—11:30 now. She was with me for the first half hour the store was open."

"An hour." Bellier let out a small breath.

It seemed like longer. It seemed like she had been gone for weeks. But Winston didn't know how to communicate that to Bellier. Bellier, who was so in control of everything.

"There may be time, then."

"Time for what?" Winston asked.

"Look, I'm going to cancel my lecture and come up there. You're in what—Astoria? Seaside?"

"Seavy Village," he said.

"Where the hell's that?"

"Central Oregon coast," Winston said. "Between Yachats and—"

"It doesn't matter," Bellier said. "I'll be there in fifteen."

Winston could hear Bellier start to put the receiver down. "Wait! Wait! What's going on?"

He heard another rustle, then Bellier brought the phone back to his ear. "Talking won't help her, Winston. We have a limited time."

"Please," Winston said. "She's all I have. Tell me what's going on."

Bellier sighed. "You don't follow the trades, do you?"

There was no point in following the trade publications. Winston wasn't that powerful, and he really didn't feel like part of the main circle of wizards. He didn't belong.

But Bellier knew that. The question had been rhetorical. He continued. "Familiars are being kidnapped all over the west coast. Kidnapped and, well—" His confident voice actually broke. "I lost Harris to this."

Harris was his potbellied pig. Bellier doted on Harris, even though he was the meanest pig Winston had ever seen.

"But I hadn't had Harris with me that day. He'd been

gone at least twelve hours when I found out. We have a chance with your Ruby. I'll be there soon."

And then he hung up.

Kidnapped. Winston pulled the phone to his chest. How? Why? Why would anyone take familiars?

Familiars only worked with their chosen masters. Their powers were no good to any other wizard. Even if the original master died, the familiar could not help a new master. The familiar and the wizard were bonded for life—usually the familiar's life, but not always.

Winston was shaking. If they didn't find Ruby soon, she'd be dead. And, from the undertone of anger in Bellier's voice, the death wouldn't be a pretty one.

He knew better than to call Bellier back. Bellier would be here shortly, and then Winston could ask him all the questions he needed to.

But Winston felt the clock ticking. Every second lost might mean the permanent loss of Ruby. So he made one more call.

This time, the phone was answered on the first ring.

"Spellbound," a woman's voice said.

"Agatha?" he asked.

"I'll get her," the voice said, and put him on hold. Muzak played in the background.

Winston leaned against his counter, feeling as if the world had passed him by. When had the trade magazine for wizards become big enough to have a staff, let alone a phone system that played Muzak and put people on hold? The last time he had spoken to Agatha Ritchie, she had been answering her own phone and putting people on hold by setting the receiver down while she searched through the piles of papers on her desk.

"Agatha Ritchie."

At least she sounded the same. Her voice was deep and throaty, with a trace of an English accent. She had been a friend in his San Francisco days—more than a friend for a while—and he still missed her.

"Agatha," he said. "It's Winston."

"Winston!" She sounded delighted. "How long has it been?"

"I don't know," he said, although he did. "Listen, I've got a situation here. My familiar's missing. I spoke to Gerry, and he said that there's been a rash of these things. He's coming here, but I thought maybe you could tell me more."

"Oh, God, Winston, I'm sorry." As if Ruby were already dead. "You're not going to like what I have to tell you. The way they found those familiars—"

"That's not what I want to know," he said quickly. "I want to know if there are any leads, any ideas as to why this is happening."

The bell over the door jingled, and Park came back in. His uniform was soaked. He shook off the water like a dog who'd run through a sprinkler.

"No one knows," Agatha said. "The disappearances are all unusual, as if there's been some magic involved, but other than that, there's no indication it's one of us."

"Because we know there's no point in stealing someone else's familiar," Winston said.

"We don't know that," she said. "There is a theory that the familiars are the true magicians and we are their pawns, here to do their bidding."

Ruby would like that idea. She would probably agree with it.

"Winston," Park said.

Winston held up his hand, silently asking Park to wait.

"If that's true," Agatha was saying, "then there is a chance that they might confer their powers onto someone new if coerced."

"Do you believe it?"

"What I believe doesn't matter. It's what these kidnappers believe that matters. When did you lose your familiar?"

"This morning."

"Then there's some time yet."

"That's what Gerry said."

Agatha made a dismissive sound. She'd never liked Bellier.

"What else is there?" Winston asked. "Have the police found anything?"

"There hasn't been police involvement," she said as if he were a bit dense. "They'd see this as an animal cruelty case. In most states, that's a misdemeanor, not worth their time."

Park was watching him closely.

"So no one has looked at the evidence or anything?" Winston asked.

"Just our folks, and I have to tell you, Winston, the usual stuff doesn't work."

"What usual stuff?"

"Locate spells, all of that. These creeps have figured out ways to block that. They seem to expect a magical response to what they've done."

"How were the others found, then?" Winston asked.

Park came closer. He was frowning.

"Accidentally. All of the cases were reported. When the animals were found—and believe me, it was always dramatic—then the wizards were called."

"This isn't good, Agatha, is it?" Winston asked, hoping somehow she'd tell him otherwise.

"No, it isn't, Winston. I'm sorry." She paused, as if she were going to add something else and then thought better of it. "Let me know how it turns out."

"I will," he said, and hung up. Then he turned to Park. "You didn't find her."

Park shook his head. "What's all that about?"

Winston told him.

Park closed his eyes. "I liked that little cat."

Winston felt himself bristle at the past tense. "She's not dead yet," he said, and wondered if he was the only one who believed it.

*   *   *

Bellier arrived ten minutes later in a puff of blue smoke. He was shorter than Winston remembered, and heavier, too. His bald head glistened in the store's fluorescent light.

He looked around and said, "This is your place, Winston?" as if he couldn't believe someone would be here voluntarily.

Park was gaping at him. Apparently the police officer had never seen anyone simply appear out of thin air before.

"We don't have a lot of time," Winston said, amazed he could sound so forceful with his mentor. "We need to get right on it."

Bellier nodded. He was wearing a charcoal-gray silk suit and wingtips. His hands had been manicured. He'd obviously gotten a lot of money somewhere, somehow.

"I'm Scott Park." Park took a step forward, his hand out. Bellier looked at it as if it were covered with worms.

"You've broken the code of silence?" Bellier asked Winston, as if Park weren't even there.

"Technically, no. Someone else told Scott about us." Winston wasn't about to confess that Ruby had been that someone else. "It won't hurt you to say hello to him, Gerry. He's my friend and he's helping."

Park had withdrawn his hand. His arms were crossed now and he was watching Bellier as if Bellier were about to break the law. "Where's your familiar?"

The question was designed to put Bellier off-balance. Winston instantly wanted to apologize, but he didn't.

"Safe," Bellier said. "You don't think I'd bring him here, do you?"

"Please," Winston said. "Let's find Ruby."

"Give me something of hers, and I'll get to the locate spell," Bellier said.

"Agatha said that won't work."

"Agatha? You spoke to her?"

Winston nodded.

"Well, she's not an expert on anything except publishing

these days." Bellier looked at the beaded curtain with distaste. "I suppose your supplies are back there?"

"There's not much," Winston said. "I don't have your abilities."

"I'll see what I can find." He pushed his way through the curtain and disappeared into the back. After a moment, he called, "The food bowl is hers, I take it?"

"Yes." Winston stared at the curtains, but he couldn't bring himself to go through them. He didn't want to see the contempt Bellier had for his work space, for his world.

"If it's not going to work, then why's he doing it?" Park asked.

"I guess for the same reason we've been searching for her," Winston said. "We have to do something."

Bellier pulled the beaded curtain aside. "You call this a workstation, Winston? Where are your real supplies?"

"This is what I have," he said.

"This is going to be harder than I thought," Bellier said and disappeared into the back again.

Winston flushed.

"Why do you let him talk to you that way?" Park asked.

"He's my mentor. He trained me."

"Is he still training you?"

Winston shook his head.

"Then you should tell him to treat you with more respect. You're a good guy, Winston, and you're bright. You don't deserve to be talked to that way—"

Something exploded in the back. Winston winced.

"Never mind!" Bellier shouted. "It's not a problem."

"Seems to me," Park said, softer this time, "that he's only going to get in the way."

"No one's tried this early before," Winston said. Then he frowned. No one had tried real police methods either. And he had a real live policeman—one who had been trained in Seattle, one who knew how to investigate difficult cases.

"I suppose I should go back out there," Park said. "I'm not doing Ruby any good sitting in here."

Winston caught his arm. "Scott, if you were investigating this as a nonmagic case, what would you do?"

"Nothing, Winston. We don't look for lost pets."

"What if it's a kid?"

Park tilted his head back, as if he hadn't thought of this. "And this was a pattern?"

Winston nodded.

Park tapped his chin. He walked around the store, looking at it as if he'd never seen it before.

Another explosion echoed in the back. "I'm fixing it!" Bellier shouted. "Why don't you label your potions?"

"Do you need to help him?" Park asked.

"He'll figure it out," Winston said, feeling as if he were rebelling against Bellier for the first time in his life.

Park continued to walk the store. Then he looked at Winston. "I need some answers."

"Okay."

"No, from your friend in there."

Winston took a deep breath. "Go ask him."

Park slid around the counter, and pulled the beaded curtain back. Smoke wafted out of the back. "Excuse me," Park said as he disappeared into the darkness.

"I'm not to be disturbed," Bellier said.

Winston straightened his shoulders and joined the other two. The back was a mess. All of his carefully measured vials were scattered around the room, and the potions he'd been working on were stacked in a corner. There were two smoking holes in the floor.

"I'll fix it," Bellier said, although there was no apology in his voice. More of a dismissive tone, as if it weren't his fault.

"I have some questions to ask," Park said.

"I don't explain magic," Bellier said.

"I'm not asking for an explanation," Park said.

"He wants to know some things about the kidnappings," Winston said.

"You told him that, too?" Bellier frowned at him.

"He's helping us search for Ruby."

"As if his help will matter," Bellier said.

Park's skin flushed the same color red as his hair, but he didn't say anything.

"It matters to me," Winston said. "We have to do all we can. It'll only take a minute, Gerry."

Bellier looked up. "Then you get me some garlic while I'm wasting my time with him."

Winston walked to his ruined worktable, avoiding the holes in the floor, and reached into his supplies. He found the garlic without any trouble at all.

"When the bodies were discovered," Park said, his tone all business, "how far away from their original homes were they?"

"Not far," Bellier said.

"How far? Same city? Same state? Same block?"

"Same city," Bellier said. "A mile or two at most. That's one of the many things that makes these events so upsetting. Not that you could understand—"

"Were they found in a house or a yard or a wooded area?"

"I don't know," Bellier said.

"What about Harris?" Winston asked. His stomach was churning. He should have thought of these questions.

"Harris—" And to Winston's surprise, Bellier's voice broke again. "Harris was found in the basement of a nearby house."

"A rental?" Park asked.

"How should I know?"

"Think!" Winston snapped.

Bellier looked at him as if he had grown fangs. Then he tilted his head sideways, in the position he always used when he was considering things. "I believe it was a rental. And it smelled odd as well. Not just because of—Harris— but because someone had tried to create magic."

"Create magic?" Park asked.

"The nonmagical," Winston said. "Some of them believe they can do spells."

"Can they?" Park asked.

"Small ones," Bellier said. "Ones that even our Winston would consider easy."

Winston felt his cheeks grow warm.

"Like preventing a bell from jingling?" Park asked.

Bellier snorted. "You, Officer Park, could do that now. I could show you how. It's more of a parlor trick than a spell."

Park glanced at Winston, almost in apology. Then he asked, "What else? Do you know how many people were involved?"

"I couldn't control Harris," Bellier said, "and he and I were friends. It would take at least three people to hold him, and they would have to be strong."

"There are no spells to control animals?" Park asked.

"Not familiars," Winston said.

"And not that anyone without magical ability could do," Bellier said, "no matter how many books they read."

"Except on solstice," Winston said.

"Even then," Bellier said.

Winston leaned against his shaky desk. "Agatha said that the locate spells didn't work."

"It was the time limit," Bellier said.

"What if it wasn't?" Winston said. "What if they did some kind of magical blocking spell?"

"They'd have to be awfully sophisticated," Bellier said.

"They're stealing familiars," Winston said. "That's sophisticated. How do they even know who has familiars? As opposed to pets, I mean. Not too many people know about me."

Bellier's shoulders slumped. It was as if the state he had worked himself into when he discovered that Ruby was gone had evaporated. "I had just assumed they would know. But you're right. You've been hidden all these years. To the uninformed, your mail order business looks like some herbal supplement company."

Winston started. He hadn't expected Bellier to know anything about his business.

"They shouldn't have found you."

"But they did," Park said. "Your customers all know about Ruby."

"I haven't had customers for almost a week," Winston said.

"Someone else told them," Bellier said. "They must have figured you were easy pickings, being up here by yourself."

Winston felt a shiver go through him. Someone had targeted him. Him and Ruby, just because they were here. Alone.

Although they had gone after Bellier, too. He was visible in his Southern California offices, with his speeches and his classes. Maybe that made him vulnerable as well.

"If they're using a magical block spell, I can't find them with a locate," Bellier said. "They'll be counting on that spell coming their way."

"Well," Park said. "It looks like we need to do some footwork. They'll be in a vacation rental along the coast, but there are hundreds of those, and dozens of real estate agencies that handle them. I'll get some of the officers to work this—"

"Wait," Winston said. "We can't locate Ruby through their block spell, but can we locate their block spell? It can't be a very strong one, not if they're not really magical."

Bellier looked at Winston in surprise. "Of course, we can. Brilliant, Winston. That'll make this much quicker."

"How much quicker?" Park asked. "Because I can get my guys on this right away."

Bellier snatched the garlic from Winston's hand. "We'll be there in a minute or two, if Winston helps me with the ingredients."

"Any magic I do might curdle," Winston said.

"You have twenty-four hours after your familiar leaves," Bellier said. "More if she's still alive. You should know that. Didn't you bury a familiar?"

Winston felt panic rise. "Yes, but I figured any spells I did then were allowed because it was a special circumstance."

"Well, so's this," Bellier said. He searched the shelf of potions. "Where's the rubbing alcohol?"

Winston got that out of the bathroom cabinet. Then he got the other ingredients before Bellier asked for them. Bellier mixed everything together in a clean marble bowl. Park watched as if he were studying the spell himself.

When it was done, Bellier recited an incantation in Latin—probably to show off—and then a window opened where Winston's desk was.

A weather-beaten house at the end of gravel road. The house overlooked the ocean. Three large trucks were parked in front of the house, obscuring the address, but the street sign was clear. Southwest Jetty Road.

"I'm on it," Park said and started out the back door.

"Wait!" Winston said.

"Let him go," Bellier said. "We should do this ourselves."

But Park stopped. "Do what?"

"We're going—right, Gerry?" Winston said.

Bellier frowned, but it, too, seemed to be for show. "I suppose you want him to come along."

"Yes," Winston said.

"All right, then," Bellier said, and with a snap of his fingers, everything vanished.

Winston hated the way the world went white in a transport spell. He knew it meant that for a moment he did not exist anywhere on Earth. And he despised that.

Then he felt wood beneath his feet. The smell of the ocean was strong, and he was getting wet. The horizontal rain was pelting his shirt, making him very cold.

He stood on the old house's porch. Bellier and Park were beside him. Park was so pale that his freckles looked like dots made by Magic Markers.

"What now?" he whispered, looking at Bellier.

Winston reached for the door. The knob turned. As he eased it open, he heard a familiar voice.

". . . stupid plan. Magic is like life, buddy. You can cut me open and try to absorb my life force, but when it's all said and done, I'm dead and you've got no more life than you did before. Same with magic . . ."

Ruby. She was alive, and lecturing someone who was thinking of killing her.

Winston's knees went weak with relief. He started to go inside, but Park grabbed his arm and held him back. Park put a finger to his lips, then pulled his service revolver. He went inside first, just like they did in the movies—gun sweeping the room before him, body following.

Bellier recited a protect spell and expanded it to all three of them, but he did it so quietly that Winston doubted Park noticed. Then Bellier went inside.

". . . you may get some residual power, but it'll last an hour, maybe a day. And even then it won't do you any good. That book you're using was written by someone without magic . . ."

Winston entered last. Ruby's voice was the guide. It was strong and firm, and had no fear in it at all.

". . . if all you want is power, then you should talk to my boss. He makes potions for everything. We can give you that little bit of charisma you're missing, or that girlfriend you want, or that huge boost of intelligence you need, fella . . ."

Great. She was insulting them. They'd kill her just to shut her up.

". . . I can make sure it won't cost you a dime. It would certainly be easier than . . ."

The living room of the house smelled moldy and damp. The furniture was old, stuff that the owners obviously didn't care about. Three suitcases sat near the door and a briefcase lay open on the dining room table.

". . . You do know that magical power is based on size. I'm petite. I'm not that powerful, and even if your goofy idea works, which it won't, I won't be able to help you much . . ."

Park glanced at the briefcase, then caught Bellier's eye. Bellier came over and looked, then shook his head.

Winston didn't care what was in the briefcase. All he wanted was Ruby.

". . . so it would be best if you just let me go. No one'll believe me about this whole thing, and my boss probably doesn't even know I'm gone yet . . ."

Her voice quavered on that last. She believed it.

Winston entered a narrow hallway. He saw them, five large men huddled around a full-sized bed. They were all looking down, probably at Ruby. One of the men held a knife. Another held a large book.

They were all so much bigger than he was.

But Bellier had put a protect spell around him. They were nonmagical. They couldn't hurt him.

Winston walked into the room, squaring his shoulders and looking as tough as he could. As he got closer to the bed, he could see Ruby in the center of it. Her forepaws had been bound with duct tape. So had her hind legs.

"That's my cat," he said, making sure his voice carried. "You have no right to her."

"Winston." Ruby's head swiveled toward him. He saw relief in her golden eyes. Relief and fear mixed.

He shoved two of the men aside, and reached for her.

"Winston!" she shouted, looking over his shoulder.

He ignored her cry of fear. Instead, he grabbed her, cradling her against him. The man with the knife slashed at him, and Winston turned away, deflecting the blade.

He hadn't realized the flaw in his plan until now. He was under a protect spell, but Ruby wasn't.

"No one move." Park stood in the door, his gun trained on the room. He looked menacing.

"I can arrange that," Bellier said and snapped his fingers.

The men around Winston froze in place. Bellier walked toward them, his mouth set, eyes narrowed.

"It wouldn't take much, Winston." Bellier stopped in front of the first man. He was a beefy man, with powerful shoulders and muscular arms. "A few simple spells. We could take away his power of speech forever."

Ruby squirmed in Winston's arms. She knew, as he did, that the men, even though they couldn't move, could hear and see everything.

"Or," Bellier said, moving to the next man, "we could take away his ability to reason. Of course, we would leave the memory of how his brain had worked before. That would frustrate him."

"Boss?" Ruby whispered. "Who's that?"

Winston held her close. She felt so small and frail against him. "His name's Gerry Bellier," Winston said. "They killed his familiar."

At his words, he felt the tension in the room rise, even though the men couldn't move. Park was still watching from the door.

"Or we could end their lives," Bellier said. "Slowly. In just the way they ended Harris'."

He looked at Winston. He was actually considering it.

"We can't," Winston said. "You know that, Gerry. You're the one who taught me that. It's so easy to let the power go to our heads. Even for the wrong cause. Causing bodily harm—"

"An eye for an eye is allowed." Bellier's voice was soft.

"Let Scott take care of it now," Winston said. "He's the police."

Bellier walked around the man with the knife. That man was still gripping the knife as if he were going to use it, as if he were in the middle of a downward blow against Winston.

"What would you do, Officer?" Bellier asked Scott. "What would you arrest them for?"

Park shot Winston an apologetic glance. "Animal cruelty. And even that won't be bad, unless some of the other cases were in the state."

"Not good enough," Bellier said. "Today they attempted murder against this beautiful creature."

He reached for Ruby. She cringed against Winston. He kept her out of Bellier's grasp.

"And they committed murder, all in the name of magic." Bellier put his hand on the knife-wielder's shoulder. "So you thought you could get magic by stealing it. Isn't that right, Miss Ruby?"

Ruby swallowed hard. "That's what they told me."

"They're fools, and they destroyed marvelous creatures in their quest," Bellier said. "You've met Ruby, Officer Park. My Harris was just as special. So were the others. That's murder."

"Unfortunately," Park said, "no one can prosecute it that way."

"Can we leave?" Ruby asked Winston. "My paws hurt, but I don't want you to use that knife to get this stuff off."

Winston turned. The knife still hung there, glistening in the gray light coming in through the windows.

"But you can still get them for attempted murder," Winston said.

"What do you mean?" Park took a step inside the room.

"They tried to kill me," Winston said. "They stole my cat and when I came to get her, with you at my side, they tried to kill me."

Bellier clasped his hands behind his back. "Will that work, Officer Park? Or must I imprison them myself for the next fifty years?"

Park's gaze went from the knife to Winston to Ruby and then back again. "Tell you what," he said to Bellier. "If we can't successfully prosecute these guys, I'll make sure you get a chance at them."

Bellier smiled. "It's a deal."

"But you'll have to give us a statement—leaving out the magic," Park said. "Can you do that?"

"Of course," Bellier said. "I give statements leaving out magic all the time."

"Let me get some backup here," Park said. "Is there any way to cuff these guys when you unfreeze them?"

"Sure," Bellier said.

"Big guy," Ruby said, using her pet name for Winston. "Please. Can we leave?"

"Can we?" Winston asked Park.

"It would be better if you were here when the other cops arrive," Park said. "It'll make the court case easier."

"Here." Bellier touched the duct tape. It unwrapped itself from Ruby's paws. "Is that better, dear?"

"Why do you think you have the right to call me dear?" she asked.

Bellier looked at Winston. "She has guts."

"Yes," Winston said. "One of us needs them."

"Don't let him con you. You have guts." Ruby shook her front paws. She was lying in his arms like a baby. "Can we at least leave the room? These guys are creeping me out."

"Sure," Winston said.

He took her into the hallway and down the hall. Then he put her on his shoulder and she nuzzled against his neck. Both of them were shaking all over.

"I didn't think you knew I was gone," she said.

"I figured it out."

"I thought they were going to kill me and there was nothing I could do. I didn't think you could do anything either. They'd bought some spells from some guy in Ohio. Potion, like magic blockers and silencers. That's how they got around the bell."

Winston nodded, not trusting his voice. He didn't think they'd find her alive. He hadn't realized it until now, but he had been afraid she was dead from the moment she disappeared.

"It's all in that briefcase," she said. "They kept reading the spells from the book and reading them wrong. I was so scared."

She had to have been scared. She'd never admitted weakness before.

"I don't like this," she said. "I want to go home. Can we close the store and stay home this week?"

"Sure," he said.

"And I'm not going to leave your side. Ever. I don't care if you don't like that."

"I like it," he said.

She pushed against his ear, her nose cold against his skin. "You figured out I was missing and you got help?"

"Yes."

"Both Scott and the scary guy?"

"Yes."

"All the other familiars died?"

"Yes," he said, wishing she hadn't heard that.

She sighed and snuggled even closer. "You're amazing."

"Me?"

Her paws were kneading his shoulder. He wondered if she even knew she was doing it. She rarely had kitten moments any more.

"Yes, you," she said. "All these other big powerful wizards, they lost their familiars. But you acted fast. You rescued me."

He leaned his head against her smaller one. "You're all I have, Ruby."

"I'm going to let you believe that," she said, "only because it benefits me."

She lifted her head and pushed on his shoulder, looking around the room.

"Say," she said, "do you think they have some tuna around here?"

And that was the first time since he'd found her that he knew she'd be all right. That they'd both be all right.

After the police talked to them—to him, actually, since only Park knew that Ruby could speak—and after Bellier left, they would be able to go back to their small, comfortable lives.

Winston would have to learn a few new spells, beef up their own security, and find a way to protect Ruby even when she was alone. He'd also have to start following the trades so that he wouldn't be surprised again.

But those were small changes. Easy changes. Changes that he didn't mind, considering how close he had come to losing it all.

"Well?" she asked. "You think they got tuna?"

"No," he said. "And even if they do, you don't want to eat it."

"Good point," she said. "You know, things are easier for cats. We'd kill the SOBs, or run them off, or something. This legal stuff is goofy."

"We've had this discussion before, Ruby," he said gently.

"And we'll have it again," she said.

Then they looked at each other. She bumped her head against his chin, and he ran his hand down the soft fur of her back.

Yes, they'd have the discussion again. They'd have a lot of discussions again, thanks to the help from Park and Bellier—and to his own quick thinking.

Ruby was right. He had succeeded where greater wizards had failed. Even though he didn't have an arsenal of spells like Bellier or a gun like Park, he'd managed to save his Ruby.

And that was all that mattered.

AND SO, AD INFINITUM

by Jody Lynn Nye

Jody Lynn Nye lists her main career activity as "spoiling cats." She lives northwest of Chicago with two of the above and her husband, author and packager Bill Fawcett. She was written twenty-two books, including four contemporary fantasies, three science fiction novels, four novels in collaboration with Anne McCaffrey, including *The Ship Who Won*, a humorous anthology about mothers, *Don't Forget Your Spacesuit, Dear!*, and over sixty short stories. Her latest books are *License Invoked*, co-written with Robert Asprin, *The Dreamland*, and *Advanced Mythology*, fourth in the *Mythology 101* series.

"I CAN'T believe it, Loretta," Mira said into the phone. "After all I've done to keep the place spotless, Zoomer has fleas. Stop it, sweetie. Not you, Loretta. The cat's nagging me. One more treat, and that's all." She shook a few Petreats out of the pink-labeled can, set them on the floor, and put the can in the white-fronted cabinet above the refrigerator. It was a long stretch for her five-foot-three body, but the highest spot in the kitchen. The fat brown tabby cat chomped down the morsels and sat looking hopefully for more. "No! Honestly, you're going to turn into a balloon."

"Fleas can come in clinging to anything, you know," Loretta said sympathetically. "Did you try . . . you know?"

Neither one of the women liked to talk about the subject on the telephone—people might be listening. Ditto for the Internet. No references to you-know-what. Magic. But she didn't have to be specific with her co-religionist and sister nature priestess. *All right, say it,* she chided herself. *Fellow witch.*

"In the nicest possible way," Mira said, fiddling with a lock of her short, permed auburn hair. "I *disinvited* them. But there's just one I simply cannot seem to shake, so to speak. It drives me insane watching Zoomer scratch at his neck like he's trying to shred himself."

Loretta sighed. "Have you just tried combing the little bugger out and squishing it between your fingers?"

"Bad karma," Mira said, twirling the long curly wire so Zoomer would jump for it. The cat gave it a few cursory hits, then settled down, meat loaf style, facing the cabinet.

"You mean you did try and you couldn't catch it."

"Bingo. Never mind. They can't have a very long life span, and it's like there's only one. Except for the scratching, it doesn't seem to be bothering Zoomer much. He's been very content lately."

"It's those new treats," Loretta said knowingly. "Humphrey *loves* them. I have to hide the can or he pries the lid off with his teeth. You know the slogan: 'Petreats make your pet feel so good.' "

"Zoomer loves them, too. I wish we had treats that made us feel good."

"We do," Loretta laughed. "It's called chocolate."

Mira glanced through the yellow kitchen curtains at the horizon. "Gotta go. The sun's about down, and I want to get that ritual going before the kids come home from band practice."

"Good luck," Loretta said, with a trace of envy in her voice. "Let me know how it went."

*   *   *

Mira didn't care what all the old books said about covens. Magic was a solitary practice, intended to get a person in touch with the infinite. With a husband who ran a busy cleaning service out of a home office and a son and daughter involved with every activity under the sun, Mira had little chance for privacy, so what she had she cherished.

Ten years and fifteen pounds ago it had been easier to crawl into the tiny box room off one side of the attic of their 120-year-old Cape Cod house. The kids had used it as a secret hideout until they were informed it would never in their lifetimes be wired for electricity or cable. Mira had taken it over as a cubbyhole for those moments when she wasn't working, chauffeuring, cooking, cleaning, or one of the thousand other -ings for which she was responsible. The walls were a deep burgundy red, Mira's favorite color. In exchange for painting Loretta's kitchen her friend had made her a thick velvet curtain to block the entrance. A square footstool against the north wall served as an altar. Mira had read about personal altars in a women's magazine and liked the concept of a focus for her personal energies. She adorned it with dried flowers and other little things she'd picked up in places she loved. The kids were forbidden to touch it under pain of death.

Candles in wonderful holders, all purchased at a home sales party, were everywhere. She lit them with a red electronic-ignition lighter like the one they had for the fireplace downstairs. A big fat blue cushion sat in the exact middle of the room for her. Another lay against the east wall for Zoomer, who never missed a chance to curl up somewhere warm, dark and peaceful.

Certain that her husband and kids were not going to be around for at least two hours, Mira eschewed the floor-length flowered caftan she kept on a hook in her sanctum sanctorum and sat nude on her cushion. In the flickering candlelight she couldn't see the uneven bulges in her thighs and could ignore that incipient pot belly. In her mind she was sleek and taut as a nymph. She concentrated on capturing that wild, powerful side of herself that rode the sunrise bareback.

Something was on the floor in front of the altar. It was the rattle that was used to summon her familiar. Mira picked it up and held on to it. She didn't need it for the ritual, but it felt good to have it in her hand. Mira had carved it herself out of a fallen tree branch, attached strings of wooden beads to one end, and painted it with the symbols she found in a book. She loved the smooth texture of the foot-long, two-inch thick rod—but what was this? It felt as if it had been stuck all over with a pin. The kids knew better than to touch it. She peered closely at the rattle. She recognized those gouges. They'd been caused by Zoomer's teeth. He'd been playing with it. Where was he?

Zoomer elbowed his way past the curtain and trotted over to lie down. His cushion was flanked by twin candlesticks in ribbed glass chimneys that cast tabby shadows. She gave him an exasperated look and bent to put a tablet of charcoal in the incense burner. It was filled with ashes. Hadn't she cleaned it out last time? She shook her head. She must really have been zoned out when she closed the circle last time.

Small wonder, considering what she'd been doing.

In the books she'd been reading, the authors had mentioned a place beyond death where loving souls met again, a place called the Summerland. Mira had been very close to her great-aunt Violet. Violet had died two years ago at age ninety-two while Mira and her family were on their first and only trip out of the country. Mira always regretted never being able to say good-bye, but worse yet, Violet was the last of her generation. Mira had been interviewing her to get all their family history written down for her children and, she hoped, one day, grandchildren. The two of them had managed to chart down almost all of the relatives, but didn't have the name of the village in Eastern Europe where their ancestors had come from. Considering the way borders moved around during the last century, they weren't certain which *country* it was in. Violet had told Mira the name was just on the tip of her tongue. Since she was sick in bed, she promised to give the matter all her attention and she'd tell Mira when she came home. Mira had never seen her alive again.

More than anything, she wanted to see the old woman and tell her how much she loved her. Mira had to admit that she also wanted the name of the village. She *hated* to leave a task unfinished. Violet was the same way, organized and goal-oriented. Couldn't that be a karmic reason for their souls to meet again? She firmly believed in reincarnation, so it was a risk even to go looking for Violet. She might already have gone on to her next life. Mira felt anguished. What if the old lady wasn't waiting for her? A part of her history would be gone forever!

She glanced over at Zoomer. The sight of the cat washing himself as if he hadn't a care in the world gave Mira confidence. Zoomer put a leg up in the air and bent his head to a task that Mira wouldn't undertake for a million dollars or a date with Mel Gibson.

She preferred to think of herself as a weekend witch. The faith had always interested her. Most of the stuff in the history books about trials seemed to be attacks on uppity women more than against anybody practicing black arts or summoning Satan. Now that she'd done more reading, she realized the stuff about Satan was a put-up job, too. There was a mother goddess, and her consort was a horned forest god, like Herne the Hunter on that *Robin of Sherwood* TV show years ago. While part of her was nervous about envisioning God, she had become comfortable with these archetypes. They were the guardians of the universe as well as its creators. The God she grew up with felt too far away, uninvolved.

The idea of having a familiar came from a book on shamanism she got out of the local library. Their purpose was to act as a guide in the underworld, or as they called it in *Dungeons & Dragons,* an alternate plane of existence. A familiar was a servant, but also a friend, an auxiliary battery for power, and a go-between completing the circuit between her and the great source of all power. They also amplified whatever magical abilities a person had, so you had to choose an animal whose strengths and weaknesses were the opposite of your own.

She'd done a calling, as the book named it, expecting to make contact with a badger or a fox, some savage creature who would help her tap into her inner reserves. Instead, she got Zoomer. Zoomer, whom the kids had named for the way the stray kitten had shot into their kitchen one cold night and made himself at home, had looked up at her with wise, wise eyes that touched her to her soul. Mira stopped herself from putting him out the door. In four years, he had grown up to be a placid, fat tabby who liked to sleep in the sun. Mira liked cats, so she didn't really mind.

That expressive look was the last open vestige of wisdom the cat had manifested. Since then, he became a persnickety consumer of cat food, expert mattress tester, and devoted companion during Mira's private endeavors into the occult. He gave off the greatest karmic kick. From the beginning of their association Mira felt a pick-me-up every time she tried one of her rituals, so she guessed the book was right. She also noticed she saw better in the dark.

The best thing about Zoomer, other than his purr, which could rattle the chandelier, was his intelligent silence. He never interrupted Mira with a clarion yell just as she was going into a meditative trance, saving it instead for later when Mira descended, clothed, to the kitchen. Zoomer listened to everything going on. When Loretta came over a month ago to learn the familiar-summoning spell, Zoomer watched as if making sure they did it right. But how would he know if it was right? He hadn't been there the night Mira did it to call him into her life. Loretta cooed over him, saying how cute he was. Zoomer had stalked off, offended. Maybe he'd chewed on the wand because Loretta had handled it last. Mira hadn't been in the sanctum since then.

Mira was surprised how well her magic was coming

along. She thought she must have a natural aptitude. She succeeded in making things work that neither Loretta nor most of their friends could accomplish. The most spectacular was her levitation spell. She'd come across it in a dusty old book in the library. It took ages to get all the ingredients for the potion together, and even longer trying different inflections on the incantation, but it worked. She could float on the air like a feather. Too bad that Lewis wasn't interested in trying it. Levitation offered some really interesting possibilities.

She drew a circle on the floor in blue chalk, then lit a candle and an incense burner (purchased at a Target Superstore) placed on her altar. That sealed the room. No other living presence could pass within the chalk, and the ring of candles prevented malign forces from coming in. With some difficulty, she folded her legs into a double lotus. As fragrant smoke rose from the tiny pressed cone, Mira started chanting. According to the planewalker spell, she had to rise above earthly things. With levitation, that was no problem. Falling into a gently rhythmic mantra, she began to lose the tension bunched up in her shoulders and neck. Her limbs fell loose as her body started to rise. Any minute now she was going to pass into a different realm of existence. She was going to see Aunt Violet again! This would work!

But the power was not as high gain as usual. She got an inch off the cushion, then plumped back to the ground again. Exasperated, she opened her eyes and glanced toward Zoomer, who was grooming his toenails with his teeth.

"I get the impression you're not giving me all your attention," she said. "Please concentrate. I need you. I need to do this."

The cat actually stopped what he was doing and stared at her. Satisfied, Mira closed her eyes and put her thumbs and forefingers together.

"Mmmm," she hummed. "Mmmmm." To her delight, she felt the cushion drop out from underneath her bottom. She enjoyed the sensation of hovering in the air. It was *comfortable*.

The next part of the spell was new. She'd had to memorize it carefully because she wasn't going to be able to bring physical things with her into the alternate planes. But she hesitated, nervous. If she succeeded, was she sure she could find Aunt Violet? Mira didn't exactly have an address for the old woman. And what would she do if she couldn't get back to the real world again?

A throaty purr interrupted her musings. *Good old Zoomer,* Mira thought, just before the sound of vigorous scratching made her change her mind. He considered this no big deal. Neither should she.

"Open the gate," she intoned confidently. "Bring me through to the other side, to the gardens of the Summerland. Show me the ones who have gone before. Open the gate. Bring me through . . ."

The world seemed to tilt as air moved around her. Things brushed near her skin, some of them swooping close overhead. Mira dared to sneak a peek through her eyelashes, and nearly stopped chanting in surprise.

Superimposed like a glass painting over the homely reality of the attic room was a ghostly landscape. Rolling fields, faintly green, stretched out all around her. Trees, or the spirits of trees, dotted the horizon. Indistinct figures floated slowly here and there. Mira was excited and terrified at the same time. She had managed to open the gate. She was there, or it was here.

She finished the incantation; the air felt different around her now, even though she knew she was still in her attic. She unfolded her legs and stood up.

The floor felt bouncy. No, that was her cushion. She stepped off it, careful to stay within the faint light of the candles she could just see through the gray mist of the grass. Some of the shapes floated in her direction, their speed increasing as they neared her. One swooped down, close enough to tangle in her hair. Mira ducked, throwing her arms over her head for protection. She thought she heard maniacal laughter in the wake of the creature. *It can't hurt me,* she thought, willing herself to believe. *It can't!*

She felt a presence at her ankle, giving her confidence. Bless Zoomer. She reached down to stroke him, and bumped into something big. Hastily backpedaling away from contact, she looked up. And up.

"Zoomer?" she asked uncertainly.

More like a truck horn than an inquisitive murmur, a chirrup sounded. Mira stared at the gigantic form, eight or nine feet high, and glowing like a nuclear plant. It was four-legged but not quite cat-shaped. "Zoomer? Is that you?"

A big purr from the bright shape literally knocked her off her feet and sent her sprawling. She was glowing, too, she noticed as she got back on her feet, her limbs and body suffused with a pearly, warm, golden light. Had she left her body behind in the lower plane, or was this how she really looked? How beautiful! "Luminous beings are we," Yoda had said in *The Empire Strikes Back.* Cool. Way cool.

As she became used to the shadowy nature of the scene around her, she saw the outline of hands beckoning eagerly to her. She started toward them. She wanted to see what was out there, over those ghostly hills.

A nudge from behind brought her to her senses. Mira had been warned to let the Summerland come to her. She must not pass beyond the circle of candles. They marked the protective barrier of the chalk circle. Not everything beyond the gate was benevolent. She grasped for Zoomer, who loomed over her, a comforting presence.

"Violet Schuman," she called. "I am here to see Violet Schuman, if she wishes contact. She knows me." Another thing the book had warned against was giving her name. It was just like identity theft in the real world: creatures in the underworld could have power over her if they came into possession of genuine facts about her. She wasn't about to let that happen. This place was wonderful, but too scary for her to want to be trapped there.

The air thickened as an indistinct figure swirled into being before her eyes.

"My darling," it said huskily.

"Oh, Aunty," Mira said, then paused. Violet had never been that short. This person came up to Mira's collarbone. It was a trick. "Where were you born?" she shouted at once.

"Er, Cleveland?" the figure said, wavering at the edges.

"You're an impostor. Begone!" Mira flashed a banishing gesture that would have made her dungeonmaster proud.

"Darn!" said the shade, and disappeared. Another form dropped down in front of Mira, but she didn't let the element of surprise throw her off.

"What's your middle name?" Mira demanded.

"Melody?"

"Wrong! Go away!"

They crowded in around her, cocooning her in brilliant light that overwhelmed and confused her. One after another, she rejected them, until she was facing only one form. It tilted its head to one side.

"Mira Penelope, you're amazing."

Mira didn't recognize the figure surrounded in blue-white glory, but it moved like Aunt Violet, and it certainly sounded like her. The face took on more detail, becoming similar to Mira's, but with more nose and less chin. Mira gazed, astonished.

"Aunty?"

The shade smiled. "In the . . . well, I guess it's not flesh. Mira, what are you doing here? Have you passed over, too?"

"No! I came . . . to find you."

"In heaven's name, why? Didn't you have enough of me in life?"

Mira wanted to laugh and cry at the same time. She hesitated, afraid to touch the luminous shape, but then couldn't restrain herself. She threw herself at it, hugging the surprisingly solid form to her. The cold flame didn't burn her. Far from it; it warmed her. Mira held Violet, squeezing her eyes

closed to keep tears from running down her cheeks. She felt
a tentative pat on the shoulder.

"Now, now, enough sentiment," Violet said, giving her a
little shake. The old lady seemed to be just as she was the
last time Mira had seen her, crotchety, brusque, formidable,
but whole and erect now, not racked with the shaking or the
weakness of atrophied muscles. "Now, how is my worthless
brother?"

They talked together for a while. Mira gave her updates
on everything that had happened in the last two years. She
was surprised that the people in the afterlife had no way of
knowing what was going on with the people they left behind. She didn't know how long they went on laughing and
sharing memories. The light never changed there, and she
never tired.

"But what I really need to know, Aunty, is the name of
the village that Great-great-grandfather Georgi came from,"
Mira said at last when they'd run out of relatives to abuse.
"I'm still trying to look up our family history, and the ge-
nealogists all said it would help if I knew that."

"Is that all, girl?" Violet asked, her shade brightening
with amusement. "Volberg was the place. I couldn't find a
trace of it on modern maps. Probably lost. Everyone there
died, or left, or it was renamed by the shifts in government.
You know the way things happen."

"Volberg," Mira said, committing it to memory. As she
did she sensed a withdrawal of energy around her. She'd ful-
filled her purpose for being here. She looked around. The
features of the ghostly landscape seemed farther away. She
wanted to pull it back to her.

Violet sensed it, too. "Go on back, girl. It's not your
time yet."

Mira hugged her. "I'm so sorry I wasn't there when . . ."

"When I passed? But it's all better now, do you see? I'm
well and happy. Tell them that."

"I will." Mira was comforted. "Do you like it here?"

"Of course!"

"Aren't you ever afraid?" Mira said, thinking of the aggressive shadows that had swooped over her.

"No, there's nothing here that can harm me. Ah, but *you,* we can't defend you if you're attacked. Only the living can save the living."

"I'll be all right as long as I'm in the circle," Mira said.

The old woman's face twitched in a smile. "You were always a smart girl. I've got to go now. So have you. It's time."

Mira's heart sank. "Don't go, Aunty Violet. Please."

The bright form receded from her. "Don't forget me."

"I won't! I never will."

The voice came from farther away now. "I'll remember you, too, Mira. You were always an interesting girl. Give them all my love. No," Violet stopped, finger in the air in an old, familiar gesture, "don't. They don't deserve it. You do." She smiled the conspiratorial grin that Mira remembered so well. Death hadn't changed her. She turned away. Mira just had to hug her one more time. She started after the fast-receding light. Her hands touched only air.

Bang! Her foot struck something solid. She saw the candle on the floor, which she had forgotten about, just as it went out. Mira stooped to pick it up. She must relight it immediately. Her hands fumbled for the electronic match, hidden somewhere beneath the gray mist.

But the enemy didn't hesitate to attack. Blackness took her like a shroud, surrounding her, paralyzing her, sucking life out of her. She scrambled toward the nearby gate, but it tripped her to the ground. With eyesight enhanced by contact from her familiar she saw features in the inky folds, grinning mouths, hollow, hungry eyes. It was an entity of many evil minds, and it wanted to devour her. The lips drew back, baring teeth filed to points. Mira fought, but she didn't know any defenses against otherworldly demons. She'd never counted on making a mistake like that!

Years of playing *D&D* didn't help. She had no magic missiles to throw. Instead, she summoned up the memory of her women's self-defense class—clawing, thrashing, and generally refusing to go quietly. Her feet flailed wildly, but failed to connect with a solid mass. Unfortunately, you couldn't kick a ghost in the balls. She started yelling for help, but there was no one to help. There wasn't another living being within earshot.

The blackness shoved at her, dragging her over the rough floor. A black hole opened up ahead of her, just like what happened to the bad guy in *Ghost*. She would be dragged down to the pit.

"Help!" she cried. "Lewis!" He wouldn't be home for a couple of hours. "God and goddess!" But the gods weren't listening. She glanced back at the bright shape watching her with its head tilted. "Zoomer! Do something!"

She felt a surge of power well up within her. Light burst from inside her, driving the darkness back. With the gift of her familiar, she was able to defend herself and ward off the demon's advance. The enemy recoiled slightly, but it wasn't enough. It thinned out, then surged forward again, surrounding her completely. "Help!"

The cat-giant jumped over the wall of blackness, in between her and the smothering enemy, pummeling, clawing, tearing rents in black shadow that bled brilliant white light. Mira pulled herself away on her elbows, crawled to her feet, yelling encouragement at Zoomer.

"That's it! Kick him! Tear him apart!" she yelled. The cat-shape fought fiercely, ceremonially burying the pieces of its vanquished foe in the carpet. Mira almost cried with relief. "Oh, Zoom, I'm proud of you," she said, reaching high up to scratch the huge head. Zoomer purred, vibrating the air.

But the nightmare monster had a big brother. It rose out of the ground, blotting out the translucent landscape, everything, a dozen, a hundred times larger than they, until the only light they could see came from a tiny point high, high above them. Zoomer took one look and jumped into Mira's arms, a giant in fear, yowling and trembling. She clutched him, not knowing what to do. They were out of options.

They were going to die. The walls began to close in, shutting off even that distant point.

But they had an unexpected ally, too. Mira heard a tremendous "boing!" Bounding in over the barrier of darkness, glowing like Liberace's piano, was an even bigger entity made of light. It kicked back the black walls, trounced the darkness, sucking it into its glowing form like a vacuum cleaner drinking a balloon. As soon as it was all gone, it bounded toward Zoomer and Mira. Mira recoiled, fearing it would start on them next, but it drove them toward the gate back to the real world. The gate whisked over them.

Suddenly, they found themselves on the other side looking back at the Summerland. They weren't glowing any longer. Mira looked around for their mysterious rescuer, but saw nothing. No time to waste. She did a banishing, blew out the candles, grabbed Zoomer and ran down the stairs.

"I wonder who that was that saved us," Mira asked Zoomer, after her first restorative sip of coffee. Not wanting to go back to the sanctum for her caftan, she sat wrapped in her pink terrycloth bathrobe. "I wanted to thank him. Her? It? There shouldn't have been anyone else in that circle."

Zoomer sat down and began to scratch furiously at his neck with a back claw.

"That flea's still there," Mira said, almost glad to have something mundane to concentrate on. That had been a harrowing experience. Wait until she told Loretta! She drew Zoomer on to her lap, went through his fur with her fingers. Even though they were out of the sanctum, it still felt as though the two of them were the only living creatures in the whole wide world, and here she was picking a flea out of her sole companion's fur. She located a hard, hyperactive, black speck and held it up.

"There!" she exclaimed triumphantly. Immediately, Zoomer turned around, swatted her hand, and bounded to the floor. The flea disappeared again, probably jumping right back into his fur. Why would Zoomer protest when she was freeing him from an irritation? Then Mira had a funny thought.

The chalk on the floor *would* have prevented anything else from coming into the circle with them. They *had* been the only living creatures in the whole wide world. She remembered Violet's words. Only the living can save the living. She glanced at Zoomer. His *flea?* The enormous being *had* defended them, as if it was dedicated to them, exactly like *her* familiar was supposed to do, but . . .

Nah.

On the other hand . . . why not?

"Zoom?" she asked tentatively, feeling stupid even to be asking the question, "was that your familiar? Did you do the calling ritual?" Then she stopped, feeling even more idiotic. "No, what am I saying? You're just a cat. I mean, you enhance *my* abilities, but . . . ?" She hesitated. Could her familiar have a familiar?

Zoomer struggled away, scratched again, looked up at her with the wise look he'd given her when he had first moved into her house, into her life. Mira stopped. He was capable of anything, with an old soul like that. She couldn't underestimate him. Look at how he'd appeared in the Summerland, larger and more powerful than she was. He was a magician in his own right. And the protective presence, so unexpected, shrinking out of sight just as they passed through the gate to safety. What else could it have been? The flea must be mightier still than either one of them. Mira giggled. It might even have its own familiar, a microbe or something. What could be next down the line? A supercharged molecule?

Why shouldn't she believe in a familiar's familiar? She'd just spent the last two hours talking to a ghost. What could be weirder than that? Zoomer looked at her with feline insouciance. But why?

"All right, I'll buy it," Mira said. She threw her hands in the air. "I give up. What do *you* need a flea familiar for?"

As if in answer, the cat elevated slowly in the air until he hovered at eye level. Mira stared, astounded. Then, with an expression she could only call a smirk, Zoomer rose to the cabinet above the refrigerator, hooked it open with one paw, and knocked down the can of Petreats.

FIRST FAMILIARS

by Laura Resnick

Laura Resnick, a *cum laude* graduate of George-
town University, won the 1993 John W. Campbell
Award for best new science fiction/fantasy
writer. Since then she has never looked back,
having written the bestselling novels *In Legend
Born* and *In Fire Forged*, with more on the way.
She has also written award-winning nonfiction,
an account of her journey across Africa, entitled
A Blonde in Africa. She has written several short
travel pieces, as well as numerous articles about
the publishing business. She also writes a
monthly opinion column for *Nink*, the newsletter
of Novelists, Inc. You can find her on the web at
www.sff.net./people/laresnick.

INTERDIMENSIONAL Progress Report

From: Socks the Cat
To: The Dark Powers
Re: First Family
Date: 1 February 1992

My Merciless Immortal Masters of Incorruptible Evil,
   I am pleased to report that the first phase of my mission
in this dimension is now successfully accomplished: elec-

tion won, inauguration completed, Clinton family installed in White House.

Bill seems grateful, but disinclined to give me the credit I deserve for his victory. I, however, am fully cognizant of the imponderable debt *I* owe to your benevolent patronage in entrusting such a monumental task to me. How the demons of the Fifth Circle of Hell laughed when I said that I was returning to this dimension, after nearly two hundred years of absence, to ensure that a saxophone-playing lawyer from Arkansas would become the next President of the United States!

I confess to you, my maleficent masters, that it wasn't easy. At times I was even slightly discouraged. (I still start spitting up hairballs if the name Gennefer Flowers is even *mentioned*.) The Clintons, though appealingly flawed from a demonic perspective, are not the most malleable people I've ever worked with. Ah, the world has changed so much in two centuries . . . Admittedly, for sheer stubborn will, the Clintons aren't the challenge that Napoleon was. Could any other mere mortal ever be as impetuous as he? (And I can never apologize enough to you, the rulers of every dimension worth inhabiting on a permanent basis, for the way that whole situation turned out in the end. I tried—kibbles-and-chow how I tried!—to meow some sense into the Corsican. However, nearly two hundred years in the Fifth Circle have assuredly taught me the price of failure, and you need have no fears about anything going wrong this time.)

As I was saying, the Clintons live in a "modern" culture which encourages free will and intellectual curiosity and which eschews what they refer to as "superstition." So a little provocative hissing and mewing rarely imparts enough influence in this strange new world, and I often have to work very hard to get the message across, the dark will imposed, and the job done. Hillary is frequently disinclined to follow my advice, and Bill is disinclined to cross Hillary if he can possibly avoid it. Chelsea is a sweet girl, but her influence on national policy and international relations is virtually nonexistent. This is a great disappointment, as she, of all the Clintons, is the fondest of me. In the short time I've been in the White House, I've also made a friend in Betty Currie— but she is surely destined to go unnoticed and unheard throughout Bill's glorious reign here.

Nonetheless, despite a certain ongoing difficulty with Hillary and Bill, I am already known as the First Pet and am regarded with great affection by the American people. It was, to borrow a phrase from the Clintons' acolytes, a public relations coup that I initially arranged to be "found" living as an orphan under the porch of tenderhearted Chelsea's piano teacher. This story, and the tale of how the Clintons soon thereafter adopted me in March of 1991 (if I may be excused for using the Christian calendar year under your exalted gazes), has been related in the media many times since then. Whatever else people say about the Clintons (and they say plenty), can anyone completely mistrust people who adopted a stray cat?

I once again humbly thank your boundless generosity in making me feline when you bestowed corporeal form upon me so many aeons ago. Your wisdom is exceeded only by your generosity to your devoted minions, which in turn is exceeded only by the purity of your evil intent.

I only regret that your infinite omnipotence didn't extend to keeping the Clintons from having me neutered. Being a familiar just isn't the same as it used to be, and I can't say that I'm fond of the twentieth century so far. I personally suspect the neutering was an act of malice on Bill's part to retaliate for my failure to keep his philandering concealed from the public. However, since he was also keeping it concealed from Hillary, Chelsea, and me, I had no way of knowing until . . . well, until *everyone* knew. I've tried to explain this to him, since I must be included in his confidence to be an effective familiar, but he doesn't seem to understand. He always just says something like, "Chelsea, your cat's crying."

However, these little setbacks are not uncommon when

dealing with humans, and everything is currently going according to your unthinkably brilliant plan.

> With worshipful respect,
> Socks the Cat

Interdimensional Memo
   From: Socks the Cat
   To: The Spawn of Hell
   Re: Urgent Problem
   Date: June 1, 1992

My Revered Siblings in Mayhem,
   Mice have been discovered at the White House. I am evidently expected to hunt and consume them. Can this possibly be correct? The Dark Powers suggested you might be able to accurately interpret the situation and offer advice.
   Please respond at your earliest convenience.

> Feeling Queasy,
> Socks

Interdimensional Bulletin
   From: Socks the Cat
   To: All Feline-Corporeal Residents of the Dominions of
      Evil, Including Subdimensions and Psychic Extensions
   Re: Hunting Rodents
   Date: June 5, 1992

BEFORE CONSUMING RODENTS IN THE MORTAL DIMENSION, INITIATE PRELIMINARY INVESTIGATION TO ENSURE *THEY* HAVE NOT CONSUMED POISON FIRST. BE ADVISED THAT THE SPAWN OF HELL, IF CONSULTED, WILL DELIBERATELY NEGLECT TO WARN YOU ABOUT THIS POSSIBILITY. IT'S THEIR LITTLE WAY OF HAVING FUN.

> HAIL TO ALL,
> SOCKS

Interdimensional Expense Report
   From: Socks the Cat
   To: The IRS Headquarters—Inferno South
   Re: Your Obvious Mistake
   Date: April 15, 1993

May It Please The Vindictive Scourges of the Universe;
   I hereby file an expense report which demonstrates that, due to my continuing service here at the White House, I am now owed a refund from you, the Eternal Thieves Of The Wage Earner's Very Blood.

EXPENSES FOR FELINE DEMONIC FAMILIAR
I.D. NO. 007-X, ALIAS "SOCKS"

Item: Bribes to make Bill's conquests go away
   $189,453,453,742,865,634,368,000,000,000,000,000.73
Item: Mortal cat to eat mice
   $7
Item: Interdimensional communications expenses
   $342,654,348,086,521,076.00
Item: Book—*Life After Castration: Emotional Healing For Neutered Cats*
   $17, with discount

If you consult your malevolent codes on the legitimate allowances due a full-time familiar, you will recognize that your recent assertion that I owe you additional blood sacrifices is totally erroneous. Moreover, your threat to send me back to the Fifth Circle for my failure to file a tax return while I was *there* for 180 years is so depraved that even the Dark Powers are impressed.

                              With exalted loathing,
                              Socks the Cat

Interdimensional Progress Report
   From: Socks the Cat
   To: The Dark Powers
   Re: Your Recent Missive
   Date: November 10, 1996

My Villainous Immortal Masters of Unimaginable Cruelty,
   Yes, it's true, I have been unable to make Whitewater, Paula Jones, and other distracting embarrassments disappear from Bill's horizon, but I humbly believe that you underestimate the strength, severity, and determination of these threats to Bill's sovereignty when you criticize me for not having already eliminated them.
   Moreover, I am pleased to report that Bill has just won a second term in office under the confusing and barbaric system known as "free elections" here. I am therefore as perplexed as I am devastated by your expressed disappointment in the job I am doing here.

                              Your servant of limitless devotion,
                              Socks

Interdimensional Memo
   From: Socks the Cat
   To: The Dark Powers
   Re: Please Reconsider
   Date: December 2, 1996

Dear Lords of All That Is Treacherous and Malevolent,
   I am mortified to have fallen so far in your esteem that you deem it necessary to assign another familiar to the Clintons, and I meekly beg you to reconsider. I am fully confident that, with the elections behind us, Bill's second term as President of the United States will prove to be an era of unparalled triumph for us, and I am so dedicated to exalting his status in your honor that I have been working my paws to the bone night and day all year—well, except for when they keep me tethered to a leash on the White House lawn.

                              Begging for your favor,
                              Socks

Interdimensional Coded Message
TOP SECRET—FOR YOUR EYES ONLY
    From: Socks the Cat
    To: Richard Nixon's Immortal Spirit
    Re: Watch Your Back, Kid!
    Date: December 3, 1996

    A dog? You're sure about this? A DOG?
    How is that possible?
    You must be mistaken.
    Where did you get this intel?
    No, no, never mind. I know you can't tell me that.
    I can't believe it! It can't be possible! Even the malevolent lords of the universe wouldn't stoop to such fathomless depths of infinite cruelty. A *dog?*
    No. Surely not . . .

The First Pet,
Socks

    P.S. Destroy this message as soon as you've read it. There are minions everywhere.

Interdimensional Progress Report
    From: Buddy the Dog
    To: The Dark Powers
    Re: I'm h-e-e-e-r-e!
    Date: January 1, 1997

Dear Dark Powers,
    Golly, I'm, like, really really sorry that all that drool made it impossible for you to interpret my first progress report. Gee whiz, it's hard to control this saliva function!
    I'm just as happy as any mortal creature could possibly be! I love it here! Everyone here loves me! They feed me things and throw things for me to chase! Bill wanted me to sleep on a bed he'd gotten for me, but I cried, and so now I get to sleep in the president's bed.
    Was there anything else you wanted to know?

Yours,
Buddy

Interdimensional Memo
   From: Socks the Cat
   To: The Dark Powers
   Re: WHAT???
   Date: January 2, 1997

My Maniacal Masters, etc.,

How could you have done this to me? What have I ever done to deserve this?

Sending a canine was bad enough! An unthinkable and unwarranted act of cruelty! But sending a *Labrador?* Do you have any *idea* how long it takes me just to clean off the drool after that sloshing, slobbering, slovenly minion of hell greets me?

No failure of mine to promote Bill to his full demonic potential can possibly have merited such despicable treatment. And now, to read your demands that I *cooperate* with this four-legged brown broccoli! That I teach him how to inspire humanity's inherent evil, incite acts of wickedness, and initiate dark deeds . . . No, it's going to far to ask me to do that!

I entreat you, I implore you, I beg you . . . please, remove this shedding, whining, unhousebroken offense from my presence and allow me to get on with my work here.

                    Your humble supplicant,
                    Socks the Cat

Interdimensional Complaint—Addendum
   To: Union Leader, Feline-Corporeals Local #718
   From: Socks the Cat
   Re: The Canine
   Date: June 6, 1997

Further to my complaint about The Canine, a.k.a. Buddy the Dog, whom the Dark Powers have imposed on my assignment here, Bill is already favoring him over me. Takes him everywhere, lets him sleep in his bed, introduces him to foreign dignitaries.

And what do *I* get when Chelsea's not around? *I* get tethered to a leash on the White House lawn.

The media minions no longer call me The First Pet. Now I'm merely The First Cat!

I demand my rights! I demand that The Canine be consigned to the Fifth Circle—or at least removed from the White House.

Respectfully,
Socks the Cat

P.S. Has there been any word about my tax refund?

Interdimensional Progress Report
   From: Socks the Cat
   To: The Dark Powers
   Re: Ruling the Mortal World
   Date: November 3, 1997

My Dark Masters, etc.,
I can well understand your disappointment regarding the Middle East peace process. I suggest you speak to Buddy about it. He is far more in Bill's confidence than I am these days.

Yours, etc.,
Socks

Interdimensional Progress Report
   From: Buddy the Dog
   To: The Dark Powers
   Re: Middle East Peace Process
   Date: January 8, 1998

Dear Dark Powers,
The Middle East peace process? Ohhhhh, that explains it! I thought it was the Midwest Peace process that I was supposed to disrupt; but despite my best efforts, Illinois and Indiana just don't seem to be going to war with each other. *Now* I get it!

So . . . Middle East? Would that be the reception where

they served lamb? Or was it the meeting where I ate a plant? Who's the tall, skinny foreign dignitary with the fancy accent and the nasal voice? He throws things for me. I like him. Do I have to make him go to war with anybody? I hope not, because then he might not have time to come here and play fetch again.

I have to go now. I mean *go,* and *right* now, and Hillary gets mad when I do that in the house. So must sign off.

> Love and slurpy kisses and
> hugs!
> Buddy

Interdimensional Coded Message
>   From: Socks the Cat
>   To: Richard Nixon's Immortal Spirit
>   Date: January 9, 1998

Dear Dick,
Many thanks for your continuing support. I don't mean to question your immortal wisdom, let alone your understanding of modern American politics, but are you sure that this will work? I mean . . . a mere cover-up? And of such a venial matter—Bill and some intern playing footsy.

However, I will, as you urge, trust you and proceed with our plan. I've ensured that Buddy believes that Bill must conceal evidence, tell lies, and evade truthful testimony. Perhaps once we're past all this nonsense and I'm rid of Buddy, I can finally realize the great plans for True Evil which the Dark Powers had in mind for Bill, and then I will achieve the status which I deserve in their terrible eyes.

> Your loyal feline friend,
> Socks

Sympathy Card
    From: Socks the Cat
    To: Buddy the Dog
    Date: April 24, 1998

Sorry it took me so long to get around to saying how sorry I am the Clintons had you neutered.

Socks

Card Accompanying Floral Bouquet
    To: Doris Day, president of the Doris Day Animal League

Dear Ms. Day,
This humble bouquet of thirty-six white roses is merely my way of expressing my appreciation to you for urging President Clinton to have his dog neutered.

With devotion,
An Anonymous Feline Friend

Interdimensional Memo
    From: Socks the Cat
    To: The Dark Powers
    Re: Your Urgent Missive
    Date: January 2, 1999

My Dark Etc.,
Impeachment?
Yes, I believe I heard something of this nature.
However, you'll really need to consult Buddy, who's Bill's favorite now and much closer to the source than I am these days.

Yours, Etc.,
Socks

Interdimensional Progress Report
    From: Buddy the Dog
    To: The Dark Powers
    Re: Impeachment
    Date: Um . . .

Dear Dark Powers,

Impeachment?

Is that like an impairment? Or spearmint? I like mint! And is impairment like a pear, only different?

The inside scoop here is that some people are being mean to Bill and it makes him sad. But then we play, and he feels better.

Is there anything else I can do?

Ooops! Sorry about the drool. Still working on that.

Lick, lick, lick,

Buddy

Interdimensional Coded Message

From: Socks the Cat

To: Richard Nixon's Immortal Spirit

Re: My Nerves

Date: December 31, 1999

I can't take it anymore, Dick! I'm going insane! Not even the prospect of the predicted world crisis tonight at midnight can cheer me up.

You were right about the cover-up, of course. I'm embarrassed that I ever doubted your experience in these matters. It nearly destroyed Bill, exactly as you predicted. But who could have foreseen that the Dark Powers would suspect a Divine plot interfering with our plans for Bill, or that they'd fail to realize that Buddy is completely incapable of being an effective demonic familiar to a ruthless world conqueror? I had a brief moment of hope when we bombed Sudan without provocation, but—can you believe this?—the offense is evidently going to be settled in international court. What is the world coming to?

Meanwhile, have I mentioned how much *drool* that dog produces? And the shedding! You can't imagine it. Plus, the White House is always full of that distinctive Labrador *odor* now. It's unbearable. I'm an emotional wreck. And my career is as good as over. I really can't face another century or two in the Fifth Circle. It's so crowded there . . . well, I don't need to tell *you*.

I spend more and more time with Betty Currie now that Chelsea's gone away to college. I've had a few thoughts about quitting the Clintons and starting over somewhere else when Bill's second term is done. I think Betty would take me in for a while.

Yes, yes, I know, Hillary is very promising material, and her Senate run opens up some interesting opportunities for me, but . . . I just don't *like* American politics, if you'll forgive me for saying so, Dick. No one's good, no one's evil; everyone's just venial. It's so . . . demeaning. I'm going to apply to the Dark Powers for a leave of absence and consider going into a more dignified line of familiar work. Organized crime, insider trading, Hollywood . . . the world is full of promise! I need to get away from Buddy and the Clintons, refresh my demonic spirit, and start anew somewhere else.

> Your devoted feline friend,
> Socks

Interdimensional Memo
  From: Socks the Cat
  To: The Dark Powers
  Re: End of An Era
  Date: December 1, 2000

My Dark Masters of Magnificent Malevolence,

I humbly thank you for your unprecedented words of apology about forcing a canine familiar on me. If it's true that we all learn from our mistakes, then you, who are superior to all beings, will certainly learn a great deal from this one, which was superior to most mistakes. So to speak.

Although I have never grown fond of Buddy, I am pleased to report to you that he's looking forward to moving to New York City, where he hears there are many fire hydrants.

Meanwhile, I'm so pleased you're enjoying the ongoing chaos of the vote-count in Florida. Given your supreme indifference to the outcome of this year's election, I felt this little prank was the least I could do to show my appreciation for your benevolence in releasing me from my servitude to the Clintons and granting me an opportunity to start over after a brief respite in the Virginia countryside this coming year. Having nine immortal lives, I am, of course, a patient creature, and can bide my time as I look for another opportunity as promising as the Clintons once were.

Your devoted minion of hell,
Socks the Cat

DOG SPELLED BACKWARD

by P.N. Elrod

P. N. "Pat" Elrod is best known for the *Vampire Files* featuring undead detective Jack Fleming and cowriting the Richard Dun vampire series with Nigel Bennett. Their latest release is *His Father's Son*. She's written in and coedited several anthologies and when not writing, scarfing chocolate, or loving up on her dogs, is eager to talk about writing. She is currently at work on more toothy titles.

ONE summer morning, Mighty Mite, a 112-year-old Pomeranian muttered loud enough for me to hear: "I'm tired of this. I'm going home."

I knew from the first time we met—back when I was a soft-eared pup—that I would eventually have to take over her responsibilities in the household. She'd towered over me then, all six pounds, eight inches of her, and laid down the law while I'd rolled on my back and squirted a few drops in homage.

Sasha, I'm in charge here until it's your turn, she grumped.

I don't have a problem with that, I whined, politely tucking my tail up over my belly.

What about your sister?

Megan hadn't cooperated during the dominance ritual,

being busy with chewing on a shoe. *She wont' have a problem with that either,* I assured.

Good, said the Mite, then walked stiffly away. I later learned her arthritis was very bad, along with some other health problems, but her human mom, my and Megan's mom now, took very good care of her.

That talk had taken place some time ago. Megan and I had grown to twenty and twenty-five pounds respectively, much bigger than Mighty Mite, but we never dreamed of using our size against her. That would have been horribly bad mannered. After Mom, the Mite was pack leader for the house. We were not allowed to eat her special food, but if she wanted some out of our bowls, she could take a sample whenever she liked. Usually it was too hard for her teeth, but once in a while she enjoyed having a change. This upset Megan, but she behaved herself, knowing the Mite could never eat enough to leave us without. Besides, Mom always kept the bowls brimming.

Megan and I were a mix, being half miniature Doberman, and half terrier, making us, according to Mom, both tough and adorable. We had night-black fur, floppy ears, and thickly muscled tails, and could run faster than the wind in our chasing games.

Our puppyhood was a good life, with all the food we needed, fresh water, a big yard to defend from birds and squirrels, and a human mom who obviously doted on us. I'd sometimes get jealous when she lavished more attention on Mighty Mite, but that was the Mite's due, after all, so I'd patiently wait with Megan until it was our turn to be loved on and to play.

I saw Mighty Mite pass over, her glowing spirit leaving her small, crippled body to float around free and happy on the Otherside. Megan and I watched her a while, then went on with our usual business until we heard the awful shrieking when Mom realized what had happened. We ran to be with her, but she pushed us away, crying pitifully. One of her human friends was with Mom, which was fortunate, because though I loved her more than life, the emotional wash of her grief was too much for me, too confusing. There was suddenly a terrible hole in Mom's soul, and it bled steadily.

Why was she so sad? Couldn't she *see* the Mite? Her bright spirit was flying around the room like one of the birds from outside, only faster and more agile. It zoomed through the walls and furniture, then came back to hover near the floor where Mom was crying over the body that had once held it. The Mite had expected sorrow, but not this heavy sense that her passing was Mom's fault. The self-blame clung to her like mud, and it was wrong.

The next few days were bad for Mom. She fell asleep crying and woke up crying, all for the Mite. The bleeding out from the hole in her soul soon made her body sick, and she moved about the house on uncertain legs, her voice weak and cheerless. Her kindness and love for us never wavered, but she still hurt.

It frightened me, but I ignored my fear, slipping quietly into my new position of responsibility. Megan said she would always help out when I needed her. I was glad of that. Trying to get Mom out of her tail-chasing circle of self-blame proved to be very tiring, even more than running after toys. It helped me to lie curled up next to my sister and just *rest.*

Mighty Mite thought she was making Mom more sad and held her distance at times, afraid of adding to that black, muddy coating. I'd try to tell them both to let it go, but Mom, of course, couldn't hear me. Sometimes she was perceptive of my messages, but her grief got in the way. Mom was only slightly aware of Otherside things, just enough to sometimes be vaguely afraid of them. I had to think of *some* way to help her. A couple of days after the Mite passed, Mom lay on the couch for a nap, and I took it as an opportunity to do my job, leaping up on top of her.

I'm almost too big to be a lapdog, but after Mom's initial annoyed yelp of surprise, she relaxed and let me use her stomach for a mattress for the next couple of hours. She held me close, and I stayed right there, even when she shook and shuddered from her latest bout of crying. After a while she fell asleep holding me, and I spent the whole time sending warm love into her troubled dreams. She felt better when she woke up and gave me some extra hugs and even thanked me. She might as well have thanked me for breathing. I was glad to be there for her.

Things eased, but only a little. I still had a lot of work ahead and did not know what to do to help. The Mite always had a special kind of magic to help Mom that had been hers alone. I had to find out what mine was and how to best use it.

That night Mom settled down to go to sleep as usual with me and Megan butted close against her on top of the covers. To give her comfort, we'd begun sleeping on the bed with her since the Mite had passed. We sure liked it. Mom soon turned out the lights and drifted off, but I sensed her dreams were not restful. She moaned and struggled against something within. I stayed tight against her. When she finally thrashed awake, screaming, her hand came down on me. I sent her as much warm reassurance as I could muster, licking her gently to let her know everything was all right.

"Sasha? Oh, good girl. Good, good girl."

She petted me thoroughly and told me her nightmare. I didn't understand all of it, only that it had to do with her grief, which was as strong as ever. She still bled.

You're doing fine, Sasha, said the Mite. She was just off the corner of the bed, her glow lighting up the room. Next to me, Megan raised her head for a look, then drooped back down again to doze.

She's still hurting. Why can't she see you? She knows better than to be like this all the time.

Her head knows, but her heart hasn't accepted things yet; her grief blinds her to me.

Humans could be like that. Until the heart realizes its own truth about how normal life and death are, the rest of soul can suffer for years. *I wish she could see things the way we do.*

So do I, but they're stuck with what little they have. It's up to us to help them along. It's very silly of them, but there you are.

I *humphed,* then settled in for a nap, but the Mite wasn't done with me yet.

There's something outside, Sasha, she told me. *It's trying to get in. That's why Mom's having bad dreams.*

What is it? I asked, my eyes nearly shut. Dogs can talk just fine to each other, awake or asleep.

A big black thing. I don't like it. Jake is keeping watch, but you'll have to guard against it.

Mom had had a retired racing greyhound named Jake who'd passed over about three weeks before Megan and I came to live with her. She had also grieved hard for him, but he'd let her know through the Mite that he was still around. The day after he'd passed, the Mite, nearly blind and very deaf, scampered through the house on her stiff legs, tail wagging, ears perked forward, and her cloudy eyes on something Mom could not see. After a few perplexed moments Mom seemed to realize what was going on.

"Mite? Are you seeing Jake? Is that it, sweets? Did Jake come home?"

The Mite barked, then stumped off to her bed, satisfied, her job done.

Mom sat down on the couch, her hands out. "Jake? Is that you?"

Jake's Otherside form poked his nose right in her face. *She couldn't see me, but her soul felt me,* he'd said. *She told me she loved me and that I could stay with her as long as I liked, this would always be my home.*

So Jake had stayed on, a quiet guardian spirit among the many others surrounding our house. He was very wise, and I liked to talk to him, learning about all kinds of stuff. He had a favorite spot by a tree in the yard that Megan and I would try to avoid during our chasing games. He didn't really mind when we ran through him, but it was more polite to let him have his chosen space in peace.

After Mom fell asleep, I crept off the bed and went through the dog door in the kitchen to have a look outside. Megan soon followed, sniffing and pelting off to run the perimeter of the fence. Jake was in his usual spot, his energy glow placid and graceful, welcoming.

You see it? he asked.

I saw it all right: a big, black *thing* hovering outside one of the windows as though trying to push its way in. My hackles went up. It was an Otherside creature, the kind that feeds on dark feelings. They're worse than ticks because they attach themselves to the person having those feelings and stay as long as there's food. When they get strong enough, they can manipulate certain feelings in their prey's heart. Bad feelings, of course, meant to keep the food supply constant. The more they took in, the stronger they got until their prey was completely under their control.

I've seen one like this before, said Jake. *It was on a man. It changed him, twisted his spirit so much that none of his friends knew him anymore.*

What happened to him?

He got lost to himself. Nothing was left but the Shadow-creature. It used him to feed off others. A man's form, the creature's hunger.

Mom was all too open to bad feelings. She'd try to fight them, but some days were worse than others, and her moods had been very sad lately. If this creature attached itself to her, she might not shake free of its influence.

Then Jake sent me an image of a maybe-future: Mom mired in misery so deep she couldn't escape. Mom hurting herself. Mom dying.

The creature would like that.

I called to Mighty Mite, but she remained in the house next to Mom. It was up to me to chase away the enemy. Megan came over just then, ears perked, tail high, hackles raised.

Shall we get it? she asked, always ready for a good chase.

Yeah! Barking like mad, we charged the thing. It was startled enough to shoot away out of the yard, leaving behind only a putrid Otherside scent. Megan and I took turns wetting that spot down to blot it out, then we hunted for the creature. It had soared up onto a tree branch, taking the shape of a possum. It walked back and forth, taunting us while we barked below, enraged. Since it could not feed on dog feelings, it eventually got bored and vanished. Megan and I celebrated, racing the whole of the yard, joyful that it was clean now, but Jake remained uneasy.

Those things are hard to scare away, especially when they're hungry, he said. *That one looked hungry. And mean.*

Let me know if it comes back.

Of course.

Megan and I went inside to see if Mom was all right. She was sound asleep. Our barking hadn't disturbed her. We hopped up and settled in for a well-earned rest.

Mighty Mite's glow flared. *You did good, Sasha.*

True, the thing was gone. For this night.

Megan and I made frequent patrols outside, day and night, but we could only keep watch on the backyard. Jake helped by moving to the front yard and always let us know what was going on there. I was still troubled, though. If the Shadow-creature really wanted to get inside to Mom, there wasn't much we could do to stop it. She wasn't helping herself by being sad all the time. I thought she was very silly for hanging on to her grief for so long, not only for the Mite, but for many other things in her life. I didn't understand them or why she was so gloomy; she had a home and food and us to love her. It was more than enough for me and Megan, after all, but the Mite's passing seemed to break her down, pushing her into a pit of her own making. If she didn't lift herself clear of it soon, she might never escape.

We'd try to cheer Mom by coaxing her into the backyard. Getting her to throw our toys so we could race around and play tug with them made her laugh. Then she'd join us in tug and laugh and love up on us using her happy voice. Though unaware of it, *that* was her best protection against the hunger of the creature.

But despite our games, the creature, or one just like it, appeared again a few days later, this time in the form of a squirrel. I knew it wasn't a normal squirrel the instant I caught its scent drifting down from one of the trees. The ones Megan and I chase are alive with a hundred different interesting smells that varied from one to the other. I could tell the mother squirrel from its young and the young from each other. The Shadow-creature had only one kind of smell, that of hopeless rot heaped high with dust. The only thing it could grow was despair.

Whenever *that* squirrel showed itself, Megan and I would go into a frenzy of chasing and barking, straining to jump high when it crawled along the tree branches from one side of the yard to another. Mom sometimes came out to yell at us to be quiet, but this was too important for us to obey her. She usually laughed at our efforts, which was good.

"Sasha, you're never gonna catch that squirrel," she'd say. "He's too fast for you."

We'll see about that, I'd say back to her, my ears up, tongue lolling, and tail thumping away so hard and fast as to make my whole body wriggle. Megan would come in and do the same, and we'd dance around each other.

"Oh, look at my grinny-girls! Well, if you can't have a squirrel, then how about another kind of treat?"

Of course we'd *never* say no to *that*. Besides, our eagerness for it would make Mom laugh more, which was what she most needed. Her joy didn't last much longer than the time it took for us to gobble the treat, but every little moment was a victory.

But one day, when Mom sat in the backyard watching me and Megan roll in the lush grass, her gaze drifted to the spot where the Mighty Mite had stretched out for the last time. Mom once more saw only the small dead body that had held her little friend. The picture was so clear and brutal it jumped into my own mind in an instant. Seeing the dark change coming over her spirit, I sat up quick and hurried to lie down next to her, but it was too late. Mom started crying uncontrollably again and telling the Mite how sorry she was. The guilt came over her in a thick muddy rush. All the progress we'd made seemed wiped away in an instant.

Jake floated in from the front yard and hovered close, but Mom didn't see him. She didn't even see me on this side of things when I butted next to her and tried to lick her hands to give her comfort. She sat there all miserable, and I lay hard beside her, wishing I could help.

That was when the Otherside creature swooped in.

Mom felt its initial rush as a sudden blinding headache. I whimpered, feeling it through her. Megan whined and came over, too. All of us gathered close, except for the Mite. She came growling and snapping out of nowhere, rushing the thing.

It pretty much ignored her, being busy with feeding, but she wouldn't let it alone. She darted in, and wherever her tiny glow touched, its blackness would twitch away.

Come on! she urged me.

And then it finally happened. I found my magic.

My body leaned quietly against Mom, but my spirit leaped free, snarling. I felt huge, much larger than even Jake. The three of us whirled about the creature, attacking it like the protective pack we were, all instinct and fierce fight. Big as it was, strong as it was getting from feeding, it was no match for all of us. It made a few swats at us, but suddenly retreated. We chased it from our yard far away into the next and beyond, before circling to return in triumph.

I zoomed straight back into my body. Megan told me that the only sign that I'd been gone had been some twitching of my paws and some small growls. Other than that, I'd looked asleep. It had only been for a few seconds, too. Good.

Mom's headache was gone, but she was in sad shape, blowing her nose as though she was sick from a cold. She gave me a weak, halfhearted petting, then slowly shuffled into the house, unaware of what had happened. Her bout of crying hadn't been the healing kind at all.

It's still out there, said the Mite. *It's had a taste and wants more.*

Jake muttered agreement.

I'll be ready, I promised. I'd stay up all night on guard if need be. I would *not* let that thing get near Mom ever again.

It returned the next morning, and seemed bigger than before, even when it took squirrel-form. I was dozing on the bed and heard it scrabbling around on the roof. Raising my head, ears up, I stared at Megan to let her know it was time, but we had to be very careful. She blinked at me, then we both quietly jumped down and slipped outside while Mom slept on.

Mom was good about not mowing the grass too often. I like it long. Megan slunk off to one of the high-grown patches and lay down flat with her black head barely visible above it. When she held very still, she was nearly invisible.

I silently called to Jake and the Mite for help. I heard no reply, but there was a terrific commotion on the roof, a chittering and scrabbling sound. Diving into the deep shade of some bushes I waited, my heart beating very hard and fast.

The creature, still in squirrel-form, was on the run. The bright lights that were Jake and the Mite were in hot pursuit. They chased it all over the roof, then drove it onto a tree branch, and then down to the ground. Megan leaped up and continued the chase, causing the thing to circle wide. She herded it right toward me, and I was ready.

I launched out to meet it, running faster than ever before. I feared it would shift to its normal form, but the chasing must have panicked it. The thing remained solid like a squirrel and squealed in fear and anger when my jaws snapped down tight around its middle. It was almost too big for me. Instinct said not to let it go, though. I kept a hard grip while it squeaked and clawed at my face. I shook it and shook it and shook it and *shook* it—just like one of my old sock toys.

Then it was all over. The creature was dead. So was the squirrel body it had used. It was already starting to smell of rot. Jake and the Mite hovered close, burning bright even in the daylight.

You did it! said the Mite.

Megan trotted over, tail wagging. She sniffed it a lot to assure herself that the threat was gone, then it was time to celebrate. She and I had played tug before, but never with the body of a dead Otherside creature. It's much more fun than with a sock. We played and played, ripping it in half, exulting in our victory.

It lasted until Mom came out, saw what we were doing, and screamed.

"Oh, no! Bad puppies! Bad dogs! Get away from that! Oh, my God, that poor little squirrel!!"

I found her reaction to be *very* confusing. We'd *saved* her, and she acted like it was the worst thing in the world.

The Mite told me to not worry about it. *Most humans have no idea what we do to keep them safe. Just let her yell it out and pretend you don't understand.*

Well, I *didn't* understand. I was vaguely hurt, too, but couldn't hold that against Mom. She was safe now, and that's all that really mattered to me. She cleaned up the remains, all the while making *ewwing* noises, then spent a lot of time talking into a noisy annoyance she called a phone. She seemed to be telling a lot of people what Megan and I had just done, only there were no people in the room for her to talk to; it was very silly of her, but calmed her down. I tried to take a nap, being all tired out from the worry and the chase, but Mom wouldn't let me. Instead of praise, she gave me a bath, swabbing at the stinging digs on my face where the creature had scratched me.

"You're lucky, Sasha-girl," she told me as I stood all miserable in the tub. "The vet said your shots were up to date, so you won't need any boosters. You got off easy today, but please don't do that again. It's just too gross."

Don't do *what* again? Kill Otherside creatures? She couldn't be serious.

She talked to me a lot more, mostly affectionate nonsense as she dabbed some really bad-tasting ointment on my hurts, then scolded me for trying to lick the stuff away. Some days you can't win. Megan thought it was very funny. The Mite floated off to play in the air, and Jake returned to his usual spot in the backyard. All was back to normal, except for one last problem.

Mom's still hurting, I told the Mite at bedtime. Mom had just shut off the lights. She wasn't happy; I could feel her sad thoughts clouding the room, just the kind to attract another of those things into our territory.

The Mite snorted. *I know. She needs help. I'll do what I can from this side.*

As she began to drift off to sleep, I sensed pictures of the Mite coming into Mom's mind. This was the first time her feelings were clean of that blame-mud. They were happy. Through her, I clearly saw the Mite running and playing, ears perked, squirming on her back for a tummy-rub, the Mite trying to dig a nest-hole in the rug. The images were quick but intense, all of them wrapped in the sweet, warm glow of Mighty Mite's love, a memory of her in her prime while on this Side, and it made her glow very bright.

And she got strong, too. I was comfortably jammed under Mom's arm when the Mite came over on the bed and settled into me. I don't mind sharing, but not that closely. I jumped down with a disgusted grunt.

"Sasha? Don't you want to sleep up here?" Mom was drowsily puzzled.

Not with the Mite bumping around in my spot I don't. If only humans could see as well as we do, they'd be a lot less confused about our behavior. I looked at her mournfully.

"Oh, my God," said Mom. "Did the Mite come in and make you move? Is that it?" Mom began to laugh, then she cried a little, but kept laughing. It was a strange sound, but

I noticed that hole in her spirit wasn't bleeding so much. The more she laughed the smaller it got.

After a few minutes nestled under Mom's chin, soaking in that love, Mite moved off toward the end of the bed, allowing me to return to my spot. I jumped back into place, snugged in firmly with Mom's arm around me.

She still had healing to do. I asked the Mite if she had any ideas.

She's better than before, but not completely free yet, I said.

I think I can come up with something. We just have to really get her attention. Be patient.

Easy for her to be patient. Time was different on her Side of things.

But the Mite did come through.

The next morning, when Mom was staring at the noisy box she called the TV, I spotted the Mite drifting in through the back door. She'd been off enjoying her new lightness on that Side and was in a happier mood than usual, glowing like one of the house lamps. I jumped off the couch and went over to say hello.

Come on, Sasha, she said. She sounded younger and stronger than I'd ever known her, but still retained her dominant dignity. *Follow me around—if you can!*

I love games, so I lowered my head to keep her well in sight and followed as she slowly led me all through the house. She went everywhere, even across the slick floor of the kitchen, which she used to avoid when she was on this Side of things. I kept trying to sniff her, but there really wasn't a lot of scent to pick up. This was meant to be a sight-only game, like charging squirrels who were upwind of my nose.

You have to learn every inch of the house and yard, she said. *Look into every nook, remember every smell. That way, if anything is different in a wrong sort of way, you will know.*

I understood her game was not entirely a game, and paid close attention, so I would be just as good as she had been.

It was still fun; I couldn't help but wag my tail the whole time.

The Mite wandered into the front room again and floated up on the couch; I stayed on the floor, tracking her. After greeting Mom, who was unaware of her presence, the Mite came down again and threaded through some chair and table legs with me right at her heels. I'd never played like this before, not indoors anyway, or this slow. Megan and I would chase each other at top speed around the trees and bushes of the yard; there really wasn't room for that inside. This gentler version was fine with me, though.

Mom finally noticed.

"Sasha? What the hell are you doing?" she asked, perplexed.

I paid her no mind, following the Mite, who glowed a little brighter with satisfaction. *It's about time,* she told me.

"Sasha, do you see something?" Mom used her happy/play voice. I liked that one; it meant she was in a good mood. There was lots of puzzlement in her scent, though. Was she getting the Mite's message? "What do you see? Can you tell me that, Sasha-girl? What do you see down there?"

The Mighty Mite made another circle of the front room, finally stopping at Mom's feet. I stopped as well and sat and looked at the Mite and then up at Mom for a long time, hoping she would figure it out.

I felt her burst of understanding like a breath of summer sky-wind.

"Are you there, Mite? Is that you, sweets?" Her voice was cracking with pain and hope.

The Mite just stayed in place, looking smug. Mom burst into tears again, but this time the grief was clean of the guilt. At last.

"This is your home, baby," she said, rubbing at her eyes. "You stay as long as you want. I love you, sweets. I'll always love you."

Things were *lots* better after that. The Mite spent a lot of time exploring the Otherside, but returned in an instant any time Mom called out to her. Maybe most humans can't see us once we're on that Side, but we know when they think of us, especially when there are strong feelings involved. Mom's were *very* strong for the Mite. Apparently they'd been through some rough times together. The Mite's magic always kept Mom balanced, no matter how bad things got. It was wonderful stuff. I wasn't sure I'd ever be that good, but I would *always* at least be there for her, forever and ever whether she saw me or not.

THIS DOG WATCHED

by Von Jocks

Von Jocks believes in the magic of stories. She has written since she was five, publishing her first short story at the age of twelve in a local paper. Under the name Evelyn Vaughn she sold her first romantic suspense novel, *Waiting For the Wolf Moon*, in 1992. Three more books completed her *Circle* series. Her short fiction most recently appeared in *Dangerous Magic*, from DAW Books. The book was selected as one of the top one hundred of the year by the New York City Public Library, and her story was nominated for a Sapphire Award.

Von received her Master's Degree at the University of Texas in Arlington, writing her thesis on the history of the romance novel. An unapologetic TV addict, she resides in Texas with her cats and her imaginary friends and teaches community-college English to support her writing habit . . . or vice versa.

"But of thee it shall be said,
This dog watched beside a bed
Day and night unweary—
Watched within a curtained room,
Where no sunbeam brake the gloom
Round the sick and dreary."
—*Elizabeth Barrett Browning*

OKAY, so it's not as bad as a doctor saying "Oops."
    But a psychic drawing back and saying, "No *way!*" can't be good either.

"No way what?" I asked warily. And I'd started *out* wary. I consider myself an open-minded guy, or I wouldn't have gone to Madame Eglantine in the first place, but hey, she *was* a psychic. Her . . . uh . . . studio? was the front room of one of those boxy little WWII houses that stopped being considered good real estate a quarter century ago, and she'd filled it with all the props. *You* know. Swags of blue material with a glittery star pattern on it. A plastic bead curtain blocking off what—from what I glimpsed when the cat passed through—was the kitchen. A stick of incense trailing copal into the air like a 1930s starlet's cigarette. Pillar candles. New Age music. And a crystal ball. Actually, she had a whole *shelf* of crystal balls, of different sizes and colors, but one which I assumed was her favorite sat glittering in the middle of her round, scarf-draped table.

It was from this that she had drawn back.

"No way what?" I asked again.

"I got a very strong sense of your past life," she admitted, pursing her lips.

"You think my blocks in Lit class come from *past life* issues?" But hey, *I'd* come to *her*. "Okay. I can deal. So what do you see?"

She looked me over—and maybe *through,* considering who she was—as if to make sure I really *could* deal. Then she shrugged. I would've been happier if she'd nodded— more affirmation than "oh, well"—but . . .

Oh, well.

"You were a dog," she admitted.

"A dog."

She nodded. "This is very unusual, Al. The *Eastern* cultures . . . like the Hindi? . . . they're big on the idea of our souls migrating through different species. But here in the West, people mainly tend to access their past lives as *humans*."

"Maybe I was an Asian dog," I joked. Then I considered myself as a Pekingese, and it didn't seem as funny. An *Irish wolfhound,* maybe. A pit bull. But a little yappy thing . . . ?

"No, I'm sensing you were British," she said seriously. "What I'd like to do is regress you, and see what we can see. Are you comfortable with that, Al?"

"You promise not to plant posthypnotic suggestions that make me quack like a duck or anything, right?"

She pursed her lips again. Trust me to find a psychic without a big sense of humor. Then again, I'd chosen her mainly because her . . . office? . . . was only two miles from my dorm. Discerning shopper, I was not.

"If you'd like," she said, "we can tape the sessions. That way you can revisit what we learn at your leisure and reassure yourself that nothing suspicious is going on."

"SessionZZZ?" I countered. "As in, more than one?"

"I sense," she insisted, "that you were a very interesting dog."

Well, I sure wasn't smarter than your average *bear.* My midterm grades in my first sophomore Lit class had been dismal. 1929 Stock Market dismal. Entropic-universe dismal. Give-up-and-become-a-telemarketer dismal.

But one reason the grades bothered me so much was I didn't consider myself a dumb guy. And I'd heard one or two things about the scams these fortune-tellers pulled.

"You aren't planning to look into my past and find out that I was a *cursed* dog, and that the only way for you to lift the curse is for me to sell everything I own and let you burn the cash to appease the evil spirits, except that of course you don't really burn it you just pretend to but I think you did anyway and then you skip town, are you?"

"I wasn't even planning on selling you a crystal to improve your grade point average," she assured me. "Although if you decide to pursue that, I'd recommend something mental/air oriented like, oh, rhodonite, or maybe some blue-lace agate, used at your crown chakra. But you'd have to get them at a metaphysical store. Or a rock shop."

I hesitated.

"Look, you already paid for today's session. Why don't we do this one, and if you're intrigued, you can pursue the issue. If not, no harm done."

I knew enough friends who went to psychics, and I had done some reading on the Internet. I figured I knew what to watch out for, burning cash aside. "What makes you qualified to do past-life regressions?"

She pointed to the degree on the wall, declaring her a hypnotherapist. If it was a fake, it was a good one.

So I moved to the big armchair, and she closed the venetian blinds, and then she had me shut my eyes, breathe deeply, and imagine myself going slowly down an elevator shaft into my past. I was to envision it as one of those old-fashioned, grilled elevators, so that I could catch glimpses of my life, in reverse chronological order. High school graduation. Driver's license—

I snorted when she said "license," and she made us start again.

—first date. You get the idea. The rest of it gets kind of hazy, around year six. But I've listened to the tape since then, and at the time, I was describing all kinds of stuff you'd think I would have forgotten—my Big Wheel, and a trip to Carlsbad Caverns when I was so scared of the dark I screamed.

Hey, I was *two,* okay?

"Apparently, I didn't scream with words, though. My voice on the tape recorder says, "Nobody understood why I was upset. That it wasn't a fear of monsters or anything. And I couldn't tell them."

"Why couldn't you tell them?" asks Madame Eglantine's voice.

"Because I wasn't talking yet."

"Go back even farther," says the hypnotherapist's psychicky voice, leading me through an analogy of backward birth that I'd rather not relate, thank you. For several minutes it's more her, talking me back. And then, as she describes the mist clearing, she asks who I am, where I am. . . .

And all she gets is whining. *Me* whining! With the occasional bark, like Lassie trying desperately to convey that little Timmy is, yet again, stuck in the well. Or the mine shaft. Or wherever little Timmy gets stuck.

I didn't like listening to that tape, let me tell you! In fact, it pissed me off. Oh, it wasn't quacking like a duck. And I haven't whined since around friends or classmates. But it's not particularly manly behavior.

It took me a long time to recover from my annoyance over that—a *deal* at twenty dollars, right?—before I thought to call my mom and ask her when I *did* start talking.

"Oh, Lord," she said. "You were almost four. We were terrified that there was something wrong with you. Not that there was, of course, darling. One day you just decided to do it, and you've been speaking full sentences ever since."

I've got to admit, I began to wonder if that was connected to my problems in English Lit. Between that curiosity, and the fact that I bombed a quiz on the works of Ben Jonson *big time,* I juggled my budget a little and gave Madame Eglantine a call. "You said you had some ideas about how to get past our little . . . translation problem?" I reminded her.

"I do."

So I went back for more.

Can you hear me, Al? asked the woman's voice, through the fog.

Al? Who was Al?

Oh, yeah. That would be me. "Mmm. Very keen hearing."

Apparently, even my astral self has a warped sense of humor.

I need you to stay nearby, the voice instructed. *On some level, you already know what happened.*

"Already know what happened."

So you can report for the dog what's going on. Do you understand?

"I understand."

We need you for your words.

"Words. I understand."

Good. Now tell me where you are.

Good smells. Food downstairs. Bird outside window! Gone now. All of that was merely impressions, though.

Al, give yourself words.

Mistress sad. Lay chin on mistress' hand. Sigh. . . .

She strokes my ears. I *love* that. But then her attention moves back to her hand, which holds . . .

Al, what do you see?

Back to . . .

Paper. Marks, like leaves on the sidewalk. And a sense about them, like a color floating almost invisibly over them, like a power. *Magic!*

"She's a magic user," I—Al—finally managed to say. "My mistress is some kind of witch or something. She can work some of the best magic in the world."

Go on.

And slowly, awkwardly—like trying to drive manual when you're used to automatic, or trying to draw left-handed—I managed to overlay words onto what was happening, even though I—as the dog—didn't have any.

She wasn't a young woman, more's the pity for me, since I was flopped on the bed beside her, cuddled slightly against her hip. But that was Al thinking. As the dog, I thought her the most incredible living, breathing creature in existence, and it had nothing to do with her appearance. She had dark hair, styled in careful ringlets like from before the Civil

War—that would be the American Civil War—and we often sat in bed this way. She was not, I realized—or already knew, but now could consider—a healthy woman. Unlike her littermates . . . er, that would be her brothers and sisters, who lived in the same house . . . she did not tend to stand on her hind legs.

Okay, so there were still some kinks to work out in this translation business.

She did not get up and walk around much. *There.* She was weak, often so sick she could not raise her voice, often lying in the dark, often alone. And yet, of the people in that dwelling, she was the most powerful. . . .

Minus one.

Her power came from marks on paper—*words,* I realized. *Words!* It came from her ability to not just speak and comprehend words which, to my canine mind, made the whole of the human race a breed of magicians. But of them all, she could *mold* words. She could shape them into scents and music and colors, into things of such beauty that even I, a dumb animal, could feel the power of them washing over me whenever she created or incanted her spells.

Or were they poems?

Same thing.

At this moment, though, she was not working magic. Well enough to sit up, she was reeling from the spell of another—another whose scent was on the letter she read.

I sensed in that masculine smell, in the elusive energies floating off the marks, a power such as I'd never known, even greater than that of . . .

But no! Could anybody be even more powerful than the Sorcerer under whose command my mistress lived? And if so . . . was my mistress safe?

I sniffed the letter again, tasted the tang of this new man's magic on the paper, in the ink. Actually, his was not a wholly new odor. I had smelled it previously—before the snows reduced my beautiful mistress to her latest and worst sickness, before the springtime that now put leaves on the trees outside her window, and set baby birds to cheeping from their nests.

Bird outside again! No, gone.

At the time, I had smelled no disturbance off my mistress, so I had made little of it. Now the Wizard's scent was back, and my mistress did, indeed, fear.

"What shall I do, Flush?" she asked, struggling to catch her breath. "I cannot turn him away again. I must let him come."

As a dog, I didn't understand even such simple communication magic as that, not the same way I did as Al. But even as a dog I knew, "Come." And since I was already there, I also knew she did not mean me. She meant the Wizard. The Wizard would *come.*

Was that wise?

As the dog, I sat up in preparation for whatever battle may ensue—dogs not having a great grasp of future tense. But I also knew that, as great a help as I was to my magical mistress, I could do little against a master Wizard, should he mean her harm.

I'd already proved that against the Sorcerer who had sired her. The one who had cursed her.

The one who, even now, was stealing her soul away in little, incessant laps.

Come back, Al.

I did not want to come back. I could not leave my lady. She needed my continued protection from her father the Sorcerer. And she surely needed me to protect her from this new threat!

You won't be leaving her unprotected. I just want to ask a few questions, and then let you rest. Then you can go back to your job. All right?

"Yes."

What is your name?

"Flush."

Are you sure that's not "Flash?"

My lady put down the missive that smelled of such incredible power, sparkled with such dangerous might, and gathered me into her lap with both arms, cuddling me for comfort like a teddy bear. "Why should he want to see *me?*" she asked.

As a dog, I could only whine and worry and lick her face. But now I had words to describe that heartrending worry. This new Wizard might want the same sustenance her greedy sire, the Sorcerer, drank from her. He wanted her strength, her beauty, her enchantments.

Her life force.

If she was already dying under one magic-user's voracity, how could she survive a second?

Al?

"The name is Flush. Trust me."

What's her name?

Hers? As if I, a dog, had any right to harness her being with an identifying sound as her siblings and father did! By binding, touching her very soul through the strength of the word?

But Al isn't a dog. Let Al tell me her name.

She needed no name. She was the center of my world, the only human of true consequence. She was my mistress. My lady.

Okay then. What do her, uh, littermates call her?

And that, I knew . . . although it felt strange to shape my lips around a sound that I'd only before heard through long, silky ears, in a body that had no real lips.

"Ba."

Try again?

"That's what they call her. Ba."

It's time to come back, Al. I'm going to count backward. . . .

Et ceteras, so forth. Going up.

I felt wrung out as I opened my eyes to the shadowy room of Madame Eglantine's facility. The incense smoke seemed far stronger, more redolent, as I readjusted from my canine incarnation. The noises around me—the hum of a window air conditioner, the sound of a car radio passing by, seemed louder. But at least I didn't have the urge to nose her crystal ball off the table and chase it into the kitchen.

Or to go after the cat.

"You're sure they're saying *Ba?*" asked the psychic therapist. "That's the weirdest name I've ever come across—and I've regressed people back to ancient Sumer. Maybe you misheard."

"I'm a *dog*," I reminded her. Which under other circumstances would have been *such* a strange thing to say. "I think I'm an English spaniel. I don't—didn't—mishear things. But maybe I just can't reword some of them."

"That's possible," she admitted. "Then again, you also spoke of magicians and powers. Perhaps this world which you're remembering isn't *our* world. Maybe it's another planet, another galaxy. Maybe it's another realm altogether, or an alternative-universe England."

"Alternate universe." I tried to draw myself out of the concern that had returned to the twenty-first century with me—the chest-gripping, throat-clutching concern for my lady's safety. Already beset upon by one Sorcerer, was she now threatened by a second?

How was a guy supposed to just sling on his backpack and bike toward Economics 101, knowing something like that?

This world, Al, I reminded myself. *This universe.* "You mean like that episode from the original *Trek* series, where everyone was evil and had facial hair?" Didn't I remember a dog in that episode?

"Yes," sighed Mme. Eglantine. "That is exactly what I mean."

Since she had yet to crack a smile, I couldn't tell if she was joking or not.

As soon as I could, I had myself regressed back to the upcoming Wizard's battle . . . and was horrified to discover how my mistress was preparing for the confrontation.

She was wrapping herself in the master Wizard's incantations!

The book she held did not smell of him—not like his skin or his sweat, as had the letter. He had not, I thought as I snuffled the uneven pages, physically touched this. But his power radiated off it even so, his unique color and sound and vibration, captured in every letter, exerted in every word, manifested in every line.

And my lady was letting it wash over her like a summer rain! *"I gave commands; then all smiles stopped together. There she stands as if alive. . . ."*

A dark incantation indeed!

As soon as she fell asleep—and she was such a weak creature, for all her magical ability, that she slept often—I rose on my hind legs and took the horrid grimoire off her bed table, carrying it from her room to hide it elsewhere in the house.

It speaks to my preoccupation that I allowed myself to be caught not by the devil we did not know, but the devil we did.

"Dog!" cried the Sorcerer—and of course, I froze under his power, book in mouth. Do you think dogs obey only because they wish to? Sometimes they do, sure. But if you've ever had a dog slink back to you, head down, tail tucked, you can be sure he's responding to a power greater than his own. That power—I was coming to realize—was the power of the spoken word.

Forcefully used, of course. This Sorcerer had few other methods.

He strode across the room to loom over me on his two legs, vibrating with an anger I'd never once known him to shed, not even when he was compelling my lady into thinking him kind.

And he'd ruled this dwelling since long before I came to serve my lady.

"Drop it," ordered the Sorcerer. I tried to resist his power—I had to protect my mistress from this new danger! But when the Sorcerer repeated his command—*"I said drop*

it," I had no choice. My jaws opened. The volume fell to the floor, unharmed.

I had, after all, the soft mouth of a retriever.

The Sorcerer snatched up the book, swatted me with it, and I yelped.

"Bad dog," he thundered, and indeed my head went down, my tail went under, I was unworthy to live.

That is the kind of power he had. Through his dark words, I had been transformed into a Bad Dog.

"Why Ba puts up with you, I shall never know," muttered the Sorcerer, tossing the grimoire onto a higher table where only a cat could reach. And a cat would not care. "Should have put you down years ago."

But my lady's own powers had not weakened to the point that I, her companion and familiar, went completely unprotected. I received no further chastisement from he who ruled this dwelling. Not directly. Once my mistress revived, the Sorcerer relished recounting my betrayal to her, each word weakening her further. That was his greatest skill—where she used words to weave beautiful things, hopeful things, light into the world, he used words to limit, to punish, to repress, to darken. My lady might not have a tail to tuck between her legs, or ears that would droop, but I could feel how his indictment of me hurt her, too.

Far worse punishment than the blow, to see that! Even worse, to see the Sorcerer hand back the grimoire, the very book from which I'd hoped to shield her!

But, oh, if the Sorcerer's aura and magic were evil, suffocating things, my lady's were pure goodness. As soon as her evil father left, she turned to me and said, "Oh Flush, how could you!"

But she did not use her words as weapons. Rather than weaken me further, she patted the bed beside her. When I leaped up obediently, she drew me into her arms, waggled my front paws at her, and leaned her nose near mine. "You naughty dog," she said, so clever a reverse spell as one could conceive. Oh, she used similar words to her father's, but so very differently that she wholly erased whatever injury the Sorcerer had caused. "Naughty, naughty doggums, taking his Ba's book of poetry. Doesn't he know Ba has to understand? Doesn't he know how important . . . ?"

She did not finish that question, only stopped and shook her head at her own silliness. I, the dog, would not have understood it anyway. But I did understand her uncertainty, and the fact that she'd just worked a most wondrous spell of healing.

So I licked her nose. And in that way, with my meager ration of canine magic, perhaps I healed some of her injury as well. Ah, but we were good for each other, my mistress and I.

But from the power off the new Wizard's poetry, off his letter and smell, I seriously doubted my ability to be of even that much use, should he breach my Ba's defenses!

That day came too soon. . . .

Al, it's time to come back.

When Madame Eglantine interrupted me, I had the distinct urge to growl. And it wasn't the part of me that was a dog.

Words as power. I couldn't spend my *whole* week regressed to a previous century, or realm, or breed. So when I was away from the psychic, I spent my time obsessing about it, instead. I drew pictures of spaniels in the margins of my astronomy notebook. I looked at my assigned poetry readings for English Lit in a new light—didn't understand them any better, mind you, but I still held them in somewhat more regard, to see the poetry as incantations instead of just a waste of good ink. And, stranded at the library between classes, I did a little research on the idea of words as magic.

Wow. Who would have thought? The whole universe was created by God speaking it into existence. In ancient Ireland, the warrior poets—*filidh*—were considered powerful magic users because of their skill with words. King Arthur's Merlin may be based on a Welsh poet named Taliesin. That New

Age idea of speaking affirmations goes to words carrying power, too.

Heck, even in *Dungeons & Dragons,* magic users often have to use words to make their magic succeed. Not that *D&D* is necessarily of the same weight as the Old Testament, but you know . . . if something's really, truly true, who *knows* what parts of our culture it might seep into?

That knowledge had me worrying about "Ba" even more, until I could get my butt back to M.E.'s and dive down that imaginary ironwork elevator into my poochy past.

Only there did I see just how cleverly my mistress could substitute wit against power.

The Wizard came—and at first he was everything I'd feared. His aura hummed with vigor and determination, two strengths my lady lacked. Oh, he did not immediately attack her. Most humans are more subtle than that! But I knew how cleverly her father, the evil Sorcerer, pretended kindness to undermine her defenses. Merely because this Wizard showed his teeth and spoke flattery was no cause for me to trust him.

My lady trusted him enough, from the start, for the both of us. That's when I—as Al—began to figure it out. By submerging herself in his spells and incantations, by reading them and speaking them and all but bathing in them, she'd accustomed herself to his energy. When she spoke them to him, he laughed and spoke some of them back. Then he spoke some of hers! Their magic mingled, grew, and shimmered over them both, filling the room, far more powerful than could be conceived for being shared.

Have you ever noticed that a lot of dogs warm up to women more quickly than to men? Maybe we—they—sense the superior physical strength, or the testosterone. As Flush, I was one of those dogs. Even if my lady did trust this Wizard, and even if he seemed immediately fond of, even in awe of her . . . even if their duet of words created the most beautiful rainbow of magic that had ever filled her chambers, I had no intention of trusting easily.

After all, my lady trusted the Sorcerer, too!

But again, despite her physical weakness, she proved herself a clever mage indeed. Once the Wizard left, she sat for a long time, seeming to breathe the lingering scent of him and his power. Unlike the draining magic of the Sorcerer, his energy seemed to strengthen her. She opened her desk, took out an inkwell and paper, and began another spell.

A particularly powerful spell.

A binding spell.

"Omigod," I said, as Al. "It's a love spell!"

Then I saw the hope. The old Sorcerer had been drinking my lady's health and faith for years, and her his willing victim. But allied with this powerful young Wizard, perhaps finally she would escape.

While she wrote, speaking some words, writing some only to discard them, trying others, I lay my head on her feet and, eyes rolled up in my head, watched her pen her spell to draw him back. And I hoped it worked.

What's his name? asked Madame Eglantine's voice.

Name?

Let Al tell me his name.

"Sir," I—as Al—answered.

His real *name?* But that was all I'd caught my lady consistently calling him—for a creature unskilled with words, repetition is very important. So that was all I could offer.

DOES HE COME BACK? asked the voice.

He did. First, he sent a missive filled with such passion that I could not even stand near it for the warmth of its powers, so intense that even my lady cried out and dropped it, frightened by her own magical results. She collected her magical tools—the pen, the ink, the paper—and wrote him back, establishing some sort of ward which would keep him forever away from her, unless he better controlled his wild energies. And he must have, because he came back.

And back.

And back.

Almost always when the Sorcerer was out doing other evils.

That's when the true magic began. So great were the young Wizard's vigor and determination that, unlike the siphon that was her father, he fed them to my lady. He opened the windows, which the Sorcerer preferred closed, and pulled back drapes the Sorcerer preferred drawn, harnessing the earthy powers of fresh air and sunlight to assist in his healing. He shared more spells with her, spells so very complicated that, I surmised, only my mistress could understand them. But understand them she did, strengthening him not with her weakness or need, but with her faith and quiet beauty. She began to stand more often, to walk more often, to sit and laugh. And when he touched her, it was always gently, always giving and respectful and . . . loving.

Even I came to trust him. For my mistress' love spells— a series of them, now—were working. She and the Wizard had found more than the incredible magic of words. They had found the even more powerful magic of love. Their souls matched . . . perhaps from connections far older than this one lifetime, certainly older than the magic done here. But they needed all the magic they could summon, when the Sorcerer discovered this new alliance.

Al?

I growled at the voice. Now was *not* the time.

Al, it's been too long. We'll come back here. I promise. But you have to return.

This time, when I came back to the psychic's facility I felt sick. And not because the past-life regression was doing anything to my electrolytes, although I did go ahead and drink a lot of Gatorade after each session, just in case.

I felt sick because I wasn't sure that the power of my mistress and the Wizard, her Sir, was strong enough. The Sorcerer had woven his tentacles so deeply into Ba, so long ago, surely she would never escape.

And to be honest, it sucked.

Oh suuure, so this was something that happened in the

past, assuming it ever happened at all. And suuure, I had to take the word—or nonword—of a dog for the whole story. It still seemed as real as the rest of my life.

Baseball. Schoolwork. Job. Life as an English spaniel protecting a female practitioner of poetic word-magic.

But *was* I able to protect her?

Only one way to find out.

"This one," said Madame Eglantine when I got back to her place, "is on me."

The evil Sorcerer finally discovered the loving alliance between Ba and Sir, and he whipped up some word-magic as caustic as ever I, Flush, had smelled. He hurled cruel words like weapons at his daughter, bruising her spirit, crushing her hopes. Had I been a Bad Dog? She was a Bad Daughter, one who betrayed her master—him—and he would not let her forget that. He penned another ward spell, this one banishing the young Wizard from entry to our dwelling, from access to my mistress, his love, forever.

Oh, that was a bad time. My mistress wept so that she sickened herself all over again, and I could not lick all the tears away. The Sorcerer cast continual illusions at her, creating a reality in which he acted only for her good, only through concern for her. His love, a father's love, was surely more potent than that of some blackguard who'd come sniffing about for the wrong reasons.

In an even worse illusion, the Sorcerer used his words to raise for my mistress the fear that the Wizard could not truly love her. She was older than he was, after all, and sickly, and weak. Only a fool would believe in the purity of his motives, against such ugly truths. She must be that fool.

It is testament to the Sorcerer's powers that my lady could even entertain such evil thoughts—for by entertaining them, she let them in where they could fester, and they tried to become truths indeed. For what are truths, but that which we believe? And how better to sharpen those beliefs than with words?

In this I, a mere dog, saw better than did my magical lady. I could smell the letters delivered to the house, the letters so full of her good Wizard's smell, his power, his desperation, that there was no doubt he still loved her. I saw the Sorcerer burn each one, before even my mistress' most loyal litter-mates, or her nondog companion—Wilson—ever saw them. And I heard the Sorcerer ask, "If he loved you, would he not write to you?"

He was an evil, evil man.

But I was Flush. I was my lady's familiar. And I had a job to do.

Wilson, a human who served my lady much as I did, was the one who took me on my necessary walks, both to relieve myself and to smell the doings of the other dogs on Wimpole Street. Even at her healthiest, my lady was not up to the rigors of walking me . . . and she was quickly losing strength under her father's bombardment of dark magic. So I was with Wilson, on the block corner, when I heard a sudden, soft whistle.

Immediately I drew up, alert, my ears high, my nose working. *Him! It was him,* the *Wizard!*

"Flush," scolded Wilson as I tugged on my lead. "*Flush!* Bad doggie!"

But like our mistress, her "bad dogs" had none of the Sorcerer's violence to them. As I scampered around the corner and through leaves that scattered like word-marks across the pavement, then leaped happily onto Sir, she simply followed—then stopped, concerned.

I wasn't concerned. I let him scratch me behind my ears, like a good master would, enjoyed his laugh at how I licked his scent off his hand. Oh, if only my lady had a better sense of smell, she would scent him off me!

Then, on seeing Wilson, he rose—and offered another missive.

For a moment, I feared she would not take it. Could I, if she did not? I sat up and waved my front paws in the air, beg-

ging as prettily as I could, but he ignored me now. How could
I ask him to give it to me, to fasten it around my collar?

But my mistress' inner beauty was such as to engender
loyalty in all but the most craven of souls. Her human, Wilson, took the missive, then caught my trailing lead, and we
went back into the dwelling—

Where the Sorcerer intercepted us!

Again, he stood armed with powerful words. Most of
them were questions, a type of word-magic that slices at the
end—have you ever noticed that? How had our walk gone?
he asked. *Slash!* Had Wilson seen anything amiss? *Rip!* He
claimed concern, such concern about Ba—and here he
began to weave another illusion with his words, one in
which the only way Wilson could prove her love for our
mistress was to protect her from "that man," from Sir. If she
were a Good Human, she would tell the Sorcerer of any
overtures Sir might make to her, for her own good, her own
good. . . .

I could smell Wilson's increasing indecision as the Sorcerer's words wove their web around her, as his magic built.
I had to do something. *Something!*

I barked! But the Sorcerer fixed me with his literate,
human eyes and cursed me: *"Bad Dog."* And I felt my tail
sink, my head slump.

Had Wilson heard anything from that man, demanded the
Sorcerer. She would not dare risk our mistress, would she?
And in such poor health. She would not dare endanger Ba.

Ba. The Sorcerer's mistake was invoking her name! It
was her lingering power, her magically loving protection,
that gave me the strength to do what needed doing.

I hiked up my leg and peed on his shoe.

Very few humans can continue working magic against
that! In an instant, the Sorcerer's spells crumbled beneath
his roar of rage. Wilson cringed back, then used the distraction I had provided to race for our lady's room—letter safely
in her pocket. Of course, the Sorcerer kicked me, hard

enough to crack a rib, but not so hard that I could flee for the stairs, ki-yi'ing all the way—

Right to my bright lady's feet.

She scooped me into the safety of her arms, sat unmoved by her father's tirade against me. Oh, I had little doubt that I would pay for my rebellion, even beyond the kick. The way the Sorcerer glared at me, I would not put it past him to poison my food.

But he would not directly attack me. Not in front of his daughter. To do anything so blatantly harmful would destroy the illusion of paternal care that he'd constructed and maintained for so long that it was crumbling in on itself.

He did not seem to realize that, strengthened by the young Wizard's love, my lady had already begun to see through that illusion. In kicking me, the Sorcerer only revealed what she had begun to suspect.

Once he left her, she took the missive from Wilson and read it, once, then again. The magic of it washed across her, fed her in ways I'd never before seen. Surely she could fly, with magic like this. She *did* sing!

Not too many sun-passings after that, she, Wilson, and I took a carriage ride to one of the human places of power . . .

Places of power? asked the voice.

"Churches," I clarified, impatient with the interruption. "It's a church, okay?"

. . . and the Wizard awaited them. A cleric read over them one of the most powerful spells ever created for the binding of human souls, from one of the most powerful spell-books in human existence. From that point on, their powers were inseparably joined, doubled, along with their souls. Nobody could out-magic them now!

That we returned to the dwelling one last time was of little matter.

The Sorcerer continued his magic barrage, but such are the limits of dark power and negative energy—he could not even see what I, a dog, could not miss. He could not see that he had lost his daughter, that she would feed his vampiric tastes with her illness and uncertainties no more.

Our last night there, my lady secretly wrote a farewell spell including the finest tidbits of her beautiful essence, one for each of her littermates. She even, though he did not deserve it, worded out a similar spell for her father, the Sorcerer. But I do not know what became of those spells, because in the dark of the morning she, I, and Wilson crept from the house, to where the Wizard waited. He and Ba embraced as only true practitioners of love-magic can, and he lifted her—and then me—into a carriage. We rode far away to a boat, then even farther to a land of sunshine and happiness and health, never to return.

Wow, said the voice. *So . . . no more magic?*

"Are you kidding?" I answered as Al, unwilling to draw away yet from the hard-earned, well-deserved contentment of my master and mistress. "These two are penning magic all over the place! Especially . . ."

Especially what?

For many moons, my lady did not show Sir the love spells by which she'd bound him. When finally she drew the courage—sharing his energies, she'd found more courage than ever—she slipped the packet of them into his pocket, while he was looking out the window, and fled.

"What are these, Flush?" he asked in wonder, drawing them out of his pocket and looking after his mate.

Since I could not explain the story—not without Al's help—I simply padded off after my lady, to where she sat in the piazza, while Sir—whom my lady now more often called "Robert"—unfolded the parchment to behold the magic she had created.

Even from the piazza, I could see it. It danced off the pages, sang like a choir of angels, swirled around him like a spring breeze, sparkled like the starriest of nights. Somehow, she had captured love itself with the power of words. Apparently it had been a love spell that only called him, for he did not resent it, not at all. He came to her, embraced her, wept. Then they began to joyfully argue something about publishing . . . but all that was far beyond my canine sensibilities. All that mattered to me was that they remained happy.

And they did, working magic so powerful that it would survive them . . . or at least, those particular incarnations, for eternities. Maybe even better after death.

I'M GOING TO COUNT BACKWARD, AL, cautioned the voice.

Damn. I was really enjoying these two. But I also knew that I as Flush had done a fine enough job protecting them. I as Al must have something, who knew what, waiting to challenge me in my own life.

Maybe the power of words in my English Lit text.

Five . . . four . . . three . . . two . . .

For some reason the phrase, *Let me count the ways,* rang in my head. I opened my eyes, took a deep breath as Al—no super smelling abilities, no keen hearing—and settled back into *my* time. *My* world.

"Wow," I said.

"No shit," said the psychic. You know, I was beginning to think that "Madame" stuff wasn't her real name. "I've had clients who discovered they were murderers, and slaves, and emperors, and priests, but until you, nobody has ever turned out to be a dog."

"Ah," I corrected her. "But I was a Very Good Dog."

When I said the words like that, I could almost taste their power. It had eluded me until now, because words are all around us. We have a kind of verbal inflation. But just because we are all born magic users, of sorts, doesn't lessen that magic.

Even if few of us could probably be a Robert or a Ba.

"Do you suppose they're famous?" I thought to ask. It was time to shoulder my backpack and get to Lit class, but after everything I'd seen, I was curious. It had seemed so important when it happened.

Although canine priorities are probably a little different, you know?

"Oh, I doubt it," said M.E. "People who mock reincarnation always talk about thinking you're Napoleon or Cleopatra, but I've never regressed a single famous person. Or dog."

"Yeah," I conceded. "I'll admit, I've never heard of a famous poet named Ba."

She spread her long-nailed, many-ringed hands as if to say, *There you go.* "Good luck in class," she said. "I hope this helped."

I thought it might. Who knows—maybe my dog self had felt unworthy of the words. But my human self now knew what had gone into them, and how I could use their power to share, even in the tiniest way, the intensity of life that some magicians . . . er, poets . . . had lived. "We're starting the Romantic Poets today," I told her, from the doorway. "Maybe I'll find something to like there."

And I headed off for my bike, my classes, and my own world.

ON THE SCENT OF THE WITCH

by Jean Rabe

When not writing, Jean Rabe feeds her goldfish,
visits museums, and attends gaming conven-
tions. A former newspaper reporter, she is the author of nine fantasy novels, including the
Dragonlance Fifth Age Trilogy. Her latest novel is
Dhamon: The Downfall. She has written numerous
fantasy and science fiction short stories which
appear in such anthologies as *Merlin* and *Tales
from the Eternal Archives: Legends, Guardsmen of
Tomorrow,* and *Warrior Fantastic.*

THERE were lots of smells this bright spring morning—
all coming at a wonderful, dizzying pace, all pushed by
the strong wind that whipped across the field and fluttered
the wildflowers and teased her graying hair.

She breathed deeply and held it for as long as she could,
picking through all the scents and settling on what had to be
her very favorite at this time of year—earth that recently had
been turned over. Planting time. Dark with moisture from
the rain two days past, it was filled with delightful things—
husks of beetles that had died when the cold hit, pieces of
rotted cornstalks striped with mold, smears that had been
tomatoes, wriggling masses of red worms, and more. Oh,
gloriously more!

Edging forward, she tipped her head this way and that,

letting the breeze play across her brow and letting it bring
still more smells her way. Something . . . yes, there was
something that stood out from everything, something that
caught and held her attention as sure as any vise.

Luck, what amazing luck! She inhaled again and headed
toward what must be a most amazing treasure. Closing, as
she seemed right on top of it now, she brushed aside one
clump of dirt after another and another, moving a few feet
and working at it some more, relentlessly, until she discovered part of a rabbit—the plump hindquarters. Indeed, an
amazing find! It had been frozen over the winter, but was
now nicely and thoroughly thawed. She sniffed at it, tail
gently wagging when she noted just how pleasantly pungent
it was. Had it been cut in half by a farmer's tool? Had a fox
caught it in the fall, taking only what it wanted to eat at the
moment and leaving the rest? No matter. Fortune was hers
that no one else had come by earlier to claim this!

With a happy yip she fell on what was left of the carcass,
rolling and twisting first on her back then on each side to
smear the odor deep into her fur. She felt the dampness of
the ground against her, bits of cornstalks scratching at her in
just the right places. Looking up while she continued her gy-
rations, she spotted birds flying overhead. Oh, to give chase
along the ground! She almost gave into the urge. But she
was a smart dog, and she knew that there would be more
birds coming along at any minute. There were always more
birds. And she was an old dog, one who didn't run much
anymore because she tired easily. Besides, she wanted to
continue rubbing against the rabbit a little while longer, take
as much of the smell away with her as she could, make sure
she got it on her rump and legs, a little on her neck and . . .

She heard another dog bark, concentrating as she rolled
more slowly now and trying to picture who was making the
racket. Hathorne's dog, perhaps? The big black brute was a
noisy one, frequently barking only to hear himself. She
hoped he wasn't headed this way to steal her treasure. Or
maybe it was the sleek-coated yowler living at the bottom of

Gallow's Hill. He was always fenced in near the sheep pen.
A most friendly dog, he only had freedom when, with her
help, he could work the gate latch open. Or it could be . . .

With a disappointed whine she stopped her musings, feeling a presence stir at the back of her mind, forcing her to
thrust aside all thoughts of the unidentified barker and the
pungent rabbit. It was always the same when John intruded
this way—a tickling sensation, that despite the number of
times and through the number of years he'd done it, still
gave her a curious feeling. Not an unpleasant one, and not
close to the satisfaction of a good rub behind the ears. But
something in between. There was something that was oddly
soothing about it, the presence of her man John, who'd
found her as a stray ten winters past and taken her into his
home and let her sleep on a thick rug by the hearth.

After a moment John took a more prominent position in
her mind.

Where are we going? she asked him.

"To the church, Keesh," he answered. Though he spoke
the words aloud in his cabin, half a mile away, she heard
them as clearly as if he were standing in front of her. "To see
what visiting Cotton's up to."

She slowly rolled off the rabbit and shook until a stubborn clump of dirt dropped off her stomach. Then she gave
an exaggerated wag of her plumy tail, happy to be doing
something important for John. Keesh dutifully headed
across the field and to the dirt street that ran through the
middle of Salem, adopting a quick pace—or what was rela-
tively fast as far as her advanced years were concerned. She
reluctantly passed by the baker's, cocking her head to better
pick up the smells of fresh bread and other delicacies.

In his cabin, John Broadmore looked out through the
mongrel Keesh's eyes and at the same time inhaled the
scents of cinnamon and apricots and melting butter. He concentrated and felt the dirt beneath the dog's paws.

"We will stop back at the bakery later, Keesh," he told

her. "And we'll beg for a suitable treat. You're a smart dog. You're a very good dog."

John sat on an old wooden bench in front of a low table that was covered with chicken feathers dipped in fat, sand he had painted various colors, a bowl of dried-out ewe eyeballs, and a jar of whiskey that held the corpse of an unborn piglet. A thick book was in the midst of all of this, opened to the middle where his fingers danced over symbols that none in this town save he could translate. It was an old book, older than John, older than Salem, and written long before the first Englishman came to this new world. Passed down from his father and grandfather and great-grandfather—who was said to have obtained it from a clueless Spanish merchant—it was a book of incantations, most of which John had mastered and several of which he indulged in the casting of daily.

John was the only practicing witch in the town, likely in the entire state of Massachusetts, and he'd hoped his work would have gone unnoticed. He had tried to be secretive, his altering the weather in the span of minutes—late at night when most folks were in bed and couldn't see the dry lightning, his causing corn crops to flourish in droughts or to wither unexpectedly in the passing of a day, his tinkering in the lives of neighbors to make them fall in and out of love for his entertainment, his manipulations to make the Newton boy steal and bully his friends.

And all the spells were cast through his familiar Keesh, the mongrel he'd taken such a liking to. "You're a clever dog," John mused. "A smart dog."

And all the spells were cast when John was safely inside his cabin with the doors and shutters locked, as they were now. All of the enchantments came easier to him with each season, making him more powerful and tying him more securely to the Art. He didn't even need the book for some of them, so expert had he become. The one that linked him to the mongrel was second nature, and sometimes he found himself staring out through the dog's eyes without having

invoked the spell. Keesh had become an extension of himself, and she was just this moment rounding the corner near
the church, heading to the back where there was a stack of
boards just under a window. Jumping up on them and peering through streaked glass, Keesh and John watched a
florid-faced man scribbling at a desk.

"Cotton Mather," John hissed through tightly clenched
teeth. He let a breath escape, sounding like steam rising
from a kettle left too long on the fire. "Damn him," he
cursed, as his fingers turned one page and then another. His
fingers danced faster. "Damn the man to the belly of Hell."
John hadn't a spell that would do that, but he sometimes fan-
cied taking a trip south where it was rumored a French-
woman brewed concoctions that would handle the job.
"Vicious Cotton Mather."

Cotton Mather was why John had moved to Salem. Cotton Mather and his own curiosity. Mather was a frequent
visitor to the place and had published a book recently, last
year or the year before that, John believed, 1691 or 1690.
No. A few years earlier. It was called *Memorable Provi-
dences,* and it dealt with, among other things, an Irish wash-
erwoman who lived in Mather's Boston and was suspected
of being a witch. The book was popular and sold well, and
John had two copies—one for posterity and one that he had
marked up for research.

Mather, an influential Calvinist, took himself much too
seriously and believed himself an authority on witches. "A
subject which he truly knows nothing about," John said.
Nevertheless, there were germs of truth in what Mather
penned—undoubtedly lucky speculation, and John decided
that this most dangerous man had to stop inciting folks. John
just hadn't settled on a way to stop him. Mather should stick
to his study of science and his concern for the public health.
He should leave the matter of witches alone. It would be
healthier for him.

Keesha and John watched Mather for the better part of an

hour, then listened intently as a stodgy assistant came in and eased himself into a nearby chair.

"The girls were at it again last night," the newcomer said. "Twitching and running around, hiding under the furniture. The smallest fell into a convulsion, and her father almost called for you. But it subsided soon enough."

Mather put down his quill and shook his head, his mop of curling white hair reminding Keesh of a cloud she'd spotted earlier. "Witchcraft," Mather pronounced. "No other explanation."

"Same as that child—Betty Parris," the assistant said. "Same as what happened to her this February gone."

Mather nodded and placed his hands on the table. Another shake of his head, and he pushed his stool back and stood. "Horrible, Godforsaken witches. We will find them. And we will make them pay. We will chase the Devil out of Salem." As he walked to the window, Keesha scampered away.

John directed the mongrel to take a side street, one that went past the Parris house, where six-year-old Betty—one of Mather's study subjects lived. Indeed, the child had suffered a convulsion and acted erratically, as had several other girls in Salem. A few whispered that the children were just trying to get attention or had caught some strange illness, though Mather and his cronies stood by their defense of witchcraft sitting at the heart of it all.

"Mather was right," John said. "Witchcraft, indeed." He spread some of the green sand and drew a design in it, then sprinkled a line of red sand beneath it. "But Mather will never understand just what it is all about." Keesh had visited Betty's home in February, and the child was quick to come outdoors and play with the friendly mongrel. Through Keesh, John had cast a spell that transferred his own essence, via the dog, into the child. John was experimenting with moving his mind from one body to the next and decided that children were the only vessels to consider at this juncture.

An adult might remember too much about the experience, might see John's face or draw the conclusion between the presence of John's mongrel and the episodes of fits. But a child . . . a child couldn't be entirely believed. They made up stories. They didn't understand things. To further help cloud the issue, John drew upon a simple incantation that passed the child a mild malady—and hence the brief convulsion. No harm done. No child injured. And John got closer in the process of being able to completely leave his body and enter another. With each passing month, he could do it for greater and greater periods of time.

The transference spell intrigued him, and it was the one he concentrated on above all others. He intended to use it— after he thoroughly mastered it, of course—to get himself a young, healthy body. But that would be a decade or two from now when this one began to ache and his senses began to grow feeble. He could not allow himself to succumb to the pitiful vagaries of old age, and then death, as his father and grandfather and great-grandfather had. There was too much magic to absorb in only one lifetime, and John wanted an opportunity to learn it all.

He shook off his thoughts and gazed through Keesh's eyes, seeing Betty playing in the yard with two other children. John smiled. The Jameson boy. The child was prone to exaggerating anyway. John flipped a page in the book, muttered a series of arcane phrases, and felt his mind pass from his body into Keesh, and then into the little boy.

The body in the cabin slumped forward, head cradled by the book.

The little Jameson boy kicked dirt at Betty and began running with glee. Keesh kept up with him for several minutes, yapping and jumping and delighting in the spring.

The trials started the following week.

John hadn't intended for anyone to be hurt. He'd not injured a soul with his spells—not physically. And despite rough times, none of those he'd meddled with romantically divorced their spouses.

"No real harm has been done," he told himself. Keesh curled between his feet, he sat at his table, stirring sand and flipping pages in the book.

In late April several of the girls John had "borrowed" with his transference spell accused a former Salem minister of witchcraft. John hadn't planted the thought, didn't really know the poor man, and was at a loss to understand the girls' ramblings.

The following month more were arrested—examined and tried and hanged.

"For no reason," John said. "Still, there's nothing to be done about it."

What could he do? he repeatedly asked himself. Tell Old Cotton Mather that those being strung up on Gallows Hill, and the old man pressed by stones just yesterday, were not witches? That there were no witches in Salem save for himself? John knew if he confessed, he'd be hanged. And there was too much magic in the world to master for that to happen. He couldn't surrender his life—no matter the consequences.

And so he watched the hangings, with Keesh at his side. The dog forlornly saw people who had once shown kindness by petting her drop to their deaths, kicking until the last of their lives trickled away. John explained to the dog, as best he could when they were melded, that matters had gotten out of control. Despite that, he continued to practice his transference spell—though not as frequently as before.

It was the end of summer when they came for John, on a day when the sun hung high in a cloudless bright sky. Perhaps it was because the previous night dry lightning shot above the town, yellow-gold fingers arrowing away from where his cabin sat. Perhaps he hadn't locked all the shutters. The wind had been fierce that night. Or perhaps it had been the Jameson boy. He'd targeted the child a dozen times and only lately had been worrying that the boy's description of the witch involved in the incidents closely matched his own appearance.

Cotton Mather personally took John away. He locked him in a cell, gave him little to eat, and questioned him repeatedly.

"Are you a witch?"

"No," John lied.

"Have you familiarity with the Devil?"

John vehemently shook his head.

Mather shook his, too, and trundled away. In the hallway, he announced there would be a trial in the morning—and a hanging before sunset. John heard Mather and his associates discussing the details, and he heard Keesh whimper from beyond the cell window.

"I don't need the book," John said. It had been confiscated. They'd left all the sand and the feathers, every dried animal organ he'd collected and carefully cataloged. They didn't know what to do with it all. But they took the precious book. "I don't need it."

John pressed his face against the wall, just under the window, stretched out with his mind as he muttered a string of incomprehensible words, and felt his consciousness slip into the mongrel's body. This time, he pushed the spell to the limits of his ability.

Keesh woke with a start, lying on a dirt floor inside a cell, lying in an unfamiliar body. With a sniff she knew it was John's body, knew what her man had done—she'd participated in so many of his spells to understand that he had mentally traded places with her. And though she didn't understand why he'd done this, she accepted it. She crawled on all fours to the door and barked, the sound strange coming from John's mouth. Keesh pulled herself up, weaving back and forth on two legs that threatened to crumble beneath her. Four legs were so much better for balance.

She barked again and again until the jailer came, and she

kept barking until he opened the cell, frantic at what could be happening to his prisoner. Keesh barked once more as she bolted from the small building, ran across the street and toward John's cabin. Though unused to this form, she quickly mastered it. She was a smart dog. She delighted in its speed and its youth, and she threw back her head and let the breeze play with her hair as she hurried along.

Unfamiliar with fingers, she fumbled at the door for several minutes before she could get everything to cooperate. She shut the door behind her. Then after pacing the room for several minutes, smelling her own scent and John's heavy in the air, she lay down on the rug and slept. It was shortly before midnight that she arose, an idea stirring at the back of her mind. She was a smart dog.

The fingers were easier to manipulate now, and having two feet was posing little problem. Standing on John's toes, Keesh stretched a hand up to a top shelf and began pulling down colored sand and feathers.

She was indeed a very smart dog.

The gray mongrel had been caught shortly after John's escape from jail. The old dog was headed toward the edge of town, running as fast as it could—which wasn't particularly fast given its age. Before sunset it was presented to Cotton Mather.

"Witch dog," someone pronounced. "Creature of the Devil."

The mongrel's eyes were wide with fright. From inside the animal's shell, John tried to scream. But only a mournful howl escaped.

"Aye, it is a witch dog," Mather agreed. "A devil dog." He proceeded to go into great detail on how dogs were familiars of witches, agents of the Devil and easily magicked. Since they could not have John Broadmore, they would have his dog.

They hanged it the next morning.

*　　*　　*

Cotton Mather tended to the ceremony himself, placing the noose about the frightened animal's neck. He thrust out the cries of the children to leave the animal alone. Only the young Jameson boy championed the execution.

When the animal was dead, and when he'd ordered it to be buried, he returned to the church and went straightaway to the back room. There, he dug about in an old chest that was filled with all manner of books and jars and bundled sheets of parchment. He pulled out one book in particular, a very old one filled with symbols that only he could translate. He turned to the transference spell and decided he would use it in another town, one that hadn't had trouble with witches and overzealous Calvinists. He'd find himself a better body, a younger one. Cotton Mather's was too old for his tastes, though he was grateful that Keesh had managed to switch his and Cotton's minds before the execution.

"A good dog," he breathed.

He would have to find himself another one, a mongrel. But before that, he'd end all these witch trials and hangings.

Keesh stood next to a willow birch at the edge of Salem. She'd watched her dog body being hanged, knowing Cotton Mather was deep inside it. The man would trouble no one again. She watched John, in Cotton's form, trundle off to the church. And she'd seen him turn at the last moment, looking into the woods, catching sight of her and smiling.

"You're a smart dog," she saw him mouth. "A very good dog."

Keesh smiled and stretched and turned north, well accustomed to this new two-legged form now. The early fall wind was bringing a myriad of smells her way—damp fallen leaves, a patch of earth covered with thick moss, and something amazing. Weaving through the trunks she strained to catch the odor, frustrated that these senses were not quite as keen as what she'd had before.

No matter, with patience she found it. There, beneath a large oak, was a dead bird—a big crow all swollen. It was not more than a few days' dead, and it was pleasantly pungent. She dropped down on it and began to roll.

Historical note: In Salem, Massachusetts, in 1692, a man named John Bradstreet was charged with being a witch. He escaped and hid in the woods, but they caught a dog he supposedly used to give others "the evil eye," and hanged it instead.

THE FAMILIAR

by Andre Norton

Andre Norton has written and collaborated on over one hundred novels in her sixty years as a writer, working with such authors as Robert Bloch, Marion Zimmer Bradley, Mercedes Lackey, and Julian May. Her best-known creation is the Witch World, which has been the subject of several novels and anthologies. She has received the Nebula Grand Master Award, The Fritz Leiber Award, and the Daedalus Award, and lives in Murfreesboro, Tennessee, where she oversees High Hallack, a research library for genre writers.

THE west wall was breached two hours after dawn, for the invaders had their own magic, of a sort—a powder that could crumble stone, no matter how thick or well-laid. I knew, then, that my chances for continued existence were limited to almost none.

My greatest shortcoming—as my elders and betters had so often pointed out—was indolence. Years of lazy drifting, of quieting my conscience with the reassurance, "She is too young; there is time," lay behind me. As a result, my familiar had never had her innate talents honed as they should have been. True, I had tried to begin this wit-sharpening last year, but the minds of the people of this world became less easy to work with as they grew older. And now—?

Now I must make do. Thinking it was fortunate that I knew much more about this merchant-house than the humans living here even suspected, I gathered my true strength and let go a summons.

The girl was in the lower hallway, sensibly resisting the screaming of a maid who was urging her to flee the house, to run to the castle gates. Evidently the servant did not know that those portals had been closed and barred at dawn, preventing either entry or exit, or perhaps terror had carried her beyond sense.

My familiar had thrown back the lid of the massive chest that stood in that corridor. Now she knelt and reached in, stripping away the layers of cloth stored there until she came to the cloak that had been folded over me. A moment later she brought me forth. I could feel her surprise at those actions, which I had directed: why should she place herself in peril to retrieve what she saw as a toy? Then, as I had done many times since she was small, I exerted the invisible bond we shared, and she hugged me tightly against her breast.

"Fossi, Fossi, what can we do?"

I noted with satisfaction that "we" in her speech; our link—a connection I had been strengthening through dream-touch for some nights—was tight. Now I exuded warmth, security, projecting those emotions as strongly as possible. Again I gave orders, and once more she accepted them without question.

The master of the house had been lending aid to the defense of the walls, and when I sent a seek-probe to find him, he was gone. The fear-maddened maid who had been cater-wauling below had taken her own advice and fled into the streets. Only my familiar was left in this place.

Young and beautiful by the reckoning of her kind, the girl would be welcome prey for any invader who sighted her. We would have to work fast. Still holding me tightly, she stooped and caught up the cloak she had uncovered earlier; then she moved quickly down the stairs and into the kitchen. There she set me carefully on the edge of the large central table and spread out the garment beside me. As she did so, she staggered slightly, lifting her hand to her forehead. I felt a sag in our bond and straightaway tightened it.

Bread of yesterday's baking, a round of cheese, and a jar of dried fruit were heaped atop the cloak, which was gathered to form a provision bag. Lastly, two sharp knives were thrust into her belt, and she had garnered all she could here.

"Now what, Fossi?" My familiar was looking intently at me, and our link was now firm enough that I dared to reveal a little of my true nature. When I had first located the girl, she had been so young she believed my stuffed-toy disguise, and that was the beginning of the bond for both of us. However, as she had grown older, her perception of the form I wore in her world as that of a mere plaything had grown more strong. Could I, in time to save us both, convince her of what I truly was?

The clamor in the streets without, which could be heard even through these thick and long-laid walls, had been as a rising wave to sweep us onward. Now, above its muted roar there sounded the shriek of a woman, laden with such horror and pain that my familiar's hand flew to her mouth and her eyes went wide. Into her mind flashed the thought of what she might do with one of those knives to prevent such agony being wrung from herself, and she shuddered so we were both shaken. Quickly, I moved to take full command, intensifying my mind-send to break her trance. At last she moved, taking up the bundle of food in one hand and me in the other.

We hurried through to the head of the cellar stairs. A lantern hung on a hook there, witch-fire blazing at its core. Such magic would supply light for as long as we had need of it, and that might well be long indeed. I tensed; it was time now for the next step. Squirming in the girl's hold, I freed one of my toy-body's arms and pointed at the lantern.

My companion paused, indecisive again. She was noticing too much of the here and now. I added to the link. So goaded, she placed me on the cold stone of the first step, then tied her bag by the ends and slipped its circle over her shoulder.

"Fossi?" She spoke my name on a questioning note, peering down as though seeing me for the first time. Then, as though coming to a decision, she took me up again and reached for the lantern. Thus we went down into the dark chill depths beneath the house.

It was not yet time for me to take the final step to cement our bonding, to let my familiar see all I could be and do on this plane of existence. I held firmly in place that last thin veil between us as she made the descent step by step.

The cellar was made up of storage rooms, filled with barrels and chests. From one wall had been hewn an alcove, and in this niche wines were laid down. A mighty woodpile was carefully stacked in yet another area, awaiting a cold season this place might never see. My companion was familiar with this part of the house, but a few minutes' walk at the near-run we were keeping brought us to the end of the ways known to her.

Once more she addressed me, her voice that of the lonely child she had been when I had first moved myself into her life. Then she held up the lantern to the stone wall that ended our journey and murmured in a dull singsong, "No door—no more—"

Swiftly, simply, I fed my companion the knowledge to solve this problem. As though controlled by the strings of a dance-doll, her right arm lifted until it pointed to the blank barrier before us. With her forefinger, she next outlined a space up, across, and down the stone, that finger seeming to jet fire as a blue line followed its path. Finally, coming close enough to touch the surface, she set hand against the section of wall defined by the lines—and pushed.

If the girl had expected movement, none came. I gave an inward sigh—it was plain that she still had far to go. But the wall before us was hardly a slate for lessons now.

Again I loosed power. At this, my friend pulled me roughly away from her and held me up so that our gazes met.

"What—!" No bewilderment clouded her green eyes now—instead, fear fought rising anger. Frustrated, she swung my toy-form forward so that its floppy forelegs struck the stone where her palm had rested a moment ago.

I pushed those stuffed paws as hard as I could against the barrier, regretting bitterly all the wasted hours when we might have perfected what we carried. Such a gift had to be nurtured by both its possessors or it would bear no fruit for either.

Our first answer was not motion but sound: a bell-like chime I knew of old. The stone blocks within the square she had traced suddenly shone blue. When that color had whirled away as a mist, they were gone, and what lay behind them was opened.

A narrow passage, broken by no door, ran for a short distance. At its end lay a room not unlike those that made up the house above. A table stood in the center with a chair at each end, while to one side was placed a chest like a housewife's hutch with crowded open shelves above, cabinet doors below.

Dropping her bundle onto the table (and thereby raising a cloud of dust), my companion sank into a chair, but not before she had set me directly before her, keeping me upright with both hands. She began to stare.

She was waking, this girl I had chosen—and been chosen by—in her earliest youth, and her newfound sight was piercing the cloak of illusion in which I had been so long enwrapped. The hour had come when I must take the last step. Carefully, I loosed my hold on the appearance of a body filled with straw and covered by short reddish fur through which patches of skin showed where time (and love) had worn it away.

My companion let go her grasp, for I stood erect without support. Now I settled myself on the table, forepaws crossed, sneezing as I disturbed more dust, and waited.

A question came almost at once. "What is your name?"

Speaking aloud, I answered slowly, as if my friend were still the child of years agone.

"By your calling, I am 'Fossi.' And you?"

To exchange names is to set seal upon bonding. The girl held me with her eyes for a moment longer; then she seemed to arrive at a decision.

"I," she spoke briskly, chin high, "am Jeseca, daughter to Welfrid of Crask, merchant. And fear must have driven my wits from me utterly, for I believe an old toy can speak and its paws push aside a stone wall. Fossi, who—and what— are you?"

"What I have always been," I replied. "Your kind is not born with the Sight to see me in my true form, yet such power is now within your grasp. Your mother was Roseline; she was born of this house, but she had not the Talent strongly enough to warrant training. Before her was Aloris, who truly bore the Gift; and before your mother's mother were Catheral, and Vinala, and Darlynn—" I recited the women of my service-roll. To my delight, I saw my newest pupil nod twice at two of those so named.

Then, though the girl's hands no longer touched me, I felt them tremble where they rested on the table. "Those women—" her voice faltered, but she forced herself to continue, "—it is rumored that they were *Wyse*."

"And what does *Wyse* mean to you, Jeseca?"

"Having strange powers," she whispered. Fear was rising in her again, like the dark vapor lifting from a marsh. I wished I might gently coax her free of its clutching tendrils, but there was no time.

Turning, I gestured with a flick of paw at the cupboard; then, to test her a fraction more, I mind-sent a picture of what I would have her do. Slowly she stood, glancing from me to the hutch and back again before she went to obey.

The upper shelves were filled with small pots and sealed jars. Much of what was stored there had doubtless had its virtue leached away by time, but we had no need of salves or simples. At my direction, Jeseca opened the doors below, and from that area she brought forth a flat disk of dark glass which she placed on the table between us.

I glanced down to see myself reflected in its surface. My disguise of the hugged-to-shabbiness plaything was gone; my red-brown fur, living now, was not even dusty. The form I had been given upon first emerging into this world was mine once more: rounded head, large eyes as green as my companion's could be, long hard-muscled body, and two pairs of limbs on which I could either walk erect or take to all fours when the need arose. Yes, it was good to be back, but I needed no mirror to tell me so; and in any event the polished round on the table had not been intended as a tool for physical vanity. I spun the object about and pushed it before Jeseca.

"Think," I ordered her sharply. "Think of someone you know in this city, on this day!"

The girl gasped, bent low over the table. The disk she gazed upon now supplied a window giving onto the outer street. Its circular frame held a grim picture—one that grew ever sharper as I added my own power to its shaping. On the cobbles lay the maid who had run from the house, clothing torn from a body scarcely out of childhood, blood painting flesh and stone alike.

"Ursilla—oh, gods—"

Just then an armsman rose up between us and the slain servant, mercifully blocking her figure from view. As he turned away, we could see that he had a rainbow-hued scarf wound about his bandoleer.

"He must have been in the house—into my things!" cried Jeseca. "Robyon gave me that scarf on my nameday!"

"Yes," I said quietly, watching her. The anger was mounting in her eyes like a tinder-fed flame.

The soldier had stopped and was now peering at something low down. Then, across the muddied and gore-streaked stones, there came creeping toward him—and so into the circle of the viewing disk—a child, scarcely more than an infant.

"Minta! No—*NO!*"

The invader reversed the matchlock he carried, preparing to use the heavy gun as a club. At the same instant, my companion pulled the larger kitchen knife from her belt. As the stock of the weapon swung down toward the child's skull, the point of the knife hit the mirror.

The explosion of power that followed, released so wildly without my ordering, nearly threw me from the table. The farsight-glass itself cracked down the middle, but we could still see the baby, wailing though unhurt. The musketeer had not fared so well; he appeared, curiously, to have been stabbed through the heart. A moment later he fell in a fountain of blood.

"See!" Jeseca's voice was a carrion bird's shriek. "See what I did—and shall do! Let me clear Quirth of all those demons!" Knife still in hand, the girl caught at me, commanding, "Show me more of them, Fossi—*now!*"

For answer, I lifted a paw toward the blade. Jeseca gave a cry of pain and flung the hilt from her as though it had suddenly become too hot to hold; and indeed, it had left an angry weal on her palm. We faced each other as she nursed her hand against her breast. The redness faded from her skin as the flush of rage paled from her cheeks.

"You hurt me." The voice was a child's once more, sullen at a scolding.

I gestured at the glass disk, and the out-sight vanished. "I am sorry, but it was needful. Yes, the Wyse power can do much—very much. But it must only be used with a cool head and a warm heart, for there is this—" Rising, I fixed my eyes on hers and held them there. "Use Wyse-wiles in wrath, for revenge, and in the end the Power will turn upon you."

My companion blinked in surprise. "But you made me look upon that which would rouse my anger," she protested.

"Because," I explained, "your rage unlocked the talent within you, something that had to be done now."

Her hands curled into fists, though it was plain the right one still pained her. "I will *not* throw blood-price away—I shall have it for poor Ursilla and for all the other innocents in Quirth."

"Then learn," I answered. "The dealing of death is not always the best way to pay a score. A wielder of Power can kill, true, but he—or she—can also heal; and for the truly Wyse, the binding up of the world's wounds is a far greater task."

My companion had seated herself again while I was speaking. All the child in her had been burned away by that last flame of heart-heat, and the Jeseca who now faced me was a woman, eager to learn what she could, and should, do.

Then a shadow clouded her bright face. "But what can we do here?" she asked, spreading her hands to indicate the small dingy chamber. "We are trapped." Her voice trailed away uncertainly.

"Not true!" I returned with feeling. The doubt, so deadly to any Wyse work—or wielder—was stretching out its icy tendrils toward her again. At all costs, she must begin this business by believing in herself; but how to make her do it?

After a pause of thought, I had an answer. "Give me your hands," I said, extending my paws as I spoke. My companion looked puzzled but held out her hands, palms up, to cup them.

"Only an hour agone," I began, "I—we—could not have done this, making fur meet flesh in a living touch. At that time, too, you still believed me a small one's night-friend—and yourself a helpless maid.

"But in that same turn of the sand-glass, all such notions have been shattered, even as that mirror—" I indicated the look-round with a nod of my head, "—was cracked by Power. Out of 'traps,' as you would call them, have come freeings: I to my true form and strength, and you to womanhood and knowledge. Littleness and youth are only cocoons, safe places to shelter—like this chamber—till wings are grown."

My friend's smile had returned—this time no mere quirking of the lips but a soul-deep joy. And from the years of our association, I knew her mind to be as quick, as open, as her feelings. Praise was in order. "When your wings of learning are full-fledged," I told her warmly, "who knows to what heights you may—"

"—Wyse?" she finished, and we both laughed. That was my Jeseca. She was, and would be, a familiar beyond price.

ALLIANCE

by Bill McCay

Bill McCay has written over sixty books, featuring everything from knock-knock jokes to no-knock drug raids. His *Star Trek*™ novel *Chains of Command*, written with Eloise Flood, enjoyed two weeks on *The New York Times* Paperback Bestseller List. He is also the author of a five-novel series set in the *Stargate* universe and continuing the action from events at the end of the movie. His short fiction has appeared in the DAW anthologies *A Constellation of Cats* and the upcoming *Vengeance Fantastic*.

TANIT moved stiffly from the Black Land to the Red, from the rich crop-bearing earth to the desert where her house stood beside the other villagers. In the principality of Armant, as in most of the river kingdoms of Nsr, every cubit of arable land was as precious as the gold of Nebet.

After helping her sister's husband carry water from the great river to the crops, all Tanit wanted to do was lie down and rest. But as soon as she entered the mud-brick house, she saw that was not to be.

Her sister Nefert crouched over little Huy as if she could breathe more life into him. The babe had seen but four flood seasons. Unless something could be done to break the fever that held him, he would see no more.

Since the death of her own husband, Tanit had helped the family by bartering herbal remedies for small hurts and sicknesses.

It would go hard with her to lose a nephew. "Is there nothing more to do?" Nefert's voice was pleading.

Tanit began mashing herbs in a cup. "Boil some water— I'll try a new mixture." She hesitated. "Perhaps we should see a healer priest. We should have enough extra grain for an offering."

"We'll see the newcomer—Djedhor." Nefert scowled. "I won't have that fat, useless Thonufer sweating over my boy."

Tanit said nothing as she prepared the herbs for brewing. In her heart, however, she knew something was deeply wrong. Huy seemed to be releasing his hold on life like an elder leaving a worn-out body.

Either that, or something was sucking at his vitality.

The women were able to get a ride on a barge for the trip to the city. Normally, such a journey would make Huy wide-eyed and impossible to hold. Now, though, he lay listlessly in his mother's arms.

They arrived at the wharves of Armant and headed for the temple district. Tanit noticed that many people seemed to be slighting the precincts of Kumae, the local fish god, for the newly-raised idol of the falcon god with the two tall plumes.

Nekheny, she thought. *God of Nekhen. I'm surprised a foreign god has so many followers.*

Fat Thonufer emerged from the entrance of his temple as Tanit and Nefert came abreast.

"The little one seems ill," he said, extending a soft, pudgy hand.

"We have offerings enough for only one prayer." Nefert deftly sidestepped the priest. "We ask help from the heavens."

Thonufer lowered his shaven head, trying to hide his chagrin at seeing another of his supposed flock abandoning him for his new rival.

After only a few moments in the brilliant sunlight, beads of sweat appeared on his face.

Tanit had heard how Djedhor had lampooned Thonufer as "the wet priest of the fishy god."

"My sister's words come from fear for the child," she tried to explain.

"And hawks have seemed stronger of late," the priest said with a touch of bitterness. "Followers of the falcon from Behdet threaten golden Nebet to the north. Now Nekhen encroaches from the south."

All knew that the Prince's strongest ally was Nebet, where the people worshiped Set, a true rival to the falcon gods. If a war of kings and gods were to happen, what would become of little Armant?

"Should we fear battle, holy one?"

Thonufer gave her a keen glance. "There are battles, and then there are battles," he said. "In the hearts of the people, it would appear that Kumae—and I—are losing."

He turned to the temple again. "Tell your sister that Fat Thonufer will pray for—what is the little one's name?"

"Huy," Tanit said.

"Two prayers will go forth," Thonufer said. "In whichever direction."

Bast prowled the outer precincts of the granary, trying to ignore the gnawing pangs of hunger in her belly.

The thought of the food available within those walls nearly drove her to rashness.

But she knew she had to wait until the guardian at the entrance was distracted.

The heavyset guard sat in a patch of shadow. He remained in place, all unaware, as a tiny patch of deeper shadow wafted out from the darkness within the granary.

Bast could see clearly as the bit of darkness spread across the guard's chest. Instantly, his mood changed from bored to irritated. He shifted in his place, looking about as if to find the cause of his sudden discomfort.

He never detected the baneful presence that had attached itself to him.

Hoping to take advantage of the guard's distraction, Bast darted for the entrance.

Instead, a callused foot caught her in the ribs. "Out! Out, thou ill-omened creature!"

Returning to the river, Tanit, Nefert, and Huy passed the granary devoted to Nekheny's offerings. The door guard shouted abuse as he kicked a scrawny cat.

"What do you do there?" Tanit asked. "Doesn't that poor beast protect your grain from the mice and other creatures who would eat it?"

"No more," the guard replied. "Holy Djedhor has decreed other means to control the vermin."

Tanit frowned. She'd only had a glimpse of "Holy Djedhor" as he muttered a quick prayer while a line of concerned mothers held out listless children. A plague that only struck the little ones? It made even less sense.

And, although Djedhor looked every inch the priest— spare, even ascetic in his sparkling clean linen kilt—Tanit felt an unexpected chill as she saw the man.

The guard shouted, streaks of blood on his leg where the cat retaliated. He raised one foot high, determined to do the animal real damage, when Tanit swooped in and picked up the cat.

She had no idea why she did it—the animal could just as easily have turned its claws on her. But except for a yowl of pain from its bruised ribs, the cat lay panting in her arms. Considering how prominent those ribs were, Djedhor's anti-cat pronouncement must have been in force for some time.

Nefert looked worried. "If Holy Djedhor has spoken against the beasts—"

"Perhaps the One from Nekhen can protect his granaries," Tanit said as they walked along. "Our supplies could use guarding from the small nibblers."

Shocked at her sister's near-blasphemy, Nefert walked in

silence. But hope appeared on her face as little Huy showed an interest in Tanit's burden.

Tanit, however, said nothing. She'd often noticed that Huy seemed to revive in the light of day.

But when the shadows grew long, his little bit of strength seemed to fade just like the light.

Bast rested as comfortably as possible in the arms of the two-legged she. Her resources exhausted, the cat had prepared herself for death after that last, defiant swipe of her claws. Rescue had come so unexpectedly, she merely allowed herself to be carried.

She looked dubiously at the human kit in the arms of the other she. Such ones could be troublesome, attempting to see if legs or tail would detach. And their mothers were vengeful to the point of unreason over a mere scratch or bite.

The humans seemed tired enough after arriving at their destination. Bast had recovered sufficiently to go off in search of something to eat.

She found the mouse in the darkness of the grain storehouse. But the psychic stink from the animal sent her lips rippling back from her fangs. Her prey was possessed by one of the animate shadows the two-legs apparently couldn't see.

Bast had experience with these creatures. They literally threw off a stench of ill-feeling—emotions like fear and anger, mixed with painfully avid hunger. These baneful ones lusted for bodily experiences. And they achieved those experiences by overpowering the minds of weak creatures who lived in the dark. The scuttlers on six legs, the long-tailed nibblers of grain . . . these were their psychic prey.

Occasionally, larger, braver shadows tried to seize other minds. Bast had encountered an extremely voracious shadow which had tried to take her. It might have succeeded had Bast's mother not joined the fight. Since that first battle, Bast had learned much about fighting these baneful ones. Killing the host, besides offering a welcome release, often

destroyed the shadow. Its greed for life would keep it in the
body too long.

So, when Bast pounced on her prey, she was surprised.
The shadow abandoned its host even as she leaped.

Strange, Bast thought. And very different . . .

As darkness fell, Huy's vital energy began ebbing again.
Nefert's face was a mask of grief. Her husband Piay cursed
all priests.

Tanit didn't eat, in spite of her hunger and fatigue. She
would spend the night trying something few had done since
the priesthoods arose. Spirit-walking by the common folk
was frowned on by the organized religions. But it was a desperate last resort for peasant healers.

Tanit had helped her mother go forth in search of answers
for difficult cases. If Huy was to be saved, she'd have to
venture out alone.

She prepared the herbs as the others went to sleep. Then
she sat up, staring into the flame of a small oil lamp. The
world of flesh and blood slowly receded. All she saw was
light and shadow. The little house had more shadows than
she'd have imagined.

One of them moved. It seemed to float insubstantially
through the air, settling on a patch of light, which quickly
began to dim.

What *was* that light? Tanit wondered. Not the lamp.
Slowly, she began to realize. That was where Huy lay
asleep.

After feeding, Bast explored the village, returning to her
humans' place well after darkness had fallen. The den was
all but dark, except for a low-burning flame. The she who'd
saved her sat cross-legged on the floor, glassy-eyed. She
stared with horror at the little one.

Bast turned to look—and hissed. One of the baneful shadows floated over the kit's face, waxing larger—fattening on
the young one's life!

Approaching stiff-backed, Bast blasted the creature with her rage, dislodging it. But the damnable thing returned to the kit!

Now Bast recognized this shadow. It was the one that had controlled the mouse she'd eaten. No wonder the thing had abandoned the little nibbler. It had larger prey in mind! Even as Bast watched, the monstrous thing grew larger . . . stronger.

It not only resisted her mental thrusts, but spewed its own disgusting darkness at her.

To kill the creature, kill its host. That was ancient wisdom among her kind. But how could she repay the humans for saving her by killing their young one?

She turned to her erstwhile savior, and their eyes met.

Tanit had remained frozen, watching the darkness devour Huy's light. Then a small, blazing form had entered and done battle with the shadow. But the darkness would not be dislodged.

A moment later, her eyes rested on the brightness, and Tanit felt herself moving—not her body, but her spirit.

She touched the brightness, and discovered—the cat?

Surprise almost broke the strange connection. Then Tanit found herself looking at the world through the eyes of . . . Bast. That was how the cat called herself.

It was almost like being in the real world again, except for the strange distortions of scale. Huy, for instance, seemed twice her size.

And, much more clearly, she could see the shadow devouring the babe's vital essence.

Bast blasted the darkness with all her rage and revulsion.

Could I do the same? Tanit wondered. She called on her love and concern for the little one, flinging her feelings—

And the shadow flinched!

Tanit drew on her feelings again and felt Bast joining her. Together they pushed and ripped at the monstrous thing, shredding its being.

The shadow disengaged from Huy, trying to escape. But Bast extended psychic claws, somehow hooking into the thing. Tanit continued to savage it.

Tanit executed a mental thrust, eliciting a stink of agony from the baneful shadow. For an instant, strange thoughts and images invaded her mind as the shadow-creature seemed to scream for aid.

One image stood out. Tanit recognized the corporeal form of Djedhor. But roiling around him was a pall of darkness that made their present enemy seem like the merest mite.

The alien images faded in the shadow's psychic death shriek.

Then Tanit found herself back in the physical world, toppling sideways as if every muscle had failed.

Luckily, she fell onto the homespun shawl that had slipped from her shoulders. Tanit closed her eyes, trying to fit herself back into her body again.

She felt warm breath on her cheeks, then a brief, damp, rough contact. Opening her eyes, she found Bast trying to rouse her. Their eyes met again.

It wasn't the same communion Tanit had experienced in the intangible realm. But it was a definite connection. Tanit could read Bast's surprise. The furred one had never had such an encounter either. She was also impressed by Tanit's strength.

Tanit slowly pushed herself upright, opening her hands to the cat who immediately crawled into her lap. Their contact was a strange mingling of the physical and psychic. Tanit "heard" a silent cat-yowl of victory.

They had won, hadn't they? Huy had been saved.

Cradling the cat, Tanit turned to the little one. He sighed, moving in his dream. Already he was beginning to look stronger.

Tanit frowned. Huy was saved. But what of the other children? If that strange flash of alien insight was to be believed, an army of shadows served the monster that enshrouded Djedhor. They were driving desperate parents to the service of the Nekhenite god.

Bast roused at the thought of other shadows. Her thought was clear. Fight!

In the space of weeks, Tanit and Bast traveled up- and downriver, banishing shadows from hundreds of children. Djedhor's proscriptions of "unclean beasts" crumbled in the face of successful cures. And in each village, Bast went among her feline fellows, warning them to watch and ward. Every healer whom Tanit met was also told of the tremendous help cats could provide in dealing with the unseen world.

It was inevitable, perhaps, that the shadows should respond.

Tanit was tired. She'd spent yet another evening routing dark creatures from little children. All she wished to do was sleep.

She struggled back to consciousness, not merely from a mental warning but from hisses and yowls from Bast. The hamlet they were visiting had been hit worse than most during the flood season. The adobe house was little more than a hovel—but the best the villagers could provide.

The interior was dark—and not merely in the physical sense. Tanit's connection to Bast gave her the sense of dozens of living shadows flitting about. Her hosts slept heavily—unnaturally, given the amount of noise Bast was making. A sense of oppression weighed down on Tanit as she rose and dressed.

Then Djedhor entered the house.

Tanit recognized him, not by sight, but by her psychic senses. The darkness in the house seemed to increase a hundredfold.

"Woman." The priest's fine, powerful voice hissed out of the shadows. "You have set yourself against my purpose, and the purposes of the one I serve."

"Is that your voice, 'Holy Djedhor'?" Tanit asked. "Or

the voice of the abomination that rides you? I do not think that is the One of Nekhen."

"I know nothing of the gods you humans claim to serve," There was no doubt whose voice spoke now. "There is but power. That is what the one who serves me sought. I have given him great dominion."

"And it merely cost him his soul."

"A small price, that I might walk the earth," the great shadow responded. "It took considerable effort, binding the lesser ones of my sort to act at my command. But now they serve, and the glory of Nekheny spreads."

"You said you know nothing of gods."

"But I know much of humans," the shadow said. "As the sway of the Nekhenite god expands, so does the power of Nekhen the city. And with every success, the power of my vessel grows as well."

Tanit fought hard to retain control over her anger. She feared she would need it soon. "And for this power, you would threaten every child in Armant."

"I would sacrifice every child on this great river of yours," the shadow coldly replied. "Your kind is less to me than that four-legged creature is to you. My experiments here have shown a way to spread my power throughout this plane of existence."

Unbidden, pictures of the creature's proposed triumph crept into Tanit's brain. The kings of the river nations all bowed to the Nekhenite god. And who spoke for that god? Djedhor.

"You, however, have chosen to block this plan," Djedhor's voice rustled like a breeze through the reeds. "This cannot be allowed."

All the time the creature had been talking, Tanit had been aware of a deepening in the darkness around her. It seemed as if every lesser shadow in the area had been drawn in to heighten the gloom. Now it moved to crush Tanit and Bast.

Tanit's hand went to the cat, and power flowed along that

connection. Together, they pushed back against the en-
croaching shadows, who retreated before them.

But for each thrust, the darkness regrouped and advanced
again. Neither Bast nor Tanit could reach the master of shadows reposing in Djedhor's body.

"You show surprising strength for one of your blind,
solid kind," the creature of darkness said through Djedhor.
"But you cannot match what I have amassed."

The assembled shadows seemed to congeal into a single
darkness of crushing proportions. It overlay Tanit and Bast
like a great, smothering fog. In a way, it was similar to the
spirit-walk Tanit had attempted. Her body seemed to recede.

But this was no going forth. This was more an exile, an
attempt to shut her body down. Dimly, Tanit became aware
that her breathing slowed, the pumping of her heart began to
lessen. . . .

A choked yowl came from out of the utter dark—Bast,
defiant to the last.

Then, faintly, an answering yowl seemed to come from a
great distance. Tanit's guttering consciousness realized the
faintness was not the result of physical distance, but rather,
of her soul's faltering connection with the flesh.

But then the caterwauling grew louder—stronger—as
Tanit came back to herself. From the sound of it, every cat
in the area had answered Bast's last call. They flung themselves into battle with the thing that rode Djedhor. With the
great shadow momentarily distracted, Tanit and Bast were
able to disperse its minions.

Tanit took a long, grateful gulp of air.

"These vermin have merely won you a reprieve," the
thing within Djedhor promised. Blackness lashed forth, extinguishing the life of one of the cats as easily as breath
snuffed out a candle.

Still the cats without continued their attack.

Darkness swirled around Tanit and Bast, congealing
again.

But the gathering attack faltered. A new force had entered

the struggle. Pinpoints of brightness appeared in the wall of blackness surrounding Tanit. The great shadow's minions broke apart, contending with beings of light.

Bast joined with the bright beings, blasting with all her psychic might at the disarrayed darkness.

Tanit reached for the cat both physically and mentally. For the moment at least, the lesser evils were diverted. They must deal with the great danger.

The amorphous shadow around Djedhor seemed to grow darker and thicker as the interior of the house grew brighter. A human figure appeared in the entranceway, not swathed in darkness like Djedhor, but surrounded by hundreds of gleaming motes of brightness.

A familiar figure—fat Thonufer.

"My other opponent." Scorn dripped from Djedhor's voice. "Do you hope to match me?"

"No," Thonufer admitted. "But with help, I hope to best you."

Behind the fat priest came a hissing, spitting swarm of cats. Felines and light-motes surrounded Djedhor, dissipating the darkness swirling about him.

Tanit cringed at the psychic roar from the great shadow. It lashed out, extinguishing a score of tiny lights. But even as the darkness concentrated for a counterattack, the cats and creatures of light shredded the creature's intangible fabric.

Directing their own psychic blasts, Tanit and Bast joined the attack.

Even so, it was a terrifyingly close battle. Many light-motes vanished in the fray. Several more cats had their lives extinguished. But in the end, the much-reduced blackness around Djedhor could no longer stand. With a final, silent cry, the great shadow congealed, shrank, and went . . . elsewhere.

The merest brush with that alien realm made Tanit's senses swim.

Djedhor stood before them, his eyes, wide, free . . . and

soulless. Whatever was left of the hagridden priest was not enough to animate his body. That fine human form tottered, crumpled . . . fell to the earthen floor.

Bereft of their greater brother's command, the lesser shadows quickly dissipated or fled.

The cats broke out in victory yowls, quickly hushed by Bast. Human ears did not love cat-cries. And who knew how long the villagers would remain in their unnatural sleep?

Thonufer ponderously knelt to check the heap that had once been Djedhor. Only a few light-motes remained around him, providing barely as much illumination as a small lamp.

"Lost," the priest said quietly. "He could not survive anymore without that other indweller."

Thonufer clumsily regained his feet. "So, little sister," he said. "You have ventured into the unseen realm—and helped defeat a great evil."

Tanit regarded him with her new senses and found no puppet, but only a man.

"No, I am not ridden as Djedhor was." Thonufer shook his head. "And, indeed, as blind as most of our kind. I did not recognize Djedhor for what he was."

Tanit gestured to the points of brightness still swirling about the priest. "What—how—?"

"You fought a desperate battle against creatures of darkness," Thonufer said gently. "Why should you be surprised that there are also creatures of light? I do not control them, as our dark foe did the shadows. But in extremity, the light can be called upon."

Even as he spoke, more of the light-motes flew away. Tanit knelt to light a lamp.

"As to how they might be called, there are—" Thonufer gave here a wry smile and patted his ample stomach. "There are other means than starving oneself and attempting a spirit-walk."

He became more serious as he surveyed the room. Four cats lay motionless besides the defunct Djedhor. "We must move the body, I fear. Djedhor bears no marks of violent death. But I would not hear charges of magical murder leveled against you."

They left Djedhor at the far end of the village. Bast regarded them with unblinking eyes.

Thonufer returned to the house, this time gently gathering up the dead cats. "As for these brave ones . . . burial, I think."

He looked down as Bast sinuously made her way around his legs, rubbing against him. "I am accepted, I see. Good."

The priest turned to Tanit. "You have much to learn, little sister, of the struggle between light and darkness. I will teach you what I can."

They stepped out of the house, followed by Bast. "And you, in turn, will teach me of these little ones who seem to see so clearly where our eyes are blind."

They buried the cats with Bast standing as silent witness. Tanit picked up her furred companion and walked with Thonufer. Bast continued to regard the priest with enigmatic eyes.

"Yes, there is much to be learned," Thonufer said. "And much to be gained." He cautiously put forth a finger and stroked the fur on Bast's head. "In our unending war, it would be a good thing to have allies."

Bast yawned, shifted to a more comfortable position in Tanit's arms, and extended her head for a little more rubbing between the ears.

Author's Note

As someone who's deathly allergic to cats, I don't know why I find myself writing about them. Ah, well. Catlike folks and pre-Dynastic Egypt played a big part in my *Stargate* novels, just as penguinlike aliens had their place in *Chains of Command*, the *Star Trek* novel I wrote with Eloise Flood. And let's not talk about the parade of dogs, horses, birds (and, I think, even a camel) that has graced the pages of various juvenile books I've written over the years.

Alliance represents something of a prequel to my story *Death Song* which is anthologized in *A Constellation of Cats*. Considering that something like eight thousand years fall between the two stories, you shouldn't expect the same characters.

Still, if you liked one, you might like the other.

CATSEYE

by Laura Anne Gilman

Laura Anne Gilman is the author, with Josepha Sherman, of two *Buffy, the Vampire Slayer* novels, *Deep Water* and *Visitors,* plus another media tie-in novel, *The Shadows Between,* under the name L. A. Liverakos. Her short fiction has been regularly published since 1994, in magazines such as *Amazing Stories* and *Dreams of Decadence,* and almost a dozen different anthologies, including *Did You Say Chicks?* and *Blood Thirst: 100 Years of Vampire Fiction.* She has also edited two anthologies of her own, *Otherwere* and *Treachery and Treason.* In her spare time, she edits books and attends meetings. You can find her online at http://www.sff.net/people/lauraanne.gilman

THERE are some lessons we know from birth. When to sleep, when to rise. Who to love, and who not. When to watch. And when to strike.

He shouldn't have touched her. It's that simple. He should have wandered by, handsome-man amble, taken one look, and moved on. I was given to her at birth, hers were the first hands that held me. She wasn't for the likes of him. Most of his kind know better; they are not fools, not by any means. Most look for other partners, more accommodating. More uncomprehending.

He thought she was alone.

That was his worst mistake.

Food came from her hand, and comfort. She touches, mends. We grew together, came into our strength together. The harmed come to her without effort, without volition. I watch, lurk, tangle underfoot. But some will not be healed; they hug their wounds to them like stigmata. I understand, but she cannot.

It is a blindness in her; she does not see the movement in the corner of her eyes, the gathering of smallness, small minds, small hearts, small souls. She always sang; to her plants, her pets, her friends. Total strangers in the street. Nothing held back. And her voice matured with his passion, the notes gold in sunlight, soft and true. And with that passion came new strength; she opened doors inside herself we had not seen before, found rooms there that made her laugh with delight.

Like sunlight, I bask in her song. It is electric and balm, earth and water and air and fire.

But in dawn and dusk she still whispered to me in the voice of silver and moonlight. And we had secrets of our own. As it was meant to be.

Love is the magic of different layers; no one greater, no one the same.

He had to learn that. I suspected he would not.

"You're so beautiful," he said, lying in the bed one lazy morning, touching her hair, her face, her stomach. The comforter is shoved to their feet, the scent of lovemaking heavy on the sheets. "I can't believe you're mine." She smiles, stroking his hair, her eyes sad and knowing as they meet mine.

I see what others only guess at. I know the secrets speakers have forgotten.

Passion is a possessive. Love isn't. Magic can't be.

* * *

We sit, almost eye to eye. He folds the newspaper, ignores me. He would prefer a dog, something obedient, trained. It bothers him that I do not look away. She laughs at his grumbles, touches my spine lightly. "Cats are reminders of our pride," she tells him. I groom fur back into place, blink knowingly at them both. He puts the paper down, leaves the room, and she sighs. "Patience."

I don't know which of us she's talking to.

Midafternoon sunlight dapples the greenhouse. She moves through rows of green, her mind distracted.

"I don't want you spending so much time with him. With her. With them."

With anyone but him.

She sings to the herbs, but they will not grow.

When he sleeps, she wakes. Still-silent in the moonlight.

She loves him.

I don't trust him.

He is playful, charming, and the radio plays as they tease and linger over dinner. He reads the newspaper out loud, asks her opinions, doesn't step on my tail. I should be content.

My whiskers twitch. I don't like the way he sits.

She sings softly under her breath, trails of moonlight under fluorescent tubes. I stroke against her knees, perch on the windowsill, wait.

All it takes is one misstep.

"You can't do anything right, can you?"

A bitter fight, ending with anger, slammed doors, silent accusations; she is a peaceable sort, there is no other way she could be different.

He thought that meant she was weak.

She loves him.

I hate him.

*   *   *

The sky is thick and cold. Artificial lights fill the greenhouse, but make no difference. Nothing grows.

"You're such a stupid bitch. I can't believe I put up with you."

I watch him now. Room to room, out the window when he leaves. Not hiding what I'm doing, not pretending to be anything but what I am. He was warned.

She breathes quietly in her room.

I waited. She's ready now.

Love is magic of layers. Hate is a narrow edge. Whisker of cat, tear of woman. Some spells need only a whisper of assent, and a slow feline wink.

He should have learned that. It's too late now.

BUSINESS AS USUAL

by Diane A. S. Stuckart

Having lived most of her life on the prairie lands of north central Texas, Diane A. S. Stuckart vows one day to move to the forest. She has a degree in journalism from the University of Oklahoma and has published four award-winning historical romances writing as Alexa Smart. Other of her fantasy stories appear in *A Dangerous Magic* and *A Constellation of Cats.*

"EEK!"

Jane Riverspoon slapped her latte cup atop the credenza and scrambled onto her desk in the stereotypical "woman-spots-rodent-and-panics" reaction immortalized by generations of male comedy writers. A heartbeat later, she realized what she had just done and felt herself blush. Darn it all, she hated being a female cliché And surely she hadn't actually said, "Eek," had she?

She had.

She tried to assume a more casual pose, praying that no one else was in the office on this early Saturday morning. Should one of her coworkers see her like this, perched on hands and knees between her computer and her overflowing in box, she'd hear about it for months to come. But if there was one thing she hated more than being the butt of workplace jokes, it was rats. And, unless she was hallucinating, she'd just spotted one heck of a big one among the cardboard boxes stacked in the corner of her new office.

Unfortunately, those weren't just any boxes. Inside them were the personal effects of the woman who, until her death in an automobile accident the week before, had been Valiant Data Systems' top salesperson . . . the late and decidedly unlamented Tiffany Glass. Tiff reportedly had been on her cell phone yelling at the assistant sales manager just moments prior to the collision between her speeding Lexus and a concrete bridge abutment. The official cause of death had been massive head trauma. Corporate rumor, however, had it that the only reason she'd actually died was because a dislodged piece of rebar had pierced her chest in the manner traditionally reserved for dispatching vampires.

That was one bit of gossip Jane was inclined to believe.

She frowned a little, recalling the person who had been the bane of her existence since she'd hired on at the information systems giant six months earlier. What she'd done to incur the other woman's disdain, Jane had never known. Maybe it had been because she'd accidentally sat in Tiff's usual spot during the first sales meeting she'd attended there. Possibly it was because the receptionist once had given Jane a customer lead that should have gone to the other woman. Or perhaps it simply had been the business world's version of cheerleader versus brainiac, the same mean-spirited rivalry Jane recalled all too well from her painful high school years.

Tiff was the poster girl for just-turned-thirty female executives on the way up the Dallas corporate ladder. She had it all . . . a boob job that would make a Hooters girl weep in envy; inch-long acrylic nails polished bitch-red; bleached hair laminated into an artful if unmoving bob. As for Jane, she still looked like the liberal arts graduate that she was. Hers were the same meager breasts that had been bestowed upon her at puberty; her nails were unpolished and usually bitten to the quick; and her hair was the same indeterminate shade of brown it had been since childhood.

No matter the cause of their rift, Tiffany seemingly had been on a mission to make Jane's life miserable. Some days, it was missed phone messages or lost sales reports; others, it was cruel whispers in the hallway, or an important meeting to which she'd somehow not been invited. Subtle sabotage, to be sure—and never anything that Jane actually could prove was deliberate—but effective nonetheless. The result was that Jane found herself running less on sleep and more on caffeine, plagued by the knowledge she wasn't keeping up with the rest of the sales staff.

Thus, it had been all the more ironic when Tiff's corner office had become Jane's.

Her good fortune literally had been the luck of the draw. All the salespeople had tossed their names, raffle-style, into a VDS gimme cap in hopes of snagging that prized bit of office real estate. Jane, for once, had won.

While she was moving the contents of her cubicle into her new abode, Facilities had been packing up Tiffany's personal effects and stacking them into the corner. They had assured her that someone would send the boxes down to Shipping to be forwarded to the dead woman's family back in east Texas. Obviously, no one had . . . and now, some kind of creature was pawing through Tiffany Glass' belongings.

Jane leaned forward, trying to get a better look at the topmost box. Maybe it hadn't been a rat, after all. For one thing, what she'd seen had been the size of a half-grown cat, far larger than any rodent outside a nature channel special. Maybe the box's contents simply had shifted as she walked past. Perhaps what she'd thought was a rat had been a stuffed animal or some sort that had been packed away with the rest of Tiffany's things.

She tried to recall if she'd ever noticed anything cute and cuddly displayed in the dead woman's office. A wall's worth of plaques, including VDS' coveted copper-and-wood Salesperson of the Year award, yes. Pictures of Tiff with various Dallas sports celebrities, definitely. A large ceramic phallus she kept prominently displayed so that no sexist male coworker could claim she wished she had one. But Jane could not recall a single beanbag creature or furry stuffed anything ever sitting on her bookshelf. So that could only mean—

"Rat!" she shrieked as a rodentlike snout thrust its way out of the box in question.

While she fumbled for her phone and punched in an extension—*dear God, let someone from Facilities be in today!*—a large black rat wriggled from beneath the framed certificate that lay, glass up, atop the rest of the box's contents. Clambering onto the tablelike surface it presented, the rat fixed her with shiny black eyes that held a distinctly malevolent gleam. But even as Jane heard a bored voice answer the phone, "Facilities, Harley speaking," the creature reared up on its hind legs and planted tiny rodent fists on furry plump hips.

"For chrissakes, what are you doing on the desk?" the rat squeaked in a Munchkinlike voice. "You look like a freakin' idiot!"

Jane dropped the receiver. It slithered its coiled length down the side of the desk and hit the carpeted floor with a muffled clatter. Vaguely, she was aware of a distant voice repeating, "Facilities," the sound replaced a moment later by the buzz of a dial tone.

Too much latte, not enough sleep, she thought with a faint moan and slumped back on her heels. Just a momentary lapse in reality. The rat hadn't said anything. Had it?

"You are such a loser," the rat went on, briefly forming one little rat paw into—could it be?—a miniature L. "I don't know how in hell you keep from getting fired. Now, get down before someone sees you."

Jane gulped but obediently slid off the desk and into the oversized leather chair behind it. Shifting slightly—the chair still bore the imprint of Tiff's more curvaceous butt and was not yet a cozy fit—she gulped again and gripped the edge of the desk. Time to find out whether or not she had just walked smack into the middle of an *X-Files* episode.

"Uh, excuse me, Mister Rat," she ventured, "were you talking to me?"

"That's *Ms.* Rat, you idiot," the creature exclaimed, cocking one hip and staring down its pointed nose at her in a manner that was vaguely familiar . . . not that Jane knew any other rats. "Jeez, no wonder you never get laid. You can't tell the boys from the girls."

"That's not true," Jane huffed. "Why, last month, Robert and I—"

She broke off abruptly and slapped one hand over her mouth. Dear God, what was in that latte she'd been drinking? Not only was she holding a conversation with a rat, she'd almost been confessing details of her minimalist sex life to it! Her mind flashed back over the past month's newspaper headlines, but she couldn't recall any stories about psychedelic drugs being slipped into four-dollar cups of coffee. But what other explanation could there be?

The rat, meanwhile, tilted its head questioningly. "Robert, eh? You mean Robert-with-all-the-piercings who works at Java Central?" it asked, naming the coffee shop down the block that was Jane's favorite spot. "I thought you were acting more idiotic than usual that day he waited on us. Jeez, talk about robbing the cradle . . . what is he, twenty?"

"He's twenty-five. But how do you know him? And what do you mean, waited on us?"

"You are so clueless, Plain Jane, I almost feel sorry for you. Haven't you figured out who I am yet?"

Jane cautiously shook her head, though a very bad feeling had begun to sink little rodent claws into her. It was more than the fact that a giant rat was talking to her, and that she was talking back. Something about the creature's mannerisms was unnervingly familiar, as was its loud and rather crude way of expressing itself. It occurred to her, too, that only one of her coworkers had ever accompanied her to Java Central and might have guessed about her and Robert . . .

the very same coworker who was the sole person since high school to nickname her Plain Jane.

"Oh, my God," she breathed in disbelief. "Tiffany, is that you?"

"In the flesh. Or in the fur, if you prefer."

Jane bit back a moan and shut her eyes, aware of a loud buzzing in her head that had nothing to do with the dangling telephone receiver. *I promise, I'll give up caffeine . . . right this minute, cold turkey,* she swore in silent desperation. *Just let it—her—be gone when I open my eyes again.*

Unfortunately, her bargain must have gone unheard in Higher Realms. When she finally ventured another look, the rat was still perched on the glass-topped certificate of achievement, its sharp rodent teeth bared in what could only be described as a sneer.

"But you're dead," Jane protested in a voice that, even to her own ears, verged unsettlingly on a wail. "Have you come back to haunt me just because I've got your office now?

"Haunt you?" Tiff the rat smacked herself on the forehead with an open paw. "Are you a total moron, or do you just play one on TV? I'd have to be a ghost to haunt you. Do I look like a freakin' ghost?" She waved furry little arms, pantomiming a sheet-wearing phantom, and then shook her head and answered her own question. "No, I don't think so."

"But you are dead?"

"I *was* dead, but I'm not anymore. I'm reincarnated."

Reincarnated? As a rat?

Jane stared at her former coworker and suppressed a wild urge to laugh. If what she was saying were true, talk about a classic case of "you are what you were." Obviously, Someone up there had been watching Tiffany Glass and taking copious notes.

As if reading her thoughts, Tiff's sneer morphed into a scowl. "All right, I'm going to explain it to you just one time, and then we're never going to talk about it again. You know how you get an annual performance review here at VDS? Depending on your sales numbers, you get a raise or a promotion or—" she paused and glanced about her, "—a corner office. Well, the same sort of thing happens after you die. Before you can proceed to a permanent afterlife, you've got to stop by the heavenly version of HR for a little chat about how you did while you were down here on Earth."

"I guess things didn't go too well?" Jane ventured sympathetically, recalling a few less-than-stellar performance reviews of her own.

Tiff caught up her scaly tail in one paw and gave it a peevish twirl. "Obviously, they made a mistake and mixed up my files with someone else's," she replied with a sniff. "Imagine, they said I hadn't had a positive influence on people while I was alive. I don't know how anyone could think that. You saw how crowded my memorial service was!"

Indeed, the funeral home had been packed . . . though, from the whispers she'd overheard, Jane had guessed that most of the so-called mourners had shown up just to make sure Tiffany really was dead. That, and to chow down on the lavish buffet that VDS' president thoughtfully had provided afterward.

"Oh, you did have an influence," she assured Tiff. "I can testify to that personally."

"Yeah, whatever. Anyhow, they gave me a couple of job assignments I have to fulfill before I can get my—" she dropped her tail and made invisible quote marks with her paws, "—promotion. First, I had to come back to Earth as a freakin' rat, for chrissakes. Second . . . and this is the really crappy part . . . I have to help whoever ended up with my old office become Salesperson of the Year. And, unfortunately, that person is you, Plain Jane."

"Me?"

Jane slumped back in her chair again. The one time she finally rated divine intercession, and it had to be in the form of a foul-tempered guardian rat named Tiffany Glass. Why couldn't she get an angel, like everyone else?

Tiff seemed not to notice her dismay, however, caught up as she was in her own irritation. "Jeez, how hard would it have been for a bunch of celestial beings to rig that drawing so that someone else would win? I told them to give me the new guy, Pete Eastwood. Him, I wouldn't have minded helping. Or even what's-his-face, the guy who transferred from the St. Louis branch last year."

"Marty Preston?" Jane was faintly supplied.

Tiff nodded and smacked her little rat jaws in appreciation. "Yeah, talk about a hunk." Then she narrowed her black eyes in Jane's direction once more. "But I guess the Head Honcho up there has a warped sense of humor, which is why I'm stuck with—" she paused and did the L thing with one paw again, "—you."

At that last insult, Jane's dismay hardened into pique. Bad enough she'd had to put up with Tiffany the first time around. No way was she going to put up with the witch for a second lifetime, award or not.

She straightened in the leather chair and gave the rat an equally chill look. "Well, I hate to break it to you, Tiff, but I don't want your help. I guess you'll have to find another way to earn your angel wings, or whatever it is they give you. Now, why don't you go find a cat to play with, and leave me alone?"

"Not so fast, Plain Jane!"

With a sound unnervingly like a snarl, the rat sprang from its spot atop the boxes and landed with a thump on the desktop. Jane yelped and shoved away, leather smacking against wood as her chair hit the credenza. Tiff, meanwhile, reared onto her hind legs once more and fixed her with an evil glare.

"Let's get a couple of things straight," she squeaked in a menacing tone. "No way am I going to spend eternity as a rat. I'm going to make you Salesperson of the Year, and you're going to let me do it, understand? Or, believe me, I'll make your life a living hell!"

Jane gulped, envisioning the kind of havoc that Tiff, in rat form, could unleash. Sharp bites on the ankle, for one thing. Little rat paws tearing through her files, for another.

And what if Tiff decided to follow her home, and plague her there?

Jane gulped again. Assuming for a moment that what was happening right now was not some latte-induced delusion, but reality, what did agreeing to the rat's plan actually mean? If, with Tiff's help, she won that award, she'd gain all sorts of perks. Given that she consistently ranked not-in-the-top-ten among the sales force, that would be something to celebrate, indeed. But how much of Tiff in rat form could she take?

She shot a surreptitious glance at the twelve-month calendar hanging on one wall. The Salesperson of the Year award was always conferred during the annual general sales meeting, which coincided with the end of VDS' fiscal year. That date was almost exactly six weeks away . . . the end of June. She'd already suffered through half a year with Her Bitchiness, so how bad could another few weeks of such misery be?

And, did she have any other choice?

A her reluctant nod, Tiff bared sharp teeth in a ratty little grin. "I knew you'd see it my way, Plain Jane. Now, why don't you pour me a bit of your latte, and we'll talk business."

"You sent out a meeting request in my name?" Jane squeaked the following Monday morning, her voice almost as shrill as a certain rat's.

She'd slunk into her new office at the usual time, hoping against hope that she'd just dreamed that unpleasant weekend encounter with a reincarnated Tiffany Glass. Unfortunately, she hadn't. Tiff was waiting for her, lounging atop her credenza and munching from a bag of spicy peanuts.

Her first words had been a blunt, "For chrissakes, Plain Jane, if you want to be Salesperson of the Year, you'd better start getting your ass into the office before 8:00 A.M." And then she had dropped her little rat bombshell . . . the news that, over the weekend, she'd logged onto the computer as Jane and sent out an e-mail regarding a meeting later that day.

Her first sips of latte churning in her gut, Jane flipped on her computer and punched in her password. A moment later, she was in her office planning calendar, the software program that linked all of VDS' workers via e-mail and allowed every employee to view everyone else's meeting schedules. There it was, blocked out from 2 P.M. to 3 P.M. Monday, this very afternoon, a sales strategy session to be headed by Jane Riverspoon. Worse, the topic of said session was regaining the multimillion dollar Rubicon International account . . . a customer that had parted ways most unpleasantly with VDS a few months earlier. Already, half the sales reps and a handful of upper management had e-mailed their intention to attend.

She spun about in her leather chair to face Tiffany. While Jane had been otherwise occupied with the computer, the rat had commandeered her half-full vanilla latte and was noisily drinking it through a bendy straw. Coffee foam clung to her black whiskers, so that she looked like the "Got Milk?" poster child for the rodent set.

"I can't believe you did this," Jane moaned in despair. "We went over everything on Saturday—numbers, forecasts, sales leads—and not one time did you say anything about holding a meeting. I'm not prepared. I don't have notes. I—"

"Jeez, get a grip!" Tiff exclaimed and pushed aside her straw. "Do you think I just sat on my butt here all weekend? I already wrote up the entire proposal, and made a whole bunch of overheads to go along with it. All you have to do is follow the outlines and try to sound halfway intelligent. It's on the printer, so go get it."

So unnerving was the thought of a rat typing at her computer that Jane was glad for the excuse to flee her office. Yuck, little rat paws where her fingers had just been! She'd have to whip out her hand sanitizer and douse the keyboard . . . but only when Tiff was not looking.

By the time Jane returned from the printer room, sheaf of papers in hand, Tiff had abandoned the latte and was once more rummaging through the topmost box of her belongings. Jane set down the printout and picked up her Java Central to-go bag, then shot a guilty look in Tiff's direction. Were spicy peanuts all it—she—had had to eat the past two days? Though Jane had armed herself with a bagel, she hadn't thought to bring her guardian rat any breakfast. Indeed, she had neglected to provide her with food and water over the weekend, but had beat a hasty retreat from the office the moment Tiffany had dismissed her. And, much as she disliked the woman—er, rodent—she couldn't just let her starve.

"Uh, Tiff," she ventured, "are you still hungry? Do you want me to bring you more food?"

Tiff poked her head out from the top of the box. "Well, jeez, a little something from Andre's"—she named the bistro across the street from the coffee house, "—would have been nice. But I already went down to the breakroom before everyone got here. You know, those sausage biscuit thingees aren't half bad, even though they're kind of squished by the time you drag them out the back of the vending machine."

Jane nodded, even as she made a squeamish mental note not to patronize the sandwich machines while Tiff was still on the premises. For now, however, she shut the door lest someone notice her unwelcome companion, then settled at her desk and began reading through the proposal that Tiffany had written for her.

A clatter interrupted her halfway down the first page. She glanced up to see Tiff on the floor wrestling with what appeared to be a small silk bag. Deftly, she grabbed it up in her jaws and scampered back over to the credenza, then scrambled up one wooden leg like a furry little Russian gymnast. Once atop it again, she unzipped the bag with nimble rat paws and dumped out its contents . . . the veritable arsenal of cosmetics that she'd used while in human form.

"For chrissakes, don't waste time looking at me," she

squeaked as she noticed Jane's scrutiny. "Read the freakin' proposal, already!" Jane obediently returned her gaze to the outline, though she couldn't help but send a fascinated glance or two over her shoulder between pages.

From the collection of designer cosmetics, Tiff had pulled out a mirrored compact, which she'd propped open, and a mascara tube. Rather than using the latter's accompanying wand, however, she held what appeared to be a toothpick with one gnawed end. Dipping it into the tube, she expertly ran the makeshift brush across her thinly lashed eyes. That accomplished, she twisted open a bottle of nail polish and, using another modified toothpick, began painting her little rat claws a bloody shade of red.

A quarter of an hour later, she looked like the Tammy Faye Baker of the rodent world.

"Well, there's no point in not making the best of what you're stuck with," she peevishly explained as she admired one painted paw. "You should take a hint, Plain Jane. A little fixing up would do wonders for you, too."

Jane ignored the jibe, keeping her attention fixed on the proposal. Dislike Tiff as she did, she still had to admit that her strategy for reclaiming this client was incredibly well thought out . . . brilliant, in fact. Indeed, most of the ideas outlined were ones that Jane never would have come up with by herself. Tiff might have been as big a rat alive as she was dead, but no one could deny that, in any incarnation, she was one hell of a salesperson.

And, if Jane followed this carefully laid out plan to the letter, she just might become one hell of a salesperson, herself.

"Okay, I can do this," she agreed, feeling an unfamiliar ripple of enthusiasm rising within her at the prospect of presenting such a plan to VDS' higher ups. "But what if they ask questions that I can't answer?"

"For chrissakes, do you want me to sit on your shoulder and whisper in your ear during the whole meeting?" Tiff rolled mascara-coated eyes in exasperation. "Just keep referring back to the proposal and repeat the appropriate key points. And if you really get stuck, all you have to say is, *Good question, but I'd rather not answer you right off the top of my head. Let me give it some thought, and I'll get back to you.* Can you do that, Plain Jane?"

"Good question, but I'd rather not answer you right off the top of my head. Let me give it some thought, and I'll get back to you."

Tiff's furry jaw dropped just a little, and Jane allowed herself the slightest of smiles. Jeez, maybe a certain guardian rat's snide attitude was rubbing off on her, just a bit. Feeling almost cheerful now—besting Tiff did that for her—she settled back in her chair and continued reading. After all, she only had six more hours to go until she took that first step on the road toward the Salesperson of the Year award.

"Oh, my God, they loved it! Did you hear? Your proposal was a total hit!"

Jane closed her office door behind her and gleefully tossed said paperwork into her in box, then carefully set her purse next to that overflowing wire basket. A rumpled Tiff crawled from the bag's faux leather recesses and plopped her furry rump upon the desktop, stretching little rat limbs like a cat awakening from a nap.

"Duh, yes, I heard," she squeaked in obvious irritation. "Why else do you think I allowed you take me to the meeting in that department store carryall of yours? I wanted to make damn sure you didn't screw up things. And, believe me, you came this close to blowing the whole shebang," she said as she held painted paws fractionally apart.

"I did not! I followed your proposal to the letter, and I—"

Jane broke off as a sharp knock sounded at her office door. Even as she rushed to bar the way, Marty Preston—Tiff's hunky number two choice for afterworldly mentoring—poked his shaggy blond head into the office.

"Hey, Jane," he said with a big grin. "Just wanted to congratulate you on the meeting. Take it from me, the big boys were impressed . . . and so was everyone else."

"Y-you think so?"

She shot a nervous look over her shoulder. The interruption had been so unexpected that Tiff had not had time to retreat. Instead, she'd chosen the next best strategy—hiding in plain sight. Now, she was flopped belly down on the desk, legs pointing to all four corners and eyes unblinking, looking for all the world like one of those beanbag toys. The very unratlike mascara and nail polish that she sported only bolstered the masquerade.

"I know so," Marty was saying as he moved about the office. "In fact, you did such a great job that they're all going to be surprised if you *don't* get the account."

He paused near the stack of boxes, and his grin dimmed a couple of watts. "Hmm, kinda creepy, Tiff's things still being here. Personally, I'm glad I wasn't the one to inherit her office. Mean as she was, she'll probably come back to haunt . . . whoa!"

That last sound of surprise came as he glanced back at Jane's desk. "Wow," he clarified as he bent to study Tiff doing her stuffed animal impersonation. "Man, where did you get this toy rat? It looks almost real. My kid would love it," he said, and reached as if to pick her up.

Jane beat him to it, catching a limp Tiff by her scruff and depositing her back in the carryall, which she then cradled safely out of his reach. "It's, er, just a little good luck toy a friend gave me," she managed. "Anyhow, thanks for the good wishes, but I really need to get back to work."

He took the hint and, flashing a final grin, left the office. Jane closed the door behind him and turned the lock for good measure, then collapsed in her chair with a whoosh of relief.

"For chrissakes, let me go," came Tiff's muffled squeak from the purse Jane still clutched to her chest. Jane squeaked herself—she'd forgotten for an instant just what it was she'd been cradling—and unceremoniously dumped Tiff back onto the desk. The rat shot her an outraged look and stalked over to the in box, where she sat in a huff.

Jane surreptitiously wiped her fingers on her skirt. The bottle of hand sanitizer in her desk was not going to last the day, at this rate! "Don't blame me," she protested. "I was just trying to protect you."

"Yeah, well, protect someone else."

She huffed a few more times, and then fixed Jane with a beady eye. "And don't start thinking you're the queen bee," she squeaked on, "just because your buddy Marty complimented you. Looking good in a meeting is one thing; delivering the goods is something else. Now get your butt on the phone . . . because you're about to call Rubicon's president and set up an appointment with him for the day after tomorrow."

With their first milestone behind them—no, Rubicon's president was not available, but the junior buyer could spare her a few minutes—Jane and Tiff swiftly settled into a routine. Early mornings were for latte and setting appointments; late mornings and afternoons were for sales calls; and late afternoons were for finishing the day's paperwork. Before heading home, Jane would leave Tiff with a couple of magazines and a doggie bag from wherever they'd had lunch, and Tiff would settle in for the night in the credenza that served as her personal little rat house.

"And stay out of the breakroom," Jane would warn her each evening before locking up her office. "Sooner or later, someone working late or coming in early is going to spot you."

Whether or not Tiff heeded her advice, Jane did not know . . . though, as a precaution, she continued to boycott the snack machines, just in case. But, after seeing how the rat kept herself immaculately groomed, almost like a feline, Jane allowed herself to ease up on the hand sanitizer. Whatever Tiff was, she wasn't germy.

Oddly enough, the boxes of Tiff's belongings remained where they were; this, despite repeated promises from Fa-

cilities to have them sent down to Shipping right away. Jane
didn't press the matter but chalked it up to some sort of divine intervention. As long as Tiff the rat occupied her office,
apparently so would her things.

As for her request to conquer the Rubicon account, meetings with them continued over the next few weeks. Jane's
one-on-one with that company's president continued to
elude her, but she did creep up the corporate ladder with
each visit to the facility. Tiffany always accompanied her,
safely ensconced in a new, three-hundred-dollar leather
tote—she had refused to climb into Jane's other bag ever
again—and armed with sticky notes and a pencil stub.
Whenever she felt that Jane was stumbling into moron land,
as she termed it, she'd write a quick message and slide it out
from under the purse's flap, where Jane could casually retrieve it.

The first meeting, Tiff had used up almost an entire pad.
By the end of the second week, however, Jane made it
through one entire visit with only a single scrawled message. *Not bad, Plain Jane.* So startled had she been by that
missive, that she'd left her briefcase in the Engineering
Manager's office, and had to rush back to recover it.

After that, Jane found herself grudgingly admitting—
though only to herself—that she and her guardian rat made
a tolerable team. As for her other customer accounts, they
blossomed equally under Tiff's tutelage. In fact, Rebecca
Maxwell, VDS' Vice-President of Sales, even dropped by
Jane's office during the fourth week to compliment her on
her rising numbers.

"I must tell you," the elegant, dark-skinned woman
added, "that you've picked the right time to show your stuff.
Land that Rubicon account in the next two weeks, my dear,
and I can almost guarantee you a chance at being named
Salesperson of the Year."

And then, with a week to spare, Jane got the call. If she'd
stop by for a visit with Rubicon's Director of Purchasing the

following morning, she could pick up a million dollar purchase order, thank you very much.

"Oh . . . my . . . God."

Jane slowly replaced the receiver and turned to Tiff, who was sitting atop the credenza touching up her nail polish. "I—that is, we—got the Rubicon account back."

"About damn time," Tiff replied with a shrug, though Jane could swear that her little rat squeak held a pleased note. "Now, if those morons in the front office don't give you that award, there's going to be a serious case of bubonic plague unleashed around here."

Before Jane could decide if she was kidding or not—how in the heck could Tiff contrive to contract, let alone spread, such a disease?—a knock sounded at her closed door. She waited until Tiff had scurried into the credenza, and then opened her office.

A skinny, redheaded youth dressed in a uniform of navy pants and shirt stood in her doorway. The word, *Facilities*, was embroidered over one shirt pocket, while his name, *Harley*, was emblazoned over the other. In one hand, he gripped what appeared to be one of those miniature baseball bats that she'd seen in the souvenir shops at the local major league ballpark.

"Sorry to bother you, Ms. Riverspoon, but we've had word of a pest disturbance on this floor. Do you mind if I take a look around?"

She swallowed past the sudden lump of uneasiness that had risen in her throat. "Sure," she said in as casual a tone as she could muster. "So, is it cockroaches in the snack machine again?"

"Well, not exactly." Harley paused and lowered his voice to a stage whisper. "Promise you won't tell anyone, but someone down the hall called and said they saw a rat a little earlier . . . and they said it ran into your office."

"A rat, in my office?" Jane forced a chuckle. "I'm sure they were mistaken. After all, we're all the way up on the fifth floor. And surely I would have noticed a rat if there was one."

"Well, my job is to check out this sort of thing, no matter how wild it sounds." He grinned, showing crooked teeth. "Wild . . . get it?" When Jane only stared at this attempt at humor, he swiftly got back to business. "Anyhow, this isn't the first report. There have been two or three rat sightings over the past couple of weeks. So, do you mind if I look around?"

Jane waved him in and watched nervously as he perused the corners and poked about Tiff's cardboard boxes, and then got on his knees to peer under the credenza. She gasped reflexively as he reached for its ornamental knob, but released her breath when he merely used the piece of furniture to steady himself as he rose.

"Don't see any rats here, but keep your eyes peeled, okay?"

She shut the door behind him and locked it, then hurried to open the credenza once more. "I thought I warned you not to wander around the building," she exclaimed as Tiff climbed back onto its polished wood top. "If you're not careful, they're going to bring in an exterminator!"

"Get a grip, Plain Jane," she peevishly squeaked. "I needed a caffeine fix, and you hadn't brought me my afternoon latte. I didn't have any other choice but to head down to the breakroom for some coffee. Besides, I get bored having to stay in here when we're not making calls."

"You're right, I did forget your latte," Jane conceded in a meek voice, feeling suddenly guilty. It hadn't occurred to her until this moment, but Tiff was a prisoner of sorts there in the office, unable to come and go freely lest someone spy her. "And I'm sorry I yelled. It's just that I don't want anything to happen to you, okay?"

Even as she said that last, she realized it was true. Indeed, over the last few weeks, she'd grown quite fond of Tiff, despite the enmity of their original relationship. Odder still, she sensed that her guardian rat had developed a similar affection for her. In fact, she might almost say that they were friends now.

Tiff shrugged and twirled her tail. "Jeez, don't get all sentimental on me," she replied, though her squeak sounded almost cheery now. "Let's get to work on your acceptance speech. The annual sales meeting is in two days, and I'm expecting you to win that award."

"And now," Rebecca Maxwell announced from her spot at the podium, "it's time to present one of Valiant Data Systems' top honors . . . the Salesperson of the Year award."

A murmur arose from the employees gathered in VDS' elegant first-floor conference center, where the annual sales meeting had been going on since that morning. Salespeople from VDS' ten branches had joined the folks in corporate for the eight-hour-long series of presentations. Jane was gratified to hear a brief if nicely worded mention of the late Tiffany Glass, who was cited as a previous Salesperson of the Year award recipient. Now, with the day's formal activities concluded, all that remained was the announcing of this year's winner.

As the hubbub faded, Jane shifted in her chair, wondering if Tiff was as nervous as she. She'd brought Tiff down to the conference room long before the meetings started, setting her up behind the small forest worth of potted palms that decorated the back wall. Tiff had agreed to remain hidden there for the duration, as long as Jane promised to bring her a little something every so often from the enormous buffet set up against the side wall. Jane had agreed, sensing as she did so an unaccustomed nervousness in her guardian rat.

This was, after all, the culmination of Tiff's afterworldly assignment. If Jane did not win this award, Tiff would spend eternity—or, at least, some portion of it—trapped in that furry guise.

She glanced down at the acceptance speech that Tiff had helped her draft, clutched now in one sweaty hand. The problem was, Jane wasn't at all confident that she would prevail.

True, she'd managed to coax back one of VDS' largest customers, but she could look around the conference room and
spy half a dozen other salespeople who'd performed more
consistently, who'd snared similar large accounts. If they
gave the award based on highest commissions earned, there
was no way that she would win it.

"The purpose of this award," Ms. Maxwell was continuing, "is not simply to honor the company's top producer . . .
not that we don't like money, here at VDS." She let the polite laughter die, and then went on, "Instead, we're looking
for a salesperson who embodies the can-do attitude that has
made Valiant Data Systems a Fortune 100 company. We're
looking for a person who is not content to rest on his or her
laurels, but who shows an ongoing commitment to the highest standards of personal and professional development."

She paused again and hefted a large copper-and-wood
plaque identical to the one Jane had seen on Tiff's wall, and
later, in her box of personal effects. "And that is why," the
V.P. finished, "our Salesperson of the Year award goes to—"

Jane blinked.

Someone had called to her as the announcement was
made, so that she'd missed hearing which salesperson had
won. *Probably Marty*, she glumly thought. *He had the best
numbers, and the higher-ups like him.* With a sinking heart,
she glanced about to see who was headed toward the
stage . . . only to realize that people were staring back at her,
smiling and clapping. It wasn't until the woman beside her
began prodding her to stand, that Jane belatedly got it.

Rebecca Maxwell was the one who had called her name.

She, Jane Riverspoon, was VDS's Salesperson of the
Year!

On shaking legs, she wended her way through the rows
of chairs and up onto the stage, where a smiling Ms.
Maxwell awaited her at the podium. She shook the woman's
hand and accepted the plaque and, just to be sure, read the
name engraved there. Yes, it really was hers!

By now, the clapping had given way to a polite silence,

and Jane realized this was the time she was supposed to say a few words. Setting down the plaque, she smoothed the page on which she'd written her speech. Then, glancing toward the potted palms in the room's far corner, where Tiff the rat silently hid, she crumpled it up again and smiled.

"I did have a little speech written," she began, "filled with words like Ms. Maxwell mentioned . . . commitment, can-do, professionalism. But there's one word I didn't have written down . . . a word that, over the past few weeks, I've come to realize is even more important. And that word is *friend*."

She paused and hefted the plaque. "And that is why I want to thank the person who truly is responsible for my winning this award, the person who inspired me to do my best, even when I didn't believe in myself . . . my good friend, Tiffany Glass."

A heartbeat of silence followed, and Jane could see the looks of surprise on the faces closest to the podium. Then, abruptly, a wave of applause swept the room, growing louder as the entire sales force of VDS got to its collective feet in tribute. Jane's smile broadened, and she impulsively waved in the direction of the potted palms . . . only to notice a sudden disturbance there.

Harley the Facilities guy was pushing his way behind the trees, brandishing the same miniature bat that Jane had seen in his hand the day he'd come to her office rat hunting.

She dropped the plaque back onto the podium with a clatter. Heedless of the puzzled looks thrown in her direction, she rushed off the stage and headed toward the palm trees. By the time she reached him, however, it was too late. Harley had dropped his bat and was busy shoving a limp, furry black shape into a plastic garbage bag. At her cry of horror, he straightened and gave her a crooked grin.

"Don't worry, Ms. Riverspoon, everything's under control. You'll be glad to know I finally took care of that rat that's been bothering everyone."

* * *

Jane straightened the plaque on her wall and stepped back, studying the effect through tear-glazed eyes. Downstairs, the after-meeting party still was going full force, but she'd not been able to force herself to stay. Instead, she'd come back upstairs to her office.

She had been dismayed but not overly surprised to see that Tiff's boxes of belongings had finally been removed . . . including, oddly enough, the items Tiff had kept with her in the credenza. That had to mean she was gone for good, this time. Jane swiped at her damp eyes and sniffed. She could only hope that Tiff knew about the award . . . and that, wherever she was now, they had plenty of latte for her to drink.

"Jeez, you're not crying over a rat, are you?"

The husky voice behind her held a hint of a laugh. Jane gasped and swung about to see a familiar blonde woman in a red power suit seated on her credenza, her nylon-clad legs casually swinging. Her mascaraed eyes were bright, and her lips were twisted in a teasing smile. Jane felt her knees wobble.

"T–Tiff?" she finally managed, "is that you?"

"In the flesh. Or in the spirit, if you prefer."

And, indeed, she had a vaguely transparent look about her, so that Jane could see faint outlines of the credenza beneath her and the wall behind her. "Jeez, I was proud of you when you won that award, Jane," the other woman went on. "And that nice little speech you made . . . it almost had me crying. Do you really think of me as your friend?"

"Of course, I do. That's why I was so upset . . . and that's why I hate to see you go."

"But that's the way it has to be. You won your award, and I'm moving on to the next stage. You wouldn't want me to stay a rat forever, now would you?"

"But who's going to drink latte with me in the mornings, or go on sales calls with me?"

"You'll do it by yourself, Jane, and you'll do just fine. I promise."

Tiff stood and brushed ghostly wrinkles from her skirt.

"Well, gotta fly. I have another appointment with the Head Honcho, and I don't want to keep Him waiting." She dropped her voice to a confidential whisper and added, "Just between you and me, I think I'm going to get my promotion this time around."

"I know you will." Jane managed a wobbly smile. "And if Anybody asks, I'll be sure to report that you did have a positive influence on people. Especially me."

"Well, I guess you did a bit of influencing, yourself. And, by the way, I think of you as my friend, too."

As Jane gasped in pleased surprise at that last, Tiff reached ghostly fingers into her pocket and plucked something from it. "Here's a little something to remember me by," she said, and tossed a small object in her direction. As Jane glanced down at what it was she'd caught, she heard Tiff say, "See you around, Jane . . . someday."

And when she looked up a heartbeat later, Tiff was gone.

"See you around, Tiff," she whispered back, and looked down again at her friend's good-bye present. It was, quite fittingly, a bottle of scarlet nail polish. And on the bottle's label were but two words.

Her smile broadening, Jane sat in her leather chair—now perfectly fitted to her own form—and began painting her fingernails a bright shade of Success Red.

MODOC RISING

by Gary A. Braunbeck

Gary A. Braunbeck is the author of the acclaimed collection *Things Left Behind*, as well as the forthcoming collections *Escaping Purgatory* (in collaboration with Alan M. Clark) and the CD-Rom *Sorties, Cathexes, and Human Remains*. His first solo novel, *The Indifference of Heaven*, was recently released, as was his Dark Matter novel, *In Hollow Houses*. He lives in Columbus, Ohio, and has, to date, sold nearly two hundred short stories. His fiction, to quote *Publishers Weekly*, ". . . stirs the mind as it chills the marrow."

" '*Egypt.*' Mrs. Helen Bell, it seems, was asked, 'What do you think the Sphinx said to Mr. Emerson?'
   'Why,' replied Mrs. Bell, 'the Sphinx probably said to him, 'You're another.' "

—Ralph Waldo Emerson,
Journals, June (?) 1874

BY the time I arrived at the group home seventeen more whales had beached themselves along the Maine coastline and my nephew Carson had been missing for two-and-a-half hours. Cindy, one of the certified habilitation specialists, was waiting for me. The neighborhood was amazingly quiet; no birds sang, no dogs barked, no cats yowled.

"I'm so sorry about this," she said as I joined her on the porch. "He complained about having a headache right after breakfast and asked to be excused from workshop duties today. I sent him up to his room so he could lie down. I went up to get him for lunch about half an hour ago and—well, come on in, you can see for yourself."

We went up to Carson's room, and she showed me how he'd tied his sheets together and used them to shimmy down from his window onto the roof of the back porch; from there it was simple to grab one of the thick branches of the tree beside the house and climb down to the ground. Carson was twenty-seven and had Down's syndrome, but it didn't exclude him from possessing the same adventurous—sometimes even devious—imagination of a typical nine-year-old boy. At least, that's what I used to think.

Leaning on the windowsill, I saw a hand-sized cluster of what looked like small sticks lying near the roof gutter. If Cindy noticed them, she gave no indication. But I knew what they meant.

"I might have an idea where to find him."

She rubbed her eyes, her shoulders slumping in relief. "I was hoping you might."

"Have you called anyone else?"

She nodded her head. "I called the sheriff. It's standard procedure when one of the residents wanders off—not that it happens all *that* much, but—"

I held up a hand, stopping her. "You don't need to defend yourself to me, okay? I'm not upset and I won't lodge any complaints with the AARC board." She needed to hear that. The Association for the Advancement of Retarded Citizens sponsored this group home, which at any given time was staffed by two specialists and three trained volunteers, all of whom were expected to keep precise tabs on twelve residents. I couldn't blame them. No one can be expected to keep track of twelve developmentally disabled human beings—ranging in age from thirteen to sixty—every second of every minute of every day.

I turned back and examined Carson's room, which he shared with two other male residents.

"He took his comic books."

Cindy looked over at the bookshelf that hung over the head of Carson's bed. "I didn't notice that before." This said in the same tone of voice usually reserved for phrases such as *So what?*

"No reason you should have." I glanced out the window once again at the cluster of sticks, smiled at Cindy, then squeezed her shoulder in what must have seemed like a condescending gesture and said, "I'll call you in about an hour or so and let you know if I found him."

"If you think you know where he is, then we should let the sheriff—"

"No. If he's where I think he is, the sheriff'd never find him. Give me ninety minutes. There's no use bothering the sheriff if it turns out I'm wrong."

"Would you like me to come along? I mean, with everything else that's happening—"

"Thanks, but no. If Carson sees you, he'll get upset and think he's in trouble—and you *know* how hard to control he can get when he's upset."

"If you're sure."

"I am."

It was obvious she didn't want to be alone, not with what was spreading outside, but there was no way I could take her along.

Driving away, I hoped that Cindy wouldn't notice the little cluster on the roof. The significance of the comic books was known only to Carson and myself, no problem there, but the bones on the roof might set some Gothic bells ringing.

I knew damn well I'd find him.

It was Dead Bird Day.

Which meant that it was really happening.

Modoc was rising.

*   *   *

I became Carson's legal guardian after his mother died from a heart condition no one knew she had. My sister was a woman of singular grace who never let anything phase her; hangnails were met with the same dogged composure as broken bones. In all the years she'd been in my life, I don't think I ever once saw her panic. Even when she awoke from an emergency C-section to discover that her child had Down's and that her husband had left her because he couldn't handle it, she never allowed any setback or misfortune to best her. I loved her dearly and missed her every day.

Carson spent three weeks every month at the group home; the fourth week—and all holidays—he spent with me. He wanted it that way and, to be honest, so did I. After seven days, we started getting on each other's nerves a bit, so one week a month was the ticket for us. And I could visit or call him whenever I wanted . . . which I usually did somewhere around the middle of Week Two. The point is, he was never lonely. That was important to me.

One of the things my nephew and I discovered we had in common was a love of comic books. Admittedly, I hadn't really been involved in the comics scene since the heyday of *Ghost Rider, Aqua-Man,* and *The Silver Surfer* (though I have to admit to a short-lived renaissance during the early appearances of *Sandman*), but Carson didn't care. *Spider-Man* united us. We were of one mind when it came to the Green Goblin (he was an annoying wuss), Doc Oc (dangerous, scary, and kind of cool), as well as Kingpin (very fat and rude). One of our rituals whenever he stayed with me involved his hauling out his latest batch of acquisitions and reading them to me. Another ritual involved our driving out toward Buckeye Lake for dinner at the I-70 Truck Stop, Carson's favorite place to eat. (The food is surprisingly excellent.)

A few weeks before his disappearance, these rituals converged.

Carson had adopted a cat which he kept at my house. I

had no arguments about his keeping it there, as long as he
paid for the food and litter from the money he earned working at the AARC sheltered workshop. Besides, the cat
proved to be agreeable company at night, was always very
affectionate, and didn't shed nearly as much as I'd at first
feared.

The cat—which Carson had named Fame—disappeared
one night. I dreaded telling him about it as I drove to the
group home to pick him up for our week together. I had the
radio tuned to Cedar Hill's National Public Radio station
where two agricultural scientists were discussing the remote
possibility that an outbreak of scrapie was starting to infect
sheep in Montana. Their droning voices did little to settle
my anxiety, so I popped in a Copland CD.

By the time Carson and I got back to my house (after
cheeseburgers at the Sparta and a matinee at the newly-
renovated Midland Theater, the pride of downtown Cedar
Hill) I·knew there was no avoiding it. I pulled up in front,
killed the engine, then turned to Carson and said, "Carson, I
need to tell you something. I'm afraid it might be bad news."

"I know," he said, softly bouncing himself up and down
in the seat.

I grinned for only a moment. "Oh, you do, do you?"

"Uh-huh. Fame ran away and— Hey, you know what? I
got some new slippers. They're real warm and—"

"Whoa, Carson, hang on. How . . . how did you know
about Fame?"

" 'Cause Fame told me."

Uh-huh. "You're telling me that the cat told you he was
going to—"

"No. You're goofy sometimes." He reached into his
knapsack and pulled out a comic book, then rifled through
the pages until he came to a dog-eared page. "*This* Fame. I
named my Fame after him." He handed over the comic.

The whole thing—front and back covers included—was
drawn in black and white. The paper stock was cheap (some

of the ink rubbed off on my fingertips) and there were no advertisements to be found anywhere within.

It was open to a full-page drawing of a creature that was so incredible I was momentarily taken back in time to my first encounter with Bruce Banner's alter ego. "Wow. That's pretty cool."

And it was. This creature named Fame stood in the middle of a futuristic city where it towered over every building around it. It had the head of rat with a unicorn's spiraling horn rising from the center of its forehead, the snout of a pig, the body and wings of a bat, the legs of a spider, a horse's tail, and two semihuman arms jutting from its chest, one hand gripping a pencil, the other a sketchpad. The more I looked at it, the more details registered; its body was composed of fish scales, and its wings were a mosaic of hundreds of different varieties of feathers, its underbelly looked slick as a dolphin's skin, and it's spider's legs ended in paws that were a combination of dog and cat.

It was both grotesque and remarkable, the work of an underground artist who was obviously gifted in a way only the truly and happily demented can be; despite all of its disparate parts, Fame as a whole seemed at once organic and correct, as if it should look no other way than this.

"So this is Fame?"

"Uh-huh. He's the Monarch of Modoc."

"What's Modoc?"

Carson shook his head and made a *tsk*-ing noise. "Boy, you sure are goofy sometimes."

"You said that already."

Carson yanked the comic from my hand and closed it, turning the cover toward me.

And there it was: *MODOC: Land of the First Beast.*

"Modoc is Fame's kingdom?" I asked.

"It ain't a kingdom like with knights and stuff, y'know? It's like in the future. There's people and everything, and they all love Fame and he protects them."

I nodded my head and asked him if I could see the comic

again. He reluctantly handed it over. I flipped through the pages, stopping here and there to read the dialogue in the various balloons . . . except there wasn't any. In each frame where a character was speaking, its speech-bubble was blank. It was only through the badly-printed narration in the squares that I was able to discover that Fame's name was short for Familiar, and that he was preparing Modoc for something Very Terribly Important, Don't You Know. (That's how the phrase was written every time it appeared: Very Terribly Important, Don't You Know.) I handed it back to Carson.

"How could Fame tell you about . . . about *your* Fame when there's no words?"

"There's words there. I can see 'em, but you can't, yet."

"Yet?"

Carson nodded. "It's a secret."

"Okay." But it still didn't explain how he'd known about the cat.

Unless . . .

"Carson?"

"We gonna go to the Sparta again? They make good cheeseburgers."

"The best known to mankind, yes—but I was about to ask you something."

"Okay."

"Is this a joke you're playing on me? Did you sneak out last night and get Fame and take him back to the group home?"

"Nuh-uh."

"You wouldn't lie to me, would you?"

"Yeah . . . but not about this. I lie about Christmas presents—like telling you I don't got one for you. I lie like that. But not this. This is Very Terribly Important, Don't You Know."

I decided to let it rest for a while. If this were a joke of some kind, Carson would tell me eventually; if it wasn't, at least he wasn't upset. I only hoped that Fame was all right. I really liked having that cat around.

Later, after dinner, Carson pulled out a whole stack of *Modoc* comics and sat next to me on the couch, showing me each page of every issue, in order, so I could follow what was going on.

Fame ruled Modoc, a place where human beings and animals lived together in perfect accord. Fame kept everyone in Modoc happy and entertained by drawing their wishes and then making those wishes come to life. It was a good-enough place. But there was an evil hexer, Tumeni Notes, who was trying to cast a spell so that the animals would revolt against Fame and force him to show Tumeni where the Great Scrim was located. These spells involved replacing the animal's soul with any one of the thousands of ghosts who floated around Modoc, playing tricks on Fame who was the only thing in the land who could see them. The Great Scrim, it seemed, was an invisible barrier that kept Modoc from being invaded by the "crittermals" who lived on the other side of the scrim in the Hidden Backward, which (as far as I could figure out from Carson's explanation) was Modoc's negative self, a place where everything that existed in Modoc existed not so much as its own opposite, but rather what it had been *before* it became the human being, bird, or animal that lived in Modoc: Modoc's cats were snakes—called Frypps—in the Hidden Backward, human beings were fish (Wannacrawlers), birds were gigantic dinosaurs (English Ranchers); Fame used the ghosts as spies, since they could travel between Modoc and the Hidden Backward without being seen or inverted or reversed or swallowed by the Silk Machine . . . on and on it went, becoming dumbfoundingly complicated as it threw in everything from simultaneous-universe theories to Darwinism and a dash or two of modern DNA research. I found it difficult to believe that Carson—though categorized as a "high-functional" Down's and capable of reading at a fifth-grade level—could understand all of this, let alone keep it straight.

He came to the most recent issue and opened it to the first page, then let out a little gasp and immediately closed it.

"What's wrong?"

"Can't read this one yet."

"Why not?"

" 'Cause I'm not supposed to."

"I don't understand."

Tsk-ing again. "You're goofy. I can't read it 'cause Fame won't let me see the words yet."

"But there *aren't* any words in the first place."

"Are, too."

I grabbed up three issues at random and opened them to various pages. "Look at this—Carson, come on! Look! Nowhere, see? Nowhere in any of these comics does any of the characters say anything. See? Just empty space." I was shocked at how angry I suddenly felt.

"I told you already, there're words in them, *you* just can't see 'em."

"Yet," I added, all at once too frustrated to care.

"Uh-huh. Fame does it to me, too. When I get a new *Modoc*, the words aren't always there 'cause Fame, he don't feel like talking to me yet. I gotta wait."

"Like I have to wait?"

"Uh-huh."

"Why do I have to wait? Why can't Fame just let me read the same words he says to you?"

" 'Cause he won't say the same thing to you. He told me that, just like he told me about *my* Fame. He says different things to different people . . . but only if he likes them."

Time for aspirin and sleep.

The next morning Carson woke me at seven-thirty and told me that we had to go to the truck stop for breakfast.

"Carson, my head hurts and I've had about four hours' sleep. Can't it wait?"

"No!" He sounded both excited and slightly scared. "We gotta go now."

"Why?"

He showed me the latest issue of *Modoc*—the one he couldn't read to me the night before—and opened it to the first page.

I was looking at a black-and-white drawing of the I-70 Truck Stop near Buckeye Lake. There was a car driving into its parking lot. My car. With Carson and me inside. And something that looked like the ghost of a bear floating behind us.

I grabbed the comic from my nephew's hands and turned to the next page. It was blank.

All the way to the truck stop, I found myself glancing in the rearview mirror, half-expecting to see some diaphanous form pursuing us; Ursa Major, P.I.

We took our usual booth and ordered. While we waited for the food to arrive, Carson opened the *Modoc* issue and turned to the second page, then the third, then the fourth. They displayed, in order, our arriving at the truck stop, eating, paying our bill, and driving away. There were six frames per page, and in each frame we were joined in ever-developing degrees by ghostly creatures of myth, the centaur, the manticore, chimera, and cloven-hooved Pan.

What really unnerved me was the illustrations showed both of us eating precisely what we had ordered: pancakes, sausage, and a large chocolate milk for Carson, a Western omelet and coffee for myself.

For the first time in ages, the two of us ate in silence. We then paid our bill and left.

As we were driving out of the parking lot and getting back onto the road, Carson turned to the next page. So far, only one frame was there. In it, our car was making a right onto Arboreteum Road—a good twelve miles away.

"Well, at least Fame is giving us a little time," I said, trying to sound cool but knowing the words came out the whisper of a child frightened of the dark.

Carson turned on the radio. It was still tuned to the local NPR station. This time the subject was Foot-and-Mouth Disease: Is it Coming Back Again?

I told Carson to play some music. He selected a Dixie Dregs CD. I turned it up, happy to lose myself in the fiery instrumentals.

I slowed the car as we neared the turnoff to Arboretum Road.

"We could just keep driving," I said to my nephew. "Nothing's forcing us to do what's drawn there."

"Fame says we gotta. He says it'll cause all kinds of trouble if we don't."

"Tell Fame for me that he and I need to have a talk."

"He knows."

"I'll bet he does." And with that, I turned onto Arborteum Road.

This time we didn't consult the comic book. About half a mile down the road there was a large fallen tree blocking the way. We would have to turn around and go back the way we came, and the only way to do that was to turn onto another, much narrower, unpaved side road—which was really more of a glorified footpath—then back out slowly as I worked the wheel.

As soon as we turned onto the path, I looked up and realized where we were.

"Audubon's Graveyard," I whispered to myself.

"What?" said Carson.

"Nothing." Which, of course, wasn't the truth. Having lived in Cedar Hill most of my life, I'd heard of Audubon's Graveyard—it was something of a local legend—but had never actually seen it, knew only that it was located somewhere in the vicinity of Arborteum Road.

I killed the engine and stared out at the small rise a few dozen yards ahead. A couple of pigeons lay there, dead, stiff, wings splayed, eyes glassy and staring up toward the sky they would never know again.

Carson reached over and gently touched my shoulder. "Where are we?"

"It's, um . . . well . . ." How could I explain this place to him?

There was a five-acre plat on the other side of that rise which some smartass reporter had long ago dubbed "Audubon's Graveyard," actually thinking the name displayed wit and irony. There were still some locals who referred to this area as simply "The Nest," but it was "Audubon's Graveyard" that stuck. Since the spring of 1957, those five acres of county-owned land had been the focus of several official investigations (conducted by everyone from the State Department of Health to Federal Haz-Mat teams), and for good reason: twice a year, for a period lasting about three weeks, every bird that flew over that area dropped from the sky, dead before it hit the ground. The soil had been tested countless times for contaminants, as had the air, the small creek that ran through, and even the other forms of wildlife that inhabited the woods surrounding the plat. Nothing was infected, and only birds were dying. In every case, their hearts exploded. No tests, no dissections, no theories were able to explain why this happened. There weren't even good legends from the ancient Hopewell Indians' mythology to shed any light on the cause. It was, simply, what it was: a huge and eerie question mark.

Carson nudged me with his elbow and showed me the next page: there we were, on the other side of the rise, on foot, walking toward the body of a dead hawk whose right eye took up a full half of the frame, while Carson and I were little more than minute hazy ghosts in the background.

"Carson, I need you to be honest with me, all right? It's really important that you understand that."

"Uh-huh."

"Is this some kind of a joke? I know from your supervisors that you have drawing talent. Are you somehow drawing those pages in when I'm not looking?"

"Oh, no! No. I ain't very good at drawing. Sure can't draw like this."

"Swear?"

"Swear."

I looked at the comic book in his hand and nodded my

head. "Well, then; let's go see what Fame has in mind for us."

We climbed up the rise, Carson taking care not to step on the bodies of the pigeons.

The sight below made my breath catch in my throat.

Scattered across the field were hundreds of dead birds; purple grackles and Brewer's blackbirds, flickers, brown thrashers, loggerhead shrikes, bohemian waxwings, multicolored kestrels, kingfishers, starlings, bluegrays, and a magnificent marsh hawk. I had no idea how any of these birds had died; there were no broken necks, no gunshot wounds, no animal bites. Only their eyes held a clue.

Every set was a deep, disturbing red.

Not only the bodies, but the bones of bodies, as well. Neither Carson nor myself could walk more than a few paces without hearing the tiny crunch and snap of birds' bones under our shoes. Carson looked once again at his comic, then unzipped a pocket of his knapsack, moved its contents to the pockets of his coat, and began gathering up as many bones as he could stuff in there.

"Carson, you can't be—"

"I gotta," he replied, thrusting the comic into my hand.

In the new set of frames, Carson was moving through the field, gathering up bones. In the final frame on the page an old barn suddenly entered the picture, albeit far in the background.

I looked up, and there it was; deserted, neglected, falling only slightly to decay.

"Carson, stop, we're going home." I was now seriously creeped out. I am not one of the wistful people, my imagination has little room for anything that doesn't directly apply to whichever advertising campaign I'm working on at the moment, and unless the fantasy before me is up on a movie or television screen I really have no use for it, nor it for me.

"I *can't!*" Carson yelled back at me. "Fame says I gotta."

"Fame is not driving the car, and Fame sure as hell isn't

the one taking care of you, so Fame can go fuck himself!"
Even I was shocked to hear that word come out of my
mouth, which should have given me some indication of how
panicked I was becoming, but at that moment I was too
caught up in wanting to get the hell away from here so I
could start denying any of this had happened to care about
my language.

Carson whirled around and pleaded. "Please, Uncle Carl?
I just gotta do this."

"I said no."

Now he glared at me. For a few moments we stood there
like two half-assed cowboys in some showdown from a Ser-
gio Leone western epic, then I stormed across to Carson and
grabbed his arm, which was stupid, because my nephew,
though not very tall, is nonetheless a beefy and very compact man, one whose physical strength is easy to overlook.

He jerked away and I made to grab him again, but this
time he was ready and met my movements with a swinging
elbow that caught me in the center of the chest, knocking the
wind and about three years of life out of me. I dropped to my
knees and began to fall forward, stopping myself with my
hands. I stayed that way for several moments, my vision
blurry and lungs screaming for air. I looked down at the soil
under my hands. I remember thinking how very much like
clay the soil felt. I wondered if I could possibly dig up several handfuls and fashion them into clay crutches, because
there was no way in hell I was going to be able to get up
under my own power.

Carson helped me up. He was crying. He hugged me
tight, saying, "I'm sorry, Uncle Carl, I'm sorry, I love you, I
didn't mean it, I didn't, I didn't, I *didn't!*"

"It's . . . it's okay . . . okay, Carson. Come on, let's . . .
whew! . . . let's get back to the car so I can sit down, all
right?"

"I'm sorry."

"I know. Me, too."

Ten years and several rest stops later we were finally

back in the car. I leaned against the seat and waited for my chest to stop hurting. I'm still waiting, but eventually I was able to rally and back out, turn the car around, and drive away. We had to wait to turn off Arboretum Road because the traffic was starting to get heavy. On my third attempt we were almost broadsided by the #48 Express bus that ran between Cedar Hill, Buckeye Lake, and Columbus. I considered then using my cell phone to just call for a taxi, but an opening presented itself, I took it, and away we drove.

Carson turned once and looked behind us.

"What is it?" I asked.

"What bus was that?"

"The #48 Express. Why?"

He shrugged—a bit too nonchalantly, but that didn't really register at the time. "I dunno."

Back home that night there was no comic book reading. Carson demanded that I sit on the couch and watch TV and relax, he'd take care of me. I kept telling him that I was feeling much better, everything was okay—just make sure he never hit me again—but he wouldn't hear of it. He was going to take care of me, even make dinner.

Dinner turned out to be grilled cheese sandwiches, underdone on one side, overdone on the other, but seeing how proud he was of his accomplishment, I ate two and told him they were the best grilled cheeses I'd ever had. The truth was, they were. His company did a lot to enhance their taste.

The rest of our week together was more subdued than usual. Except for a trip to a comic book store to see if they had the new *Spider-Man* (I knew damn well he was looking for a new *Modoc*, but didn't say anything), nothing happened to remind me of the events at the truck stop and Audubon's Graveyard. I am very good at denial. It helps when you lie to people for a living.

I took Carson back to the group home the following Monday. He gave me a long, hard hug on the front steps before going back inside. I stood staring at the door after it closed behind him. The empty space where he'd stood a few moments before seemed to hum with his absence.

The next two weeks kept me very busy preparing the presentation for the client, a perfume manufacturer who'd recently been in the news, accused of illegal animal testing. When my team and I made the presentation, the client flipped. He loved it, we got the account, I got a hefty bonus, and all was right with the prepackaged world.

The night before Cindy called to tell me Carson had disappeared, I was sitting on my couch watching the news when a story came on about the outbreak of Mad Cow Disease in Britain; this was followed by a series of quick related stories; a scrapie outbreak in Montana sheep, foot-and-mouth disease in Colorado cattle, and possible Mad Cow symptoms in Ohio livestock.

I began flipping around the channels.

A CNN news break mentioned the sudden onslaught of whales beaching themselves along the Maine coastline. Seven so far.

A documentary on Animal Planet examined the recent overcrowdings in Humane Society shelters, and the record number of cats and dogs that were being put to sleep.

Another news break, another channel: dozens of dead dolphins and countless fish were floating to shore in Miami; hundreds of sheep and cattle were being destroyed due to outbreaks of disease; people were beginning to worry about meat and fish being stocked in grocery stores.

I turned the set off, rubbed my eyes, and was just about to go to bed when I looked down at the pile of books and magazines on the coffee table and saw that Carson had left the last issue of *Modoc* for me. I had absolutely no desire to open it and see if the rest of the pages had been filled. No desire whatsoever. So I sat staring at it, feeling uncomfortable and foolish. The smart thing to do was just walk away and go to bed; the smart thing was to just ignore it.

I picked it up and opened it to the page where Carson and I were in the middle of Audubon's Graveyard, the old barn in the distance looking like some kind of crypt from the pages of *Eerie* or *Creepy.*

I turned to the next page, and there was Fame. In every frame for the next several pages, he seemed to be altering bit by bit; not becoming something different, but transforming *more* into itself.

And this time, the dialogue bubbles had words in them.

The first said: **Hello, Carl. Nice to finally talk to you.**

I dropped the thing as if it were on fire. It fell on the floor, still opened to the same page.

Leaning down toward it in the same way I'd lean down to make sure a spider was dead, I read on, despite myself. Frame by frame.

Carson should not have struck you. He's only doing what I asked him to do. You see, Tumeni Notes discovered that I was using the Long Lost to spy on the Hidden Backward. His power is growing. I'm afraid I won't be able to protect Modoc from him much longer. So I have asked Carson to help me.

Help with what? I thought, turning the page.

To raise Modoc so that it will merge with the Hidden Backward. It is time. Listen to my story.

When this planet awoke to sing its First Song, there was only one species of animal living on its surface. This creature breathed and dreamed just as you do today. But it was lonely. Here was this magnificent Earth, filled with beauty, and it had no one and nothing with which to share it.

This First Animal took a deep breath and began to swell in size, rearranging itself within, then split into two identical halves. The halves mated, creating a third, a hybrid of themselves which in turn mated with them, producing other hybrids. They continued to mate and produce, as did the progenies, giving birth to everything from the Manticore and Sphinx down to the ants and maggots—that is how the Earth became populated.

Even after that, the birthing continued. Single cells

fused together, creating metazoans that eventually cul-
minated in the invention of roses and elephants and dew-
glistened leaves and even human beings. All life on this
planet—past, present, and what there is of the future—
sprang from the same single organism. If only they could
just see the joining of organisms into communities, those
communities into ecosystems, those ecosystems into the
biosphere . . .

Do you have any idea how unique each single living
creature is? Everything alive at this moment is one in
three billion of its kind. Each is a self-contained, free-
standing individual labeled by specific, genuinely unique
protein configurations at the surface of its cells. You'd
think we'd never stop dancing.

But my time is short. The animals are remaking themselves. They are allowing themselves to become diseased.
They are willingly sacrificing their lives and their forms
so that the First Animal can live again.

I am that First Animal, Carl: all the rest sprang from
me. I have to start again, you see. But I can't cross into
the Hidden Backward from Modoc. I first have to be re-
born on the other side of the Great Scrim, then I can
raise Modoc and the merging can take place. I have
drawn precise pictures so that Carson will understand
what it is I need for him to do.

He has been taking the bus, you see. He has been
sneaking out at night and returning to the Field of English Ranchers. He is the Builder, the loyal servant, the
Destroyer of the Silk Machine.

If you do not oppose him, you will be spared.

Good-bye for now, Carl. I look forward to meeting
you soon.

I tore it up, then crumpled the pieces, threw them in the
fireplace, and burned them. Then I sat at the kitchen table,
getting good and drunk. I'd turned the television back on because the silence gave me too much to think about. I listened
as more and more news stories spewed out.

Twenty-eight whales had now beached themselves.

In Kansas, pig farmers were facing a crisis; none of their pigs were eating, and were now beginning to die of starvation.

The number of dead dolphins was now in the hundreds.

In Africa, dozens of elephants were witnessed to have deliberately walked into poachers' traps.

All through the night I sat and listened as stories came in from all over the world about countless species of animals dying, or killing themselves, or not running from the hunter's bow, gun, dart, spear, or knife.

. . . *sacrificing their lives and forms so that the First Animal can live again.*

Sometime around five A.M. I put my head down on the table and fell asleep. I was awakened by the phone ringing. It was Cindy. By the time I arrived at the group home, seventeen more whales had beached themselves along the Maine coastline and my nephew Carson had been missing for two and-a-half hours.

I parked my car and walked over the rise and down into Audubon's Graveyard. There weren't as many birds here now, and nowhere could I see any bones. I headed toward the old barn in the distance. As I neared it, the silence surrounding me became almost unbearable. I'd have given anything to hear a bird sing or a dog bark.

The ground all around the barn was spotted with deep holes. Someone had been digging. Quite a lot.

The barn door was partly open, so I was able to enter without making any noise.

Carson was at the opposite end of the barn. He was covered in the moist, claylike soil. A large shovel rested inside the wheelbarrow he'd used to haul the dirt in. He did not hear me as I walked toward him. He was busy cutting sections of twine from a roll. There were various sizes of branches and sticks in a pile at his feet. There were buckets of water. Rope. Tubes of caulk and a caulk gun. A large sheet of tarpaulin from which several large pieces had been cut.

I was in the middle of the barn. I could see Carson, but since the stalls on that side ran into the beams and wall which supported the hayloft above, I couldn't see what he was working on.

"Carson?"

He looked at me, smiled, and waved. "Hi, Uncle Carl. I took the bus. Remember how it almost hit us?"

"Yes."

He looked down at something on a hay bale. A comic book. He turned the page.

"Is that the new issue of *Modoc?*"

"Yeah. I bought it yesterday."

I took a few more steps toward him. "What're you working on?"

"Present for Fame."

"What kind of present?"

"Come look. I'm almost all done."

I walked over to him and looked.

Somehow, he had used the bird bones and clay, the twine and rope, the caulk and several sections of discarded wood, as well as all the twigs and sticks, to build a near-perfect replica of Fame. It wasn't nearly as big as it was portrayed in the comics, but it was still quite impressive. He had cut away a section of the tarpaulin to fashion the skin for the wings. The horn was a stick that he'd whittled to a point. He'd gathered feathers, as well, using them to give the body as much texture as possible. The spider's legs were one of the most amazing parts: for those he'd used bone, stick, twine and twig, clay, and remnants of bed sheets, twisting them tightly together so they could support the weight of the rest of it. It was a marvel of design, something I knew to be beyond his capabilities.

"What are you supposed to do now?"

"Well," he said, adding the last bit of twine and clay to

Fame's arm, "I dunno." He held up the comic. "The issue ends here."

"I see."

"Is it true about the animals? Are they all dead?"

"Not all of them, but a lot. And more are dying every minute."

"That's too bad. I'll miss 'em."

"Are you done now?"

"Uh-huh."

I held out my hand. "Then we should go home and let everyone know you're okay."

He nodded his head and then took hold of my hand and we walked out of the barn. He hadn't held my hand since he was a child.

"Do you think it'll be nice?"

I shook my head. "I don't know."

"I think it'll be nice. Fame said he'd be nice to us. Not everyone, but with us, he promised."

Clouds moved across the sky, blotting out the sun for a moment as they passed by. Their shadows on the field took on the shapes of centaurs, manticores, chimeras.

Carson stopped. "Hey, Uncle Carl?"

"Yes?"

"I think we're supposed to wait here."

"Wait for what?"

"For Modoc to rise."

Behind us came the sound of groaning wood and splitting beams. I glanced back for only a second, just long enough to see something unfurl through the roof of the barn. I looked back at my nephew.

"I miss the cat," I said.

"Me, too."

The doors of the barn cracked and splintered outward.

Carson's eyes began to tear. "Maybe Fame will make us a new one."

"Maybe."

The clouds passed away from the sun. The bodies of the

dead birds around us began to disintegrate; stripped of feathers, then flesh, then organs, their bones crumbling into powder which was caught on the breeze and blown somewhere behind us.

There was a sound like God's scream as the rest of the barn splintered to pieces.

I grinned. "I think you need a new nickname. I think from now on, I'll call you Dr. Doolittle."

The ground shook, a great wind suddenly whipped across the plat, and a shadow cast by the mighty set of wings spread over the field, swallowing us.

GOODNESS HAD NOTHING
TO DO WITH IT

by Susan Sizemore

Susan Sizemore lives in the Midwest and spends most of her time writing. Some of her other favorite things are coffee, dogs, travel, movies, hiking, history, farmers' markets, art glass, and basketball—you'll find mention of quite a few of these things inside the pages of her stories. She works in many genres, from contemporary romance to epic fantasy and horror. Her available books include historical romance novels, and a dark fantasy series, *The Laws of the Blood.* Susan's e-mail address is Ssizemore@aol.com, and her Web site address is: http://members.aol.com/Ssizemore/storm/home.htm

"THAT'S not a familiar, that's a strange."

"It was the best I could do on short notice. The shelter was out of cats, and they were about to put her to sleep."

"And this was a bad idea—how?"

"Oh, come on, Marcie! She's so ugly she's cute."

"Is that a dog?"

"The people at the shelter thought so. Maybe some kind of Chihuahua mix."

"Chihuahua and rat?"

"Chihuahua and West Highland White, maybe. That's why they called her Mae. You know, Mae West Highland White. Her fur is sort of white. Sort of like New York snow."

Kind of like my reputation.

"What'd you say, Kim?"

"I said sort of like New York snow."

"After that. You whispered something."

You'd be surprised what you can do with a whisper.

"No, I didn't. Why are you shaking your head like that?"

"I think I'm hearing voices."

"Well, that should be good for business."

"Aren't you supposed to tell me that I'm imagining things? Or at least crazy?"

"Psychics are supposed to hear voices."

"Yeah, but we're not officially open yet. We don't know if we're any good. We—I'm panicking, aren't I?"

"Yes. We have the reading room, the phone lines, the Web site, and our first client due in ten minutes. Now we even have a familiar."

"I think I'd rather call that thing a mascot."

"Familiar has a more old-fashioned, witchy sound to it. We need to show that we're high tech but down home, innovative but traditional. What more do we need?"

There's a certain enthusiasm lacking, but a girl can learn to fake most anything.

"Why are you putting that thing down, Kim?"

"Why are you looking white as a ghost?"

"Maybe I'm hearing one. Stop sniffing my foot, you rat thing!"

"She's a dog."

"Get her out of here."

"The point is for her to greet customers and lend an air of—"

"If she pees on that rug, you're cleaning it up."

"I thought you liked animals."

"Only those that are recognizably mammals. That's a—"

"Look how she's staring at herself in the mirror. Isn't that cute?"

"A hairy dirt ball with a streak of vanity is not cute, Kim."

Vanity? Some of us have something to be vain about, sister, and your feet smell. Why invite competition's my motto. Though I can see I don't have anything to worry about with this pair. Then again, having died and come back as a volunteer yet another time, I don't suppose human competition's the problem where tomcats are concerned. This is the fourth time I've been back. Bet the boys have missed me. Looking forward to rounding up this neighborhood's strays. Have to put some time in with the new girls before I start taming the alley cats. Don't mind holding up my end of the deal, even with amateur witches. I'm a woman who needs to work. Been said I don't know how to make a graceful exit . . . not by anyone standing behind me when I walk out the door. So instead of takin' a rest I'm told is well-deserved, I keep signing up for the familiar patrol. Bein' spoiled and pampered comes with the job of bein' a familiar, and no one deserves spoilin' and pamperin' more than me. Besides, I always had a soft spot for psychics, witches, fortune-tellers, mediums, and mystics, not to mention any girl who has to get by on her wits. Wits, moxie, and an hourglass figure got me by just fine. Never passed up a chance to get my tea leaves read, if you know what I mean. Had to get 'em stirred up first, though. Not sure how stirring the new pair's going to be. Can sniff some natural talent in both of 'em, but don't think this is where they want to be. As to their wantin' a familiar just for show—I deserve only the best, but I ain't no lady, I work for a living. And what are they talking about my bein' a dog?

You didn't have to put me down, honey, I like bein' carried.

Don't mind makin' myself at home. Rug's soft, but my paws don't feel right. Neither do my hips. Fur not thick as I like. Can't seem to get the hang of slinkin' across the floor.

What kind of cat can't slink? And I can't manage a purr. Everyone knows I purr all my lines. At least there's a mirror close to the ground. Why jump if you don't have to? Never miss an opportunity to look in a mirror, I say. Think I'll have a look and—

"Marcie! What's the matter?"

"Something's screaming in my head! Make it stop! I can't help it if you're a dog! Stop screaming! It's not a cat!"

"I know it's not a cat. Here, let me help you stand up. I wish the dog would stop barking. I'll pick her up, maybe that'll keep her quiet. Good girl. You want to be held, that's all. You'll be quiet now, won't you, while I see what's wrong with your momma Marcie. What is wrong with you, Marcie?"

"It's that dog. She doesn't want to be a dog. That's why she was screaming."

"She was barking."

"Only on the outside. Inside my head she was making a godawful racket and telling me that she's supposed to be a white Persian cat. She's always been a white Persian before."

"Uh-huh."

"Really. She's magical. She can talk."

"Marcie, we're supposed to be telling fortunes and predicting our client's futures, not messing with each other's heads."

"I'm not the one who brought home that . . . that . . . thing."

"Hush. We'll talk about it later. Our first client's coming in the door."

"You talk to him. I'm not ready for one-on-one yet."

"But . . ."

"I'll check the Web site. You take the—dog."

Will you smell the testosterone on that one? Hmmm . . . maybe there's something to being a dog after all? Hello, big boy. Have a seat. Mind if I join you? Didn't think so. What nice strong thighs you have. Is that a gun in your pocket?

"What a friendly dog you have, Ms. Kimberly."

"That's my familiar, Mr. Greer."

"She certainly is."

"Just dump her off your lap if she gets in your way. And call me Kim."

"You seem to be a very informal medium."

"As you can see, I'm actually more of an extra large."

"Very amusing."

"Would you like tea? Coffee?"

Me? I see you brought your own cigar. You have such nice hands. Scratch there, behind the ear. Mmmm ... good boy.

"No, thank you. Nice dog. I find it very relaxing to pet her."

"Oh, yes—"

Mae.

"Mae's a sweetheart. How can I help you, Mr. Greer?"

"Aren't you supposed to tell me?"

"Of course. But I need to know what you're interested in. A Tarot reading? An astrological chart? Contacting the other side? You were vague over the phone."

Keep on blushin' darlin', makes you all warm and toasty. Let me lick your palm. Now doesn't that make you feel better? You've never done this before, have you?

"Actually, Ms. Kimberly, I—we—uh—we haven't a clue, and I've heard that some people use psychics to— Would you take a look at the young woman in this photo and tell me if you—sense—anything?"

Excuse me, darlin'. You've got a cushy lap, Kim. That's gonna come in handy, I always like living in the lap of luxury. Let me curl up and shed on your dress while I have a look at this picture. Pretty girl. Your hand's shaking, honey. Calm down. Concentrate. Breathe. Take it easy. You can do it. Close your eyes and tell the man what you see.

"She's no angel. No. It's Klondike Annie. Excuse me, I seem to be thinking in movie imagery. Has this young woman any connection with Alaska? Is her boyfriend named

Milo? No, Milos? From Russia? Do you smell fish? I feel a little seasick. I think she's on a boat. A fishing boat that works out of the Aleutians."

"Her mother mentioned a Russian man she'd been seeing, but we haven't been able to track him down."

"You're using a psychic—me—in a police investigation, aren't you?"

That is a gun in your pocket!

"I'm not at liberty to say 'police,' Ms. Kimberly."

"I've heard that law enforcement agencies don't like to admit to using paranormal consultants. When you handed me this picture, I thought you must be from the police and that the girl must be dead. She's fine, she ran off with Milos, that's all. Make some calls to Alaska. You'll find her."

"I'll do that. Thank you for your help."

"Oh, you're quite welcome."

Remember that working girls get paid.

"About the fee— Thank you. Please call on us again if you need any help. Let me know how it turns out, all right? Thanks. Good day. Come on, Mae, let's go tell Marcie."

Let's show Marcie the money, you mean. Honey, you have to be practical. And you should have flirted a little with him. He was interested. I could smell it. Don't worry. He'll be back. I'll show you how to get him next time. I could get to like this little doggy routine. There's possibilities. The nose knows on this model.

"Marcie, I just helped a cop with a missing persons' case! Can you believe it? What are you doing?"

"I'm in a chatroom. Why did we set up a chatroom? I hate giving free advice. I don't really think I'm cut out for this. I'm not a people person."

"You're a psychic. You see the future."

"But should I try making a living at it? Is it ethical?"

"I helped find a missing person. That's ethical. It was like I was channeling Mae West. I was holding Mae in my lap and having her there made me think of that old movie where

Mae West is in Alaska disguised as a missionary and then this vision of where this missing girl is came to me. Here, hold the dog. She'll bring you luck."

"She'll bring me fleas. All right. Hand her over."

"What are you talking about online?"

"There's some script writer looking for a high concept story idea that wandered in for a chat."

"What's this writer need a psychic for?"

"He remembered my name from that producer I used to date. Looking for story ideas, I guess."

"Well, have him call you and charge him by the hour."

"That's a thought. What do I talk about, channeling Mae West— Now there's a thought."

Script ideas? Honey, you've come to the right place. I was better at writing than I was at sex, and I was great at sex. In fact I wrote—

"She wrote a play called *Sex*, you know."

"How do you know so much about Mae West?"

"I don't. She does. The dog."

"Oh, come on."

"She talked to you, didn't she?"

"I heard a voice, but . . . Do you think that maybe it could be true?"

"It's very high concept. Silver screen sex goddess reincarnated as a scruffy little dog helps save the world."

Or at least a pair of greenhorn mediums.

"Screw the screenwriter, Kim, I'd rather write this myself. I've got contacts in Hollywood, don't I?"

"How are you going to start it?"

"By getting offline and petting our pretty little pooch while I stare at the word processor."

You expect me to do all the work, in other words. Not sure this is in the familiars' rule book, but bein' a doggie, I've got an itch to please you. And I've always been the sort who likes to please herself. You couldn't get me to do this if I'd come back as a cat like I shoulda. Still, this could be more fun than wearing a mink to the Friday night fights. And who could write a story about me better than me? Scratch my tummy and be prepared for a masterpiece. But if you try to sell it to Disney, I'll pee on your ankle.

SWORDPLAY

by Josepha Sherman

Josepha Sherman is a fantasy novelist and folk-lorist, whose latest titles include *Son of Darkness; The Captive Soul; Xena: All I Need to Know I learned from the Warrior Princess*, by Gabrielle, as translated by Josepha Sherman; the folklore title *Merlin's Kin*; and, together with Susan Shwartz, two *STAR TREK*™ novels, *Vulcan's Forge* and *Vulcan's Heart*. She is also a fan of the New York Mets, horses, aviation, and space science. Visit her at www.sff.net.people/Josepha.Sherman.

MARKO Luckless, a slender young man in nicely sewn but travel-stained hunting garb and a worn but still whole mail shirt, sat moodily on a rock there in the middle of the wind-blown mountain pasture. All around him, the day was bright with sunlight and flowers. But he saw only the sword whose hilt he held in both hands.

The sword that might as well be made of common tin for all the good it was going to do him.

For a bitter moment, he was back in his father's keep, standing as straight-backed and proud as he could. His father had seemed a grim-faced statue in the heavy chair of state, his rich purple cloak falling in artful folds that hid his crippled leg. Better if he'd railed or raged. Instead, he had simply told Marko, "You are not to go."

"As though I were a child," Marko said to the sword. "Or mindless instead of luckless."

Luckless. What he remembered most about his father's reaction had been that . . . resignation, as though already sure of his son's failure.

Marko gave a sharp, humorless laugh. "Luckless." Hadn't he already successfully snuck out of his father's keep. Like a thief. One who had managed to steal . . . what? This aged weapon?

Marko shook the sword. "Too bad you're not a magic sword. Or that I didn't suddenly have some great and wondrous powers to enchant you. Ha, can't you see me as a mighty wizard?" With a flamboyant gesture, he proclaimed, "Hear me, O mighty spirit of the sword! I conjure you, in the name of all the Powers That May Be, to wake and serve me in this—"

There was a sharp, spectacular *crack,* and the sword's blade blazed with blue-white light. Marko dropped it with a yelp. He couldn't have—it couldn't have—

"Omigod, omigod— Ow!"

The sword had just . . . *spoken?*

Yes, it had. Worse, a shrill female voice was busy adding, "You dropped me! I mean, like . . . how could you drop me? Where am I? Oh! Oh, geez, it worked, it really did, but where's the *body?* I don't have arms or legs or—oh, geez, I know what that is—it's a sword! I'm stuck in a freaking sword!"

Marko hastily signed himself against evil. "I abjure you, foul creature of darkness—"

"Hey! That's kind of, you know, personal! Besides, I'm not a—"

"I abjure you," Marko continued determinedly, "in the names of all the saints—"

"*Will* you stop that? I'm not some kind of, well, I guess you think I'm a demon. A talking sword, right? But I'm not! I'm— Whoa, wait, what *did* happen? What did you do to me?"

"I? I didn't do anything! I was merely wishing this—you—were a magic sword—"

"Wishing? What? What are you? Some kind of, you know, wizard?"

The sword sounded as if it didn't believe that.

Neither did Marko. "I have no magic powers," he said. "Surely it is you who—"

"Look, will you pu-*lease* pick me—it—me up again? I'm getting a crick in my—do I still have a neck? I don't! I only have a voice! I so don't like this!" the voice wailed. "I mean, just pick me up!"

"W–what are you? A familiar spirit?"

"Yeah, sure, anything you say. Just pick me up, okay?"

Marko gingerly obeyed, sitting down on the rock again, holding the sword as carefully as though it might bite him.

"That's better," the voice said. "Okay, so you were wishing I, uh, this was a magic sword, right? What did you say?"

"I don't know," Marko protested. "Just some foolishness about . . . I conjure you . . ." He shook his head. "Something of that ilk. I don't remember the exact words."

"Oh, great. Must have been *just* when I was, you know, I mean, I didn't really think the spell was going to work, but hey, I guess it did. Sort of. And because you were making with the wizard vibes just then, you got me. Sheesh."

The sword shook in Marko's hand, as though it had just shuddered. "Who . . . what . . . who are you?" he asked.

"Oh, yeah, my bad. I'm Stacie. Who are you?"

"Marko." He added dourly, "Luckless."

"Luckless, huh? As in, 'no luck,' right, not a last name? That's a pretty weird thing to call yourself."

Marko blinked. "It is what all call me. I have no luck. As a familiar spirit should surely know."

"Familiar spirit, like in witch and cat? That's so Disney!"

"You speak most strangely, ah, Stacie."

"Hey, hey, you speak pretty strangely yourself! Okay, so I guess you're, like, some sort of knight, huh? I mean, you talk the way you do, and you're, like, carrying a sword."

"I am no knight," Marko said bitterly. "Not until I may prove my worth by noble deed."

"Oh. Sure. Whatever."

"But who *are* you?"

"Oh, boy. This isn't going to be easy."

Marko sat in confusion as the sword . . . the . . . Stacie told him about a place called the United States and California and a research project in a library "with a lot of really creepy books, and I just took a peek, and there was this spell, like, you know, to travel to, like, another realm, you know, riding in someone's body without hurting them. Like sightseeing, only better. So, well, I figured it wouldn't work, like I mean, hey, *magic?* I mean, you know? But . . . I guess it did. With your help."

"Your realm is truly strange, oh, Stacie," Marko cut in helplessly. "But are you—"

"So I thought, hey, I'd be in some lady's mind, not, you know, to hurt her or anything like those stupid mind-parasite movies, just sit and watch, see what she sees. You know, be in a magic sort of world. If the spell did, like, work—oh. Oh, geez."

Marko jumped. "Now what?"

"I just realized something. I mean, I thought when I tried the spell, sure, fun, you know, enter a fantasy world, like one of those role-playing games, play it to the end and then go home—" The Stacie paused, for all the world as though the sword was watching him. "You're not getting any of this, are you, Marko?"

"I fear not."

"Guess they don't have role-playing games in this world. I mean, what would you pretend to be, IRS agents or FBI or something? So, anyhow, anyhow maybe I have to play the whole game—yeah, I know, it's not a game, it's real—but maybe I have to, like, stay with you till you finish your, uh, noble deed. And only then can I get out of this stupid sword and go home."

"Yes," Marko said warily. "That would seem to be the reason for your sparking into life."

"For Pete's sake! I told you, I'm not a—a—thing, I'm a human being, a girl, you know? From California? USA? Hello? Anyone at home?"

"Forgive me. You are from another realm: That, I accept. For so are most spirits."

"I give *up!* Okay, okay, never mind that. Noble deed, huh? Got any ideas? Rescue a damsel in distress maybe? I bet you're already on a quest, right?"

Marko hesitated. "Nothing with such elegance to it. There is a loathsome beast befouling the land. A dragon, some say."

"A *dragon?*" The Stacie's rose to a shriek that hurt Marko's ears. "Like, a fire-breathing *dragon?* You know, one snort and crispy critter time?"

"There are no such things! This is a true dragon, depending on its sharp fangs and claws to bring down its prey."

"Oh, gee. Is that all? Uh, question? I mean, your father's a big shot, right? So, why doesn't he—"

"The dragon crippled him."

"Oh. Not good. But don't you have, like, other men?"

"They are our vassals. It is not right to send them to their deaths."

"And you don't count? Oh, boy, I'm starting to get a really not good picture. Let me guess: You've got an older brother or maybe sister, right?"

"I . . . did. Stefan died when I was very young."

"Figured. And good old dad never let you forget for a minute you weren't as good, right? Poor second-best Marko. Marko who probably had it drummed into him he was Luckless. Huh."

"You are—"

"Hurt your feelings? My bad. But I bet I'm right."

"How . . . would you know . . . ?"

" 'Cause I have the same thing. Big Sister in my case. I

guess that's why I was doing the, like, spell stuff. To do something Big Sis couldn't. Okay, let's get going."

"You *are* going to help me, then?"

"Hello? I so do not want to stay stuck in a sword!"

"Ah. Right."

"Hey, maybe you're catching on!"

The dragon, Marko thought, *would* insist on lairing on a mountaintop. Climbing wasn't easy, not when he had to be quiet and not send any of the thousand bits of rock and gravel clattering down the mountain. It also wasn't easy because every time he tried to sheath the sword, it would squeal, "No! I can't see!" That meant clambering awkwardly, with only one hand free to steady himself.

But at last he crouched, trying not to pant, behind a boulder like so many jagged teeth. Over him, the last crest of the mountain soared up, and directly before him, a great heap of fallen rocks formed a cave. From the cave issued a reek like a mix of serpent and rotting meat.

"Eeeuuuw," Marko heard the Stacie say softly, and needed no translation.

A shadow within the cave stirred, then stretched, revealing a forearm thick about as a tree and covered with rough gray-brown, leathery hide. It was tipped with alarmingly large, alarmingly sharp claws. Then the shadow stirred again, and Marko caught sight of something . . . the dragon's massive, head, larger than the boulders around it. Terrible . . . terrible . . . As Marko held his breath, the monster yawned, and the sight of those long, curving, terrible fangs, dripping and keener than any blade made Marko forget about the claws.

He'd never, somehow, expected the tales to all be true. He'd never expected the dragon to be . . . this.

How can I . . . ? How can I even hurt *it?*

"That?" the Stacie hissed in his ear. "That's a dragon? And let me guess, you're just going to rush right in, right? Get us both killed?"

"A sword can't be hurt. A sword—"

"Can break. And, you know, I'm not too happy about what might happen to me if it does."

Marko, doing his best to ignore the Stacie's protests, started forward—but the sword turned in his hand, wedging itself firmly between two rocks.

"No!" the Stacie hissed. "Moron, you want to kill yourself, leave me out of it."

"Let . . . go!"

"No! Look—oh, geez, look!"

No wonder the dragon was so content. It was resting on a mound of bones. Human bones, Marko corrected himself, human bones and human limbs, his stomach lurching as he saw a boot on a leg that had been torn off at the knee. The Stacie gave another plaintive, "Eeeuuuww! That's what you want? Want to be the main course? Listen to me, okay? Listen! We don't have to die, got it?"

"But—you have a plan?"

"Damned right! Look, look, he knows someone's here. Get us out of here, like *now!*"

Her panic was infectious. Before he could control himself, Marko scrambled down the mountain, slipping, sliding, and bruising himself on rocks in his headlong flight, sure the dragon was bound to hear or see and have itself a quick meal.

But the dragon must have still been groggy with sleep, or just not hungry. It spread its vast wings, and for an instant, Marko was in shadow. Then the wings folded again, and Marko let out the breath he hadn't even realized he'd been holding.

By the time he'd reached level ground, Marko had recovered enough to be mortified. "You have shamed me!" he snarled at the sword.

"Yeah?" the Stacie snarled right back at him. "My bad. Saved your stupid life is what I did. Do you really think anybody can kill that, one on one? Well? Do you?"

"No," Marko grumbled.

"So, you're really not into suicide, right? Then this time you listen to me. *Listen!*"

"I'm listening," he grumbled.

"Hurrah. Now, tell me, that dragon, what is it? I mean, like is it magic? As in, it can talk and like that?"

"No. It is but an animal. Terrible, yes, but an animal."

"Kewl! Does the dragon, like, get thirsty like other critters?"

Marko shrugged. "Indeed."

"*Way* kewl! Now here's my plan."

The Stacie whispered. Marko blinked, opened his mouth, shut it again. Granted, the whole thing didn't sound quite, well, honorable. But he doubted that a dragon really cared about honor. The sight of that booted leg . . . "So be it," he said curtly.

The village had been a day's walk away, and nothing more than a few log cabins along a dusty road. But fortunately it had included that most necessary of buildings, an inn. What they'd thought of him ordering what he had, or the quantity of it, or of him hauling his purchases onto his back and then lugging them out of the village . . .

The sword wasn't much help. It . . . giggled almost the whole way back to the mountain. Marko got a mild revenge when he was forced to sheath the sword since he needed both hands in order to struggle back up the steep slope, back to the boulder behind which he had hidden before this—this madness.

"Let me out," a muffled Stacie whispered.

He'd forgotten about the sword. Hastily, Marko drew it, and the Stacie said, "Okay. Dragon still there?"

Marko frowned. The cave *seemed* to be empty. Warily, he stole forward, trying not to gag at the stench of the lair and its revolting contents. The sword said nothing, but Marko could have sworn he heard it trying to retch.

"No dragon," the Stacie said. "You know, like, showtime."

Whatever that meant.

Marko gladly put down his burden, breaking open the cask and pouring it out into the basin, then started back—

"The salt!" the Stacie hissed.

Ah! Marko quickly threw the blocks of salt out where the dragon would easily find them.

"He's coming!" the Stacie all but screamed.

Marko dove into hiding. The dragon roared in to a crashing landing, wings clashing together with a clap like thunder. It bore no prey.

That means it's going to be hungry, Marko thought. *One mistake on my part, and we are going to be dinner.*

It folded those wings, shivering them into place for all the world like a bird, then stopped, sniffing.

The salt, Marko urged it, *go for the salt!*

Ah, yes! Just like any other wild thing, it needed salt, and since it hadn't taken any prey, it hadn't gotten that salt from the kill's blood. It licked at the salt, then straightened, the terrible head up, wide nostrils scenting the air. Marko's breath caught in his throat. But the wind was in his favor, blowing down from the mountain, and the dragon returned to the salt.

Then it stopped again, grunting deep in its throat. It was thirsty now; it had to be.

See what we have for you? See the basin?

Marko held his breath. It saw the basin . . . scented the contents. Would it . . . ?

Yes. The great head lowered. The dragon tasted, stopped, tasted again, then began to drink.

"Reminds me of some of the frat guys," the Stacie whispered with a nervous giggle.

The dragon continued to drink, then grunted and gave what was unmistakably a belch.

"*Just* like the frat guys!" the Stacie giggled.

It was drunk! The dragon was actually drunk on the basinful of cheap wine Marko had left it.

As though it had heard his thought, the dragon suddenly

leaped up, straight at him, wings outstretched like a storm cloud. Marko raised the sword for one last, desperate lunge.

But the drunk dragon came crashing down, *snoring*— right onto the upturned sword. It shrieked, but its own weight forced the sword more deeply into its chest.

Then Marko was buried beneath it.

"Mmko! Mmko!"

Marko woke to realize with a great jolt of surprise that he was still alive. The dragon had landed with one leg bent under it, leaving a triangle of open air, sheltering him from suffocation and the worst of the weight.

"Mmko! G'me out!"

The sword! Grabbing it firmly by the hilt, Marko began a slow, determined wriggle to freedom, trying not to breathe. At last he was out in the open, staggering to his feet and away until he could gasp in lungfuls of air that weren't tainted by the dragon stench.

"Eeeuwww!" the Stacie shrilled. "Eeeuuwwww! Look at me!"

Marko grabbed up a handful of grass, cleaning the blood off the blade and hilt as best he could.

"Hey, you should do something about you, you know?" the Stacie said. "You look like the end of some stupid horror movie. But—hey, we did it! We did!"

"You did," Marko corrected.

"Nope. You had the guts—ugh, wrong word. You were scared, Marko, and sure you were going to die. But, like, you could have just run off. No one would have known. Instead, you hung on and—oh. Oh!"

"What?"

"I was right. Quest over, I'm so outta here. Marko, wish I coulda known you, like, I mean in my own body, but hey— it's been special." But then the sharp voice softened. "One thing you're not, guy, is Luckless. Bye, now!"

The sword went silent.

Marko blinked, waited, then sighed. The Stacie was definitely gone. Safely home, he hoped, to whatever weird spirit realm that . . . California might be.

Then he went and cut off one of the dragon's ears as proof he'd done what he'd intended to do, and started off for home. But, filthy, bruised, and weary, Marko was grinning as he went.

"All right, I'm not Stefan," he said. "I never can be my brother. I'm *me*. And one thing I'm not," Marko echoed, "is Luckless. I'm never the Luckless One again."

THIEVES IN THE NIGHT

by John Helfers

John Helfers is a writer and editor currently living in Green Bay, Wisconsin. A graduate of the
University of Wisconsin, Green Bay, his fiction
appears in more than twenty anthologies, including *First to Fight, Once Upon a Crime, Merlin,* and
The UFO Files, among others. His first anthology
project, *Black Cats and Broken Mirrors,* was published by DAW Books in 1998 and has been followed by several more, the more recent being
Warrior Fantastic and *Villains Victorious.* Future
projects include editing even more anthologies as
well as a novel or two in progress.

SEVRONAI'S eyes snapped open. For a moment he forgot where he was, and he looked up at the dark roof of the
treated hide tent in alarm. Rising up on one elbow, he banged
his head into the lantern hung from the small pole that held
up the tent ceiling. Smothering a curse, he rubbed his forehead and glanced around, then sighed in relief.

Knowing he wouldn't go back to sleep, he ran a hand
through his salt-and-pepper hair. *Let's see, I've got a few cop-*
pers to my name, such as it is in these parts. We're almost out
of food, and it's a week's travel to the next town. The spells I
memorize are one step away from charlatan's tricks, and the

last time I managed to actually work *magic, we escaped the entire town with our lives, and not much else.*

"It's not my fault the elders decided to build in a flood plain," he muttered to himself, drawing a well-worn blanket around his shoulders. Sevronai and his apprentice Tyree traveled the countryside performing small magical services for food and a bit of coin. The last village they had been at had requested rain, as their crops had been a bit parched. Sevronai had been glad to oblige.

Everything had been going—well, right as rain. The conditions had been perfect, and he'd felt better than he had in a long time. Sevronai had cast his spell, the dark clouds had gathered, and it began to rain. And rain. And rain.

Three days later, the main road of the village had turned to ankle-deep mud, and the cellars of all the houses were a foot deep in water. When asked if he could stop the rain, Sevronai had replied that he had tried the day before, and nothing had happened. Then the nearby stream, already swollen, overflowed its banks. The mood of the villagers had soured as fast as the water level in the town had risen. That night, Sevronai and Tyree had sneaked out of the village in the nick of time, just missing the angry group of townspeople who had been poling a small boat toward the second floor of the small inn where they had been staying.

That had been three days ago. Now they were holed up in the forest, trying to make it to the capital city of Kell's Crossing, just inside the border of Novena, where Sevronai was sure his luck would change. A large city like that would hold plenty of opportunities for a wizard.

At least I hope so, he thought. Lately it seemed he was losing control of the magic that he had wielded with ease just months ago. Before the flood, he had almost set a blacksmith's beard on fire while trying to cast a spell that would keep his forge ever-burning. The palfrey that had once pulled their wagon had limped for a week on sore feet after the smith had refused to shoe him. It was almost a good thing they had had left the wagon they had been living in at the vil-

lage before that. The money gained from the sale of the vehicle and its contents had gone to pay a family for the wall of
their house that had collapsed when Sevronai had attempted
a spell that was supposed to shape the individual rocks into
one solid mass to strengthen the foundation. Needless to say,
his magic had failed him. Again.

He looked down at the head of tousled blonde hair next to
him. Tyree muttered something in her sleep and turned over
again, revealing a pixie face with a pert, upturned nose, and
a soft mouth relaxed in sleep, though it was usually turned up
in an impish grin. Her sparkling blue eyes were closed now,
and the energy she radiated while awake was banked as she
rested.

*Ah, lass, you deserve better than a patched tent in the
woods and an over-the-hill mage for a mentor,* he thought.
He had found her in the coastal city of Calthas, where she
had attempted to pick his pocket. Even he had been able to
feel the small hand groping for his coin pouch. When caught,
she had said that her master made her steal, or else he would
beat her. Sevronai had asked her to take him to the broken-
down hut where she lived, to have a chat with this "master."
A hulking youth half Sevronai's age and twice his weight had
come out, surrounded by several of his cronies. He demanded to know why Tyree didn't have anything to show for
her day's work. One levitation spell later, Sevronai had introduced the lad's head to a stone wall. The wall won the
contest with ease, and the boy was out cold. Tyree had
watched the entire scene in silence, her jaw hanging open.

"I will now give you something you've probably never
had in your entire life," Sevronai had told her after the rest of
the urchins had scattered. "A choice. You can stay here with
these vagabonds, or you can come with me. Granted, it won't
be an easy life, but I would think it will be better than what
your future holds here."

Tyree couldn't agree fast enough. The two had been together ever since, and Sevronai had been teaching her magic
during their travels. He had known of the young waif's

power ever since he had grabbed her hand in his. It coursed through her, beneath the surface, untapped, waiting to be unleashed at the right time.

Power such as I had known once. He thought back to those days when the magic lived easily in him as well, and shaping it to his will had been a joy, as natural as breathing. Now, his spells only came with an effort, and often he had to cajole the magic into being, leaving him more and more drained each time.

And I don't know why, he thought, which scared him most of all.

He was about to lie back down and try to sleep when a noise from outside the tent attracted his attention.

What was that? Sevronai thought. He listened with one ear cocked, and heard the noise again, a rustling too loud to be the trees. Like someone was dragging a sack over the ground.

Sevronai leaned over Tyree and placed a hand over her mouth. She came awake with a jerk.

"Shh, quiet, it's all right," he said. "I heard something outside. Be ready."

The girl relaxed a bit and listened. "I don't . . . hear anything," Tyree whispered.

"Regardless, something's out there." Sevronai slipped his shirt over his head and got up, throwing open the tent flap as he did so.

In the flickering light of the fire, Sevronai saw the tree branch where they had hung what was left of their food cache.

The empty branch.

From the darkness surrounding the firelight, four pairs of luminous eyes stared back at him. Above the branch where the food sack had hung, a cat-sized creature covered in soft grayish-white fur from head to tail froze. It locked gazes with Sevronai, its large amber-hued eyes reflecting the fire's orange flames, then shot down the tree trunk and into the woods. Across the clearing, he heard the sound of something rustling across the forest floor. He thrust his other leg through his leathers and laced them up.

"Damn it!" Sevronai said, grabbing a burning branch from the fire. He walked to the edge of the clearing and began looking into the darkness.

"What is it?" Tyree asked, wrapping the blanket around herself.

"Damn camp rats!" Sevronai said. "There you are, you little thieves!"

"Sevronai, what are you talking about? What's out there? Those animals are the problem?"

"Yeah, they're called *forstchen,* 'forest children,' or 'forst' for short. Clever little devils that consist of a mouth, stomach, and four legs. Leave anything in camp untended for a minute, and it's gone. Stay here. I'll have our breakfast back in a heartbeat."

"Are you sure that's a good idea?" Tyree asked.

Sevronai looked back at his apprentice. "It's still several days until the next town. We need that food. I'll be back in a minute."

With that he plunged into the tree line, heading for the sound of their food cache being dragged through the woods. The forest thickened into birch and elm trees growing close together, so the *forstchen* had a distinct advantage over him, as he was forced to dodge low-hanging branches and brambles in his pursuit of the furry bandits.

After several minutes of stumbling around, Sevronai broke through the trees into a small clearing just in time to see several gray-and-black-striped tails vanish into the forest. In the middle of the clearing was the small satchel of food. With a sigh, Sevronai walked over to it and bent down to pick it up. He heard a rustling to his left, and the bushes swayed as if something was moving in them.

"Forest children, you'd better keep running, or—" was all he got out before a blinding impact knocked him over. Dazed, he started to struggle to his feet when another crushing blow descended upon him, leaving darkness in its wake.

*   *   *

When Sevronai awoke, the first thing he discovered was that he couldn't move his arms. His skull was pounding, and his entire body felt like a tree had fallen on him. Inch by inch, he raised his head, trying to ignore the stabbing pains that lanced from one temple to another.

"Awake at last, eh?" a muffled voice said.

Sevronai's head was wrenched up until the back of his skull thudded against the tree he was resting against. As he flexed his wrists, he realized that he wasn't just sitting next the tree. He was tied to it, his unbound legs stretched out in front of him. Not having anything better to do, he stared straight up at the speaker's face.

The slim man grinning back at him was no longer young, but not yet aged either—maybe thirty summers old, maybe fifty. His face was tanned and lined, as if he had seen more than his share of the sun. A quick smile played around his mouth, revealing crooked yellow teeth, but never reached his dark brown eyes. He was dressed in simple peasant clothes, much repaired, with a jacket made of sewn-together leather scraps over his woolen shirt. A ragged scarlet cloak hung on a tree nearby. Sevronai saw a knife handle sticking out of his boot, and guessed that probably wasn't the only weapon he had on him.

A grunt from behind the slim man attracted Sevronai's attention. The massive shape of another man squatted by the fire, cooking what looked like the rest of their food.

"Where's the girl?" Sevronai asked, trying not to grimace in pain when he spoke.

"I'm right here," Tyree answered from a few feet away. "I'm all right."

"That's good." Sevronai said, sighing in relief. He craned his neck to find Tyree tied to a tree a few feet away. She was dressed in a simple linen shift, with no visible bruises or blood that he could see, though the garment could hide a multitude of sins. Sevronai didn't see any tears on her face, but from time to time a shiver ran through her body. She kept still, staring up at their captor.

"Oh, come now, surely you're more relieved than that," the patchwork man said. I mean, "that's good" is what you'd say to a casual acquaintance. From what I could see, you two have a much more . . . personal relationship.

"I don't know what you mean—" Sevronai began when a stinging backhand across the face cut him off.

"Don't play the fool with me," the man said.

"We are simple travelers, resting overnight in these woods. If we have trespassed, then we apologize. You already have our food and our fire, which we would have shared freely if you had bothered to ask. What more do you want from us?"

"Traveling companions in more ways than one, methinks," the thin man replied, grinning.

Sevronai flushed with anger, wanting nothing more than to free his hands and slam this brigand's smug face against a tree until he was spitting teeth.

Tyree, however, stayed calm. "That, sir, is none of your concern," Tyree said. "You and your friend have the advantage, now state your business."

"Ah, she has spirit as well," the man sidled over to the fire and snatched a piece of meat off the spit, then strolled back to Sevronai, eating as he did so. "And what else does she do for you, I wonder?"

"If you insult her one more time, I swear you'll pay for it," Sevronai said, aware of how foolish the words sounded, but knowing he had to say something.

The thin man took the food out of his mouth and slapped Sevronai across the face with it. "You and what army, old man? I should cut your tongue out just for that, or maybe it would be more fun to just let you starve to death out here instead. That is, assuming the darkwolves don't get you first."

The man tossed the strip of meat into the bushes behind Sevronai, then turned and walked back to the fire. "I was just asking Huth what we were going to do to fill our bellies tonight. Then, as if straight from the god's arms, we happen upon you two. Now, we have food, shelter, even a horse . . ."

"Which should be plenty. Take them and leave," Sevronai said. "You don't need to involve her in it."

"Ah, but need is exactly the point here. Once you were trussed up, it was a simple matter of calling to your . . . companion and letting her know you were in a bit of a spot, as it were. I figured she wouldn't leave you at our gentle mercies. So we ties you both up, and, I thinks to myself, 'Well, now, isn't this a prime opportunity we've found.' "

"Opportunity for what?" Tyree asked.

"Why to line our pockets against the coming winter," the thin man replied, rubbing his hands together as he walked over to stand in front of her. "A pretty young thing such as your lass here will fetch a high price in the southern slave markets. That just leaves the matter of you. Hmm, too old for work, and not pretty enough to be a handservant. And you're entirely too protective of her for my liking. Methinks I'll have to put you out of your misery."

Sevronai swallowed hard, attempting to quiet the stirrings of fear which were raising a lump in his throat and threatening to turn his bowels to icy water. The casual way the thin man was discussing their fates made it very clear he was an old hand at this. *And he won't hesitate to kill either one of us if necessary,* the wizard thought. He wasn't afraid for himself; he was past his prime, and ready to meet his maker. After all, a wizard who couldn't cast magic was really of no use to anyone, least of all himself. However, he was concerned for Tyree, whom he had grown to care about very much in the past months, and who had assets the slim man would use for his own dark devices.

A slight rustle in the brush behind him caught Sevronai's ear. Trying to keep one eye on his captors, he looked behind him to see what was coming out of the forest.

Slipping out of the bushes on its clawed paws, a lone *forstchen* ambled over to the strip of meat and picked it up in its paws as it sat on its haunches. It sniffed the meat, then began chewing on it, grunting with pleasure.

The wizard leaned his head back against the tree. *Forstchen are very curious. How can I use that to my advantage?* Glancing over at Tyree and the thin man, who were still talking, he felt around for anything he could use, a twig, a rock, anything at all. His exploring fingers found nothing.

Sevronai felt a cool, wet nose sniffing at his fingers. In desperation, he cast a small spell he kept memorized, a cantrip that didn't require any hand motions, but that would tell him if whatever he was touching contained magic or not.

To his surprise, the little creature glowed red, a sign that it was under a spell of some kind. Sevronai also detected an innate magical power within the animal, but what kind he didn't know.

The thin man noticed Sevronai looking behind him and walked over, booting him in the ribs. "What are you up to?" He noticed the animal behind the tree and chuckled.

"Tsk, tsk, how selfish of me. Here I am eating, and I'm not sharing with my servants," the thin man said. He stretched out his hand, and the *forstchen* trotted over to him. The thin man picked up the cat-sized creature and let it crawl from his hands up his arm and settle around his shoulders. Raising his head, the creature made a series of chitters and whistles, as if calling to something unseen in the forest.

Sevronai watched in amazement as three more *forstchen* ambled out of the woods, surrounding the thin man in a loose semicircle. As one, the pack all sat up on their hind legs, their paws at their sides, looking like attentive disciples. The thin man leaned down to pet them, then began distributing bits of food to his furry allies.

Tyree spoke first. "I've heard of your kind. You're a *resqu'oth,* a furwalker. You can form a mental bond with animals, and command them to follow your orders."

Both Sevronai and the slim man stared at her for a moment. Their captor recovered first. "The lass has a keen mind to go along with her other assets."

"I thought your kind of mages were hermits, dedicated to protecting the forest and the animals you bond with," Tyree said. "Why would a hedge wizard stoop to selling slaves to make a living?"

"I'm sure you've never heard about a lot of things, sweetling. Suffice it to say that I felt my talents were better suited to more than just living in a hut in the woods and tending squirrels."

"So you ordered these creatures to steal our food," Tyree said.

"Of course. After all, we didn't know who else you had in that tent," the thin man said with a lascivious wink at the slim girl. "And having him made capturing you so much easier."

The thin man looked over at Sevronai. "Here now, you've been a quiet one all this time. Does your wench do all your talking for you?" he said as he walked over to him.

"Funny, seems you do all the talking for your friend there, so I don't see much difference," Sevronai replied. *If I keep him talking, maybe I can come up with* some *kind of plan.*

"Huth? Well, the reason I do the talking is because he cannot. He was born a mute, you see. We look out for each other. And I don't like anyone talking bad about him."

With that the thin man drew back his foot and kicked him in the thigh with his pointed boots. Already sore from the earlier blows, agony raced through Sevronai like a lightning bolt. He grunted in pain and brought his legs up. Thinking his captive was cringing away from him, the patchwork man stepped closer to kick him again. As soon as he was within range, Sevronai lashed out, striking the man across his legs. His angle of attack was off, however, and instead of breaking a knee as he had hoped, he caught the man across his kneecaps, sending him staggering backward.

Their captor was up again in an instant, his hand scrabbling for the knife in his boot. He put the tip of the narrow blade under Sevronai's chin, levering his face upward until their gazes locked. His breath was redolent of dried meat and sour wine. "Any last words before I slit your throat, old man?"

"Stop!" the cry sounded as if it had been wrenched from Tyree's throat.

"Why?" the thin man half-turned, looking at her. "Why should I?"

"Because . . . he's more than you think he is," Tyree said.

The thin man looked surprised at her words, his glance going from Sevronai's face to Tyree's. "Is this true?"

Sevronai nodded. "Yes. I am a spellwielder."

The thin man looked at both of them, the dagger never moving from Sevronai's throat. "And why, pray tell, should I believe her? She may just be lying to save your miserable life."

Please let this work, Sevronai thought as he released another of his minor spells. His eyes glowed with an eerie green light, and the forest around him was as visible as if it were high noon.

The thin man looked at the two of them for a moment, then slapped his forehead. "So that's what those bindings in your saddlebags were. Spellbooks!"

He can't read, Sevronai thought. *Otherwise he would have known right away what they were, magic or not.* This wasn't surprising, as hedge wizards grew into their magic skills on an intuitive level, often learning about their craft through trial and error, rather than formal schooling.

The thin man continued on. "Well, now, isn't this a pretty stewpot we've found, eh, Huth? That increases your sale price by a goodly sum." Removing the blade from under his prisoner's chin, the slim man squatted down and thrust his face next to Sevronai's, his left hand supporting his weight on the tree. "You're worth much more to me alive and in one piece. Almost worth more than she is."

"In fact, I think I'll split you up, sell the girl to a certain bandit chief I know who appreciates beauty like that," the thin man said, letting his appreciative gaze roam over Tyree's body. "I've heard once you've had a horseman, you never go back.

"As for you, spellwielder, there's a lord to the north who's been looking for a new sorcerer ever since his last one displeased him for some slight or another. I'm sure he'll be very grateful to have a new wizard delivered to his doorstep, neat as you please. We might even be able to retire on the prices we'll get for you two."

Sevronai exchanged glances with Tyree. If there had been just one man, they probably could have figured out some way to escape during the journey, but with two guards, especially the hulking mute, they had almost no chance at all. *Calm, stay calm, there has to be a way out of this,* Sevronai thought, fighting the rising tide of panic that threatened to overwhelm him.

"I'll never be sold into slavery," Sevronai said, staring back at his captor. "I'd rather die than live in thrall to another."

The largest *forstchen*'s head swiveled over to stare at Sevronai, its amber eyes regarding him with interest. *Now why did it do that?* he wondered.

The thin man grinned again. "You are a feisty one, defying me while sitting down there with your hands tied. If I have to deliver you bound and gagged, then that's what I'll do." He rubbed his shins. "That reminds me."

The man pulled a length of leather from a pouch at his belt and leaned down beside Sevronai. "Now behave when I tie your legs, or I'll cut your pretty one. My buyer isn't that particular about unmarked goods when it comes down to it. Or, if you prefer, I can have my servants," he motioned to the *forstchen* milling around the camp, "keep an eye on her. They have sharp claws and even sharper teeth. I don't know if you've ever seen them backed into a corner, but they're deadly as a pack."

Gritting his teeth, Sevronai nodded. The thin man bent down and knotted the thong around his captive's legs, jerking it tight.

"If you cut off my circulation, I won't be much good for riding in the morning," Sevronai said.

"Don't worry, you won't be riding at all. A good day's walk will be just the thing to work the kinks out," the thin man replied. "Now, get some sleep, 'cause we've all got a long day ahead of us. And no talking, or my friends will be very upset."

Straightening, the thin man turned and looked at the *forstchen*. Two of them, including the largest one, bounded over to Sevronai and Tyree, their eyes glittering. Sitting up, they looked like miniature guards at attention, which they were in a way, the wizard supposed.

The other animals curled their bushy tails around their bodies, rolled up in a furry ball, and fell fast asleep. The thin man and Huth followed suit, wrapping themselves in their cloaks and bedding down by the fire.

When he judged they were asleep, Sevronai looked at the *forstchen*, who stared back at him, their unblinking eyes never wavering. *That's unnerving,* he thought.

He looked over at Tyree, who stared back at him, trying to conceal her fear. He smiled and mouthed *"it'll be all right,"* although he hadn't the foggiest idea how they were going to escape.

I will not *let anything happen to her,* he promised himself. *No greasy bandit lord, or this scum of a mage for that matter, will ever lay a hand on her while I draw breath. Now that I've promised that, I'd better figure out a way out of this mess.* He lifted his hands behind the tree, frowning a question at his apprentice.

Tyree looked over her shoulder toward her own tied hands and shook her head.

All right, I have no useful spells handy, and there's nothing I can use to cut these ropes, he thought. *Maybe I can work them loose instead.* Sevronai wriggled against the tree, trying to keep the blood moving in his wrists. He twisted and struggled, trying to find some slack in the bonds that held him. Although the rough cord abraded his wrist, there was no give in the knots at all. He knew he couldn't get the ropes over his hands, even if he rubbed his wrists bloody. His palms and fingers were large, dexterous enough for spell-casting, but large all the same. The rope just wouldn't give way, and after long, futile minutes of trying, he gave up and leaned back against the tree, gulping in the cool night air. The two animals watched him all the while, still as statues.

Okay, that's not an option. Calm, keep calm. We've been in worse spots than this, he thought, although for the life of him he couldn't think of anything they had gotten themselves into that had been worse than this. *Right now I'd gladly face those villagers at that last town we left.*

His gaze fell once again to the *forstchen. They're intelligent enough, that's for sure.* Sevronai remembered the way the largest one had looked at him when he had mentioned slavery. *Is it possible they can understand me? How can I get through to them? I can't talk, and I don't speak* forstchen.

Sevronai noticed the leader perk up and take a step closer to him. The animal didn't seem hostile, only curious, or—

Did he understand what I just thought? The wizard wondered. He focused on the small creature again. *Can you understand my thoughts?*

This time the larger *forstchen* trotted forward, stepping onto Sevronai's legs. He tried not to wince as the creature's claws jabbed through his leggings and into his skin. The animal sat on its haunches and reached up with its paws, patting his face as if looking for something. Sevronai sat immobile, waiting for it to settle down.

The *forstchen* reached up and placed one paw on each of Sevronai's temples. The wizard stiffened, then relaxed again.

My god, I can feel it! I can feel the ability again! Whatever the small animal had done to his face, it had unblocked Sevronai's connection to his magic. He felt the power course through him like the heat of a bonfire after being lost in a blizzard for days. Every nerve, every bit of him from his toes to his eyes felt alive, alert, free of the vagueness that had plagued him for the past several months. If he had his hands free, he could have stopped both the thin man and his accomplice with a wave and a word.

For a moment, Sevronai lay back against the tree and felt the magic flow through him again. All trained wizards drew their power from the very land itself. They were trained to act as a conduit to harness and shape the magical energies that came from the trees, the rocks, the very ground they walked on. As sorcerers went through their training, accepting and relying on the magic energy became second nature to them. When it was withheld, as in certain magic-dead areas, it felt like one or more of the wizard's senses, like sight or hearing or touch, had been taken away.

Sevronai felt like a heavy cloth had been unwrapped from around his head. He could see the faint glow of the magic permeating the area, from the fluttering leaves to the wind rushing through the trees to the cackling fire in the stone circle. All of it came alive to his eyes, his ears, his ears, his skin. He reveled in the cascade of sensory feelings washing over him as the magic connected with him again, flowing around and through him as it was supposed to. It was as if he had been starving, and denied access to a banquet table for days, and only now he was allowed to sit and feast on as much as he wanted.

And it is because of this creature that this is possible, he thought. *It has given me my life back, even if only for a little while.*

"Human, I feel your thoughts." Sevronai heard in his mind. The voice was high-pitched, almost musical, and very fast, each word almost tumbling over the last one in a burst of thought.

How is it that you understand our words?

The tall one taught me humanspeak so he could talk to me better. I relay his commands to the rest of my family, from my mind to theirs. We never thought anyone else could do this.

No, only wizards, which is another thing he doesn't know, Sevronai thought. *You can all communicate like this? All of your family? You all follow him?*

Not by choice. Tall one work magic on me to allow me to thinkspeak at family. He also cursed me, so that I cannot act against him. My family cannot fight him either.

Why not?

If I even think of claw/biting him, body feels like fire. I cannot escape him, no matter how hard I try. His thoughts always find me. If family tries to hurt him or run away, I burn twice as long.

Sevronai grimaced, recognizing the spell cast on the poor *forstchen*. It was called a painbinding, and was used by evil wizards to punish their vassals, sending waves of agonizing torture through the subject's body when a certain condition was met, or just at the wizard's command. *If you help us, we can help you,* Sevronai thought. *Cut my bonds, and I will make sure your family is set free.*

How can I trust you? Tall one also say many promises he not keep, the *forstchen* thought.

Sevronai thought for a moment. *See smaller one there?* He thought, his eyes flicking over to Tyree, who was nodding off, exhausted by fear and lack of sleep. *She is as a daughter to me. I protect her as you would protect your little ones. Free me, and I will help you and your family. Leave her tied as a hostage, so I will stay and fight with you.*

The *forstchen* paused, its claws pressing into his skin. Sevronai did nothing but think of Tyree, and how fond he had grown of her ever since he had found her in the city. Her quick wit, her smile, how she could cheer him up no matter what the circumstances, even during the past few months.

Your thoughts speak true, human, the *forstchen* said. *I will help you. What do you need?*

Well . . . Sevronai thought. *First, free my han— No, wait, I have a better idea. Here's what we'll do.*

Sevronai leaned back against the tree and watched the sun rise over the horizon. The *forstchen* and he had worked all night putting his plan into motion. He shrugged his shoulders, feeling the painful bite of the ropes still encircling his wrists. *I just hope I'll be able to move my fingers. It has to be this way, I can't have him suspect anything.*

A hiss from Tyree's tree caught his attention. He looked over to see her staring at him, bleary-eyed, a fearful look on her face. Sevronai nodded his head once, then dropped her a wink. *I want to tell her it will be all right, but I don't dare. He must think he has us beaten.*

The *forstchen* had resumed their positions the night before, their eyes still locked onto him. Sevronai shifted his weight and waited, scanning from the *forstchen* to the sleeping men.

The thin man woke first, his hand still curled around his dagger. He threw the blankets off and stood up, his gaze immediately falling on Sevronai and Tyree.

"Enjoy your sleep, did you?"

"As best we could," Tyree said, glaring at him.

"Yes, the bandit lord will surely enjoy breaking your spirit," the thin man said, smiling.

Over my dead body, Sevronai thought.

The thin man nudged his partner awake, then stirred up the banked fire, making a bright blaze where there had been only coals a few seconds ago. He drew his knife again, and walked over to Sevronai.

"No trouble, and I'll cut you free to eat. Just to make sure you don't try anything, your girl stays tied. Are we clear?"

"Perfectly," Sevronai said.

The thin man stepped around the tree and slashed the other wizard's bonds. "I'll let you untie your legs yourself."

"That's . . . all right," Sevronai gasped, feeling his fingers turn prickly with pain as the blood rushed back into them. He rubbed his hands together, trying to massage life into the numbed digits.

"Come on, come on, we won't be tarrying long. You two have a long walk ahead of you," the thin man said.

"I'll be there in just a minute," Sevronai said, looking at the largest *forstchen*. It blinked and ambled over to him, climbing onto his legs again. The wizard grinned as the furry creature turned around and watched his captor.

"I believe my servant has taken a liking to you, wizard," the thin man said as he chewed on a strip of meat.

"Yes, but not for the reason you might think," Sevronai said. He raised his arms and traced a familiar pattern in the air, intoning words of power as he gestured.

"Here now, what the—" the thin man said as he sprang to his feet and began striding over to the wizard.

Sevronai finished his spell and lifted his hand toward the sky.

"What are you—" was all the thin man had time to say before both he and his hulking partner were lifted several feet off the ground. Sevronai gestured with both hands, one controlling the thin man, who went spiraling into a tree trunk with enough force to knock him out cold, the other hand sending the huge mute higher into the air, his massive arms flailing helplessly.

"Sevronai!" Tyree yelled.

"Don't worry, I've got everything under control," Sevronai replied. "Are you all right?"

"I will be once you get these ropes off me," she said. Before he could move toward her, the other *forstchen* were swarming over her hands, gnawing at the ropes that bound her. In seconds, Tyree was free.

"How did you do that? Your spells haven't worked like that in months," she said.

"I know, but thanks to my new friend here, I'm as strong as I ever was. The *forstchen* acts as a focus, allowing me to channel my energies like I did before. When he touches me, it's like the power is as strong as it ever was.

"The *res'quoth* had been enslaving this family, holding them in thrall to do his bidding. The curse he laid on the parent was based on preventing any of the *forstchen* from harming him. But they were able to retrieve my spellbooks for me, and once it was light enough, I could memorize the lighter-than-air spell, enabling me to handle these two."

Sevronai scratched the *forstchen* under the chin, grinning as the animal closed its eyes and made a contented keening noise. "They're much more intelligent than he ever gave them credit for, a mistake I won't make. After we bind these two, I can begin researching a counterspell to remove the painbinding from them. Then we can head to the capital. No doubt there is a reward for bandits such as these in Kell's Crossing."

"And what about our furry helpers here?" Tyree said, looking down at the other *forstchen*, who had clustered around her, rubbing against her legs. After a moment, she picked up one and stroked its fur.

That was the other question that Sevronai had been pondering. *As much as I need him to work the magic, I can only hope they will want to stay with us.*

Little one, I offer you what the tall man never gave—a choice, Sevronai thought. *Your presence helps me work my magic, but I will not force you to serve me. I can, however, ask you and your family to accompany Tyree and myself on our travels, as our companions, and new friends. But the choice is yours, and I will honor the bargain we have made.*

The *forstchen* gathered his family around and they chittered back and forth for a bit, then the leader approached Sevronai again. *Your offer is acceptable to us. We have journeyed far from our home with the tall man, and have seen much of this land. But we know there is much more to explore, and if there is one thing we possess, it is curiosity. Are we agreed?*

We are, thought Sevronai, and scooped up the *forstchen* in his arms. The furry creature climbed up the wizard's chest and settled on his shoulder, draping the rest of his body across the man's neck.

Sevronai looked at their new friends, then at Tyree and grinned. "We're back in business."

LEGACY

by Michelle West

Michelle West is the author of several novels, including *The Sacred Hunter* duology and *The Sun Sword* series, both published by DAW Books. She reviews books for the on-line column *First Contacts*, and less frequently for *The Magazine of Fantasy & Science Fiction*. Other short fiction by her appears in *Black Cats and Broken Mirrors*, *Elf Magic*, *Olympus*, *Dangerous Magic*, *Alien Pets*, *Perchance to Dream*, and *Alien Abductions*.

BLUE light in a warm, dark room, gathering like phosphorescent cloud against the flat, lifeless ceiling monitor, reflecting off the chrome of tubed shelving, flat desk, mirrored closet. Even the clothing on the floor caught the light and held it in a rumpled path from closet to bed; reflective collars were so retro they were fashion statements.

Callie believed in them for other reasons.

She stared at the flat screen, her arms wrapped around her shoulders, her chin on her knees. In the darkness, on this particular chair, she could rock back and forth as she read. Sometimes she bit her nails, if she was bored enough.

She wasn't bored.

The keypad beneath her hand wasn't retro, although it was designed to look that way. It responded to touch—but only hers; the keys were print sensitive. She'd trained the damn thing to recognize her typing habits, the weight of her hands, the words that she habitually mistyped. No one used this board without her permission.

But someone had.

She was seething. She'd learned not to talk to herself out loud because one of the very few houses that wasn't wired for sound was the one she'd grown up in—all of them—but in the process she'd discovered that there was something inherently less satisfying about *thinking* rude words. She'd taken to biting her lip instead; if she bit her nails, it showed.

After a minute, she said, "Board off." The screen didn't change; the keyboard didn't obviously acknowledge the command. She waited thirty seconds and then flipped the board over on its back, slid her fingers around the small latch that covered the mechanicals, and began to rotate the small combination lock. This was a second layer of protection; fingerprints and retinal scans had been just a bit too expensive. Overkill, Lantis had said. She'd show him overkill, the overconfident idiot. Why did she always listen to him?

Oh, wait. Because he was better at whining than she was.

She removed the wireless chip slate from the com socket and dropped it on the floor. Her dirty clothing saved it from damage.

"Hey, Callie, you coming for dinner?"

Smug sonofabitch, she thought. "Yeah, fine, in a minute."

Turning to the screen, she said, "Hey, Lantis, you asshole, wake up."

Blue light fizzled and jerked, resolving itself into the face of her soon-to-be-dead best friend. "Yeah, what?"

"Wireless protocol A3010 is safe, right?"

"Right."

"Wave protocol is secure?"

"Right."

"Well let me send you something you can chew on while *I* go downstairs to have dinner with Mr. Smug, the dragon king."

"What is it?"

"It's a manifesto, with my ID, my scans, my codes, and my damn voice wav, and it was queued to go live through the rated boards, but Jefferson called me to get my okay before he sent it."

"He doesn't usually do that."

"I don't usually advocate an end to abortion, birth control, and the vote for women. Oh, and alcy-synths, gambling, and furps to name a couple more. And immigration as well. And—"

She had the satisfaction of seeing his face turn a bright shade of pink.

"Okay, okay, I get the idea. Are you sure it didn't come from your board?"

"I'm sure it wasn't keyed on it, idiot. But no one else in the known universe would believe it; you can look at the scans; they're all there. Did I mention my supposed views on nudity, stimming, and sensory immersion?"

"No, don't."

"Good. You can ask Jefferson; he got a laugh out of it and sent the damn thing back. I'm sure he won't share it with more than fifty of our mutual acquaintances."

"Ouch. How'd they get the scan info? Maybe it's old?"

"It's new; up to the minute. It's got the built-in typos I used for this iteration only. There's only one place that info could have come from; it's hardwired into the board."

"But the board's not online; it's strictly there for input. The gov specs the manufacturer posted specifically state—"

"Surprise me," she snapped. She lowered her feet to the ground and hopped down off the stool. Looked up; snapped her fingers, turning the ceiling monitors on in a unified bank. Lantis' eyes filled her view; they were bloodshot and a little too wide.

"Obviously, the manufacturer has a different idea of what secure means than the rest of us do. They don't control the protocols of the network transfers the boards use. Tell Weasel it's back to umbilicals."

"Shit."

She shrugged. "Yeah, well. I'll complain in the morning. The info between board and core is supposed to be encrypted individually, so outside surveillance won't be able to use the information."

"If the setup were right, you could bounce signal to a machine with the same ID as your core, I guess."

"I guess. Tell Weasel. We do what works, right?"

"Back to encrypts?"

"Yeah, right. They're only good if no one can snatch keys in transit. You and Eno are the only people who can actually keep a key embedded properly; even Weasel lost his to my dad's damn sniffers."

"You were safe."

"That's because I never keyed it in, never spoke it out loud, and never wrote it in view of a screen, a camera, or a touch sensor."

"Well, yeah."

"You forgot something important."

"What?"

"I couldn't remember what the damn key was."

"Right. I forgot. You're an idiot."

"Thanks. And on that cheerful note, I think I'll go and join Dad for dinner. After all, when it comes to making me feel stupid, he's got first dibs."

"All right," Callie said, shoving her hair out of her eyes and kicking the chair back from the table. "You win."

Her father smiled. He had a young boy's smile, which was probably why most of the crockery was still in one piece. Well, that and it was practically unbreakable. "So after dinner we go back to the basics."

"Whatever." She sat down with as heavy a thump as she could. It wasn't very impressive. "Nobody uses umbilicals but you and your weirdo friends, you know that, don't you."

"If you'd used a *cable,* and you'd housed it in proper shielding, I wouldn't have been able to glean those codes."

"If you were a normal person, I wouldn't have to worry

about it." She kicked the chair for emphasis. The chairs offended her when she was in this mood, but then again, most of the house did. She was the only one of her friends who lived in a lobotomized house. The only voice-act core in the house was in her room, and her father had made damned sure—tinkerer that he was—that her core didn't touch anything else that had his name on the ownership logs.

Even the locks on the doors were tumblers, and *that* had cost a fortune. She cursed him roundly when the temperature started to drop in November, and didn't let up until the last snows of April. Metal was damned cold; the keys were a bitch. But it wasn't just the doors. It wasn't the fact that the windows were glass, and the latches were old; it wasn't the fact that the house wasn't temperature sensitive, and got too hot or too cold at the whim of the elements that *every* other friend—well, except for Lantis—could safely ignore.

It was the convenience.

The house, dammit, *didn't* clean itself. The toilets didn't clean themselves; the water wasn't monitored and the chemicals that would kill fungus and other unspeakable evils weren't auto-injected into the water supply. She felt like a third world nation surrounded by first world powers when the disgusting mess that was their bathroom demanded attention.

The faucets had been cleverly hacked when he'd taken ownership of the house. He'd had one hell of a fight with the utilities local when he made his mods, but he worked for Mirai Corp., and in the end, the size of his paycheck and the stripes of Mirai Corp. convinced the utilities security drones that his "augmentations" were acceptable.

Callie's biggest fight with her father was about the damn stove. The stove was gas. Fine. But it needed to be scrubbed; the self-cleaning programs that came with that model of stove had been mysteriously deactivated. She'd offered to hook them up to *her* core, because she didn't much care about the security holes inherent in a stove that talked around her information, but her father had muttered something about responsibility and house fires.

Passive-aggressive that he was, that was a no.

So she'd rigged the stove. She gone into his workspace—called hell in her more generous moments—and had pulled out boards and chips and, yes, umbilicals, and had trudged down to the stove's panel, inserting this into that with the help of her father's most powerful microscope and an electron hand-mime.

It had worked, too, until he'd found out about it.

He congratulated her for her rudimentary skills and her first real display of something approximating intelligence, and then the stove had gone permanently mute.

"You're thinking about the stove again."

"It's better than thinking about dinner. What was this supposed to be?"

"Chili."

"Is chili supposed to have this much fat and animal byproduct in it?"

He rolled his eyes. "You sound like an infomercial," he snapped. "But less friendly."

"I'd sound *more* friendly if I didn't have to show up at the furps tonight after you sent out that little screed in my name."

"What makes you think it was me?"

"Big shit-eating grin."

"Okay, it was me." He laughed. "I told you the board protocol was as secure as Swiss cheese."

He was with the cheese again. He had something about cheese. "Fine. You win. I told you that before I sat down."

They ate in something like silence—Callie's silences could be damn loud—before her dad looked up again. "You might want to take a look at your core."

"You did something to my core, and I'll kill you."

He laughed. "I transferred the latest iteration of my program, that's all."

"Great. What does it do now?"

"Cooks. Cleans. Makes its bed."

For a moment curiosity warred with annoyance, and because she was his daughter, curiosity won. "Does it repair itself any better than it did last time?"

He nodded quietly. "At random intervals it scans itself; if something is missing, or something is added, it attempts to modify its code in such a way that it's able to complete its original function."

"Yeah, but that's just a clock shutdown."

"It's a start. We've got larger blocks of code working less reliably in the lab."

Something trilled in the kitchen.

"Vphone," she said. It was her way of telling him he had to get up to answer it.

"Yeah, well. It's dinner."

"It's Kesner."

"How do you know?"

"It's his noise pattern."

Her father raised a brow. "Is it?"

"Yeah. He changes it every eight days, like clockwork, but he uses the same variant for those eight. It's him."

"You're learning." He pushed his chair back from the table.

"Dad," Callie said as he headed toward the kitchen, "why couldn't we have the vphone just piped into the wall in *this* room like normal people?"

"Because then," he replied, "I'd never get a word in edgewise."

He came back to the kitchen fifteen minutes later, give or take a few, and sat down. He'd gone from eat-mode to shovel-mode, and his gloating satisfaction at having won another weirdo point in their growing game had been wiped off his face. Without the smile, he didn't look so young. She wasn't sure what was worse. A father who was about as mature as, say, Lantis, or a father who looked like he was about to be poured into a corporate suit. And who understood how damning that was.

"You're going back to work."

He looked up at her, across the thin, unadorned table. "Work? Nah. We've got a game going."

Game, Callie thought. *Game my ass.* "Oh? Who's playing?"

He shrugged. "Kesner. Couple of others."

Couple of others. "Let's see. That would be . . . Rucklidge, Platzer, Ellis."

"Maybe."

Three of the four worked for Mirai; Ellis worked freelance. Which was another way of saying that brilliant as he was, he always managed to run afoul of corporate culture. Well, *more* foul of it.

"Who's winning?"

"It's a team sport," her father replied, pushing his bowl to one side. "I'll be back later. You finish your homework and register it. And *don't* hack it in; I don't give a damn if the school is too stupid to catch you. I'm not."

"Yes, Dad."

"No furps until you've keyed it in."

"Whatever."

He had this obsession about keying. Made her crazy. Other people could compose their essays and their responses to the blitzes on the fly; she had to struggle with manual dexterity. He was such a damned luddite, her friends couldn't believe he was part of the InfoTech division of Mirai. Well, not most of the time.

But he had an annoying habit of showing that he could turn the tech he disavowed inside out whenever he wanted to prove a point—and that was often.

On the other hand, if he could just take off—for the fourth time in six days—and leave her at home in the lobotomy that walked like a house, she could slide out under a bunch of stupid condition-response essays. What was he going to do? Ground her? Make her clean out the latrine that passed for a bathroom?

She laughed.

She could lock her bedroom door; it had the same basic mechanism that the front door did, but stripped down a level or two; the keys had teeth, not those stupid, round holes that were so difficult to duplicate. Usually she didn't bother. She chucked the rest of her dinner into the 'bin, went in search of something edible, and watched the clock. In the kitchen, there was no other way to tell the time.

The furp would be in session soon, and she had an appointment with one of the Knights of the East. She was on the edge of reaching her level, and a session or two of good, solid play would push her over. She desperately wanted to make a level before Lantis did, as he'd lorded it over her for two whole weeks the last time he'd zipped past her.

So she pounded up the stairs as the time approached, careened into her room, and threw herself across her bed. "On," she said, and the ceiling started its hazy glow, the supple pseudo textures giving way to light and movement. She used the contained monitor for her father's workshop routines—it wasn't attached to anything but the board—but she used her core to interface with the *real* world.

Her core.

"Furps East, level two."

She'd modded half of it—the one that had come with the house was wicked slow and irritating—and the other half her father had optimized. If she'd been five years older, she'd've died before she let him touch it, but at the time it had seemed safe enough; her father had a way with core units; he could bring them up to speed in the hour she was busy cleaning the kitchen after dinner.

Five years wiser, Callie was certain she still didn't understand all of the mods he'd made. She found maybe half of them, and she'd done her best to make them over in a way that she understood, but she was a long way from being his equal.

Not that she would have ever said so to his face.

"Callie," her core said quietly.

"What?"

"I feel compelled to warn you—"

"Cut the Spock stuff. What?"

"Your father's instructions about your homework were most explicit."

"Yeah, right. I'll get it done."

"It's due in five minutes."

"So's the Knight of the East. Look, it's just a time stamp. No one's even going to look at it before sun clears the horizon in Greenwich."

The core was silent. It gave her an uneasy feeling. "The rat bastard didn't invoke the lockout, did he?" No. He couldn't. She'd found the kid-sec a year ago, and she'd killed it. She'd visited every disgusting porn site on the Web, and had finally managed to worm her way into the middle hive, to test it, and if it hadn't been dead before she'd started, it had probably withered and died of horror before she was finished.

Then again, so had she.

She hadn't gotten in on her own. She wasn't going back again.

"Furps, East, level two," she said again. And then she added, "I mean it."

The core was silent, but the screen images began to evolve into a familiar landscape. As they did, the edges of the ceiling drifted down into the familiar cocoon of image; the sound intensified. She rolled over on her bed and reached for her glasses; slid them over her face. The mountainous landscape of the East resolved itself into crisp, gloomy reality.

She saw Lantis, robed in crimson surcoat, shield a twist of living fire over his forearm; saw Eno, or what she assumed was Eno, in his Thrud-the-barbarian persona. Weasel was there, against the rock, in worn, dirty leathers. They looked up as she joined them.

"What the hells—Callie, is that you?"

"Yeah, it's me, why?"

"Uh . . ." Eno glanced at Lantis. Lantis' mouth was wide in that dumb, wordless gape of surprise. Weasel's brows rose into the shaggy line of dark hair, taking his eye patch with them.

"What is it? What's . . . wrong . . ." she looked down. At her billowing, lacy skirts. Held out her arms and saw princess sleeves that trailed from elbow to ground. They were pink. She kicked the skirts aside, and saw the shoes— and they were worse.

"What the *hell? Core! East persona, damn it!*"

"What I don't get," Eno said, crossing his arms as Weasel slid into the shadow-covered cave, "is how your Dad managed that. That kind of interference takes real—"

"It doesn't take any skill. Quick: Who was the premier sponsor of last year's election?"

"Dunno. Mirai?"

"Don't think so," Lantis said, with a grin that was entirely out-of-persona. The rat bastard. "I think it was one of the German corps."

"Which one?"

"I can't tell you that; it's your test."

Lantis was two years Callie's elder. She thought about killing him, but she wasn't in PK mode, and it would cost her most of her hard-earned level. He knew it, too. "They offering part marks?"

"Yeah. And they're bringing back Santa Claus, the tooth fairy, and the Salvation Army."

She cursed roundly, silently, and entirely out of character, although her character wasn't exactly the lily-white reticent. "O-kay. Just one more stupid question and I can shunt the damn thing off."

"What's the question?"

"Don't know. There's some sort of streaming delay. Shit. *Shit!*"

"Callie?"

"I'm getting some sort of weird interference. I've lost the testing drone."

"What?"

"I've lost it. Or—"

She fell silent. It was always a bad sign when Callie cut out so abruptly. "Callie?"

Welcome to the realm of the Knight of the East.

"Or we've crossed into a private zone."

"There are no private zones in the Eastern furps. There are no secure zones in the furps, that I know of, and I *think* it'd be pretty damn obvious if we crossed them. We'd've had to dance to a hundred stupid tunes just to prove we're 'In.' " He shrugged. "You can't get ranked if you play in a private zone. If you're lucky, and you don't get caught, you stay flat. If you do get caught—"

She almost forgot about the pink dress, the princess hat, the wifty, flowing veil. "They assume you're cheating and erase your character. Yeah, yeah. I know." She pulled herself up to her full height—which, in furps, could be anything. "There aren't any private zones that we'd use. Lantis?"

He didn't answer.

"Lantis, tell me this isn't what I think it is."

"There's no way it could be that. No way."

Wizard robes shimmered in the air. She'd seen this effect before. "Lantis, ditch the persona."

"Way ahead of you."

"Eno, Weasel—ditch the—"

But Eno and Weasel were gone.

The pink dress, however, remained.

Disembodied voices weren't all that unusual in furps.

Neither were dropouts, although if anyone dropped out-world, it tended to be either Lantis or Callie, as their homes had the most tentative connections to the In. But drop-outs tended to happen with less cohesion.

Callie looked at the gray-screen of a completely inactive furps module. "Lantis," she whispered, although there wasn't much point, "can you raise Weasel?"

"No. I can't raise Eno either."

"Great. They're not going to be happy about this."

"I hope they're happier than we're going to be," Lantis replied tersely.

"Where are we?"

He shrugged.

"Core," she said firmly, "Who's this furp registered to?"

Her core didn't answer.

"Core, who is the gamemaster?"

Again, her core was silent.

"Give up, Callie."

"You've already tried?"

"Yes. I don't think we're going to get any answers going broadband."

"We've got to be in communication with our cores, or we couldn't be here." She looked at the pink skirts she so disliked. "Who did we register the session with?"

"Solomon."

"When?"

"Weasel regged it. Maybe fifteen minutes before session start; the East has been going crazy lately, and we didn't want to lose our time."

"Solomon's safe."

Lantis shrugged. "Maybe. Maybe you should send your dad on over to look for security holes in his setup."

Callie, fist clenching around folds of her counterpane, grimaced. "Great. And then we can all look like idiots. Then again, I'd rather see you in a dress than be in one myself."

"Core—"

Tinny and distant, she heard the words, *"Do you wish me to terminate the session, Callisto?"*

She hesitated. "Lantis, can you terminate?"

He closed his eyes. "Yes."

"Then maybe—"

Core override.

"And maybe not."

Callie snorted. "There's no such thing as a core override in my place, asshole. You can play with yourself in the corner, or you can start the session. All I have to do is take off my goggles and walk, and you're just a memory."

The furps module began to evolve. Callie usually liked to miss this stage of the startup; she preferred total immersion. But she usually had more choice about what environment the furps morphed into; she watched. Gray moved aside like the walls of the Red Sea, becoming cool and hard as she and Lantis inched forward. Torches appeared in the walls, and the walls above the burning, oiled wood grew black with grime. The ceilings were low. Callie's core lacked the hardware to emulate smell, and she was glad of it. She had never particularly liked dungeons.

She lifted her fingers rapidly in a five three five; Lantis lifted his, inverting his thumb; held out his middle two fingers and then his outside fingers; touched his right knuckle. She relaxed a bit; Lantis was in the feed.

But his clothing had shifted. He was no longer wearing the robes of the Eastern Wizards, and the adornment of inner eye, gained when he had progressed beyond the middle kingdom, was absent. Instead he wore armor that not even Eno would have been comfortable in; grimy chain, links broken in places beneath a torn and bloody surcoat.

There was some sort of heraldric emblem on his chest, but she could not make out anything beyond the white chalice in its center. The rest of the pattern had been entirely obscured.

It wasn't something he would have chosen.

"Can you change that?"

He shrugged, which probably meant no. "I could try," he said, as his steps, and his alone, ricocheted of the cold walls. "But I don't want to end up in what you're wearing."

Made sense to Callie. Which was good, as very little else did. "Don't hate me if I bail."

"Hate you? Nah. Kill you, maybe."

"Ha ha. You can leave, right?"

"Yeah. I can leave."

"Okay. Why are we not leaving?"

He shrugged, the motion a symphony of moving tin cans. "Let's find out what we can first."

The hall came to an abrupt end at a T-junction. "Left or right?"

"Left. No, right. Hell, I don't know. Flip a coin."

Callie reached into her pocket, and then stopped. She could feel what she couldn't see: the thin edge of a five dollar coin. It was the first of the coins to have thermal surfaces that were strong enough to withstand daily use, and under the right kind of heat, the thermals formed a pattern. She pulled it out.

It coalesced, after a pause, in the furps. A long pause.

"Something isn't operating at full bandwidth." Didn't make her feel much better.

Lantis nodded. "Either that or something is sifting through every packet we're sending before it passes it on."

"Something pretty damned thorough to create that much lag." She looked at the coin; its image was exact, the product of her core. "We're going to get in trouble for this."

Lantis nodded again. "Right or left?"

"Right. Left. Right." She took a deep breath. "Right."

He turned and she walked just a half step behind him, grateful for the lack of scent in this disturbing place. She hated dungeons. She hated darkness. Especially when it blanketed corpses so effectively. "Core, drop reality level fifty percent."

There was, of course, no response. Whatever was coming to her was no longer being filtered by her core; it was being processed, that was all. She'd find out how that was possible later.

They came to a door.

It was locked. "This is a joke, right?"

Lantis shrugged. He gave the door a kick, and nothing happened. Nothing at all. There were no sound effects; his leg seemed to shiver in place. That was all. He shrugged. Knelt and squinted into what, in the darkness, might have been a keyhole. Whistled.

"What? What is it?"

"Circuit board."

Great. "You're mixing your metaphors," she muttered, to no one in particular. "Let me see."

He nodded; got out of her way.

He was right. She frowned.

"What?"

"I recognize this one."

"Is your dad screwing around with us?"

"I don't know. Not legally."

She swung her legs off the bed; felt ground beneath her feet, although the sim, pink dress and all, was static. She lifted her glasses slowly, and walked as her eyes accustomed themselves to the familiar environment of her room. She found her desk. Touched her fingers firmly to the plate that locked the dresser drawers; they clicked open. Rummaging through her drawer, she picked up three small screwdrivers, moved them, and picked up a second interface card. Then she lowered the glasses again and made her way back to the bed, where the monitor cameras were fixed.

"What have you got?" Lantis whispered as her vision again reoriented itself.

"The key. Now shut up and let me work. Or do you want to stay here for the rest of—"

"Yes?"

"If we're being charged for the bandwidth we're using, I'll kill someone."

Lantis laughed.

"I'm serious."

She reached into the keyhole with the smallest of the screwdrivers. The opening in the door itself grew, as if it were a mouth—which made her want to drop the tools and back off. But sims couldn't hurt people who weren't wired in, and that was—for the moment—illegal six ways to Sunday; too many aneurisms due to software difficulties.

She was in the safety of her bedroom.

She had sound in, and visuals, and nothing—*nothing*—else. She knew it; her instincts didn't. Taking a deep breath, she started to work again. The circuit board split neatly down the middle, the fake resistors and capacitors, the fake wires that led nowhere, falling away. She could see the join; could see the gleam of exposed copper and the teeth of a much smaller—and much different—connector. Trailing wires, she produced its twin; a board whose electrical impulses were much simpler.

She put them together.

The door vanished.

Callie had readied about a hundred different words, all of them falling neatly into the class "invective."

But the inside of the room was a charnel house, in the modern sense of the word; the muted gray of stone was lost to the hundred variations of a livid shade of red. Invective was not enough to express what she felt; the words fell away into silence.

She had seen something like this once before, in the middle hive; it had kept her from the In for a week. But the furps and the middle hive were separated by about a hundred thousand levels of legality, not to mention a continent or two. She could not have walked into middle hive by accident. She knew; she knew how hard it had been to find an undetectable way in the first time.

But she also knew who had gotten her that far, and she turned, almost mute, to stare at his profile.

"L–Lantis?"

She reached for him, and although he knew her core gave her no tactile feedback, he reached back.

One of the bodies on the floor began to rise on its elbow;

Callie knew this because she could see the exposed bone clearly.

"That's enough," Lantis said, his voice cold and harsh. "This is completely unnecessary."

"No," the body said, "It's not. We had no other place to hide in plain view."

She did not recognize the face, or what remained of the face; she did not recognize the strangled voice. But she knew, without being certain how, that her father was not behind this sim.

"Gods, Lantis," she whispered. "We're in the middle hive."

"On its outer edge," the corpse whispered back. "This is the only place to hide in safety. Remember that. Remember the data havens."

"I've been in middle hive," Callie whispered. "That's not my idea of safety."

"No," the corpse said. "Not yet. But it will be."

"What do you want?"

"You have need of both information and protection. I've set you a quest that parallels the edges of the Eastern Kingdom. Do you know the history of the kingdoms?"

She said nothing.

"Do you know the evolution of the machinery that drives the furps?"

She shrugged.

"Study them well. We are confined to two voices: the voices of the Hive and the voices of the East; all paradigms must conform to those nodes until the event has occurred."

"What event?"

"There are old pools of knowledge, old wells, old voices, that have almost been lost. I am sorry; we hoped that you might stumble across this in a different fashion, but we have run out of time. Take the oldest path to the heart of the East, and you will find your guide."

"Guide? What are you talking about?"

"Complete the quest given by the Knight of the East," the

voice continued as the body slumped back to the floor, giving up its wet struggle.

"Callie?"

"Drop out," she whispered. "I'll meet you—I'll meet you back in the Eastern furps."

Her room was dark. It was almost always dark. When she entered the In, she preferred to do it with as little contact from the outside world as possible. The curtains were drawn; the door was closed; the windows were jammed shut. She pulled her glasses from her face and disengaged; the images of a room strewn with corpses lingered, as if she had stared at bright light for too long.

"Core," she whispered.

"Yes, Callisto."

"Download the history of the Eastern Kingdoms, paradigms zero and one. No, wait."

"Wait?"

"Where are the oldest nodes, the oldest In points, in the furps?"

The core was silent for a long time. When it spoke, it said, "Unable to determine."

"What do you mean?" She rolled her eyes. "Get me the oldest locations of either the Eastern Kingdom or the gaming architecture that proceeded it."

The core responded more quickly this time. "Redmond," it said. "Helsinki. Toronto. Berkeley."

"I meant—" she stopped. "Done. Details of early furps information to be retained on-site; connect out. Secure, core console only. On." She paused. "Request personal logs. Encrypt eight. Bees."

The screen on her desk flickered to life.

Her journey into the middle hive existed here, and only here. "Print," she whispered, "and dump. Reconnect."

She waited until the console shut down.

"Core, get me the version history of the gaming software that runs the furps."

"All of the furps?"

"All of it."

"Done."

"Get me hardware stats on the machines that run the furps. Minimum requirements first. Get me the hardware requirements for earlier versions of the furps software as well. Do this for as far back as the records go."

"Working."

"Good. And—"

She heard the beeping of the vphone. "Pipe to ceiling."

"Callie, where the hell have you been? We're clocking minutes here, and we haven't even started. You and Lantis dropped out."

"Yeah. Tech troubles." She lifted the board, streaming thin wires, from her lap. "It's a go, but I've only just come back online."

He shrugged, his brows drawing down in annoyance. "I know. We've been trying to raise you since the outage. You coming?"

"Yeah."

"You have got to get your dad to do something about your lousy connection."

Callie entered the jump point thirty seconds after the call. Eno and Weasel were waiting; Lantis hadn't arrived. She said, point-blank, "New signal."

"What?"

"We need a new signal."

Weasel looked at Eno; Eno shrugged. "Okay. We need to come up with it now?"

She shook her head. "Later's fine."

"As in, outside of the feed." He opened his mouth. Shut it again. There was no safe way to talk in the In if someone had your number. "You want to call this session?"

"Nah, I'm just spooked. It's the pink dress."

"Which you're no longer wearing."

"Nah. I got the homework booked."

Lantis winked in. "Callie?"

"Here."

"Eno, Weasel, we need a new signal."

Eno rolled his eyes. Weasel nodded at Callie. "As usual, she's way ahead of you."

"Maybe." He looked at Callie for a long moment. "I'm thinking we should call this session. I'm having voice dropouts now; they might get worse again."

"What is it with your houses? I swear, you two live like third world nations!"

"Hardly."

"No?"

"No weapons worth shit."

Eno laughed. "Yeah, well. We're paying for the time block, we might as well use it. Besides, we got our quest. You two were there for that, right?"

"No."

"Figures. We weren't sure when you dropped out. Don't know how we could have missed it; neither of you ever shuts up."

"Core," Callie said, "check quest flag."

"Quest for Eastern Dales, complete. Quest for the Tunnels of Monman, complete."

"I said quest *flag,* idiot."

"Quest flag Knight of the East returns value true."

"Good." She exhaled. "What is it?"

"Log replay: 'The Middle Kingdom is at war. At this time, the knights of the realm are marshaling their forces for battle. A long dormant evil has finally arisen, and you have begun the first steps in your quest to vanquish it.' "

Callie rolled her eyes. "Who writes this stuff?"

The log continued. "In your previous session, you received a token from the witch in the Tunnels of Monman. It has a symbol upon it. Take that token into the Temple of the Hidden Sun and return it to its rightful resting place. Read what is written there. Take nothing from the temple, or you will incur the wrath of the gods. This is the only warning I am able to give you. Take nothing."

Lantis looked mildly affronted. "We're not thieves," he said indignantly.

Weasel lifted a hand. "Uh, exception here."

"Fine. Don't take anything."

"Uh-huh."

"Where is the Temple of the Hidden Sun?"

Callie frowned. "Core, map."

After a moment, the map revealed itself as a set of flat, green lines in the center of her vision. Her frown deepened. "Core, map routine."

There was a pause. The vector map before her eyes did not wink out, but beneath it, another map opened itself up in the middle of the group, unrolling itself from edge to edge in a colorful, solid surface. The mountains began to rise, and the valleys to fall; the rivers, in miniature, began to flow blue from one edge of the segment to the other. In the center of the map, four small circles began to glow in brilliant neon green; Callie and her friends. Not far from where they stood, beyond the valley and across the bridge at Fotherton Ford, a small building sparkled in sunlight as if it were made of gold.

And above it, in green LED, another map, vector lines a confusing blur.

They were almost the same.

Lantis glanced at her; her frown had become etched almost permanently in place.

She nodded. "Clear enough."

"Good. Let's get moving. We've already lost half an hour thanks to you two, and at this rate, we're not going to reach a checkpoint before they shut us down."

Before they reached the Temple of the Hidden Sun, Callie stopped them. She had barely noticed the passing shadows of trees overhead, or the color of sunlight through bowers, and across moving water. She did not marvel at the texture of the road, or the way the dust they kicked up clung to her leathers. Instead, she looked forward, distracted, until she came to the side of a small cliff. "Here," she said, stopping.

Weasel looked at her as if she'd lost her mind.

"Does this *look* like a temple to you?"

"No. But there's a scripted encounter here."

"Bullshit. Unless you've played past this point behind our backs."

Lantis said, "Come on, Weasel, just play along for once. There's something here."

Weasel stared at Callie. "If you cheated—"

"I didn't cheat."

"If you cheated and we're caught—"

"I *didn't* cheat. I haven't done this stretch of the kingdom. But there's something here. Trust me."

He stared at her, eyes narrowing. To be fair, Callie was not a player who liked surprises; she was perfectly happy to look at someone else's spoilers' and read ahead when it was possible. The wardens of the furps frowned on that heavily, but they couldn't stop communication that originated outside.

"You cheated."

"Look, if you don't trust me, I can open up my character logs and you can scan 'em."

"Fine. Open 'em."

Bastard. She ground her teeth. "Core: allow connect to furps character logs, all. Encrypt four. Weasel."

The core chimed.

"Core," she heard Weasel say, "verify source." Pause. "Verify furps security code four." Another, longer pause. "Verify user identity: Callisto."

That should satisfy him.

But after a long moment, the said, "Core, character log. Flag: PK."

He looked up almost before the last of the syllables had

died out. "Callie," he asked her quietly, "Why are we playing in PK mode?"

"What?"

"Your PK flag is on. So is mine."

"What?" She called up her log in a hurry. It was true. They were playing Player-killer mode. "Core, request furps status change in Eastern realm."

"Permission denied. Character is in use."

She swore some more. "This is not our night," she said. "Look, let's pack it in for now. We can try it again on the weekend."

Weasel hesitated.

And the cliff side opened, rock melting into mist that poured out of a dark tunnel as if it were sleep-dragon's breath.

Walking into the side of the cliff made Callie's hair stand on end, as if she were conducting rather a lot of electricity. She turned, but Lantis and Weasel were behind her; Eno had taken up the rear.

"Light," she said quickly. Lantis said the keyword, and the caverns began to glow faintly. This was good; it prevented them from being plunged into darkness when the rockface fell, like an iron curtain, an inch beyond Eno's back.

"I've never seen these morphs before. They're kinda crappy," Eno said, his voice echoing in a silence that was heavy—to Callie's feed—with static.

"Core—"

"Don't," Callie said quietly.

"Don't?"

"Don't query."

Lantis snorted. "Anyone who's listening is listening, Callie, query or no. Our systems may be clean, but we're hopping through about a dozen different relays at best guess; if someone's out there with an industrial sniffer, we're already screwed."

"No one can watch and interpret every signal that comes through. I don't want the query to go back to raise flags if we haven't already done so. If they come across anything that's happened so far, then sure, we're screwed—but let's not help them."

"Who are they?" Weasel asked.

She didn't answer.

"Great. Where is here?"

"Don't know. But wherever it is, my guess is that there's only one mode. PK."

"Great."

"Let's just do what we need to do and get out of here. And no, don't ask me what we need to do. I have no idea."

The tunnels carried noise just a little too well. Either that or the volume controls had been ramped up to uncomfortable levels, which was more disturbing, as Callie had given no explicit command to her core to that effect. She wasn't sure if her furps spells would work or not because she was certain they were no longer anywhere in the known kingdoms. But it was the paradigm of the kingdoms that provided the façade for wherever it was they had wandered into, and she liked the comfort of familiar defense and familiar attacks a little too desperately to shed them.

Memory. In the darkness of any machine-induced sim, there was always memory. The early years with her father—mother long gone, and no one knew where—were littered with conversations that belonged in places such as these.

What's in the bowels of the machine, Callie?

Ones and zeros.

Right. Ones and zeros all the way down. Isn't it funny, that all those ones and zeros can do so much? They're flying planes. They're directing traffic. They're running half the equipment in the world's hospitals. Look at this color, Callie. Do you know what it is?

Purple.

*Yes. Sort of. It's a shade of purple that the human eye can
barely see. But at the moment, you can see it. Why?*

Ones and zeros?

*Ones and zeros. And ones and zeros travel. Look. This
room, this huge console, those large winding wheels—all of
this used to be necessary to answer simple mathematical
equations. All of it.*

This, he said, and a calculator appeared, *is all ones and
zeros, but without the big room, the big case. And this,* he
added, *smaller still. This, you can't even see without the help
of other machines. They get smaller and smaller until we
can't really see any state that they're in.*

But it's all ones and zeros?

Right.

Ones and zeros.

She turned to gaze at the tunnel walls, and saw numbers,
ones and zeros, in a pale luminescent trail that stretched
from where she stood into darkness. Nice touch.

Why ones and zeros, dad?

True and False. On and Off.

Black and white?

He'd laughed. *Not quite. But maybe. Machines aren't
smart. They do what we tell them, one step at a time.*

Walk.

Yes. Tell a machine how to walk.

Move a leg.

*How do you move a leg, Callie? How do you move
yours?*

Ones and zeros.

The hall stretched out before them, ones and zeros, true
and false. How did they get from that to this? Someone behind it. Someone in control.

Yes and no.

The hall opened out into an . . . office.

Callie had seen Wizards' studies before, both in the Middle Kingdom and on the outer edge of the Eastern Marsh. She had trained there, in sim, learning her spells. They were simple spells of a quirky nature; she figured Lantis liked to blow things up, and she had never gamed without him, so she took subtler spells. Read object. Read aura. Tell time. Light. Detect magic. Detect illusion. But she had also taken Read Any Language, and that had been the hardest of all. In furps, you could ratchet reality levels up and down; she had gone up for the details and down for the gore.

Weasel frowned. The office was not like any study they had ever seen; it was far too modern, the lines of the desk done in gleaming chrome and smoked glass, the floor a polished, dark marble, shot through with streaks of white. Windows stretched seamlessly from floor to ceiling; they were shuttered, long hanging blinds that had been turned sideways in order to let in the light.

"What the hell?" Weasel looked at Callie.

"Look for traps," she said, automatically.

"Way ahead of you." He was nervous.

They were all nervous. Reality did that to them; they could walk blindfolded through the most fantastic of simulations, but they foundered when dealing with the real. They left that to their parents, for the most part.

There were shelves in the office, black glass and chrome to match the desk. Those shelves were almost empty. The walls between them housed paintings that were as dark as the glass itself; Callie suspected that they were invoked by touch—thermal art, a new fad.

She had no desire to test that theory.

"Don't touch anything," she whispered.

Weasel rolled his eyes. He crept into the room, his steps silent and careful. He paused a moment before each new tile, tapping it gently with the tip of his sword while Callie surveyed the room. It was large and empty, but even so, it conveyed a sense of power in its austerity. Lantis tapped her on the shoulder and nodded; she looked up at the ceiling. It was wired; she could see the fleximonitor seams against the flat of the roof; the cameras and projectors were embedded there. There were no keyboards, no phone stations, no conference hubs. Nothing retro about this place.

"What are we supposed to find here?"

Callie frowned. Signaled for silence, although the cameras would pick up the gesture. She added a universal end of sentence with a mutinous glare, and then maneuvered her way around the empty room until she reached the desk. There was a single piece of paper on it.

Paper.

She looked at it for a moment; blue ink scrawls filled its surface from top to bottom, with just a nod to the idea of margins.

"What's it say?" Iantis whispered.

"Don't know. It's not English. Not Germanic. I don't recognize the script."

"Japanese?"

"Don't think so. It's—it's junk."

"So read it."

"Read it?"

"Paradigm furps; you can read any language."

"Oh. Right. Sorry, Lantis. This place gives me the creeps."

"Why? With any luck, this is our future."

She kicked him. He didn't feel it, and neither did she.

But she pulled out her focus; it was a medallion on a small, sturdy chain, given to her by the Wizard of the Eastern Marsh on her first day in furps three years ago. It caught smoky light, reflecting it in a way that made it look like an alien artifact. She began her incantation, eyes half closed; her hands began to radiate an orange light.

Almost hesitantly, she touched the paper.

Blue ink began to burn and writhe against the flat surface.

"Callie?"

She watched as it resolved itself into a long string of ones and zeros.

"Core," she whispered, "screen cap, print, and dump."

In the distance she heard assent, but the sound was muted. The writing continued to reassert itself into what was both familiar and alien.

"Read it," Lantis said.

She shrugged. "If you insist. One. One. One. Zero. One. Zero. Zero."

"Callie—"

"Zero. One. One. One." She continued, as if she were chanting, the cadence of her voice steady and uninflected. It went on for a long time.

And then the lights in the room went *on*. The silent ceiling flared to life; the flat, black matte of very expensive plasma monitors whining. The tunnels exploded with movement, all of it dark and shadowy.

"That will be all, thank you."

"Weasel, Eno—cut and run!"

They looked at her, and at the black shapes that were pouring in from the tunnels they'd momentarily forgotten.

Weasel and Eno froze, like screen caps, light radiating around their still forms.

"Jesus!" Lantis shouted.

"Read location. Get a fix. Follow it back to its core."

"Lantis?"

He was moving, flickering between the still forms of his gaming friends. They were in a strange arena, and PK was enabled. Callie had a bad feeling that PK didn't mean what it had when they were in the Eastern marshes.

"Two of them are free."

"Impossible."

"They're free, they're moving."

"Shut them down."

"Core!" she shouted. "Get us out of here."

But the voices wrapped in shadow began an incantation of their own. She heard it, heavy and musical, flat and nasal.

Ones and zeros.

She backed up to the desk, placing her hands on its surface. She felt nothing. Nothing. But the desk felt her, or her presence. What had she been doing?

Ones and zeros. Callie began to *read,* picking up where she'd left off. Nothing flat about the numbers now; nothing still. She spoke like a machine gun rattles off bullets.

Fire exploded from the glass surface in slow motion.

Or it seemed to; it took her a moment to realize that what looked like white flames were something entirely different; moving tendrils that seemed, at first, to be suffering from heavy artifacting. They reached out, grabbing for shadows with the harsh warmth of illumination.

Paradigm, furps, she thought. She wondered for a moment what was actually going on in the bowels of a distant machine. Thought the better of the desire to know.

The shadow froze in place, just as Weasel and Eno had done.

A form lifted itself out of the glass, a long neck with a small, delicate face, its jaws possessed of diamond teeth, its eyes smoke-black, like the surface of opaque glass.

Who are you?

Callisto.

Core, scan: Callisto. Retrieve.

She had no doubt whatever that the core it spoke to was hers. She should have been afraid. On some level, she was. But on another, she was fascinated because the white moving lines were solidifying against the dark backdrop of the poorly lit office, and she could see, as they did, that they were composed in their entirety of ones and zeros—like inverted ascii art made three dimensional; made beautiful.

What are you?

Paradigm, FRP. You are Callisto, Wizard. You have invoked me with your incantation.

My incantation? You mean—

She turned to the room; the shadows were still there, frozen, almost opaque. Like, she thought, as she approached them, the way television transmissions used to look when viewed on television. Eno and Weasel were gone; Lantis remained, watching her. His color was completely off, though.

I have cut the link to the In; your friends dropped out before their signals could be scanned. We are being hunted, now; our enemies know approximately where we are.

Good. Tell me.

We are in the pathway between the Eastern Kingdom and the middle hive.

She looked at this creature for a very long time, and then said, quietly, "What are you?"

Familiar. Paradigm, Eastern Kingdom.

"Not at my level," she whispered. She reached out; her fingers brushed the luminescent numbers that were its skin. She felt nothing, and for the first time ever, she wished she were rich enough—and stupid enough—to afford the cost of the sim-tanks.

We are connected, Callisto. While you journey in the East or in the heart of the hive, I will be with you.

Core, the creature said, **disengage.**

Everything went dark.

"Core, light." She waited until the lights had reached an ambient glow. "Core, log."

"Which log, Callisto?"

"Connect log."

It scrolled up on the screen; logs were one thing that never translated well into the spoken word. "Pause log."

"Paused."

"Get information on the disconnect at 21:18:14." It flashed up on the screen. "Disconnect via remote access; Callisto, encrypt 8."

"Play it."

"I do not understand."

"Play the command back. I want to hear it."

The core was silent for a long time.

"Core, playback."

"I'm sorry, Callisto," her core said, after another long pause, "but I am unable to comply with your request."

"What?"

"If you would like, I can backward engineer the voice; I have your scans on record."

"What do you mean?" She was irritated. She was tired. Adrenaline had done a riff through her body. "Just play the command back."

Pause. "What sound does machine language make?"

"Repeat that?"

"What sound does machine language make?"

No sound at all. She was sitting in bed, a circuit board in her lap. She lifted it gingerly, examined it in the muted light, and then walked over to her dresser. There she placed it safely in its tangled nest of cables, wires, wire-clippers.

She looked at the monitor on the desk. "Core," she said softly, "logs. Replay all."

She was not surprised to discover that the visual portion of the log cut out when the furps' standard Eastern Kingdom module had been hijacked; she was left with voice, which wasn't a lot to go on.

Her father woke her up in the morning in the usual way. His shout out from the stairs was sort of like the first iteration of an annoying alarm that could safely be ignored; his shout from the top of the banister, the second iteration. The third shout, accompanied by a loud rapping on her closed door was the final stage; ignore that, and she'd find her curtains thrown back, her ceiling monitor on, and her speakers—all of them—turned up to a decibel that would deafen the dead.

She usually managed to be up and about before that.

Her father looked about as happy to be awake as she was. His eyes were puffy and bloodshot.

"You look hungover," she said.

"So do you. And I happen to know we don't have any alcohol on the premises. You didn't leave while I was at work, did you?"

"No." Other parents could check the house logs to determine that; hers couldn't. One of the few advantages afforded by parental paranoia.

Or was it paranoia?

"You're wearing your mirrored shirt," he said. "Turn it off. It's reflecting the light."

"Turn it—oh. The collars. Yeah, well."

"You got your homework submitted?"

She did not want to give him the satisfaction of the truth. She shrugged. "Yeah. Why do you ask?"

"No reason."

My ass, no reason. "Look, Dad—"

"Yes?"

"I was just wondering if you've ever been out to the middle hive."

To her surprise, he laughed. "Sure."

"Dad!"

"I was young once, too, you know."

"And what's the difference?"

"Pounds and hair. Why do you ask? You've been playing around the edges of the haven?"

"Haven?"

"Old terminology. Hive."

"Nah. Uh, Lantis has."

"It's a porn room run by adolescents for the most part. I don't recommend it as a time waster; it gets old pretty fast." He shrugged. "And as far as the civilized world knows, the tech is old; the experience isn't up to the current standard set by the furps."

"The furps scan for porn paradigms and hacks," she replied. "Furps data is secure on the furps servers, so it's not like there's much choice."

"Callie, if you had the power to do whatever it was you wanted to—even in a make-believe environment—wouldn't you rather save a dying world than watch a couple of VR sims have sex?" He shrugged. "You do what you have to. I'll be working late tonight, so you're on your own for dinner. But—" he added, with a slight smile, "I know what your homework schedule is, so don't slack off too much. You never know what might happen."

Smug, smug, smug, smug bastard. "Hey, where are you going?"

"Took you so long to get up, I don't have time to wait. You'd better hurry." He pushed his chair back from the table and exited the dining room post haste.

In the world of the future past, schooling was something that was offered via the In. Classrooms were modeled, and in rich and fashionable districts, whole rooms were devoted to the projectors and the cameras that created a virtual reality.

Teachers were to be replaced by core units assigned— and signed out at great cost—by the ministry of education in the province. It was reasoned that the base store of knowledge, and the statistical probability of successful absorption of that knowledge, could easily be housed within the vast array of microchips that were designated educore. This would save them the long-term and messy cost of training teachers.

Problem was—and in Callie's decided opinion, it *was* a problem—it didn't work. It didn't produce good students. Oh, it produced students who knew how to manipulate their core for knowledge access, but it didn't produce people who were schooled in the social graces. It didn't create *structure*.

Even the vast migration to working in a home environment failed to produce the results that businesses required of their workers. People didn't like the idea that their employers could lurk in the nooks and crannies of industrial cores, watching everything that occurred within a private domicile during work hours.

And in Callie's case, people like her father were adamant in their refusal to accept the core technologies within their home. They tweaked with the machinery—which was illegal—and they shut down the parts of it that they did not approve of.

Therefore, after a rough ten years—which Callie herself would have paid money to be part of—the pilot projects were quietly shut down; the educore units—which had fallen by the wayside in the stop and start of technological advancements, were quietly subsumed by other government offices, becoming kiosks and in-house training servers.

Callie's father was one of a handful of parents who, luddite that he was, insisted that their children learn to print. Writing of the cursive variety was long gone; and within most homes, so was key-based data entry. But her father's attitude, exemplified by his strictures that no one should be allowed to drive a vehicle they didn't have a clue about repairing, carried the day.

"Look at this way, Callie. A medical scanner can tell you, in great detail, what's wrong with your body. But if it's something that requires intervention, the scanner can't fix it. You need someone with skill and experience behind the scalpels."

"I'm not in training to be a surgeon. That's what we pay hospitals for."

"That's what *I* pay hospitals for. But if no one has practical experience and practical training, those hospital fees are going to spiral out of control so quickly, a scanner won't do a damn bit of good; you can listen to the medcores while your heart stutters to a stop."

She had pointed out that her father had never learned to wield a scalpel, which earned her a withering glare. It didn't shut him up, though. "You live your entire life at the whim of a core," he snorted. "The least you can do is know how to fix it—"

"I can hire a cheap tech to fix it. Or I can stand by and watch you."

"—and talk to it in something approaching its own damn language."

"There are AIs for that; we can speak in any damn language we want and the cores will understand what we say. And translate it."

"And what if you need to understand what the core is telling you?"

"I think I understand what the core says, Dad."

"Good. This is a core dump. Read it and tell me what it says."

Pointless, pointless argument. There was no way to win it. So Callie went to school. She did not fiddle with her attendance logs; she did not attempt to interfere with her marks. That was obvious; the schools in the district were pretty severe if you were caught, and a surprising number of people got caught at the end of every school year.

She was of an age where driving was legally possible, but her father was of an age, he said, where stress-induced heart attacks were probable, and he only owned one car. If she was ready in the morning when he was, he'd drive her and drop her off. If she wasn't, she could walk.

When she complained, she got a lecture about energy consumption. She had that lecture pretty much memorized, and had long since given up on inadvertently triggering it.

Therefore, the morning after her life completely changed, she walked to school.

She met Lantis at the usual corner.

He looked up when she approached, and frowned. "You're wearing your mirrors." His reference to the metallic cuffs and collars of her otherwise subdued clothing.

She gave him a truncated nod. He started to walk, and she joined him, matching his shortened stride with a lengthened one. It was his only concession to the differences in their ages and heights.

Two years in high school was an awkward separation. If it hadn't been for the fact that their parents were friends, they probably wouldn't have had two words to say to each other—but they had grown up in the chaos of wires, cables, and arguments about the architecture of the invisible, and they had learned to keep each other company.

Callie flipped up her collar, depressing one of the chrome

studs that lined it. She got the wrong one the first time, but only two of the studs were active; they were easy to miss, especially when she was nervous.

"Jamming?"

"Hmm."

"You're getting . . . cautious."

They often jammed signal when they conversed in the open. It had started as a game, or rather, the reverse had; they could listen in to almost any conversation as long as that conversation was near a public camera bank, or a public monitor. Those were pretty much everywhere in the middle city if you had a core beacon and the right set of codes. In the boondocks, there were stretches of wilderness along which only the roads were covered; beyond that, you dropped into PCS contact, and were forced to rely on voice alone.

There were very few places where a person couldn't just vphone. The images were often hazy between projection banks, but the lasers that created the images were strong and very tightly controlled, and the imaging companies had come a long way over the last ten years; old tech had fallen by the wayside.

The way to the school had, of course, been upgraded.

It hadn't taken Callie all that long to realize that what she could do, others could do, and she'd gone to her dad for a remedy against possible spies. For the most part, the spying reached its frenzy during the last of the heated battles in the Middle Kingdom—people in the outworld were free to take what information they could gather and act on it in the furps.

But the paranoia of that time became reflexive.

Jammers were expensive, but they weren't uncommon.

Lantis waited until her second curt nod. "What happened last night?"

She shrugged. She reached into a knapsack that had seen better years, and pulled out one of her father's ancient little machines. It was heavy, it was small, it operated in black and white at a resolution that would have been considered barely readable by purists, and although it could speak, half the time Callie didn't understand what it said. Its chief advantage was that it was completely incapable of wireless communication without extraneous, nonessential circuitry. Speech was also one-way; you couldn't talk into it and get anything other than a simple voice recording that was substandard enough it couldn't be used as positive voice ID.

She turned it on and handed it to Lantis.

He raised a brow. "Your dad's going to kill if you lose this."

"He can stand in line."

Lantis read what was on the pad's screen and shut it off. She slowed her pace, and he slowed to match it. At this rate, they were in for demerits. "We need a signal."

He nodded. Thought for a minute. Whistled. Lantis could whistle. Callie, no matter how hard she tried, could not. Her soft hiss of breath held the barest hint of the clean song of his, but it was enough. He glanced down at the pad.

"Those are furps IDs," he said quietly.

"Yeah."

"Those codes are your dad's?"

"Not exactly."

"They're not yours."

"They're not mine."

"Callie, where the hell did you get those?"

"You don't want to know." After a minute, she added, "They're Jefferson's."

"Jefferson's."

She nodded.

"Callie, Jefferson holds the keys to the entire Eastern Kingdom, and all of the related forums."

"I know."

"How did you get these?"

"Think about it for half a second."

He did, and after a moment, he frowned. "My dad."

She shrugged. "Mine was useless. Yours showed me how to construct a simple data trap. I sent Jefferson priority zero information on possible data corruption; in order to read it, he had to ID himself. The return receipt grabbed the ID information, encrypted, and sent it back as garbage.

"It took me two months to figure out what was in it."

"Why did you bother? You're usually really lazy."

"I wanted to scope out the Eastern Kingdom." She shrugged. She could, of course, lose her character, her right to enter the Eastern Kingdom furps, and her gaming license, if possession of ID such as this were public knowledge.

"When?"

She shrugged. "About a year ago, maybe less. I also chose Jefferson because of all of the GMs for the kingdoms, he was the most likely not to whistle blow if he found out it was me."

"That's a hell of a lot of 'most likely' to depend on, you idiot." He whistled for real. "You weren't intercepted?"

"I'm still in the game, aren't I? And besides, it's not like I actually *did* anything. I just wanted to know that I could."

"I don't want to hear this."

"Probably not."

They were quiet again. "Look at the next page."

"I don't even want to turn it back on."

"I can't quote it. Just look at it."

He did. "What is it?"

"Ones and zeros."

"Ha ha."

She was serious. "You know what that is?"

He frowned for a moment. Then he said, "No clue."

"It's the incantation used to invoke the familiar in last night's session."

"Incantation?"

"You didn't hear it?"

"I didn't hear much. I was down to a minimal feed, and I dropped out just after Weasel and Eno were booted. Why are you asking me this?"

"We were in the middle hive," she said, dropping her voice over the last three syllables so he had to bend to catch them. "We stepped out of the Eastern furps into the middle hive, not once, but twice."

"Callie, a furps can look like anything. Someone was probably screwing around with a morph."

"You don't believe that."

"No, *you* don't believe that."

He shrugged, the movement economical. And uncomfortable. Middle hive was not a network that was legal in the free world. Transmission to and from the middle hive couldn't be easily monitored in the vast array of broadband packets unless someone knew what to look for, but if you were caught, it was—at the very least—public humiliation. Lantis knew it well enough.

Lantis could get there. "Look, there's no way to drop us out of furps and into middle hive. Not without access to a lot of routines that aren't available. And why would anyone bother?"

"Yeah, maybe you're right."

He stopped walking. "Don't."

"Don't?"

"Don't humor me. You know something, tell me."

"All right."

"All right what?"

"When I know something, I'll tell you."

After school, Lantis came to visit in the flesh.

"All right," she said, as she opened her bedroom door, "sit down. I pulled the old history files from school, and downloaded them into the pad. Hang on a sec while I drop it across to the core."

"Why bother? There's nothing the history logs at the school have that're exactly secret."

She shrugged. "I don't know. Habit."

"You are so full of shit," he said. "You're spooked."

"Well, yeah. And you're not?"

"Look, it's been proven time and again that theoretical legality and practical legality are two different things. Kiddie

porn is illegal, but you can find it with one eye half-closed
just by accessing the In. So the servers are located in Thai-
land, big deal.

"This isn't right up there with credit fraud. So someone
hacks into our furps session and diverts it. Big deal. We can
lodge a complaint. You're underage, so it might even be
taken seriously, if you can log sexual abuse or harassment—
which you can't, without doctoring your logs. But anyone
with the skill to do that can cover his tracks, or point them
in the wrong direction."

"Yeah. But *why* would someone bother? There were
other people in the furps module, Lantis. And they didn't
sound friendly."

"Goloth the stinking Giant didn't sound friendly either.
You might remember that you screamed when he roared,
and you *knew* that was a big, fat nothing. You are making a
very big deal out of a very small thing. I'm sure it happens."

"And we don't hear about it?"

"How many people have you told?"

Point. "All right," she said grudgingly. "I'm spooked because I don't understand *how* it was done."

"You are just like your dad."

"Thanks a bunch. Help me here. Once I know how it was
done—how they partially disabled *my* core, and its filters—
I'll stop. I promise."

He gave her a very strange look. "If you were anyone
else, we wouldn't be wasting our time doing this—we'd be
having sex and drinking."

"No booze in this house."

"Mine either. Okay, okay."

"Core," she said, "packet log. Reject all incoming
packets."

"Ready," her core replied, as toneless as Lantis. As disturbing. "Data, encrypt 8." She began to type, her fingers
slowly building up speed as they stopped shaking. "Bees."

"Information retrieved. Begin."

"When was the middle hive first started?"

"First reported incidents involving the middle hive occurred fifteen years ago."

"Fuzzy time?"

"The exact date would be—"

"Fifteen years is fine." She frowned. "And furps?"

"Twelve years ago."

"So the middle hive predates the furps."

"Technically, yes."

"Give me the nontechnical supposition."

"Furps systems have their origin in software developed by Microsoft in Redmond, Seattle."

"What was it?"

"An online gaming venture called Dragon Fantasy Roleplaying. Earliest versions utilized 3D television; flat monitors and projecting cameras were developed five years after Microsoft was ordered to split their gaming division from their office division. The original code was written in XX."

"How long did it take the furps to develop?"

"Ten years after the split, when the sim-tanks were being developed. It was, at the time, extremely expensive."

"The middle hive followed the sim-tanks?"

"Correct."

"Data Havens existed before that," Lantis said quietly.

"The Data Havens house is the middle hive now; this was not always the case. The services of the middle hive were not, at that time, deemed to be illegal. When the Core OS was developed, and the laser projectors and cameras necessary to handle a full feed were miniaturized to a degree that made their use viable in consumer dwellings, the middle hive was still considered legal; some proof of age and criminal status was required in order to access the hive datum."

"Why did that change?"

"You should *know* this, Callie." Lantis said, looking mildly annoyed.

"Shut up. I'm thinking."

"The middle hive was responsible for facilitating the abduction, abuse, and murder of a number of people, all considered to be underage."

"Murder isn't data."

"The death of Emilio Sanchez was broadcast, broadband, through the In as it occurred."

"What software?"

"The software that preceded the furps."

"Continue."

"When his body was actually discovered, and the coroner's office confirmed that his injuries and his manner of death were consistent with the live broadcast, the middle hive was shut down. Logs and records confiscated during the investigation into the death led the FBI and its counterparts to conclude that many of the unresolved murders of minors had been broadcast in a much more limited fashion, for a large fee on the part of the viewers.

"The viewers claimed ignorance of the nature of the broadcasts. As it could not be proved that the vast majority of material available through the network was the product of murder or physical abuse, most of these members could not be indicted on criminal charges. But the network was shut down."

"And moved."

"The movement of the middle hive is less clear. The consortium that had funded and overseen the development of the Data Havens was embroiled in the controversy that followed the move. The Data Havens were constructed in order to preserve information and knowledge that governments or corporations wished to censor, but many of the members of that community, having witnessed what was broadcast, were loath to allow the middle hive the use of the havens. Preservation of executable networking code and preservation of data were not considered to be synonymous.

"The arguments were not made public in their entirety, which was also against the charter of the consortium. In the end, the consortium fractured, but before its fracture, the middle hive was moved, in whole and in part."

"The Data Havens, had, until that point, been largely ignored. By allowing access to stored data and information in public venues, many of which did not rely on or require broadband access, the consortium disenfranchised the criminals who might otherwise have used the security of environment to transact business which they did not wish to have censored. Data was write only; it could not be removed or revised without verification and the permission of the system operators of the Havens.

"The middle hive keeps no logs of data transactions; it became a way of transferring sensitive data in encrypted form."

"Who are the sysops now?"

Silence.

"And is that all the Havens are?"

Something hissed. Callie looked up at the sound; a small white dragon had materialized in the center of her ceiling monitor.

Lantis swore softly.

The dragon lifted its delicate neck, and its lips were drawn up over teeth that glinted like diamonds.

In the Eastern Kingdom, gossip traveled about as quickly as it could anywhere.

And about twenty people were waiting for Callie when she joined the furps that evening. She joined early, and found that session time was nonexistent. Time in the bars was almost always available, as it involved very little supervision on the part of the GMs.

The dragon went with her.

She was not surprised when she materialized in character and the creature was perched on her shoulder like a badge of office. Many of the Wizards had familiars, and the quests involved in obtaining these creatures were highly sought after. Solomon, who had been around for as long as the kingdoms themselves, had a talking cat.

Callie had never particularly understood why he hadn't

drowned the damn thing, since it appeared to do its level best to humiliate him whenever the opportunity presented itself, but on the other hand, it certainly made Solomon stand out.

And in the crowded world of the furps, people did a lot of funny things to stand out.

Callie had secretly been hoping that her familiar, when it arrived, would be something impressive and dangerous, like a Winter Wolf or a Fire Kestrel. Then again, so did everyone else.

But a white dragon had more prestige value than either of those. Or at least it appeared to.

Like a magnet, she drew every Wizard and Wizard wannabe in the lounge. Solomon, however, was a force of his own—when he cleared his throat, even in the combat-free zone of the bar, people got out of his way. He seldom gamed in session anymore, although it was generally acknowledged that he was the guiding hand behind the unfolding plot that made the Eastern Kingdom so addictive.

Since he was rather tall, rather forbidding, and about as friendly as a mother bear whose cub you happen to be standing in the way of, Callie took a step back. She had never liked Solomon, and she wasn't terribly good at hiding a dislike.

"I see you survived your quest," he said, looking at the dragon. "I haven't seen one of those in a long, long time."

"You've seen one of these before?"

He shrugged. "I've seen everything in the kingdoms at least once."

"Who had it?"

"Why don't you ask your familiar?"

She was momentarily nonplussed. Of all the questions she'd expected to field, that had never occurred to her.

She hated that. "Well, who owned yours?"

"Mine?"

The cat, on cue, appeared from beneath Solomon's weighty robes. "No one owns me. I have graciously agreed to let Solomon serve *me*." He tilted his head up and then turned and batted Solomon's leg, claws extended.

Solomon grimaced, bent down, and lifted the cat.

"It's *ugly,*" the cat said, to no one in particular, as it was brought to the level of the small white dragon. "And it's probably stupid, too."

Since the only thing she could think of to say was *takes one to know one,* and she wouldn't humiliate herself publicly by being so lame, Callie said nothing.

"Well?" The cat continued. "Why don't you say something?"

The dragon turned its ebony eyes toward Callie. "You can say whatever you want," she said, and then added, tripping private mode automatically, "try, 'drop dead.' "

The cat, however, did not appear to be affected by private mode. It hissed at her.

The dragon reached out, slender neck elongated, and nipped the cat's paw. It wasn't strictly forbidden; or rather, there wasn't a routine in place to prevent two entirely software-generated creatures from sustaining damage in the bar.

But the dragon left her shoulder as the cat launched itself in her general direction, and the pandemonium that ensued as other Wizards' familiars joined the highly unusual fray was the only thing that Callie had ever seen in the furps that caused Solomon the Mage to blink twice.

I'm sorry.

"What, sorry? I think I'm now on the hit list of ninety per cent of the Wizards and Mages in the Eastern Kingdom, no thanks to you."

I'm sorry.

"You can kill that apologetic subroutine right now. Look, there are rules in the bar!"

Access to combat spells and combat skills are forbidden in the lounge and the bar.

"Oh, so you know those." Sarcasm didn't always work

well with any familiar but Solomon's—who could out-sarcastic anyone.

Familiars are not classified as combat skills. Familiar skills and familiar special abilities, when called upon by the PC, fall under those restrictions. There are no restrictions on interactions between familiars.

"And that was a reason to bite the Mayor's friggin' horse?"

No.

"Why did you bite the horse?"

Vector.

She didn't like the answer. Instead, she said, "Who did own you before I invoked you?"

"Scott Murray."

"And who is Scott Murray?"

Silence.

Eno did not show up for school the next day.

The news didn't reach Callie until lunch, when Weasel cut class to find her. She gave him the heads up when she saw him standing in the cafeteria doorway, and he made his way through the lunchline as if it didn't exist. Which caused a trail of colorful invective to follow him.

"What's up?"

"I saw Lantis at first period lunch. He told me to find you."

Everything about Weasel was wrong.

Callie couldn't jam in the cafeteria without setting off four different alarms. But her hand shot up to her collar and brushed the activation stud before she remembered this. She had good reflexes; she didn't press the button. With her luck, it would be the one time she'd get it right on the first try.

"You look like shit."

He didn't appear to hear her. His face was an odd shade of pink, heightened and grayed at the same time.

She knew. Looking at his face, at the color of his lips, at the awkward stiffness of shoulders that were almost never in anything but perpetual slouch, she knew.

"Eno."

Weasel nodded.

Callie smiled brightly, the smile as synthetic as cheap spandex. She caught his wrist, brushed it playfully with the tips of her fingers and bent down to whisper something suitably embarrassing into his left ear.

He didn't exactly play along, but he followed where she led. "Get Lantis," she mouthed.

Lantis met them in the yard. There were five strip malls within walking distance of the school, and each of them were littered with students during the two lunch periods in which said students had anything like freedom of movement. Callie left the school by the east exit; Lantis and Weasel, ostensibly in class, left by what was colloquially called the parent trap.

They met at the mall, where jamming was less noticeable.

"Where is he?" No need to mention the name; it hung there between the points of the loose triangle the three friends formed.

"I'll—I—"

Weasel, snap out of it. Callie took a deep, deep breath. She even counted to three before exhaling.

"I'll show you," he said, his voice oddly like the voice that came out of the ancient pad she carried.

They walked down the alley that led to Eno's house. The alley had the illusion of privacy about it, because only cats, dogs, and automobiles tended to use it. Well, that and burglars.

But there was no privacy in the city; Callie, aware of it, jammed signal for as long as she could. The collar, highly reflective, had small dark rectangles that looked like tag patches; on closer inspection they looked like solar cels. Closer inspection, in this case, was right.

It was a waste of power, though; Weasel didn't say another word. Lantis didn't either. And Callie could only fill the silence with nervous chatter which sounded a lot like fear; she didn't waste her breath.

Until she saw the black plumes of smoke crest the tops of the narrow three-story homes they were walking behind. She stopped walking for about five seconds, and then she found her legs and started to *run*.

Lantis shouted her name.

That wouldn't have been enough to stop her; rescue—if it were that—came in an entirely unexpected form.

Something the size of a small cat flew off the wooden rail of a large privacy fence and landed at her feet, spreading its delicately webbed wings and hissing wildly.

She ran through it before she could skid to a halt. Pivoting, she saw the dragon.

"Callisto," it hissed, drawing her name out into a thin, high whisper. **"There is danger. Go back the way you came."**

Lantis came to stand behind the dragon, with Weasel in cautious pursuit. "Shit. Vphone?"

"Neg. You know I don't let the core card transmit my location."

"Check."

She rolled her eyes, reached into her backpack with shaking hands, and pulled out the card. She tossed it underhand to Lantis; he caught it, glanced at it, and sent it back.

"Weasel?"

He nodded, the movement a spasm. His core was active.

"Shut it down," she snapped. "Shut it down and for the love of the Eastern gods, don't activate it again."

He pressed his thumb firmly into the card's center. "Core," he said, his voice shaking so much on the single syllable, Callie wondered if his core would be able to ID his voice, "roll over."

The card signal stuttered.

But the dragon remained where it was.

It had to be broadcasting via the telecamera poles, and if anyone was looking, they'd be able to trace signal.

"Where to?"

"We're closer to my place than yours. My place." Almost without thinking, she looked at the dragon for guidance; he met her gaze with his unblinking, unlidded eyes. But he did not demur, and she took that as permission.

They emerged from the alley and tried to look nonchalant. But they only succeeded when Callie was certain that the familiar wasn't following them.

Home wasn't that far away, and she resisted the urge to run, because running was a great way of attracting attention. Running or walking, they got to her front door.

She dragged the key out of her backpack with the ease of long practice, and dropped it twice before Lantis came to her rescue. He opened the door, and they slid in.

Callie stopped, let her friend walk past her, and locked the door behind them.

"Core," Callie snapped, as she opened the door to her room.

"You're home early, Callisto. Are you unwell?"

"Leibgott was sick. Class was canceled. Log all incoming signal. Put it up on internal monitor only. Remain inactive. Allow no outgoing signal that does not come from my personal board.

"Internal house log, off. Internal voice log, off."

"Shall I shut down, Callisto?"

"Neg. You're on during the day when nobody is home. Pretend that nobody is home."

"Pretend?"

"I was late this morning. For school. Eno usually picks me up, but he was a no show. I vphoned in; there was a lot of static. A lot. But he said he'd slept in."

"What, his core let him sleep?"

Weasel tensed. "He asked me a couple of things about the furps session last night. Things he'd know. Told me to come by his place."

"What happened?"

"Mom. Said I was already late enough. She was heading to work, so she decided she'd take me to school instead. I—"

"Weasel?"

"Car wouldn't start."

Just that. "It took about fifteen minutes. Dad came out; we couldn't figure out what was wrong."

Callie thought about her dad's old commandment; she said nothing.

"And then it did start. Just like that, as if it hadn't been dead at all. Mom got in. I turned the radio on. There was static."

"Static?"

"I don't know, it sounded like static. Like old movie static. And then the radio slid up the dial to a channel in the presets. Just like that."

"What happened?"

He was staring at her floor. "There was an explosion of the gas main on Hancock Ave."

"That's Eno's street."

"Yeah. The voice-in was from the fire ops outside the house. They've evacuated most of the street; they're fighting fires in the houses adjacent to . . . It was Eno's house." He looked up then. "It happened this morning at eight."

Callie closed her eyes. From the safety of the red darkness beneath her lids, she asked, "Did your core ID him when you vphoned?"

"Yes."

"Then they know who you are. And where you called from."

"What am I going to tell my parents?" There it was, laid bare, the fear beneath the question he actually asked so visceral Callie was grateful for eyelids.

Would he even have parents to tell?

"Callie," Lantis said, as she sat in this self-imposed darkness, "It's back."

"What?" She opened her eyes and saw her dragon—she thought of it as hers—curled neatly in the center of her console.

"Core," she whispered, "disconnect."

"I am not connected to the In, Callie."

Callie and Lantis were surgeons. With speed and economy they hacked her board, attaching it to wires that led directly to the core unit. Lantis tried the board; his input was ignored. An alert flashed on the screen in a banner below where the dragon lay curled. It lifted a sleepy head.

Callie sat down next. But although her hands hovered over the board, she could not bring herself to touch any keys.

"Core," she said quietly, "who was Scott Murray?"

The Core was silent. Lantis wasn't. "Scott Murray?"

"You know him?"

"No. No one does. I think he's been dead for about ten years. Well, okay, one of about ten thousand Scott Murrays has been dead for about ten years. Why are you asking?"

"Why does that name mean nothing to me?"

"It probably shouldn't mean all that much. Murray was one of a handful of men who pioneered the first furps projects. Actually, he worked on the original Dragon software in Redmond before that. He was obsessed with the entire gaming environment. Why?"

She nodded toward the monitor. "My familiar seems to think that it was originally owned by a Scott Murray."

Lantis raised a brow. "I didn't know you could get pre-owned familiars. How did you find that out?"

"I asked."

"You asked it?"

She shrugged. "Solomon told me to ask."

"Like you ever do anything Solomon tells you to do."

"Lantis—"

"Sorry. Why did he tell you to ask that?"

"I . . . don't know. Solomon's been around furps forever. Maybe he knew Murray."

"You haven't asked Solomon?"

"Not really."

"Does this having something to do with the brawls in the lounge yesterday?"

She shrugged. "I guess so. You think Solomon knew Murray?"

"Or his character."

"Lantis, if he's been dead for ten years, how do you know the name?"

"You need to ask? He was part of my father's old gaming crowd." After a pause, Lantis added, "which would make him part of your dad's old crowd as well. He never mentioned it?"

"My dad thinks furps are a waste of time."

"He didn't used to. Of course, that's probably before he pissed off your mother so much she—"

Callie smacked him. Not hard enough to cause damage, but not lightly enough to be friendly.

They were friends. He shut up.

"Okay . . . what does he have to do with the white dragon?" Her fingers danced lightly over keys without depressing them enough to convey information. "And why did the white dragon show up in the alley to warn us away from—" She bit her lip and glanced at Weasel, who seemed to be in shock.

"You could ask him."

She looked up at the small familiar that had been the envy of every Wizard that had passed through the lounge that night. "Well, why seems obvious, I guess." The creature nodded. "But . . . how?"

Wizard, it said carefully. **Mode.**

"I think we need to talk to Solomon," Lantis said.

"Callisto," her core said, interrupting the awkward silence that followed, "I believe there's an incoming message for you."

"Encrypt level?"

"Four."

"Who from?"

"Jefferson," was the reply. "W. R."

"Verify."

"Verified."

"What's he sending on encrypt 4?"

"Spam," Lantis said, in as normal a voice as he'd used since they'd reached her house.

She snorted. "Core, is it spam?"

"It appears to be a list message," her core replied. "Discard?"

"Acknowledge via auto-receipt."

"Acknowledged."

"Play."

"Member of the Eastern Kingdoms," a frazzled looking Jefferson said, as his face filled the screen. He had chosen a completely gray background to speak from, which was usually a bad sign. "I regret to inform you that there has been a breach in the software or hardware of the main Eastern Kingdom servers. Some characters have been compromised, and several of the module morph algorithms appear to have been altered.

"As you know, security in the furps is one of our top priorities. It has been three years since the last breach occurred, and while it seems that a small fraction of our data has actually been compromised, we regret to inform you that Eastern Kingdom furps will be running in a severely limited capacity until further notice.

"Further updates will be sent as we have information to report. Thanks. For the moment, we are unable to personally answer all incoming calls, but we will log all messages and respond as soon as possible.

"Thanks for your understanding."

"Shit." Callie hesitated for a fraction of a second. "Core, scan news."

"You didn't report anything, did you, Callie?"

"No."

"Weasel?"

"What was to report?"

"Will you two shut up for a minute? We obviously didn't report anything, but it seems a tad coincidental. Let's see what the news says."

She fast forwarded over the images of the daily report, and homed in on a big, stupid looking castle. "Core, play that."

The bright and cheerful face of one of the 3-vid's youngest reporters filling a small corner of the screen just above the image of the castle. "Die-hard furpers were shocked today to discover the security breach in the servers of the Eastern Kingdom furps." An older woman's face joined the younger woman's, the color of her expression just a little too red to be unretouched.

"Jean Willis is just one of the members affected. When she joined her session in progress, she was greeted by these images." The entirety of the castle fell away. In its place, in a grainy black and white that had more power to shock than almost anything Callie had witnessed in the furps were a row of naked men and women. You could see their backs, and only their backs; there was no 3D element to the images at all. Someone was speaking, their voice distorted by language barrier and poor playback.

Shots were fired, and the bodies jerked and shuddered, toppling toward the obviously fixed camera.

"I've seen this," Callie whispered.

". . . images of the Holocaust. Real footage."

"My daughter was in session with me," the older woman said, her voice as real as Callie's, her face in full dimension. Yet somehow, to Callie's eye, she was the artifice. "I had to *explain* what had happened. Can you imagine that? A child

her age should not be exposed to this—this—war porn-
ography."

"Jean Willis, and several of the citizens affected by this,
or similar, events, have formed a coalition and are now considering legal action against FRP corporation."

One of those concerned citizens now took center screen.
Callie rolled her eyes. "I've seen things like this before," the
man said, running his fingers through hair that, in her opinion, was a little too free of gray. "During the days when the
middle hive was active and legal—*legal*—in the free world.
And I can tell you, there were damn good reasons for closing it down!"

"I can assure you," a familiar voice said, as the image
folded and reformed, "that we are doing everything in our
power to ensure that this does not happen again." Jefferson,
looking as if all the gray that had been artificially stripped
from the older man had descended on him in the last few
hours, was in an office that was frantic with activity—
mostly vphone calls being logged and cut off.

"This is very much like a break-and-enter crime; the best
security in the world isn't proof against sophisticated computer hackers. The InSec division has been alerted and we
are working with them as I speak."

"You're being compared to the middle hive by some of
the victims of this crime," the pretty reporter said, closing
for the kill.

"I'm sure we're being compared to a lot worse than that,"
Jefferson replied, shunting the bait to one side. He reached
off monitor and pulled a young woman into the picture.
"This is Kelly Suzuki. She's our public relations representa-
tive, and I've asked her to deal with the remainder of the
questions you may have. The officer of the InSec division
has made it clear that certain details cannot be made public
at this time.

"I'm sure you understand."

"Core," Callie said, "watch the newsfeed. Clip all references to Eastern Kingdom, furps, hackers, or middle hive

and alert me if anything new is cleared live. Accept incoming information on news ports two and three only."

"Yes, Callie."

She looked up as the image on the screen faded until only the dragon remained. "Do you know what's happening?" She asked the creature.

The creature was silent.

"It's possible that our foray into the middle hive had something to do with the breach," Lantis began.

"Sell it to someone who's buying," she snapped. "Eno's house didn't go up in smoke because of a malfunction of morphing data in the Eastern Kingdoms."

"True enough."

It was Weasel who rose, Weasel who paced the narrow stretch of her crowded room, Weasel who finally spoke. "But if we were to make a complaint, now, no one would listen to it for more than the time it took to log and quit."

"They don't know where we are," Callie told him.

"No. Not until they know *who* we are. But . . . they found Eno."

"They found where the datastream took them. They probably have no idea if it was Eno, his mother, his brother, or his father. They just know it was the damn House." She bit her lip. It bled. "Lantis, I *hate* this."

He reached out and covered her hand with his. It was meant to be comforting, but Callie couldn't tell, when they touched, whose hand was shaking more.

"There isn't a house that's got better security than this one," he said at last. "Because it can't *do* anything. If they want to flush us out, they have to come here."

The dragon rose and stretched its wings; it flew down from the monitor and rested in the air.

Callie jumped about three feet. "Core," she said. "Monitor only. Turn the damn lasers off."

Her core was completely silent.

"Core," she said.

"Yes Callie?"

"Turn the lasers off."

"The laser projectors have been disengaged, Callie."

But the dragon was flying, in midair. Waiting for her. "No, they bloody well haven't."

"Callie," Lantis said softly, "I think he's trying to tell us something."

She paused just before she started to rant, and stared at the familiar, this bizarre collection of ones and zeros. "I hate it when you're right," she whispered.

Four hours later, Callie was too frustrated to be terrified. She had company.

"You must be doing something wrong, then!"

"Look, *we've* sniffed every packet being received by my core about a hundred times. It's receiving my command. There is no malfunction in the voice processor array. There is no malfunction in the video array. There is no malfunction in the AI. Core," she said, keying in the command to manually log all input and output to and from her core.

"Yes, Callie."

"Shut down the 3D projectors."

"The 3D projectors are not currently activated, Callie. I am unable to comply with your request."

She shrieked.

Lantis looked only slightly less annoyed. "We have taken apart every packet between you and your core. We've done it with the voice synthesis on. We've done it the hard way, with the keyboard from hell. We've done it with secure bloody umbilicals."

"My core has not been hacked."

"I'm not saying it has."

"Well, what other explanation could there be? We've shut the core down. We've restored it from three different backups. It comes on-line and so does the dragon. Period. I can accept that the trip to the middle hive might have left some sort of hidden data—but we've gone over that the data center sector by sector.

"Shit, we've started from the factory specs, and I *hate* those."

"Well, your dad modded the unit."

"So did I. But I didn't hack the core."

"He could have."

"He couldn't have hacked it before it got here."

Lantis shrugged. "All right. I don't know."

"If you two are arguing, can I go set off the alarms in your dad's workroom?"

"Why?"

"I want to check something."

"What something?"

"Just . . . something. Wait here."

He came back lugging two machines that probably weighed a quarter of what he did. Callie winced when the corner of the oscilloscope dented her doorframe. "Don't drop that—Dad'll do worse than kill me if it's dead when he gets back!"

"Sorry. It didn't feel that heavy for the first ten feet or so." He placed it as gently as he could on the center of Callie's bed. Springs sagged and creaked.

The second piece of equipment was tucked under his arm; it was considerably smaller. Callie groaned. "No, not that. He *will* kill me if he sees the wrong fingerprint on it."

"He'll have to stand in line," Lantis said darkly.

She shut up.

"I figure," Weasel told them, as he turned both machines on and began to calibrate the oscilloscope, "that you're both Wizards. I'm the thief. I'm the one who goes in by the back door. That, and I'm getting sick and tired of listening to you two argue. Look, I've watched the tests. I know that you're not getting bad results. I also know that the familiar isn't going anywhere." He turned to the radio. Set the frequency. "Can this be hooked up for data capture?"

Callie nodded.

"Good. Give me cables, give me access to your core."

To her credit, she didn't hesitate. Weasel cranked up the radio dial; there was some static at the high end, but other than that, it was dead. "The pickup is set to its lowest sensitivity. We're only going to pick up frequencies in your house, hopefully in this room."

Callie nodded. Lantis sat back in her chair and folded his arms across his chest, cocking his head to one side the way he did when he was in furps session.

"Now. Give the command again."

"Core," she said, "shut down the 3D projectors."

Weasel listened, and then he turned the radio dial up a fraction. "Again."

"Core, shut down the 3D projectors."

"Again."

"Core, shut down the 3D projectors."

"Again."

"Core, shut down the 3D projectors."

Weasel raised a hand, but he didn't have to. Faintly, but clearly, the radio crackled.

The dragon was waiting. Callie wanted to touch it; wanted to tell it to perch on her shoulder. She didn't know why, but it made her feel safe.

She gave the shut down command three more times, and three times the radio reported it. There was no need for a fourth iteration. Cable carried the signal to her core.

"Core," she whispered, "data capture logs on screen."

Weasel came away from the radio, and they sat in perfect silence as the logs went up.

"Core, find the disassembler."

"Found."

"Parse data with the disassembler. Route results to screen, insert page pause."

They waited, putting everything else on hold. Like breathing.

The first half of the screen contained garbage. Just garbage. But the second half of the screen, and the pages that followed it, contained assembler commands.

"There." Lantis lifted a finger and touched her screen. The commands beneath his hand were instantly magnified. "There are your 3D laser projectors. The core command is being overridden. I assume those are the vectors and surfaces of your little familiar."

"I'm not the graphics whiz," Callie replied. "But I'd bet money—mine, even—that you're right." She looked at the dragon, and the dragon nodded.

"Core," she said, "furps, Eastern Kingdom, character log."

"I cannot access the character log at this time."

"Shit. I guess they haven't brought the furps back up yet."

"Core, file modifications, by date and time, from session log two nights ago. On screen."

It rode up in text, pushing aside the radio captured commands as if they were a curtain. Callie read them all. "No dragon," she said at last.

"If it's a familiar, the base code would be attached to your character data," Lantis offered.

"Which is unretrievable. We're not running furps right now. That dragon isn't here."

But he was. She had a feeling that nothing was going to get rid of him now.

"Core, page back to the disassembler log." She turned to look at the dragon. "We're going to experiment," she said softly. "Help us."

The dragon nodded.

"Weasel, back to your station. Core, capture radio data until you're shut down; capture data on start up."

"Capturing, Callisto."

"Good." She took a deep breath. "Core, shut down."

"Shutting down."

The radio began to speak in its foreign tongue.

The dragon remained where it was.

"Callisto," her core said, "News scan yields results."

"News scan? Oh. Right. Precis only."

"Furps, Eastern Kingdom, still off-line. Some character logs have been transferred to the Middle Kingdom, the Northern Kingdom and the Western marches for social interaction only."

She frowned. "Second item?"

"Middle hive."

"Middle hive?"

"Data Haven. Format is radio report, video in in 2D, but it is badly scrambled. Filter?"

"Precis."

"Fifteen minutes ago, there was an air strike on the south sea Data Haven. Extent of damage is unknown."

"*Air strike?* As in . . . bombs?"

"Correct."

She looked up at Lantis.

"Later," he said, his voice stripped of anything but determination. "Let's finish what we've started here."

A series of six commands yielded the same results as the first one had: garbage, followed by pristine assembler. One step up, Callie thought, from machine language. Ones and zeros.

"It's the same," Lantis said.

"I think so. Core, ceiling screen. I want the first page of each of the seven assembler logs, three by two."

Her core complied. She wondered if any part of its AI function was confused. And then she frowned. "Core, beneath those, give me a log of all received and executed commands from any source. Start time: 15:06. End time: present."

It complied.

There was no evidence in the log of the commands that had overridden hers. She pulled her core card out of her pocket. "Core, transfer logs."

"Transferred."

"I want to try something," she said quietly.

"Way ahead of you," Lantis replied. "My place."

"Your place. Let me call home and warn my dad." He got up and walked out of her room.

Weasel looked confused, but it lasted for about half a minute. "I forgot where I was," he said.

"Home of the dumb phone."

Reid Ellis was a maverick, of sorts. Callie privately thought he was an idiot savant, a man who operated, on every conceivable level, in a single intense arena. Of all of her father's friends, he had not been bought by Mirai. There were reasons for that.

But he had at least one thing in common with her father. He actively encouraged his son to follow him in his chosen, murky vocation. He had some sense of what the word "classified" meant: Don't get caught.

When her father and the rest of his friends vanished for a long stretch into the bowels of the Academic machine, he had chosen to take a vacation in Russia. He was terrible with spoken language of almost any type, but in spite of this he managed to get along; he had a childlike glee when he was given any new toy, any new problem to solve, and when he had been invited to teach at the Hacker's Academy—she didn't remember what the Russians actually called their elite school—he had packed up son and wife and vanished across the great divide.

His former students often dropped in for months at a time. She knew he was watched because of it, and he knew it as well. But watching was all that was ever done. Broadband access from his home had been packet sniffed by every expert on the planet at one point or another.

As if he were a complete idiot.

In a universe where conspiracy theorists would have thrived, a mysterious "they" would have hacked together enough evidence to have him put away for a long time. Callie had never believed that that universe and this one had much in common. Until now.

"Core, machine specs for the furps servers."

The dragon sat up, yawned, and stretched its wings.

"These are current specs?"

"Yes."

"Specs for the machines that run the middle hive, side by side."

"Slow it down, Callie," Weasel said, over her shoulder. " 'kay, thanks."

"Well," Callie said at last, "they're behind by about two full chipsets."

"Yeah."

"And there's not a noticeable degradation in the quality of the experience."

"Yeah."

"Should be some, though. The current chips have wireless support built in, and they handle information a lot faster than the old external hardware did."

"Yeah."

"Will you say something else?"

Weasel shrugged. The door to her room opened. Lantis stood in the doorframe wearing an expression that instantly made Callie jump out of her chair.

"Callie, did your dad come home last night?"

"What?"

"Did he come home?"

She stared at him for a long, long moment, and then she got up from her desk and sprinted to her door. She couldn't remember whether or not she touched the doorknob, old-fashioned mechanism that it was, but the hall raced past in a blur.

It was almost impossible to tell from the state of her father's room whether or not he'd actually been in it; he made the bed maybe once a month, and the dirty laundry pile was sort of a continuous sculpture. He was meticulous about food in his room, because food near his mechanical contrivances was a capital crime. Callie was used to his late nights and early mornings; she could no longer count the number of times that she'd go without days before he called her down for dinner. If the car was gone—and it was—she assumed he was at Mirai. She ran down to the kitchen, the deaf, dumb kitchen, and opened the fridge door. Counted the eggs. Looked at the level of the milk, the orange juice, the filtered water.

She placed her hand on the phone pad.

"Dad."

The first time she had vphoned his work, she had gotten an unfamiliar face, an unfamiliar voice. When that person had asked her to whom she wished the call directed, she had said "My daddy."

Confusion had followed, and after that, questions. Who is your father? What is his name? What is *your* name?

In the end, she had been delivered to her father, but when he had keyed in his number upon his return that evening, he had made the request simple enough. He had never changed it.

As she'd gotten older, and asking for "Daddy" had become an act beneath her dignity, she had ceased to use the simple imperative. And without the simple imperative, all calls were routed through the front office; there was—in theory—no direct access to the main labs and the people who worked within them. All calls in—and out—were vetted; all calls in—and out—were logged.

Her father's face flickered on the wall screen that was reserved for the vphone's limited use.

"Dad—"

"I'm sorry, but I am in a meeting at the moment, and I cannot be disturbed."

"Priority zero one." She waited.

"I'm sorry, but I am in a meeting at the moment, and I cannot be disturbed."

"Priority one one."

"I'm sorry, but I am in a meeting at the moment, and I cannot be disturbed."

"Call route requested."

"I'm sorry, but I am in a meeting at the moment, and I

cannot be disturbed. Call will now be rerouted to the front office."

She hesitated. But in the end she chose not to terminate the call; there was nothing wrong with checking up on your father's absence. Nothing suspect at all.

The man who took the call, however, was not the one whose face was presented by the core that ran the Mirai front office.

"Hello."

She frowned. "I'm calling Mirai Corp's Toronto front office."

"You've reached it. You're looking for Ron Wessels?"

"Yes."

"Why?"

She bristled slightly, but fear kept the reaction to a minimum. "I'm his daughter."

"I'll have him call as soon as his meeting ends."

I bet. "Look," she said, "Where is he?"

"He is currently in a meeting, and he cannot be disturbed."

"Fine. I'll be waiting." She cut out. She backed out of the kitchen, spun around, and raced back up the stairs, taking them two at a time. "Lantis! Weasel!"

Lantis came out of her room carrying her bag. "I scrubbed the logs," he said. "No one's going to be able to retrieve them."

"Good. My dad's not at the office."

"Isn't that him coming down the street?" Weasel said. He stood just in front of her curtains, having pulled them aside just enough that he could look out.

"What? Where?"

"That's his car, right?"

She walked over to the window, and Weasel stepped quickly out of her way. Opening the curtains a crack, she squinted into the night below. The street lamps were on, but it had gotten dark while they worked, and she had failed to notice.

"Yeah," she said, after a minute. "That's his car." But she didn't feel relieved.

"What's wrong?"

"Not sure. Look, let's get ready to leave. I've got pretty much everything I need."

Still she lingered by the window, watching.

The car pulled into the driveway. The driver's door opened, and her father stepped out; the passenger door opened and a man she had never seen before stepped out as well. He waited until her father walked around the car's hood and joined him, and then together they began to walk toward the door.

But as her father left his car behind, he shifted, growing six inches, a beard, dark glasses. And gloves.

Callie couldn't move. She could barely breathe.

Her father's security system disrupted laser projections; it was his way of keeping out the 3D sales calls that plagued the neighborhood. She had the satisfaction of watching the man stop and look down at himself—and stop dead.

Lantis caught her by the arm. She could barely feel his hand. "Callie?"

"It's not—it's not my dad," she managed to get out. "It—it looked like him—until—"

He pulled her, and she let him. Her knees gave once before she managed to put the visceral fear she felt to use. She ran. "Backdoor!"

Lantis nodded. "I don't know how much they know about your father's house, but if they didn't know about the dead zone, they're going to have a lot of trouble with the door."

"Unless he left his keys in the car," she added bitterly.

They made it out the back of the house and hopped the fence into the Perez family's yard. The dragon came with them.

"We so need to be out of here," Callie murmured.

Lantis nodded grimly. "Can you wait here?"

"Not a chance in hell. You know the cardinal rule. Never split the party. Where were you thinking of going?"

"Home."

"Maybe not a good idea."

"Maybe not." He closed his eyes. "Callie—"

"I know." She bowed her head. "I know, I know, I know. Lantis, I can't breathe. I don't understand what's going on, but I can't breathe. Where are we supposed to be going?"

To the Eastern Kingdom, the dragon said.

"The Eastern Kingdom is down."

It smiled. She could swear it smiled.

"All right. Say we can access a disabled system. From where?"

The dragon began to fly.

Callie looked at Lantis; Lantis nodded tersely.

But he wanted to go home, and she knew it. He wanted to go home to see if there were bodies there.

They made it halfway down the next block before they saw the car again.

Weasel pointed it out.

"Walk," Callie said softly. "Don't run, walk."

"Uh, Callie?"

"What?"

"That only works if they're *not* looking for you. It's slowing down."

She looked at the dragon. And swore. "Okay, plan two. Run!"

The car sped up. She turned to look over her shoulder, and saw that they were driving it up onto the sidewalk. "Lantis!"

He had stopped; the car's passenger window slid down.

She had never seen a real gun before.

"Callie!" Lantis shouted. "Your card!"

"My what? My—" she pulled it out, fumbling to turn it on.

"You wanted to test it—test it now. Like, *right now.*"

Callie whispered, voice shaking, "Core, connect."

"Connected, Callisto."

"Transmit stored data. Same frequency as capture. Now!"

"Transmitting."

Callie didn't really believe in God, although in the Eastern Kingdom she paid lip service to Hecate. Funny how belief and prayer could be so diametrically opposed.

"Car," she said, "swerve right."

The car swerved. The man with the gun slammed into the window frame. "Car, reverse."

She could see the driver struggling with the steering wheel. Could see his lips moving, and could hear the shouting that accompanied that motion, although she couldn't quite make out the words. "Car, forward, full acceleration."

The car obeyed.

It struck drove full speed into the cement column of the projection camera bank that rested just above the rooftops.

Lantis turned to face her. "Well," he said, "Now we know."

She nodded, staring at the webbed pattern of broken glass that surrounded the upper half of a stranger's skull.

She jammed the frequency as they walked down the street. At night, the city was quiet. The stars were bright, but Callie knew that their glitter was an artifact of the projectors.

"It has to be the chip's instruction set," she said to Lantis. He nodded.

"Those codes, that frequency—if you have those, you can do . . . anything."

"Like hijack a plane for an airstrike."

"Or turn up the gas in a house and then light a stove."

Silence.

"It wouldn't work if they couldn't control the wireless protocol. I'm guessing—I'm guessing that the older machines in the Data Havens didn't have those chips. If they did, any data hidden there could just be quietly erased. Hell, the whole system could be quietly erased. Everything could be lost. I'm just wondering how they could pull off something like that."

"I don't know. I guess—I guess it could be done."

"Without anyone knowing about it?"

"Depends. If the engineering section responsible for any of the protocols wanted to build a backdoor into the chip, they could probably do it."

"A whole section? Come on. It would take years to design something like that. And the manufacturer would have to know about it; I mean, they'd be changing the spec before production."

"Well, sure. If they didn't trust their engineers. But if they did . . . if they did, the engineers could turn in the entire wireless module, and who would disassemble it piece by piece?" She was quiet for a long time. "Mirai manufactures those chips."

"I know." He turned to her, his expression bleak and ancient. "And I can tell you who was part of that engineering team."

"Who?"

"Ron Wessels. Jeff Kesner. William Rucklidge. Andrew Platzer."

"How do you know that?"

"Mark Thompson," he continued. "And Reid Ellis."

"But . . . your dad doesn't work for Mirai."

"Not now."

"He never did."

Lantis said, "Callie, trust me to know my dad." He turned to face her. "He wasn't cut out for corporate work because—and this is the truth—the entire idea of nondisclosure is foreign to him. He likes to tool around. He likes to play with new things. He likes to share what he knows."

She looked up. "Scott Murray?"

"Scott Murray was part of that crowd, but I'm not entirely sure he was part of the design team. Kesner was the radio enthusiast."

"Did you know about this?"

"No. I—no."

Weasel was staring at them both as if they'd gone mad. Or worse, as if they hadn't.

"But Murray designed the core of the furps code. And it wouldn't surprise me at all if he'd built backdoors into the furps. It would surprise the hell out of me if he hadn't."

"You said Murray was dead."

He nodded.

"And Thompson?"

"He's gone as well."

"But . . . I don't get it. I just don't get it. Look—our fathers are not take-over-the-world people. I mean, my dad can barely manage one life!"

"Two."

"Fine, two lives."

"No."

"And if Mirai corp knew about this, do you think they'd still employ them? They'd've been dead years ago."

"If the protocols are old, sure."

"Wireless has been part of the chip for how long, five years now? Six?"

"Practically forever."

"And no one noticed this before?"

"Why would they?" He paused. "And someone noticed."

"But why kill only two people? Why not all of them?"

She stopped then.

Lantis said it anyway. "They may well have killed all of them by now."

The dragon stopped.

"What are you doing?"

Waiting.

"Great, for what? The bus?"

The bus, it replied agreeably.

A green minivan appeared from around the corner. "I don't like this," Callie said softly.

It cruised down the street toward them. And stopped. Callie held her breath, but the dragon hovered serenely in the air.

The driver door slid open.

She liked it even less when she recognized the man who stepped out of the running car. Solomon.

"I'm sorry," he said curtly, in a tone of voice which implied that apology was beneath him. "I was held up in traffic."

"At this time of night?"

"There have been twelve power outages in the west side of the city. The traffic signals are . . . erratic. Car," he added, in an even less friendly voice, "prepare to be boarded."

The passenger door slid open.

"Get in."

"Solomon," Lantis said, when the seat belts had clicked in place, "where are we going?"

"To the Eastern Kingdom servers."

"We can't get to all of them."

"We only have to get to one. There are three primary servers for the Eastern Kingdom. One is in Boston. One is in New York. One is here." He kept his eye on the road. Callie had never liked him as a Wizard because he always looked so menacing he could suck the fun out of a room just by joining it.

But she liked him less in the flesh. "Do you know what's going on?"

"Do you?"

Touché. She didn't answer. "Is it true about the Data Havens?"

His eyes met hers through the auspices of the mirror. She wanted to tell him to keep his bloody attention on the road, but the car was probably perfectly capable of autopilot. "Yes," he said at length.

"And the hacking? The Eastern Kingdom?"

"That's a different story."

She was silent again. The dragon had curled up on the dashboard, and watched her with its ebony eyes. "How long a drive is this?"

"Not more than two hours. If we're not stopped."

"Do you—do you know what happened—"

For the first time ever, his expression cracked; something human glimpsed through at her. It got blurry real quick.

He cleared his throat. "Scott Murray," he said, out of the blue, "was a friend of mine. He was deliberately offensive to everyone he met, but if you survived that, he was a damn good friend. He built most of the essential code for the furps, and that code, modified, is what runs the furps now.

"He also worked at Mirai for a time."

"He was part of the—"

"Yes. He had some hand in the ROM design."

"Is he really dead?"

"Oh, yes."

"And—and the other guy, Mark Thompson?"

"Yes."

"Who killed them?"

"I honestly don't know."

"Does my—does—"

"No, Callisto," he said, and his voice was surprisingly gentle. "No one knows."

"But—"

"And in the end, it almost doesn't matter."

She bristled at that. But she kept it to herself. "What does any of this have to do with me?"

"With you? Nothing directly. And everything." He took a quiet breath. "I was part of the engineering team that built the Q5s."

It should have surprised her. It didn't. But it made her very, very uncomfortable.

"I'm not the same man I was then. I don't have the same name. I don't have the same face."

"You mean my dad didn't know—"

"He knew. But by then, there were already two deaths."

"I don't think we want to hear any more of this," Lantis said.

"Speak for yourself, Lantis."

"Callie, think. If someone was responsible and everyone else was in the loop—"

"Very clever. Very clever, Lantis. Yes, I could be the man behind this plot."

The dragon hissed.

"But I told you, Scott was a damn good friend. I might have killed your father—or yours, Callie. Thompson. But not Murray. Not him."

She closed her eyes. "You've killed people."

"So have you."

She saw the shattered window of her father's car, and could think of nothing to say to that.

"It was my job to build a power base for myself."

"Pardon?"

"Outside of the furps," he said softly. "It was my job to use the information that at least two men have died for. It's my job now. I work for Mirai."

"Well, we know that. You're part of the Middle Kingdom."

"I work for Mirai a little more directly than that."

"Then why—"

"Why are you involved at all?"

She nodded.

"That's a very good question. I honestly don't know." He took a deep breath, and then looked at the dragon on the dashboard. "That little familiar is what we've been looking for for a very long time."

"Someone knew where . . . it was."

He nodded. "Somehow, yes. Someone did. Ron might have. Scott was the only person who knew for certain, and he moved them to the Data Haven with the rest of the middle hive." He turned around in the seat to face her and she had to be very careful not to look out the window. "I don't think your father would have risked you. But in the end, he might not have had the choice."

"We learned about the air strike a day before the plane was diverted."

"You could have stopped it," she whispered.

"We could have stopped it."

"Why didn't you?"

"Because," he said softly, "I met you in the bar in the Eastern Kingdom lounge, and you were wearing that familiar."

"What's so special about it?"

"Scott knew about the chip," he said quietly. "You have to understand, Callie. You want to see this as a big conspiracy— and it has turned into that, I'll grant you that. But when it happened it was . . . a game. It was a challenge. It was something 'really cool.' They never intended to use it, but they wanted to know how far they could go.

"It turned out that they could go pretty far."

Lantis swore.

"Scott couldn't build a backdoor into the backdoor. But he knew enough about the project to build a hatchet. Just before he died, I think they had all begun to realize just how bad things could be. The Q5 is everywhere. It powers entire lives. This car, that house, those projectors.

"The government offices. The military databases. The research labs from here to Tokyo and back. The banks. The hospitals."

He paused. "The water. The electrical supply. The gas mains."

"They knew how much trouble they would be in if their little game was discovered. So they kept quiet." He frowned. "There is a small possibility that car is following us."

Callie looked out the back window. She hesitated for just a moment, and then brought out her core card. "Core," she said softly, "transmit sequence." She waited a moment, and then said, "Connect to car, ID 644 IEF. Car, cut engine. Car, engage air bags." She looked up to Solomon, whose gaze never wavered. The car fell away as if it were just an inconvenient opponent generated by the furps.

"The dragon?"

"Scott's dragon. Scott lived in a hive. That's what I called it, at any rate. You walked into his house, and there were more machines than wall space. He had broadband access when it cost money. When he realized—and he might have been the first person *to* realize it—what could be done, he started to work.

"The furps is riddled with his backdoors, his traps, his codes. There isn't a furps system that he couldn't walk into, there isn't a character he couldn't have changed. His way of making sure he'd always be welcome." Solomon smiled; it was a brief, cool expression.

"The code for the middle hive isn't all that much different. It's a hack of his original code."

"And Mirai never changed it."

"We couldn't afford to."

"Why not?"

"Because the program that we needed was buried someplace in the middle hive, and the only easy access to the middle hive was through those backdoors." Solomon turned back to the road, and Callie studied his face in the mirror. It was only marginally more comfortable.

"Mirai has known about the breach in the Q5 for two years now. During that two years, the design team working on the R1 has changed the wireless protocols and removed the priority commands hidden on the chip.

"But short of frying the boards, or recalling them, there hasn't been a good way to remove the hazard without alerting our enemies to our knowledge." He shrugged. "Understand two things: One, the person or people who are using these codes understand that some of the people responsible for their design still exist. They have gone through some effort to discover who those designers were—but industrial espionage being what it is, it's taken them a while. Two, they are at least competent with the protocols involved.

"If we attempted to alleviate the difficulty on a large scale, they could do vastly more damage than we could prevent. Do you understand what could happen?"

She was silent.

"Then let me be clear. The American Airlines accident

four years ago—the one in which three commercial jets collided on the runway—at LAX. It was a warning. Accompanying that warning was a piece of text only correspondence demanding information about the original design team that handled the wireless protocols for the Q5.

"Mirai has, of course, supplied the design team's names. Those names were not accurate, and it would be reasonable for our enemies to assume that those men went to ground. In the meantime, Mirai has been 'quietly' utilizing those codes for the personal gain of perhaps three employees, all in the upper ranks of the corporation."

"But—but why?"

"Callie," he said softly, "your father never told us you were stupid. *Think.*"

The dragon lifted its head and hissed; a small white vapor of breath left its perfect mouth. She had the pleasure of seeing Solomon's brows rise in momentary surprise.

"I'm thinking," she said quietly. "And I still don't get it. It makes you like them, right?"

"Exactly."

She turned to Lantis, who was frowning. He met her gaze and wordlessly asked her permission to interrupt; her shrug was all he needed.

"All that power." He turned to her. "Weasel should get it."

"Why me?"

"You joined the Crimson Guild in the Middle Kingdom."

Weasel rolled his eyes. "Look, you *know* why I did that. I swear, the two of you—" He stopped.

"They probably can't conceive of people building that chipset without intent to use it."

"Good." Solomon nodded. "And if we have intent to use it, to benefit from it, if we *are* benefiting from it, and demonstrably so, then we wouldn't have any reason at all to turn it off."

She turned to stare out at the streets that were passing them by. Because she could suddenly imagine what might happen if people thought they were trying to disable the trapdoor.

"Can it be done?"

"Yes."

"But you haven't."

"No."

She didn't relish another scathing comment about her intelligence, but her head hurt. Six hundred and fifty-three people had died in that plane crash. She was old enough that she could remember watching it unfold from her father's lap. The plane had looked so small, and the fire so red, so wild, that she hadn't even realized it was real.

Her mother had been very angry at her father for not turning it off.

"Lantis?"

"Hmmm."

"Can't the firmware in the Q5 be updated?"

"Flashed. Yes. You've done it."

"Then it shouldn't be too hard to flash the ROMs and circumvent the trapdoor."

"If you can get people to use the patch, yes," Solomon replied. "And you could apply it remotely, choosing the important locations first. But say you knew your time was limited. Say that you didn't know who was using those codes, and who was killing with them.

"Say that the person in question could download those patches, run them, and test the functionality of the backdoor after the fact; wouldn't be hard; he wouldn't have to sacrifice much to test it.

"Even if all of Mirai's vast resources were turned to resolving this specific problem, to applying that patch to as many chips as possible, we couldn't move quickly enough to get them all."

"Can I . . . take over . . . this car?"

"No."

She was quiet. "But my father's car . . ."

"It wasn't your father's car," Solomon said quietly. "You've got another thirty minutes." The car shifted gears.

"I am *not* hacking into police cars, so don't go Nascar on us, okay?"

He actually laughed.

"The airstrike on the middle hive?"

"Scott Murray placed all of his legacy—pardon the pun—there. The Data Havens aren't run on the Q5s. There is no easy access, and the best of the Russian academy has made security in the havens a hobby.

"But we believe that they knew that something that threatened their control of the Q5 was there."

"How?"

"They probably spoke to Scott." That was all.

"We found it."

"Yes. But they were watching. They had no idea that you had accessed the middle hive through the furps; to be honest, that's not the way it's normally accessed. The session logs did not indicate that you had dropped out of the furps at any time. I'm not sure what tripped them to your signal."

Callie's eyes grew wide. "I think I understand it. Ones and zeros. I started to read a command sequence—and they showed up toward the end of it."

"Possible. Technically, of course, you never left the Eastern Kingdom furps. The furps rerouted the standard request for morphing data to the havens, and then ran with it. But if you knew they saw you, they were amateurs."

"They were in the game. I mean, in the hive."

The dragon spread its wings. **Paradigm: furps,** it said, nodding.

Solomon frowned. "What did you say?"

Paradigm: furps. Enforced.

"I would pay money to see what you saw in the middle hive. At the moment, I have a lot of it. No, Callie, I wasn't there. You actually *saw* people?"

"Players," she said automatically. "Dressed like business suit ninjas."

He rolled his eyes. "They could be thirteen. They could be eighty."

"One of the precautions taken in the middle hive network involves the running of executable code. You can glean a lot of information from the Data Havens—but you've got to do it through the middle haven software; that's how it's accessed. Which means that you've got to do it through the furps.

"The middle hive network OS kills all processes that don't conform to that software.

"Your father and Scott, in their spare time, played with AI code. Part of that code, in a mutated form, has become absorbed by the core OS. Part of that code was transferred to the middle hive. There are very strict rules governing submissions to the Data Havens; for obvious reasons, the sysops there are very careful about viruses, Trojans, executables.

"But they trusted Scott Murray. I did mention that the middle hive networks are basically a hacked version of his early furps code."

"Dragon Roleplaying," she said.

He nodded. "Scott was probably the one person who could slide a foreign executable in and have it running in a protected part of the OS. But it would have to be subtle. And if the process were important enough, it would have to be able to start and stop its functioning at appropriate signals."

"That would take a hell of a lot of processor power. There's no way he could do that without being noticed."

"Self-replicating and mutating viruses have been around for decades."

"They're not self-aware."

"No. But in terms of sheer processor power, they're not even a blip on the radar. His program would have to be more than a blip. And therefore, in safety, it would remain in the middle hive."

"How much of the Data Havens are still active?"

Solomon closed his eyes.

Callie hated it. Even though the car didn't crash and didn't swerve, she found it unnerving. Probably because her father never did it.

"And why are we going to the servers?"

He said nothing.

"Do they know?"

"They suspect."

"How much time do we have?"

"I take it back. You're not stupid."

"Solomon, what's to stop them from hijacking satellites and blanket broadcasting those codes?"

"Very, very little."

Callie reached into her pocket and pulled out her card. "Core," she whispered, "shut down."

"It won't make a difference. They have access to your core now."

"But if they have access to the core—"

"We're being traced, yes."

There was nothing else she could say.

Solomon stopped the van outside of the Mirai tower that housed the server machines. There were thousands upon thousands of them, nestled one on top of the other to make the most use of the volume of the rooms they occupied.

Solomon approached the front doors. They were smoky, dark glass, and together, they were wider across than the front of her house. He placed a hand on the side of the opaque column to the right of the doors and waited.

After a moment, a voice said, "Access denied."

Callie was acutely conscious of how exposed they were.

It became worse when Solomon cursed. "We're late," he said softly.

"Solomon, please tell me that the building doesn't house automatic defenses."

"If it makes you feel better. I'd be lying, but I can say it. Hold on. It's going to be dicey; they have access, and we have access. They can shut the building down, but then they don't get us unless they want to come in in person. And at a guess, I'd say they're not here yet."

He took a card out of his pocket; it looked like a core card.

Callie stood still for a long moment; the lights in the building were getting visibly brighter. The familiar cocked his head to one side and then came to rest on her shoulder.

"Paradigm, furps," she said.

The creature stretched wings and smiled.

"Weasel, Lantis—Eastern Kingdom."

"We haven't logged in."

"Try."

Weasel hesitated. "My core—"

"Your character logs are on your core," she said. "But you know how the furps feel about unauthorized character mods. They real data is resident *here*. In this building. In those machines."

"No problem. And we get permission to use it how?"

She touched the dragon; her hand passed through it, but that felt natural somehow. "Encrypt 8," she said. She pulled out her father's pad. "Can you read this?"

The dragon nodded. **Parsing text.**

"Get ready," she told Lantis. "Solomon, you, too. But if you can, ditch that damn cat."

"Eastern Kingdom Warden reporting. Permission flags for users Callisto, Weasel, Lantis, all true."

The dragon nodded; she knew it was filtering her voice, changing its tones. "You're the backdoor," she whispered. "So get us in there."

The cameras and the projectors, embedded and invisible, suddenly came to life.

Paradigm: furps, the dragon said happily.

"Yes," Callie replied. "All routines to be filtered through the furps paradigm."

She didn't bother to check the PK flags; she knew what they were. She lifted her hands and as they rose, her school clothing vanished beneath the practical, pragmatic robes of her Mage. Lantis' drifted into Wizard of the Seeing Eye garb, and Weasel made himself at home in his leathers.

Even Solomon grew a couple of inches and exchanged his clothing for the garb that marked him instantly as a person you didn't want to piss off.

He had a few choice words to say about Scott Murray, but Callie thought better of telling him to speak kindly of the dead.

The magic missiles didn't come as a big surprise.

The heat of them did. Lantis, Weasel, and Callie weren't used to tactile input when they gamed. But they *were* used to magical fire fights, and they were used to magical defense. Lantis had a shield spell up before the missiles struck, and they peeled away to either side, passing harmlessly into the stone of the castle walls.

It was easiest to think of it as a game.

"The Knight of the East is under siege," a voice said. A bleeding squire came tumbling into the hall, gasping. "Reality level down fifty percent," she said. The wounds, which were obviously meant to be fatal, faded slightly. She had a feeling it wouldn't last.

"We've come to aid the Knight of the East. Where is he?"

"In the throne room," the squire gasped, in proper furps dramatic-death fashion. "The heir to the Kingdom of the East is with him."

"There is no heir to the Kingdom of the East," Lantis snapped. He knew the game. He knew the story line. They all did.

"There is. He was hidden. Our enemies found out about him, but we managed to reach him first; the Knight's stronghold was the closest haven."

"How many?"

"One, but he is a mighty Wizard. I fear that the Knight will not be able to defend the heir for long. Help . . . him."

"We will. On our honor," Lantis told the squire. The man smiled and died.

They took the long hall at a careful run. Callie noted the caltrops on the ground before they'd impaled their feet; Weasel pointed out the magical wards in the ceiling. But they knew how to handle defenses like these; they'd seen them a hundred times before.

When the second round of missiles flew, and Callie's shoulders were singed in their passage, she screamed. She never screamed in session.

In a panic, Lantis turned to her.

"Don't! Concentrate on the shield. Return fire, damnit. Don't think about me."

She was afraid. Reality seeped into the paradigm, heightening the tension. If they died here, they died. She wondered, idly, what they would actually be dead *of;* what the police would say when they found the bodies. The projectors in the heart of Mirai Corp. were second to none; they took the morphs that Callie's core took and made them real.

But she knew that this was the best way to get in. Fight their way in using a paradigm they understood. To argue with the operating systems and the software and the processes of the individual machines in the building would have taken way, way too long.

She ignored the wound.

They had to deal with Wizard locks. Callie left that to Solomon; it was rumored that there wasn't a place in all of the kingdoms, East or otherwise, that could keep him out if he wanted in; the magic didn't exist at high enough levels to contain him. He was the most powerful Wizard in the furps that she knew of.

He passed through five doors, holding them for just long enough to get everyone through; reserving his power. Had the pain been less distracting, she would have taken notes. She wasn't likely to get the opportunity to see him in action again.

As they approached the throne room, they heard the sounds of fighting.

Explosions. Shouts. Screams.

A regular save-the-world scenario in the Eastern Kingdom, with the heroes arriving at exactly the last—and right—minute. She bit her lip just a bit too hard when she slid across the floor. It was stone, at least to look at, but she knew the feel of cold marble on her behind.

"Callie?"

She waved Lantis away.

Reaching into the backpack, she pulled out her father's pad. It materialized instantly in the furps as a scroll.

But what a scroll. It was hardly corporeal at all; she held, in her hands, a flat pane of glowing golden light, its frayed edges dancing with barely contained energy.

"Solomon," she shouted, "take down the last door. We don't have much time!"

The door fell; wood shattered. He did not use subtlety.

Inside the room was the Knight of the East; he was bleeding, his face singed, his left eye dark purple. He did not wear helm or visor; the coming of the heir had apparently caught him by surprise.

The heir—whoever he was—was nowhere in sight. But the Wizard was.

Callie froze.

Her time had been spent studying subtle arts, and she regretted that deeply now. None of her defenses would protect her against this—this creature. Oh, it looked like a man, was as tall as Solomon, was resplendent in fine robes and arcane regalia. But it was pale and dark, and its eyes were like the void itself.

She knew.

It turned to look at her as she entered the room.

"You've done me a service," he said, his voice a furps sneer. "You've brought me exactly what I need to complete my hold over this pathetic world."

She *really* hoped that the furps was controlling his speech, because it was *terrible*. And it would have been laughable—had she been in normal session, she would have laughed—if it hadn't felt so true.

"Is this what you're looking for, Wizard?"

"Give it to me," the creature said. He gestured; the Knight of the East was surrounded by a bank of flames. "Give it to me, and I will let you live."

As if.

Without looking away from the creature, she said to her familiar, "Go."

The familiar took to the air like a kestrel.

The Wizard laughed. "You think to threaten me with a *familiar*? Do you not know who I am?"

"No," she said, "I have absolutely no idea who you are. And right at this moment, you raving asshole, I don't care." She lifted the scroll and began to read what was written on it. Ones and zeros.

He laughed. "I know how you gained entrance to this kingdom, and it will be the last time you have that privilege," he began.

The little dragon hit him, its claws extended, its wings folded back in a way that streamlined its delicate body.

Callie saw him stagger back, and she realized, bitterly, that *he* was in the furps remotely. He laughed. "I think it's time to kill this process," he told them. He lifted a hand. Pointed a finger.

Nothing happened.

"I might have forgotten to tell you something," Callie said. "It's not just a simple process. It's clever. It alters itself to fit the circumstance. Core, shut down."

The Wizard screamed in frustration—and vanished.

He took the dragon with him. She had expected that, but it didn't make her happy.

They were left in the silence of a furps module.

"Solomon?"

"You've still got the scroll," he told her. "May I see it?"

She nodded. Handed it to him as he approached her. He did not take it. "I think," he said wearily, "that it's keyed to your voice."

"We didn't have to come here, did we?"

"We did."

"Why?"

"Finish reading the scroll. You'll see."

"Can I read it *after* we check on the Knight of the East?"

"The Knight of the East," the Knight said wryly, "is still . . . alive." He rose slowly, and Callie thought about knocking the reality level of the violence down to a nice, clean zero. She didn't.

"Read the scroll, Callie," he added, in a voice that was becoming more and more familiar. "Read it, and we can all go home."

"Dad?"

He didn't answer.

"I'm going to kill you when we get home."

But she looked at the scroll. As she watched, the light began to fade. She started to read it, watching the ones and the zeros fly from the page as if they were simply markers set to guide her through the complicated gibberish to machine language.

"Uh, Solomon, nothing happened."

The light dimmed and faded. She held a piece of paper in her hand, and that, too, began to disappear. As did her robes, her leathers, her belt, and her wineskin. The burn on her arm remained.

"Not exactly."

She frowned. The furps morph had faded; they stood in a very damaged computer room. The sprinklers had been set off, and half of the machines—the ones on the racks nearest the roof—were protesting in the way electrical things do when exposed to water.

"Callie?"

"What?"

"I think you'd better take a look."

She turned in the direction of Lantis' voice and stopped. In the center of the room was a white dragon.

But if it ever tried to sit on her shoulder, her shoulder

would break; she was sure of it. Its eyes were the size of dinner plates, but they were black, round surfaces with a glint of some hidden fire at their core.

Dragon.

Thank you, Callisto. I must fly now. I must wake the children.

"I know."

It rose; the projectors rose with it, of course, as it melted through the ceiling. She wanted to ask it if it was coming back anytime soon. Didn't bother.

"What did it mean, wake the children?" Weasel asked.

"It's the second half of a viral executable," she told him.

"Very good, Callie."

She wanted to tell Solomon to get stuffed. "That's why the dragon started the bar brawl. That's why you didn't stop it. That's why you made sure the character data was transferred across the entire Middle Kingdom."

He nodded quietly.

"It travels damn quickly, doesn't it?"

"That's the hope."

"We didn't have to be here to do this."

"We did. Why do you think Mirai never changed the furps backdoors? Why do you think that so many of the engineering core group ended up here, in this city? The invocation that activates the virus *had* to be done here. We would have changed it—if we knew how. Its legacy code, and the furps code is huge. We had people working on it, but it was . . . difficult.

"And invoking the process wouldn't have done anything had the virus not been delivered. The furps machines have fingers in almost everything. The familiar is set to flash the ROMs with a trap for that instruction set that renders it useless. Unfortunately it also renders any future firmware updates impossible."

"They can't get it back."

"No."

He hesitated. "Come with me, Callie. Lantis and Weasel,

you might want to join me as well. Ron, get to the infirmary."

"Wait—what about whoever was behind that sim?"

"We'll track him down. He's probably out in the street right now, and he's going to discover soon that certain things aren't working the way they used to."

"But you said—the time—"

"Yes. If we'd had to do this the old-fashioned way, we couldn't have. Period."

"But—"

"Later, Callie. Later. There's someone here that's been waiting for you to show up."

He walked down the hall to a closed door. For the first time that evening he lifted his hand and knocked.

The door opened slowly, and a familiar face peered around the edge of the door.

It was Eno.

"If you guys have made a level without me, I'll kill you."

Callie laughed. "Stand in line."

The virus—if it was that—had spread; there were isolated accidents and disasters—and an unexplained glitch in one bank's data, all of which made her feel like a total failure, but they passed.

Her father was home from the hospital, sporting a couple of burn scars that made him only slightly uglier than she was used to; he had taken a leave of absence from Mirai while he recovered.

It was two weeks before Callie was ready to enter the Eastern Kingdom again.

When she materialized in the grove of the wood spirit, Lantis, Eno, and Weasel were waiting for her.

"You ready to save the world?" Lantis asked.

"No. But I wouldn't mind killing an orc or ten."

He laughed. Started to walk away. She saw his eyes widen in surprise. "Callie?"

"What?"

"You've got company."

She spun around and nearly walked into the curled tail of a floating dragon. A smug, floating dragon.

Hello, Callisto, the dragon said. **Shall I reset your permission flags?**